W9-AVQ-982

Praise for Come Clean

Anthony Bidulka, Author of *Amuse Bouche* and *Flight of Aquavit*.

"From the nail-biting first chapter to the breath-taking conclusion, *Come Clean* has everything you'd expect from a masterful mystery."

Beverley Simons, playwright: *Crabdance, Preparing.*

"Moving through layers of mystery in plot and character, Parker blends horror, humor, and grace with rare professionalism."

Bob Lind, Yahoo Book Group.

"*Come Clean* is one of the most original, suspenseful and outright 'terrifying' mystery novels I have ever read."

Dean Figg, Associate Publisher, Xtra West.

"*Come Clean* has one of the best, if not the best beginning, I have ever experienced."

Dr. Jennifer Hurd, Senior Consultant, Houghton Mifflin.

"Poignant and riveting, *Come Clean* takes the reader to the heights of suspense."

Ronald L. Donaghe, author of *Common Sons.*

"In the grand tradition of the PI and police procedure, Parker treats the reader to a whodunit that keeps the reader guessing until the very end."

Come Clean

John F. Parker

Quest Books

Nederland, Texas

Copyright © 2005 by John F. Parker

All rights reserved. No part of this publication may be reproduced, transmitted in any form or by any means, electronic or mechanical, including photocopy, recording, or any information storage and retrieval system, without permission in writing from the publisher. The characters, incidents and dialogue herein are fictional and any resemblance to actual events or persons, living or dead, is purely coincidental. Where real persons, places, or institutions are incorporated to create the illusion of authenticity, they are used fictitiously. The author apologizes for the outspoken opinions of one of the main characters towards a few celebrated actors with whom he is obsessed. They are not the author's impressions, but the distorted speculation of a wildly opinionated villain. All registered trademarks mentioned in this book are the property of their respective owners. No infringement is intended or should be inferred.

ISBN 978-1-932300-43-7

First Printing 2005

9 8 7 6 5 4 3 2 1

Cover design by Donna Pawlowski

Published by:

Quest Books
PMB 210, 8691 9th Avenue
Port Arthur, Texas 77642-8025

Find us on the World Wide Web at
http://www.regalcrest.biz

Printed in the United States of America

Acknowledgments

I would like to thank the following readers of early and later drafts of *Come Clean* for pushing, cajoling, stretching, and ultimately helping me to make this publication a reality: Mary Parker, Roseanna Rudolph, Elaine Kronhaus, Beverley Simons, Bob Lind, John Crossen, David Parker, Sylverre Serenade, Rob Edler, and Robert Fong.

— John F. Parker

Up and down, up and down,
I will lead them up and down;
I am fear'd in field and town.

—Shakespeare

Chapter
One

THOMAS HENRY KING slipped a razor blade out of his jacket pocket. Without hesitation, he slashed his right eyebrow — through hair and flesh — and threw the blade out the window of his speeding car. His pursed lips broke into a radiant smile.

He knew that on the same dark road about a thousand feet behind, college instructor Nancy Henderson was heading to her cottage a mile beyond the sleepy community of Deep Cove, in British Columbia, Canada. Except for her car, he had seen no one else since the turnoff to Swallow Lake. *I bet you're singing along with Boy George. I know what you like, Nancy.*

Blood brimmed over his blond eyebrow and dripped onto his high cheekbone. He enjoyed the feeling of each drop's release and fall. "I will make her 'thank me, love me, and reward me.' "

For the past month, THK had been Nancy Henderson's shadow, learning her every move from her waking up, to her daily traveling to the college, to shopping for groceries, coming home, and preparing for the night.

He shook his head, drops of blood spotting his clothes, the seat next to him, the dashboard. He smiled. "For the last three Friday nights," he mused, "I have followed you to Swallow Lake. Directly from your last class." He laughed deep in his throat. "You're ever so precise, Nancy Henderson.

"You didn't see me a few minutes ago, did you? Parked in that deserted Chevron Station in Deep Cove. But I saw *you* coming down the main road. That's when I pulled out and turned onto Lake Road. That way *you'd* be well behind *me*. I am truly brilliant."

He had always loved the excitement of the chase; but, of course, never more than the actual climactic kill, seeing death overtake his...

Nearly three miles along the darkened road, he began turning the steering wheel to the left, and then to the right, and back to the left.

NANCY BECAME AWARE of the car in front of her; she stopped humming "The Crying Game," leaving Boy George to finish alone.

"Some drunk!" she said out loud. "Disgusting!" She was only five hundred feet from the driveway to her cottage. Relieved, she flicked on her left-turn signal. "Good riddance!"

She watched in amazement as the car—instead of following the road's gentle turn—flew across the road and crashed into one of the florescent-painted log posts that signaled her driveway. Nancy automatically braked and stopped within five feet of the other car—its horn blaring, shattering the silence of the peaceful setting.

Motionless, she sat, breathing hard. "Darn!" Everything told her to pull around him and go straight on to the security of her cottage, snuggled fifty feet ahead among the cedars. *Who cares about a drunk hitting a post? He will probably sleep it off, wake up in the wee hours of the morning, and continue on his way. Why should I get involved?*

HE CAREFULLY LIFTED his right hand and switched off the ignition. And waited. *Everything is working perfectly. She'll open her car door any minute now.*

NANCY SAT PERFECTLY still, listening to the horn continue its cruel night screech. *If the Mounties pass and see the car, they're sure to knock on my door and ask questions.* She could imagine their questions: "Didn't you hear the guy's horn? It'd wake the dead. What kind of a citizen are you? Is that the way you'd want to be treated if you were in need?"

"Darn it anyway," she whispered. She sensed that her quiet evening was about to be ruined. She loved her Friday night routine: collapse for an hour or so, have a long soak in the tub while sipping a gin and tonic, prepare and eat dinner while listening to a favorite CD, and enjoy a good night's sleep in preparation for a weekend of hiking alone with random rest-stops to enjoy John Milton, Ernest Hemingway, or Scott Fitzgerald. Heaven!

She grudgingly snapped open her car door. A chill September gust stopped her breath for a moment. *Don't be a fool. He could be bluffing. You don't want to end up raped and murdered. Stay in the car, stupid! There's plenty of room to drive around him and go into your safe cabin.* She blinked. *But what if he's really hurt? What if...?*

She pondered her options. Guilt took over, and she stepped out of her car, leaving the door wide open in case she needed to make a fast getaway. She started to walk over to the dark-colored car, and then she stopped cold. *My pepper spray! I've always carried it with me and this might be the first time I have to use it.* She went back to her car, rummaged through her purse, and pulled out the small canister. She tiptoed over to the driver's side of the other car, ready to spray the second anything looked suspicious.

She peered through the window. *A woman!* Nancy was surprised and, in a way, relieved to see a woman slumped to the right of the steering wheel, her head directly over the open ashtray, her blood dripping onto the coins. *She uses her ashtray to hold parking money, just like I do!* Nancy breathed deeply for a few moments and felt the tension and fear that had taken hold of her give way to concern and a desire to be helpful.

Nancy saw that the woman's left hand was squeezed between her body and the horn. She touched the handle and slowly opened the door on the driver's side. A burst of fragrance collided with the crisp night air. *Obsession! My favorite.*

She wasn't allowed to wear perfume at work because Brent Barnes, her office mate and mentor, was allergic to fragrances. On her first day at the college, she had tentatively knocked on the office door. When he opened it, the first words he tried to say to her through a cacophony of sneezes were, "Go wash off that smell before you come in here." Some greeting. But he was so handsome and she was, after all, the rookie instructor, so she had rushed to the ladies' room. She scrubbed her wrists and behind her ears to get rid of the scent, then returned to the office. He gave her a big smile and said, "I won't ever sneeze you off again. I promise." They'd both laughed. Within minutes they were joking; a mutual magnetism had been established.

For a full minute Nancy stood beside the car, looking at the still body of the woman. She didn't know what to do. *Should I touch her? I don't want to. I don't need this. I want to get into my cabin and relax.* Unsure and still a little frightened, she slowly closed the door. The inside light went out. "Oh, poo," Nancy said out loud. She put the pepper spray into the pocket of her London Fog and opened the door fully. Leaning in, she touched the woman's shoulder. Then she gave it a quick shove. The woman fell effortlessly away from the steering wheel back against her seat. The horn stopped shrieking. *Thank God. Silence!*

HE HAD BEEN watching her through slitted lids. *You're mine, Nancy Henderson.*

NANCY STOOD VERY still. *Blood.* She saw that the right side of the woman's face was covered with blood. *My God, is she dead?* She looked closer. *Nice hair.* Wavy, blonde. *Beautifully made up. Perfect for her complexion.* Nancy felt a twinge of jealousy, quickly stifled as she continued examining the woman's body with her eyes. *Broad shoulders. Big breasts. Tight stomach. Nice legs. This lady is a looker in spite of the blood. And obviously athletic.* She liked a woman to look like a woman, to take care with her appearance. This woman obviously did. She jumped when she heard a soft groan.

"Are you okay?" she asked.

The woman's eyes fluttered and slowly opened. "What happened?"

A cultured voice. *Wonder if she sings?*

"Where am I?"

"You are..." Nancy trailed off as the woman stirred; the slight movement made the blood on the right side of her face glisten in the dim light.

"Who are *you*?"

With hesitation, Nancy answered, "You smashed into that post." And then," I think you've had too much to drink."

"I don't drink."

"Yeah. Tell that to the judge. I saw the way you were driving." No matter how pleasant she looked, Nancy was not about to be blamed for the other woman's misfortune. *No way, sister.*

"No, really. I had one of my dizzy spells." The blonde looked up with tears in her eyes. "I felt myself going under and tried to stop my car in time. I really, really...tried to stop."

Nancy's face flushed. "I'm sorry. How are you feeling now?"

"A bit shaky, but I'll be okay." She wiped a tear from her mascaraed eye. "I better get on my way. Thanks for stopping. Many people wouldn't have. You're a very nice lady." She managed a shy little smile. "I must look a mess." She touched her forehead, then looked at her bloodied hand and stifled a tiny scream.

Nancy stared at the woman. *Oh, damn. Well, she seems a nice enough sort, and it's probably not a great idea to send her off down the road all injured and dizzy, miles away from anywhere. Who knows what might happen?* "Maybe you'd better come in and clean up. That's my cabin through there."

"Is it really?" The woman followed Nancy's pointing finger. "You live right here?" Then she focused her attention on Nancy. "Are you sure you don't mind if I come in — I mean, so I can clean up a bit?"

"No, of course not. It would be my pleasure."

"Thank you." Perfectly painted lips curved in a smile. "I have a change of clothes in my overnight bag. It won't take me long." A toss of golden hair. "Do you think I damaged my car much?" A manicured hand slipped the key into the ignition. "Phew. It still runs. Lucky me."

"Yes, you are. You broke that post, though." They both looked at the broken post illuminated by the headlights. It was snapped in half.

"Careful," Nancy yelped as the other woman began to back up.

"My car is right behind yours."

"Oh, dear. I didn't see it."

"You hold tight," Nancy shouted back over her shoulder, on the way to her car. "Let me lead the way." She maneuvered around the brown Toyota and pulled into her driveway.

HE FOLLOWED THE sandstone Infiniti. *I'm behind you, Nancy. My favorite position. We'll try that one first. Or last. Or first and last. Because it's my favorite. Bitch!* Dark red lips parted in a whisper as his car pulled into the driveway, at 6:32 on Friday evening, September 25, 1998. "I'll have her, but I'll not keep her long."

Chapter
Two

"LOOK, KEV, I know something terrible has happened to Nancy. She wouldn't let her students down like this. It's panic stations here for me. I'm going to have to go to her classes and cancel them, and then run like hell to my own. I'll be late. And you know I hate being late. You've got to help me, for God's sake. The police won't do a damn thing. 'Call us tomorrow,' they said. 'If she doesn't turn up tomorrow, call us.' Why the hell do they..."

I'd been listening to Brent's breathless griping for the past two minutes. Ever since he was made assistant head of the English Department last year, everyone brought their problems to him. And in most cases he solved them expertly, admittedly often with Nancy Henderson's input. Nearly every night during dinner, he would tell me about the day's inter-departmental problems and how he and Nancy had solved them. If I didn't know Brent as intimately as I do, I'd accuse him of having an affair with her.

He shouted, "Kev! Are you listening to me? What are you going to do about it?" Brent was getting hysterical. I could picture his intense, concerned eyes. Almond-shaped, but full, so that the whites completely encircle his dark-brown irises. And his chiseled Roman nose. Aside from Brent, I'd never met an Asian man with a magnificent Roman nose.

I'd long learned that silence was the way to calm Brent down. It was only ten fifteen a.m. and Nancy Henderson had missed her nine o'clock class. No big deal. Let him wind down.

"Aren't you listening to me, for God's sake? I need you to find Nancy. Would you please go over to her apartment and see if she's there? She may be terribly sick, or may have had an accident, or God knows what."

It was time for me to speak. "You really think something's wrong?"

"Duh! Haven't you been listening to me? In the past two semesters, Nancy has missed only one day. And when she did, she not only — "

"Yeah, yeah. She not only told you the day before, she also gave her students an active-learning library assignment so they'd be no bother to any of her colleagues, including the librarians."

Brent's voice became quiet. "Sweetie, I know something is wrong. There's no answer at her apartment and I can't phone her at the lake." Nancy unshakably refused to get a phone for her cabin even though Brent had tried to pressure her to have one put in. He had even offered to pay for the installation. What a mentor!

"Lots of people come in late Monday mornings. She probably had a great weekend and is running a bit behind. I'm sure she'll turn up."

Brent was not going to let me brush off Nancy's absence so lightly. "Look, I think you should go over to her apartment. And if she's not there, would you be a darling and go to her cabin?"

I didn't respond immediately; I was calculating how much time I'd be wasting by driving all the way from the West End to Swallow Lake. Brent and I had been there only once before, and the trip from downtown Vancouver seemed to take forever. "You know, Brent, traffic is insane at this time of the morn—"

He ignored me. "Maybe you can pick me up at the college and we can go together."

I recognized his tactics. He had no intention of skipping class to go to the lake with me. It was a familiar ploy. He'd have to be near death before he'd leave his students in the hands of the department head or any of his colleagues. "Brent, Nancy has been missing for only one hour. I think you're overreacting."

"As far as I'm concerned she's been missing for three days, two hours and fourteen minutes. When she left the college on Friday, she said, 'See you Monday morning, eight thirty sharp; I've got a surprise for my nine o'clock class and need to get the room ready.' Did you hear that, Ms. RCI? Nancy is bright, beautiful, and always..."

"Yeah. And always punctual." Brent could get me to do anything, if not through bribery of promises to spend extra time with me then through drowning me in bitchy sarcasm. *Ms. RCI. Really!* He still uses the fact that I'm a Retired Chief Inspector of the Royal Canadian Mounted Police to needle me.

When I first met Brent, I thought those tactics endearing little idiosyncrasies that I'd soon get used to. The truth: I'm still not used to them.

That man of mine never lets up until he gets what he wants. I know him too well; and worse, he knows I know him. I don't really mind, though. The moment I saw him, I knew we were destined to be soul mates. "I'll call you from Nancy's apartment."

"Thanks, Jessica. You're a doll. Love you." He hung up before I could tell him to stuff his *Jessica*.

AFTER RINGING NANCY'S number on the intercom at the front of her apartment building on Barclay Street and getting no response, I punched in the manager's number.

"Yeah?"

"This is Kevin Porter. I'm a friend of Nancy Henderson and I am concerned about her. She didn't turn up for work this morning. Have you seen her today?"

"Nope."

"Could you let me in? I'd like to talk to you." The manager buzzed me in.

After a few minutes of haggling, he and I were standing at Nancy's unanswered door on the fourteenth floor. "I told you. I don't have a key to Miss Henderson's apartment. All the owners have their own door keys." He gave me an impatient piss-or-get-off-the-pot look. "So, how long are you going to stand here staring at the door?"

"Who does she leave her extra keys with? In case of emergencies."

"Search me. I don't know all the owners' friends, for Christ's sake. I keep the place looking clean and mind my own business."

I lifted my leg and slammed my heel against the door near the lock. The molding shattered and the door flew open. I limped into the apartment.

"What the fuck? I'm calling the police." The manager scurried to the elevator in his scruffy slippers, not wanting to tangle with a crazy senior who kicks down doors.

I hadn't kicked down a door since I was a corporal in the Mounted Police. A million lifetimes ago. It felt kind of good, but my big toe hurt like hell. Little knives slashing around inside. Ignoring the pain, I searched through the four-room apartment like a bloodhound bitch in heat. Just as I thought, everything neat as a pin, and quality stuff everywhere. French provincial furniture throughout. Venetian glass everywhere. Bed made. Probably not slept in since Friday. I looked in her closet. It was full of smart designer clothes, all in basic colors.

Nancy keeps her home as neat as she keeps the office she and Brent share. Before I left, I checked her digital answering service. The number 3 blinked in the message window. I pushed the Play button. The message window glowed: Friday, Sept. 25, 5:08. "Hi, Nancy." *Brent's voice!* "I'm sorry I left you standing in the parking lot. But you know I had to hurry off to my big weekend. I'm really looking forward to it. I bet I'll enjoy my weekend more than you'll enjoy yours. Ha! Ha!" I admit I was surprised that he would share his weekend experiences with her.

The next message flashed: Sunday, Sept. 27, 10:01. "Nancy, it's Mom. I know you probably won't be home until after your classes on

Monday, but I'm just reminding you that your Dad and I are both looking forward to seeing you tomorrow. Don't forget, Flight 8344 arrives at two p.m. Tuesday. I hope you can still get to the airport between classes. We'll be waiting for you in the Air Canada First Class lounge. Don't be late. Love you." Then I heard a man's voice: "Me, too." *Nancy's father.*

The message window flashed again: Monday, Sept. 28, 8:45 p.m. I waited a couple of seconds for a message and then the screen printed out: "Hang up." And it printed out: Brent's office phone number.

I hurried out of the apartment block, hoping that the manager was still busy giving the police my description. I had no desire to be stopped at the door by an overzealous Vancouver cop. I was off to Swallow Lake.

CAUGHT IN A bumper-to-bumper crawl through Stanley Park, inching toward the North Shore via Lions Gate Bridge, I caught a glimpse of myself in the rearview mirror. I actually had a stupid grin on my face. Was I enjoying playing detective? "You silly old bastard. What the hell do you think you're up to? You retired twelve years ago, Ex-Chief Inspector Kevin J. Porter. The RCMP drummed you out on your ass, you idiot."

It was true. Twelve years ago my Commissioner, Sam Wheetley, made me an offer I couldn't refuse: "I suggest you resign with no questions asked. I'm not promising anything, but I'll try to get you a full pension. After all, you've been in the Force for over thirty years." I accepted his offer. I had no choice.

I resigned in disgrace, giving them one week's notice. After a little in-office retirement party, Sam called me in and muttered, without looking me in the eyes, "Ottawa says no deal on the full pension. Against RCMP policy. Case closed."

The next day I wondered what in hell I was going to do with the rest of my life. I was only forty-eight, strong as an ox, and had more energy than most of the thirty-year-old rookies who had looked up to me as their chief. I regularly whipped their butts on the racquetball court, to remind them who was boss.

I'd been married to Martha for twenty-eight years and we'd raised a good crop of kids who were now scattered around the world with their own families. At last count, I have nine grandchildren. With one daughter in Hawaii, one son deep in a nasty divorce in San Francisco, twin sons in England, making a name for themselves in show biz, and a daughter in Winnipeg, I have three exotic places to holiday whenever I want, and then there's Winnipeg. Life there was and still is one of extremes: so hot in the summers the mosquitoes choke on your scalding blood and so cold in the winters your spit turns to ice before it hits the ground and leaps back to stab you in the eye.

So there I was twelve years ago, not having a clue what to do for the rest of my days. Up to then, the RCMP had been my life. I was in denial. I was suffering. Martha got a job exactly one week after I retired. She pulled no punches. "You'll definitely crimp my style, being home all day."

During the next two years, she held down several jobs, ultimately settling into a small business she created for herself. Seeing many apartments standing vacant while their offshore owners waited to move to Vancouver when Hong Kong reverted back to Mainland China, she opened her own rental agency. Martha approached business people, lawyers, movie moguls, and found out they needed accommodation on a short-term basis. Within the first six months she had taken over the rental leases on fifteen West End apartments and had purchased lots of chic-looking furniture for them. She soon had them filled with wealthy yuppie tenants. And she had a waiting list.

Her successful business kept her away from home most of the day and well into many evenings. Every morning I kept my distance as I watched her get ready to leave for work in a whirr of activity. When she got to the front door, she'd turn and shout, "Don't know when I'll be home. Ciao!"

And what did I do while Martha was out in the world making a life for herself? I puttered in my North Vancouver garden, a pebble's throw from the RCMP detachment office that had been my second home for twenty years. But after terrorizing every weed to death on my one-acre lot, and producing more vegetables than all the local green grocers could sell in a year, I grew bored with my home, my garden, my neighborhood, myself. No longer sure of who or what I was, I was fast becoming an asexual recluse. Martha and I hadn't had sex since—Hell, I couldn't remember when. And neither of us was complaining.

Then one morning, instead of her usual farewell greeting, Martha announced, "I want my freedom." Without taking a breath, she said, "I've been having an affair, and Hank wants me to move in with him. I'll sell this place and we'll split things fifty-fifty. Is that all right with you?"

I looked at Martha in disbelief. What the hell was supposed to be *all right* with me? Selling up? Splitting fifty-fifty? Having my wife leave me? "Who the hell is Hank?"

"My young man."

"Young? How young?"

"He's in his twenties." She beamed. "And he adores me."

"Christ Almighty, woman. You're old enough to be his mother. He's after your money. He couldn't possibly be in..."

"Look, Kevin. Hank and I have been lovers for just over two

years."

"Two *years*?" I said in disbelief. "You mean that you were having an affair before I retired?"

"I was sick to death of being a grass widow. You were married to the Force, not me. Right? I needed companionship, Kev. Someone to cuddle up to."

Who was this confident, attractive businesswoman standing in the doorway in a smart suit with a briefcase under her arm? Happy. Beautifully made up. Youthful with her new dye job. Dancing, alive eyes.

Looking at her as if for the first time, I didn't recognize my wife. Where had the old Martha gone, the plain, middle-aged housewife who aged significantly as each of her children left the nest? "Don't wait up for me Kev. Ciao." Martha closed the door. Our marriage was over. Just like that.

What kind of a chief inspector had I been? I had been able to solve every crime in the book. I graduated from the Saskatoon Mountie Boot Camp over thirty years ago. Top of my class. I received my first promotion within two years. And I was the youngest Detective Sergeant in the Force. Hell, back in the late '60s, I was known throughout Canada as the RCMP prodigy. I'd been decorated for bravery four times. I had personally brought in forty-eight murderers. I'd single-handedly convinced the Squamish Indian Band to give up their blockade of the PGE Railway. I've always been a meat-and-potatoes kind of cop. Leg work, paper work, nose to the grindstone. But I was too filled with me-me-*me* to see what my wife had been up to for over two years. I had always trusted Martha. No, that's not accurate. I took our marriage for granted. I didn't work at our relationship and it was apparent that she'd stopped working at it too. She had no idea why I was forced to leave the RCMP. And I was too much of a coward to tell her or even to admit to myself why the Commissioner Sam Wheetley had showed me the door. You see, in those days I had thought I was only a bit bisexual. But not gay. Never gay. If Sam had seen Brent and me last night, after being separated the whole weekend, he'd have seen my true rainbow colors.

My thoughts and the stupid happy grin on my face disappeared. I was at Nancy's cabin.

I GOT OUT OF my Lincoln Continental and stood for a moment in the driveway, taking in the setting. Shaded beneath primordial old-growth cedars stood a beautiful little log cabin. Parked on the well-packed driveway to the left, Nancy's Infiniti looked like an anachronism. A heavy dew covered her car, the sun's rays not strong enough to evaporate the gathered moisture. I could feel a cold breeze blowing down from the Cascade Mountains, hinting an early freeze for the Deep Cove district. I had an instant premonition of tragedy.

I walked hesitantly up to the picturesque cabin and knocked. No answer. Did I expect one? I knocked again. Louder. Silence. Stepping down off the small four-by-four landing, I decided to look around. *Hell, I might as well. I'm here.*

I walked around the back. Trying, unsuccessfully, to look in the windows. Arguing with myself. *I should get the hell out of here and phone the RCMP. You're already here, Porter, so go on inside. If I open that door, I'll contaminate the scene. Especially if she's in there. Dead. You're contaminating the scene just by walking around the cabin, you old fart. Hell, I've already contaminated the scene by being here. What's a little more? Fuck. I pray to God she's not inside.* I walked back to my car, but instead of getting in, I turned around. The cedars stood around the cabin, several of their branches bending towards it, embracing it, protecting it. *Stop thinking such crap.*

I decided I would go inside even though I knew I was about to break all the rules that had been drummed into me over thirty years ago when I was a green rookie at Depot Division barracks in Regina, Saskatchewan. In that most ball-breaking of boot camps, you learned one thing: Don't Contaminate a Crime Scene. *That means, get the hell out of here and wait for the forensic boys and girls to do their thing.* I stood still for a moment. *How do I know there's a crime until I see it with my own eyes? You're just doing a friend a favor.* I walked toward the cabin.

Once more on the landing, I hesitated again. I looked at the healthy growth of impatiens on either side of the steps. The lush green foliage was broken by white, pink, red, and a few variegated blooms. *Another frost and they'll turn to mush.* I looked down at the Welcome mat and wiped my feet.

I knocked again and waited. As I expected, no response. This was the only door, so I turned the handle. Open. I didn't think I could have kicked down this solid door; besides, the gout in my toe was still hurting like hell. I opened the door slowly, an inch or two at a time. "Nancy? Are you here? It's Kevin." Silence. I opened the door fully and walked in.

An antiseptic pall filled my senses. I smelled a conglomerate of disinfectant, furniture polish, and laundry soap.

Everything in the main large room, which included kitchen, dining area, and living room, looked normal, if spotless can be normal. *She keeps this place as neat and tidy as her apartment.* I took out a pad and started making notes.

I looked at the only interior door. Memories flooded my brain. I'd opened too many bedroom doors and had been greeted by blood-soaked beds, blood-stained walls, graffiti in bold dripping letters bleeding obscenities.

I reached for the bedroom door handle. *Fingerprints!* I shouldn't use a hanky because I might wipe off any prints that might be there. *Get the Hell out of here, Porter, while the getting's good!* The door was ajar, as if inviting me to enter. I heard a scream in my brain like some prehistoric bird. *A killer has been here!* I smelled terror. I tried to shake the thought away and elbowed the door a little. It swung open easily.

Nancy was cuddled in her bed. I was sure that the reading light on the bedside table had been deliberately left on because of the way it was focused. It acted as a movie key light, illuminating her face in the darkened room so that she dominated the scene. The room itself could stand in for a film set; I sensed a line of dialogue. I could hear it clearly: "Too bad. You missed a great show."

I stared at Nancy, knowing that I had come too late.

Her head facing me in the open doorway, her left thumb tucked into her mouth, her duvet cocooned around her body to below her chin, Nancy Henderson looked as though she were enjoying a peaceful sleep. "Nancy!" I whispered. "Open your eyes and say, 'Fooled you!'"

I walked towards the bed. "Nancy," I breathed hoarsely. She didn't move. I walked closer and leaned down to listen for breath. Nothing. No sound. "Nancy, it's Kev." Still no movement. *Not good.* I placed my hand on the duvet above her shoulder and gave her a gentle shake. "Nancy." Again, nothing. Not wanting to disturb the position of her thumb, I put two fingers on her exposed carotid artery. I knew the moment I touched her deathly cold skin that I wouldn't find a pulse. I looked at the still, dead body of Nancy Henderson, her thumb still firmly locked between lips that glistened with newly applied gloss. I bent closer to look at her makeup. No doubt about it. Professionally applied. I could smell greasepaint. She was wearing theatrical makeup. Probably Leichners. And her skin had been carefully powdered down.

I'd seen more than a hundred dead bodies in my job but, standing alone in this cabin, staring down at Nancy's lipstick-stained thumb between her full red lips, I felt weak and suddenly old. My throat was dry and I felt that I was going to be sick.

I stepped into the adjoining bathroom and knelt in front of the toilet. I thought I was going to empty my grapefruit and bran breakfast into the bowl, but only spat out the taste of bile. I flushed the toilet and stood up to wash. I was aware of the pristine appearance of the bathroom. Everything was spotless. The bathtub was sparkling. The taps gleamed. I bent to smell the towels, precisely hung on the towel rack. Freshly laundered. Instead of washing, I wiped my mouth with my hanky.

I used it to lift the lid of the clothes hamper. Empty.

I forced myself to write more notes. It helped. It gave me incentive to go back into the bedroom. This time, I was aware of a distinct odor of burned candle wax though I saw no evidence of candles, burned or otherwise.

The neatness of her bedroom increased my suspicion that something wasn't right about this picture. There were no clothes to be seen. I walked over to the armoire and, with my special pen and its versatile built-in clip, easily opened the door. I'd been out of harness twelve years but I knew damn well that I was contaminating the scene of a homicide. I should have walked out then and there and phoned the RCMP. But I was in a no-contest battle with my curiosity.

My eyes avoided the bed. I sat on the floor and wrote furiously. I had to remove Nancy from my mind. The laughing, happy, cheerful woman who entertained Brent and me, here, last Labor Day weekend. I took several breaths until I could feel the air filling my lungs, sustaining my life. Making me feel useful. I could feel a change coming over me. I became centered and stood to attention. *Chief Inspector Kevin J. Porter, reporting for duty.* Hammy, but it did the trick.

I moved again to the armoire and looked inside. Among a few designer jeans and tops, I recognized the same cherry skirt and jacket I had seen Nancy wear so often when I had paid the occasional visit to the college to take Brent to lunch. Her clothing spelled quality. I made a mental note: "Check to see if she wore this outfit on Friday." Beside her suit hung a white Valentino blouse. It looked so fresh that I took it off the rack to examine it. It looked like new. I smelled it. Newly laundered and perhaps ironed, that is if a Valentino needs ironing. I put it back in the exact same position. I knew I was going to get shit for poking my nose around. I looked down. The sight pierced my heart. There, neatly placed, was a pair of black suede Rockport pumps. Shoes Nancy would never wear again. I had to take a few more deep breaths. I had to admit I had become soft. Vulnerable. I closed the armoire.

Walking over to the dresser, I opened a few drawers with my pen. All her lingerie and pantyhose were spotless, fresh, and neatly folded or ironed. There were no soiled clothes anywhere. I couldn't imagine anyone washing, ironing, and putting them away before going to bed. Plus making up as if going out on a heavy date. I looked over at Nancy. "You've been murdered, my darling. By a neatness freak. Take your thumb out of your mouth and talk to me. Tell me who killed you." I was talking out loud to a corpse like in the old days when I worked a case.

I looked at the bedside table. Beside the lamp sat a digital clock radio. Checking the alarm, I noticed that the setting for six thirty had been turned off. She had planned to be on time for her first class at the college. Notes. Notes.

I turned toward the bed. Nancy's brown hair was carefully arranged in a bouffant style, the lamplight enhancing her natural red highlights. "I'm sorry, sweetheart, but I need to see what's under the duvet."

Not wanting to disturb the position of her head, arms, and especially her thumb, I lifted the duvet from the bottom of the bed. Curious. The cover had been placed with great care and attention. Perfume wafted up and filled my nostrils. I recognized the smell: Obsession. Nancy's hips and legs were curled up towards her left side.

She weighed approximately one hundred twenty-five pounds and was about 5'8". Even in death she was voluptuous, well-defined waist above curvaceous hips and a full white bosom. Her brown nipples had red highlights. Could it be lipstick? Or blood? More notes. "How did you die, Nancy?" The sheets and pillowcases had been freshly laundered and, for God's sake, ironed! What had the killer done to Nancy once she was dead? Position her? Move her limbs about as if she were a mannequin? Dead, she had to do his bidding in her clean bed without a word of complaint. Without the overwhelming feel of terror.

Her right hand rested on her slim, taut stomach with the little finger covered by her dark pubic hair. She had cherry-red polish on all her nails but I couldn't see any part of her pinky nail. Why had he buried it? I had to find out. My pen easily parted her dense growth. The nail had absolutely no red polish on it. *Why leave this nail unpainted?*

"Because...because..." There I was, waiting for answers. Like the old days, expecting corpses, places, and events to fill me in with details.

I covered her, placing the duvet in the exact same position it had been in originally, making sure not to tuck any of it under the body.

I drew a sketch of the room and closed my pad. Then I went out to my car to use my cell phone. I dialed the North Vancouver Detachment Office. "Give me Chief Inspector Riley, please. This is an emergency."

"This is Joan Riley."

"Joan, Kevin Porter here. I'm at Swallow Lake. There's been a murder."

Chapter
Three

AFTER I HUNG up, a wave of conscience engulfed me. I was about to break another rule: leave the scene of a murder, after contaminating it. But I had to see Brent.

It didn't take me long to get across the Second Narrows Bridge. In fact, I was going to be at the college too quickly. Traffic at noon in East and South Vancouver is seldom a problem. Although I wanted to make sure that I caught Brent during his lunch hour, I needed some time alone. I slowed down.

My big toe was still tingling, a sure sign that my gout would act up big time before night. I reached into the glove compartment and took out my bottle of colchicine tablets. I never leave home without them. With my right hand, I snapped off the lid and, with difficulty, fished out one of the tiny yellow pills. As I started to pop it into my mouth, I spilled the whole damn bottle all over my lap. "Shit!" I pulled over. It took me damn near fifteen minutes to collect the last of the little yellow devils. "Gotcha!" Snapping the lid on them, I threw the bottle back into the glove compartment.

I sat for a few minutes, breathing deeply. "Shit! Shit! Shit!" I couldn't remember whether I had taken a pill or not. I decided I hadn't and reached into the glove compartment. I wasn't going to take a chance on missing my medication. Of course if I take too many, I get diarrhea. "Bloody Hell." I popped one in anyway.

I started the car and continued on my route. Realizing I needed all my wits, stamina, and concentration to get to the college in one piece, I kept my eyes glued on the traffic, obeying every red light and stop sign. I drove like the careful senior citizen I am. I was on auto-drive. Part of me watching the road, part of me lost in past thoughts...

Not long after Martha walked out on me, she came over one morning and said, "Sign this," handing me a real-estate listing agreement. That afternoon, she showed the house, and by the evening, she'd sold it. When Martha gave me half the proceeds from our family home, it took her only a week to find me a one-bedroom apartment in the West End. "Buy it," she said.

Still in my mid-life crisis, I did as I was told. Paid cash and still had a bit left in the bank to add to my meager pension. I cursed Commissioner Sam Wheetley the first of every month.

Once settled in Vancouver's West End, I got into the habit of biking around the sea wall of Stanley Park in the mornings and walking around English Bay in the evenings. I got back into racquetball by taking out a membership at the macho Club in the Sky, playing two or three fast and furious games a week. I intended to keep fit and trim till they put me in a box. My first two years of living in the apartment passed uneventfully. I gradually regained some of my confidence and learned to enjoy my independence. To be myself, for the first time in my life.

One September night while strolling along English Bay, I passed a young, very good-looking Asian man who gave me the eye. Although I'd had occasional looks from guys before, this was a look that stopped me in my tracks and, after a couple of seconds, I turned around in a blur of disbelief. At that very moment, he turned too. The second look literally arrested me. Talk about electricity in the air; his eyes sizzled the autumn chill. As he started slowly walking towards me, my throat became tight and dry. Perspiration poured from every pore. I could feel drops of sweat under both my moustache and scrotum. What could this gorgeous twenty-something man possibly want? He opened his mouth and said, "Where have you been...?" Pause.

"What?" I asked stupidly.

He blushed. "I was going to use the old-pick up line 'Where have *you* been hiding all my life?' But I really mean it this time. Where *have* you been all my life?" An Australian accent.

I don't care whether you're straight or gay, you probably haven't had many greetings like that. I know I sure as hell hadn't, and I knew I wasn't going to let this beautiful man slip into the darkness of the shadows surrounding English Bay.

Last Wednesday night, Brent and I celebrated our tenth anniversary of that auspicious meeting. Now that I'm a sixty-year-old senior, Brent calls me his cheap date. He has always insisted on picking up the tab. "I'm not a boy toy, Kev. I've always wanted a senior toy all to myself, and now I've got one." Inter-generational lovers! Go figure.

In my job, I had met all types. But before Brent, I was so far in the closet I was in danger of becoming a garment bag. During these last ten years, Brent has shown me that I probably always was gay.

Still living in Vancouver and still bumping into each other occasionally, Martha and I are now the best of friends; both with our young men. I remember what she said the first time I was brave enough to tell her about Brent: "Now you know what it's like to cuddle up to a firm young bod." She smiled reflectively. And then with a laugh, she poked my "slight" paunch.

I was sure our kids would never understand or appreciate their parents' activities, but their grumbling was worth it. Every time I saw Martha's smiling face, I was confident that we had both finally learned how uncomplicated, blissful, and beautiful real love can actually be and...

The college loomed to break my thoughts. I knew Brent would be waiting for me.

ENTERING THE SIDE door of the college at ten past noon, I walked down the long, ever-crowded corridor. Brent's office door was open. I could see my lover at his desk. He had a carrot stick in one hand and a deviled egg in the other, alternately biting a bit off each and munching the mixture. Was it only this morning that I had prepared his lunch while he sleepily spooned in his corn flakes? Brent is not a morning person. I usually make his lunches, otherwise he'd be satisfied with a bowl of cafeteria noodles.

Our eyes met long before I reached his office. He knew I'd turn up. Jostling the milling students, I noticed the tension in his jaw as I got closer. He stopped chewing, dropped the rest of his carrot and egg on the desk, and stood in the doorway of his office to greet me. "What?"

"Mind if I close the door?"

Brent backed up to the far side of his small office, eyes searching for good news but afraid to hear the worst.

"I'm sorry, Brent. Nancy is dead. I found her at the..." I looked into his grief-stricken eyes. His body started to shake uncontrollably.

Tears flew out of his eyes. Literally. They did not roll down his cheeks. They careened out of his eyes and splashed on the lino floor. His face screwed up like a little kid's in such grief that I rushed to him and took him in my arms. I sensed that my shoulder was being covered with tears and half-chewed carrot and egg.

I could feel his heart pounding into my chest. We stood quietly for two or three minutes. I waited for him to deal with the death of his young friend and colleague. Finally he released me and looked into my eyes. "She's too young to be dead, Kev. What happened?"

"I'm sorry to have to tell you this, my love, but I'm positive Nancy has been murdered."

The tears stopped. He pushed himself away from me and gripped my arms. "Murdered? Are you saying someone killed Nancy?"

As I told him all I knew, I was amazed to see Brent's kind, sensitive eyes harden with rage and hatred. "You find that fucker," he yelled through gritted teeth. Then he looked me in the eye. "Find him and fry his ass. Promise me, Kev!"

"I promise." Then I added, "The RCMP officers are probably at the cabin right now. I'd better get back there. You should let the administration know about Nancy's death; and I suggest you call her parents before the police do. You know the Henderson's are coming here tomorrow." Brent nodded. "It'll be better coming from you. And Brent, don't tell them or anyone else that she's been murdered, not until the RCMP announce it. I got to run."

Halfway down the hall, I remembered a question I had to ask him. I tapped on the door. Brent, fresh tears bouncing out of his eyes, opened the door a crack. "One more question, love. What was Nancy wearing when she left for the cabin on Friday?"

Without hesitation, my fashion-conscious lover said, "Her cherry suit and a white blouse. My favorite outfit. She always wore suits on Fridays. She said they were comfortable to drive in." He bit his lip to try to halt another waterfall of tears.

"Thanks." I whispered, "Keep your chin up, my manno." I called Brent *kiddo* once during our first month together. He had grimaced. "I'm a man, not a kid."

I knew that he'd sit in his office and weep for the rest of his lunch hour. Then, he'd emerge, dry-eyed, to spread the word of Nancy's untimely death.

I now had to hurry back to Swallow Lake because I wanted to get there before the RCMP investigative team. On my way back, I tried to recall past cases that I had worked on with similar MOs to this one. But I couldn't get my mind off my lover's distressed face. No matter what case I tried to conjure up, all I could think of was the first time I'd seen Brent cry. Five or six years ago, we were in a Thai restaurant on Davie Street, about to enjoy an extra-special hot pot that the server had set down before us. Casually, I asked Brent, "If I ask you a favor, will you promise to do it for me?"

"Sure." He smiled, as he put a heaping forkful of rice, veggies, and chicken into his mouth. He'd always refused to use chopsticks.

"I made a living will today. I want to be cremated and I would like you to sprinkle my ashes down Ridge Runner." We'd been skiing the last five years, and Ridge Runner was, without doubt, our favorite blue run on Blackcomb Mountain.

Well, the tears sprang from his eyes and bounced onto his plate of food. I'd never seen anyone cry like that before. I didn't know what to do, so I stupidly continued to clarify what I'd been wanting to say all day, hoping that he'd stop crying. "I'm more than thirty years older than you, and I'll certainly die long before you, so I want to make sure that you know what to do with my ashes."

"Shu...d...up for p-p-pity's sake," he sobbed, particles of food dropping from his mouth, co-mingling with his stinging, salty tears.

I became aware that the eyes of close-by patrons and even our server were on us. Watching, listening. Talk about a bad sense of timing. Brent had pointed out that fault in me on several occasions, but I obviously hadn't learned.

Once he'd emptied his mouth, he let me have it through clenched teeth. "Why are you talking about dying now? When we were having such a nice time. You're not going to die. Not now. Not ever. I don't want you ever to leave me. Anyway, I'll probably die before you. You're in great shape. Stop talking about dying." Sobs were interspersed between each of his short statements. I sat there like a fool, patting his leg under the table. He'd never allow me to touch him in public, my manno deeper in the closet than I ever was. By this time, all the patrons in the crowded restaurant had grown stonily quiet. There were eyes on us from all directions.

"Brent, everyone's looking."

"I don't care," he howled. "Why did you ask me to scatter your..." He couldn't finish the sentence.

"I'm sorry. I'm sorry."

He excused himself and went to the restroom. Everyone's sympathetic eyes following him to the john. When the door closed, all eyes moved accusingly to me. *What did you say to that poor boy, you old bastard?* I lowered my head, heaped up my plate, and dug in. I wasn't going to let a perfectly good meal go to waste. I could sense they hated me more for eating while the poor boy repaired himself.

After a few minutes Brent came back, a fake little smile on his face. Seeing me eating, he picked up his fork. Smiles all 'round us. I expected the damn restaurant to break into applause when he swallowed his first mouthful.

He leaned over. "Do you find your dinner a little salty?" We both roared with laughter.

From that moment, all was forgiven. Brent was like that. He wouldn't forget though, and I knew that if the time should come, Brent would scatter my ashes. I was sure, though, that several patches of icy tears would surprise those unsuspecting skiers who followed him and *me* down Ridge Runner.

Chapter
Four

"LET ME EXPLAIN something to you, Mr. Porter. The Royal Canadian Mounted Police have rules, in case you have forgotten. We certainly appreciated your call to the Detachment, but Chief Inspector Joan Riley is far too busy to personally investigate every death case. She can't make house calls when someone has died of natural causes."

I was quite proud of myself for keeping my cool and sitting quietly on the steps after this smart-ass corporal had barred my way from entering the cabin. *Damn.* I should have hot-rodded it back here. I should have been waiting for them, not the other way round.

I was in a bad mood and knew that I'd probably say something I'd regret if I opened my mouth. So I kept my unfair, cheap thoughts to myself. *When will this power-hungry twit shut up? She's been talking down to me from the moment she opened her trap.* I was feeling much better now, having had the opportunity to rest a bit. After rushing around all morning, I had been feeling a bit pooped. And my sore toe was reminding me that I'd better take another colchicine tablet pretty soon.

"You must realize, Mr. Porter, that Chief Inspector Riley is a very busy woman. She's got a huge territory to oversee now that Ottawa's dumped Swallow Lake in her lap and she couldn't possibly come all the way out here." I concentrated on the white bubbles that were sprouting in the corners of her mouth. "I don't know how you ever got through to her this morning. She never answers the phone. That's not like her." *Will this woman ever turn off the tap?* "You should feel very honored, Mr. Porter. Ever since I was posted under her command, I have been impressed by the way she..."

I stared into the corporal's fulsome face with her unmoving, unblinking eyes and her ever-flapping chapped lips. I tried to find something positive to think about. Ah, yes. It was comforting to know that my replacement was well respected by this flunky. After all, I would have been the first to recommend Joan Riley take over my job, if they had asked me, which they wouldn't have and didn't. All RCMP promotions are made by the higher echelons in Ottawa. Anyway, she took over my position as Chief Inspector. Twelve years ago, Joan Riley was my best Inspector and deserved the promotion to Chief Inspector.

"Chief Inspector Riley has assigned an experienced officer to this case, so you can go along home. If we need you again, we'll call. Sergeant Spivic is now in charge."

"Barry Spivic?"

"The same," replied the corporal proudly.   "Do you know Sergeant Spivic?"

Christ Almighty.   Spivic in charge of this case? I couldn't believe my ears.

"I asked you a question, sir. Do you know Sergeant Spivic?"

Two ambulance attendants appeared from the cottage, carrying a full body bag on a stretcher. My sentinel ran to open the door. For a moment I watched as they put Nancy Henderson's body in the waiting van, but I took the opportunity to steal into the cabin for another look about.

A monster's presence still lingered in this once happy second home of Nancy's. I walked around, sniffing, tracing a killer's steps from the time he entered.   I walked towards the bedroom door. Sergeant Barry Spivic stepped out, hitching up his belt over his beer belly, which had grown significantly since I'd last seen him twelve years ago.

"Chief! I mean, Sir! Long time no see."   We smiled, both of us remembering I had been his boss ever since I moved to the North Vancouver Detachment.   Both of us knowing that each year I had turned down his request for even *applying* for a promotion. And now he's sergeant. *Christ Almighty!*

"What?"

"Nothing. Good to see you again, *Corporal* Spivic."

"Sergeant now," Spivic beamed.

"Sergeant? Really?"

"Ya betcha! Whatcha doin' in these parts? Joan told me that ya found that corpus delicious." He winked.

Oh, my Lord!

"Yes, that's right." I hesitated. How much should I tell Spivic? That my lover asked me to come out here to see if Nancy was okay? No, I didn't want to get into that. "Where are you taking the body?"

"To the morgue, where an autopsy'll be performed.   I don't suspect any foul play, but it's routine t'perform an autopsy when there don't appear t'be no obvious reasons fer death." Spivic drew a liquid breath through his bulbous nose, his ruddy cheeks puffing out.

"Really? I didn't know that, Barry."

He ignored my sarcasm. "Do ya know if this chick lived alone?" Spivic was basically a well-meaning, amiable fellow who could always be counted on to say the wrong thing at the right moment. I had always thought he pretended to be thick in order to get a suspect to drop his guard. But, let's face it, I really didn't get to know Barry very well. I had always made a point of keeping my distance. He was low man on the totem pole in the Detachment when I arrived and was still low man when I left. *And now he's a Sergeant!*

Gazing into his perplexingly bland eyes, I thought I'd better be more circumspect in my judgment of Sergeant Barry Spivic. He must have put forth a massive effort to study and pass that nut-crunching sergeant's exam. Underneath his lack of social graces and native ability must beat a strong drive to succeed.

Spivic's tone changed. "I've asked ya two questions, Kevin. How 'bout coughin' up answers? What brought ya out here in the first place?"

"A favor. I was doing a favor for a friend. Brent Barnes. He's an instructor at the college. That's where Nancy teaches and he was concerned when she didn't turn up to the..."

Spivic's eyes lit up. "So ya knew the dead woman."

"I'd met her a couple of times. Yes."

"I see. Did she live alone?"

"As far as I know she did." He was interrogating me, goddamn it. I had my own questions, screaming for answers.

"Well, that's it then. Let's git out o' here, Kevin."

"Wait a minute, Barry. What about the condition of the cabin?"

"Whatcha mean?"

I could see he still needed help. "Barry. Think for a minute. Doesn't it look suspicious that everything's so neat and clean? Did you see any soiled towels?" He looked dumbly at me. Déjà vu. Looking at his blank face, I suddenly remembered what used to irk me so much about him. I remember griping to Martha night after night about Spivic's inability *to rise to any level of incompetence.* Barry continued to look bored and bewildered. I tried a new tack: sounding patient. "They are all freshly laundered, Sergeant. And her clothes. They are all hung up neatly in her closet or folded neatly in her dresser drawers. There isn't even a tissue in the wastebasket. The place is as sterile as an operating room, for God's sake. That surely proves that something suspicious has been going on here?" I walked into the bedroom. The first thing I noticed was that the light was off.

I pointed over at the bedside lamp. "That was on when I was here."

"Ya. I turned it off. No point in wastin' 'lectricity."

Scat. Get out of here. Let me take over this case. I want to be alone. Leave me alone.

"Didn't it seem odd to you that it was on?" He looked blank. "And focused on her face?"

He sighed. "Let's go outside fer a minute, Chief. I mean, Kevin."

He lumbered outside; I followed.

He sat down on the step and patted it. "Sit." I was going to be in for one of his paternal patters which I'd seen him unsuccessfully and embarrassingly perform on gang members in the '80s. "There's nothin' odd about clean towels, and many people wash their clothes at night. And many people leave a light on fer security." He continued to prattle on as he put his heavy paw on my shoulder. I looked at it and smiled. He removed his hand quickly, then he looked at it. Bits of Brent's carrot and egg stuck between his fingers. He looked puzzled as he tried to figure out what it was.

"Bird shit," I grinned. "We're in the country now." Disgusted, he spat in his hand and wiped it clean on his pant leg. I asked, "Barry, how many women do you know who make themselves up to the hilt before going to bed?"

"It may be a bit unusual, Kev, but it's not significant." *Now he's calling me Kev? The son of a bitch!* "I heard that Marlene Dietrich never went t'bed without makeup on. What the hell would she want t'do that fer? She always vanted t'be alone." He guffawed.

"Greta Garbo."

"Huh?"

"Greta Garbo wanted to be alone."

"Whatever. Anyways, there ain't a shred o' evidence that Nancy Manderson—"

"Henderson."

"Whatever."

"Spivic! She was made up. With stage makeup. Leichners. Surely that must seem odd to you."

"Like-ners? When did ya dream that one up?" He had already made up his mind and was not about to listen to me. "That chick wuzn't murdered. I seen the babe's bod and there ain't a mark on it." He looked into my face with concern, and I thought how lucky I was to have got out of the Force. "Kev, if she wuz murdered there'd be some evidence of a struggle. Some disturbance. Somethin' broken. You could eat yer dinner off o' the damn floor, it's so clean." He looked at me as if I hadn't a clue what he was saying. Spivic needed to see broken dishes, tipped-over furniture, and pools of blood to convince him that a murder had taken place. "She hasn't even got a hickey on her. Now, are ya gonna answer my question or not?"

"What question was that, Barry?" I looked at him with feigned surprise.

"Did the Henderson dame live alone or what?"

"Yes, she lived alone." Either he had already made up his mind that a murder had not been committed, or he didn't want to share his suspicions with me. At any rate, I was tired of playing games with him. I didn't even want to tell him that she only spent weekends here in the cabin.

"Does she have any relatives livin' in the Lower Mainland?"

"No, they are all back east. Brent told me they lived in Halifax."

"Who's this Brent guy?"

"I told you. He teaches at the college. Where Miss Henderson teaches...taught."

"Oh, I see." Spivic gave me one more of those enigmatic looks. "Brent and Nancy were having a thing, eh?"

Christ, I was being sucked into a vortex that could drown me any minute. "I'm sure Miss Henderson's parents' address and phone number will be on file at the college where she taught. I know they own this cottage." The way he locked on my eyes, as if he knew something more, was pissing me off. So I didn't tell him that the Hendersons would be in town the next day.

"She was a school teacher. They sure don't make 'em like the cows I got stuck with in school. Bet she could o' taught me a thing or two. Eh? Eh? Ya know what I mean, Kev? You're not too old to appreciate a good-lookin' broad. Or are ya?" He chuckled contentedly.

I ignored him. "She was a *college* instructor," I mumbled.

"I suggest ya leave now an' phone the Detachment with the address an' phone number of her next o 'kin. No. Forget that. I'll get my assistant t'phone the college after she does a last-minute check-up here. Ya don't wanna be messin' around with Mountie stuff anyways. Yer retired."

"Have you taken photographs?"

"Of course, Kev. It's routine. I told Abby to take a picture or two of sleepin' beauty."

"Abby?"

"The corporal out front, Abby Davis. She's the one ya were talkin' to. Good gal. Still can't get used t'broads in the Force. Ya know how it is nowadays? We gotta swing with the times, so they tell us. I'll never git use t'them Mountie turban-heads. Stupidest damn thing I ever seen. But seriously, Kev, let me assure ya that there's no case here. Henderson probably had a heart attack. It happens, ya know. Even to the healthy ones. Remember that Russkie skater? Dropped dead on the ice."

I don't believe this guy!

"Will you at least seal off the cabin so that no one will disturb the evidence?"

"That's routine, Kev, for murder cases, or have ya forgotten how it's done? But this ain't a murder case, so I don't think it's necessary."

"Humor me. Order Abby to ring the scene with tape. And lock the door. She'll respect you more for giving her orders."

"Ya think?" I gave him a knowing wink. "It's a done deal, Kev. Now, why don'tcha run along and do whatever you seniors do t'keep yerselfs out o' mischief," he chuckled. As I walked away, I kicked some of the gravel and immediately regretted it. *Idiot. Shithead. Bastard. I may be sixty, but I'm not dead yet. Ask Brent.* I limped towards my car.

"Kev?" I turned to look at Spivic. "C'mon over here fer a sec." I walked over to him, trying not to limp. "If this turns out t'be a murder, and I'm not sayin' it is...the — how can I say this delicately — the shit'll hit the fan."

"What do you mean?"

"You contaminated the murder scene, Mister Porter. Then disappeared. Then came back." He looked at me with a small, nearly undetectable smirk. "Off home with you now. I'll call you if I need you, Porter."

I got into my car and hurriedly popped a colchicine. *No doubt about it. Spivic is an enigma.* I noticed that he conveniently dropped his colloquial vernacular when he was reprimanding me.

Before I closed the car door, I heard Barry say to his corporal, "Accordin' to ex-Chief Inspector Porter, 'Clean towels equals a clean murder.'" I left the laughing pair to continue their fun.

Have I lost my touch? Twelve years is a long time. Things have changed. Electronic surveillance has replaced routine leg work. I hoped Spivic wouldn't get in touch with me. I didn't want to take on a murder case at my age. Besides, I had plenty to keep me busy.

Brent had bought me a computer last year and begged me to start writing down some of my more interesting cases with the RCMP in the form of a novel. He had a notion that the results of my labors would open the door to a new TV series: a gay Jessica Fletcher. He said, "Imagine, darl', we'll be sitting in our lazyboys and flick on the TV. The screen will glow to life with *Murder, He Wrote.*"

I've always felt a bit testy about his devising activities to keep me involved, and in truth, out of his hair. A year after we moved in together, he thought that I could easily become a leading light in Vancouver's theatre community so he enrolled me in an Arts Club acting class. The only acting jobs I ever got were — you guessed it — detective roles. I played three different detectives in Agatha Christie chestnuts at Metro Theatre. My British accent left a lot to be desired, but I must admit I had a lot of fun. And it kept me off the streets at night and gave Brent some time to mark his essays or do whatever it is he did while I acted my heart out to an adoring public.

And for the past five years, I'd become a bit of a private eye. It started with a fan who came backstage one night. After heaping me with kudos, she asked if I could track down her hubby who went out one night for a tub of caviar for one of her soirees and never returned. By the end of the month, I'd found him shacked up with an eighteen-year-old bimbette. Gave the old lady the info and she handed me a hefty check. She was eternally grateful and is living happily ever after, alone in her Marine Drive mansion. The old dear asked, "Is a private investigator also called a dick?"

"Yeah. A private dick."

"Well these are for you, Mr. Porter." She presented me with five hundred business cards.

Kevin J. Porter
Experienced Private Detective
Call 555-469-DICK for services

When I showed Brent, he split a gut. "I wonder if the old dear understood the significance of her rebus."

"Her rebus?"

"No one's going to forget: 'For a good sixty-nine, call DICK!' " he howled. "Get it?" He handed me the phone and dialed our number: 469-3425. I groaned.

Since then, the old dear's told the entire Metro crowd about me and now I get at least half a dozen calls a month to track down lost wills, suspected disappearances, runaway puppies. Most of the calls I receive, however, are obscene or heavy breathers. They've figured out the rebus.

Anyway, without any other form of advertising, I keep busy through word of mouth and dropping off an occasional business card. Unlike the life of a Mountie, a private detective can take a job or leave it.

Driving home, I tried to talk myself into letting the RCMP handle the case without Private Detective Kevin J. Porter's assistance. But I knew that Brent wouldn't give me any peace until I had found Nancy's murderer. He was thoroughly convinced that I was the best of Sherlock Holmes, Inspector Morse, Hercule Poirot, and Jessica Fletcher all rolled into one. At this moment, I felt more like Inspector Clousseau.

On my way home, my thoughts turned to a long soak in the Jacuzzi. I soon tired of that self-indulgence and turned my attention to poor sweet Nancy Henderson, lying there all perfumed and fully made up in a dark body bag. "Tell me how you were murdered, Nancy."

Chapter
Five

NANCY HENDERSON GLANCED at her watch as she drew the key from the cabin door lock. Just habit, Thomas Henry King knew. *It isn't as though you have anyplace you need to be, Nancy. You planned a slow, relaxing Friday night like the last two Friday nights. Isn't that right?* He held his breath as the cabin door opened. *Stop, Nancy. Stop and enjoy the quiet night air. Smell the autumn leaves before you go inside. Because this will be your last chance.* He nearly cracked his pained expression into howls of laughter when Nancy ushered him into the cabin.

"The bathroom is off the bedroom. Through here." She threw her coat and purse on the maple chair near the door and carried her guest's suitcase into the bathroom. She was back in the living room area in a moment. He enjoyed watching her sympathetic smile. He gave a little groan as he leaned against the door frame. She said, "You look as though you could do with a good soak."

Perfect.

Nancy laughed. He could tell she was just trying to cover her awkwardness. "Hey, maybe you should tell me your name," she said. "I've never had anyone in my bathroom without knowing her name first." She laughed again, this time more nervously because THK was now smiling and gazing into her eyes.

He enjoyed studying this reserved, strikingly beautiful, young woman. She had a natural look of wholesomeness that belied the need for makeup. In fact, one would assume she never wore any at all, so subtly did she apply it. Most days, like today, he detected only a touch of mascara and a bit of natural gloss on her lips.

"Nikki. Nikki Henson." *I've never been a Nikki or Nick before. "Old Nick" has arrived in the nick of time to become your passionate horny weekend lover.* His thoughts began to arouse him. *It wouldn't do to have Nancy see a bulge under my skirt.* He started to walk toward the bedroom.

"Same initials as mine. That's a coincidence. My name is Nancy Henderson."

Yeah, what a coincidence! He reached for the bedroom door frame and leaned against it, as if he might faint. To the trained eye, his performance might have seemed a little over-rehearsed, but here it achieved the desired effect.

"Are you okay?" Nancy moved to offer help.

"Yes. Thank you. I'm feeling much stronger now, Nancy. The bath should do the trick."

"Well, you take your time. Would you prefer a shower? There's a shower, too."

"No, I think I should be lying down."

"Well, make sure you use plenty of bubble bath. It's right there on the side of the tub."

I know. "Thanks. You're very kind." He entered the bedroom slowly.

"In the meantime I'll make a pot of tea. Do you like tea," she called to the bedroom, "or would you prefer something stronger?"

"Stronger would be great."

"Scotch, vodka, gin?"

"I'm a gin-and-tonic woman."

"Me, too. I love sipping a G&T while I'm soaking in the bath."

I know. He poked his head out the door. "That's the only way to drink gin." He closed the bedroom door behind him. Then he strode quickly to the bathroom. *Shit! I already told her I didn't drink, when I was in the car. Careful now. You don't want to blow your cover.*

He heard Nancy singing happily as she prepared the drinks. *Not to worry.*

Relaxed, he closed the bathroom door and opened his suitcase. He took out a camcorder and set it on the counter beside the sink. He focused it on the closed door and then draped a towel casually over it. All except for the lens. Then he took out a large garbage bag and silently peeled it open. He stripped and put into the bag all of his clothes, even his stylish pumps. He whipped off his blonde wig and threw it in, sealing the bag and putting it back into his suitcase. *Bye-bye, Nikki.*

Standing naked, he looked at himself in the mirror. The cut over his right eye had stopped bleeding, but his right eyebrow and cheek were covered in near-congealed blood. He liked razors; the cuts produced a lot of blood, but healed cleanly. Leaning closer to the mirror, he examined a thin, but completely healed scar on the left side of his face. With the fingernail of his right pinky, he carefully surveyed his hairline. He tenderly traced a near-invisible two-inch scar. Then he slowly, lovingly stroked his finger down the side of his face and over to his nose. He pressed his nose to the right to see a sign of the once-deep, razor-thin cut he had given to the underside of his left nostril. *Knavery's plain face is never seen till used.* The remembrances of each scar that had prefaced delicious adventures opened his eyes with expectation.

He moved back from the mirror. Now he could see his entire

body. He gave himself an approving, full, lips-apart smile.

He focused his attention admiringly on the right side of his bloodied face and began caressing it with both hands. His nails were beautifully manicured, but only his right pinky was painted a dark cherry-red. His little explorer of hidden mysteries.

Moving some of the blood to his stomach, he worked it into his skin, rubbing harder and harder. He whispered to the mirror, "There's only one thing I love rubbing on my skin more than my own blood." He knew exactly how to please himself. For two full luxurious minutes he indulged himself while he continued to take bits of blood off his face and, mixing it with his spittle, worked it into his skin. *Damn handsome man. Brilliant and handsome. What woman wouldn't die to be taken by a body like mine?* He wrapped his tongue around his little finger and drew it into his mouth. He watched himself sucking rhythmically, giving himself delicious pleasure.

He stole a glance at his erection. His mood changed abruptly. *Too soon. Too soon.* He removed his pinky from his mouth and flicked the engorged head of his penis. He groaned as he continued to snap it harder. Hissed, "You put that thing away, you little faggot!" He stood still, closed his eyes, and took several deep breaths.

Opening his eyes, he looked in the mirror, relieved. He smiled and winked. *Good. I've got work to do before I can have some real fun.* He stepped into the tub and pulled the shower curtain closed.

After turning on the taps and holding his fingers under the nozzle to make sure the temperature was right, he snapped on the shower button. He knew exactly what to do. *It really helps to know the territory.*

He loved the feel of water splashing on his face. He squeezed his eyebrow where he'd sliced himself with the razor. He knew that in a few minutes the cut would completely seal. Looking down, he saw his blood circling down the drain. *That will get rid of most of it. And I will soon be clean again.*

After a couple of minutes he looked down and smiled. The water was draining clear.

Kneeling, he put in the plug, turned off the shower, and opened the shower curtain. He stepped out and pushed the Record button. Returning to the tub, he closed the curtain and sat down. He reached for the bubble bath, pouring a generous portion directly under the tap. Instantly the top of the water started to foam. "Bubble, bubble; boil and bubble," he chanted. *Bubble baths make a real man real horny. Nancy, you're going to be in for such a treat tonight.*

Lying back in the bath, he watched his most proud possession disappear under the bubbles. *Inch by glorious inch. Bye-bye, my beauty!* He leaned his head on the tub's edge, closed his eyes, and mused.

Then his eyes opened cruelly, and THK called out in a husky

feminine voice, "I'm ready for my gin and tonic." *Dive, thoughts, down to my soul; here Nancy comes!*

Chapter
Six

I HAD A GOOD view of the mourners who came to Nancy's funeral at St. John's United Church. Well, actually it was a memorial service.

When Brent broke the news of Nancy's death to her parents in Halifax, they were devastated. They had been in the throes of packing for a two-week holiday in Hawaii and a quick visit with their daughter during a layover in Vancouver. After several phone calls with the grieving parents, Brent persuaded them that Nancy would have wanted them to continue with their plans. He told them that he would arrange the funeral to coincide with their layover, pick them up at the airport, and take them back out to the airport later in the day to catch their plane to Hawaii. He assured them that they would be able to say their farewells to their daughter in private, and that she indeed would look like a beautiful, sleeping princess.

As I suspected, we found out that they would not be able to see their daughter at all. In fact, Nancy's body would not be present at the church. It was still being held by the RCMP. "The bod's on hold," Spivic told me in his brief phone call this morning. I was convinced that the autopsy report had proved that Nancy had been murdered.

I told Brent not to tell Nancy's parents or to make public that she was murdered. "There will be enough sorrow at the service, so why compound it?"

Brent had been on the fly all morning and, the master organizer, he'd managed to change all the funeral arrangements to a memorial service. New bulletins. Floral casket blanket dismantled to make individual bouquets for the end of each pew. The church looked beautiful.

Immediately before the service, Brent caught me unexpectedly by the arm, pulled me behind a pillar, and whispered, "I really wanted an open casket so that all her students could see her. She would have looked so beautiful under the blanket of flowers I designed." He gave me a furtive kiss and then was off to be with the Hendersons. He looked handsome in his suit; black always looked good on him.

I was surprised to see the little shake-and-stucco West End church packed with so many mourners that they had to open the church hall next door. Nancy Henderson was well respected by her colleagues and well loved by her students.

Anyway, I was glad to be on my own during the service so I could do a bit of surveillance work. I would be able to bounce from the sanctuary to the church hall easily to look over the crowd. It wouldn't be the first time, or the last, that a murderer turned up for the funeral of his victim. His ultimate high. Sick weirdo.

What do I have to do to get on this case? Eat crow? When Spivic called that morning, I asked him if he'd mind letting me take a look at the autopsy report. For old time's sake. He laughed. What was I going to have to do to read the damn thing? *Become friends with Spivic? Well, if that's what it takes...*

Nancy's distraught parents sat in the first pew, next to Brent and his department head, Jane Edwards.

"Thank you for coming today, to glorify the life of Nancy Henderson." The minister of St. John's began the service. "I can see that Nancy will be greatly missed by a large circle of friends, colleagues and students. In Nancy's short twenty-seven years, she lived by God's commandments. Her parents related to me that she was always an ideal daughter and that she..." Having never met Nancy and having just met her parents half an hour before the service when Brent deposited the grieving, travel-weary couple in his study, the minister was still able to heap Nancy's short life with praise. Like so many ministers, he had the knack of speaking of the dead in intimate terms, whether he knew them or not. Few of the mourners would doubt that he had known and loved Nancy and the Hendersons all their lives.

Surveillance is difficult at the best of times, but standing at the back of the church and not being able to see the faces of the mourners made this self-imposed task pretty futile. I decided to try out the hall next door.

SITTING IN THE church, close to Nancy's parents, Thomas Henry King wasn't the slightest bit concerned that he might draw attention to himself.

The ultimate turn-on would have been to attend an open-casket funeral so that he could look into Nancy's face once more. The face he had so carefully made up. The undertaker wouldn't have needed to do much. Maybe not even a touch-up. He had hoped to bend down and give Nancy one last kiss before she became worm fodder. His farewell kiss. *I would come in my pants for sure if I could put my painted pinky in her mouth one more time.*

He wanted to get up and leave. But he didn't want to draw

attention to himself. So he sat and brooded, silently cursing. *I wanted a God-damn funeral. With a God-damn fucking open casket. I probably won't even get a boner at this rate.*

He felt perspiration run down his cheeks. *Easy. Take it easy. You don't want your mascara to smudge.* As he daubed his face with his lace handkerchief, he remembered exactly what he had said as Nancy took her last breath: *Good night, Queen Bitch, / And flights of hellions sing thee to thy rest!*

WHO AM I looking for? A man? Yeah, I'm sure it was a man who murdered Nancy. My eyes were working their way to the back of the right section of the church hall when I spotted Spivic standing against the wall. What was he doing here? Attending the service of a woman whom he claimed died of natural causes. And out of uniform so that he might blend in with the mourners. Big joke! *Spivic doesn't know what surveillance means, standing there at Mountie attention in his tight, size fifty jeans.* Every inch of him smelled cop. As I began to work my way over to Spivic, I heard Brent's voice over the loudspeaker.

"Twelve years ago, when I stopped off in Vancouver on my world tour to 'find myself,' I fell in love with this beautiful city and decided to apply for a teaching post at the college instead of going home to Sydney..."

The college was lucky to hire Brent. A clever man, he completed his master's in English and Drama at twenty-three. His intelligence, clean-cut look, and cheerful personality got him a term contract. Within three years, Jane Edwards offered him a full-time position and the next year she asked him to be her assistant department head. Oh, yes, she had a crush on him too. That's probably why she hired him in the first place. She liked having his young, handsome face close by. *And so do I.*

"I have had many highlights at the college," continued Brent, "but, without any doubt, my highest of highs was the day that Nancy came into my office. She was a constant source of inspiration, always presenting me with a new challenge, a new adventure in literature. On Friday, while we were strolling around the campus, she read to me an excerpt from her favorite Emily Dickinson poem. I'd like to share it with you now."

I went into the church to be nearer Brent, hearing him recite. "Because I could not stop for Death,/He kindly stopped for me./The Carriage held but just Ourselves/And Immortality./We slowly drove—He knew no haste/And I had put away /My labor and my leisure too,/For His Civility./We passed the School, where..."

A tear sprang from Brent's eye. He tried to continue. "We passed the...college..." He broke down and whispered, "I'm sorry, I can't finish. I'm sorry." Mouthing, "Goodbye, Nancy," he took his place beside Mr. and Mrs. Henderson, who comforted him.

The effect on the congregation was intense. Even a few of the strongest jocks shed tears. The service continued with "Amazing Grace," sung by a quartet of Nancy's students who were music majors. Most of the lyrics were drowned out by sobbing students.

I got caught up in the emotion too. Standing misty-eyed at the back of the church, feeling uncomfortable and curiously self-conscious, I decided to step outside to wait for Spivic. I wanted Nancy's killer.

"OBVIOUSLY NOT AN official call," I said to Spivic at the end of the service. I had caught him slipping out to get a look at everyone leaving. The surprise on his face clearly indicated that he hadn't noticed me in the church hall. And he was on surveillance duty?

"Kev! How's it hangin'?"

"So what brings you to Nancy Henderson's memorial service? Have you released the body yet? Is the autopsy completed? Have you found out she was murdered after all? Is that why you're here?"

"Hold yer horses, Kev. I'm not about t'answer yer questions 'cept t'say that we now suspect foul play. I'm here jist t'have a look-see." He continued to check out the crowd. I surveyed his unreadable face, trying to figure out what made this man tick. His eyes held a depth that I couldn't fathom. "T'morra mornin' I'm gonna visit the college in my official capacity. I wanna have a chat with them teachers and students there. Joan don't want me steppin' on any Vancouver Police toes, so she's okayin' things with the powers that be herself. We don't want that Anne Wyner chick blabbin' on the tube and givin' things away about our murder investigation."

"So Nancy was murdered."

"Ya betcha."

"Come on, Barry, fill me in. Let's have a cup of coffee and chew the fat a bit. Like old times."

"Like old times?" Spivic shot me a disbelieving look.

Ignoring his eyes that registered the fact that we never had any "old times," I was about to get chummy with Spivic. I'd always held a secret hope that one day Joan would ring me up and ask for my help on an especially difficult case. She never did phone. I suspect my old boss saw to that. And I knew Sam was still the commissioner. "Let's have a coffee together and talk about the case. I live around the corner."

Spivic stared incredulously at me. I tried again to read his face. I made an executive decision. Spivic needed my help whether he

knew it or not. I convinced myself that Joan must have been short-
staffed to have put him in charge of this investigation. I was sure she
realized he didn't have a clue as to where to begin. *I bet she put him
in charge because she knew that I'd be doing my own snooping and feeding
my discoveries to Spivic.* I'd always known Joan was a clever cop.
Whether she planned this or not, she was going to get two detectives
for the price of one.

I could see that Spivic would never ask me for anything, but he
wanted to look good for Joan. "Jist one cup. And then I'm off t'do a
bit o' research."

*Research? Spivic wouldn't know a microfiche from a microwave. He
probably came to the church to find me.* "I promise, Bear. Just coffee."
He gave me a fulsome smile. His wife called him Bear, her Teddy
Bear.

On a hot afternoon at one of our annual picnics, Spivic and I
happened to get out of the pool at the same time. The hair on his
chest and back was like a shag carpet, and at least two inches long.
Millie, who was his size, came running up. "Hi, Chief. Hi, Bear."
"Bear?" said I. Millie giggled and blurted, "When we make love, I
hang on to Barry's back hair. I call him my Teddy Bear." Both Mil
and Bear had nearly punctured my eardrums with their loud hoots.

I tried not to conjure up an image of the Spivics, all five hundred
and twenty pounds of them, making wild, passionate love.

Once most of the congregation had left the church, Bear and I
walked the two blocks to my penthouse in silence, except for the
sounds of a mouth breather struggling up the gentle incline. I tried
to pin down this man, what made him tick. He was much more like
the stereotypical bumbling, affable TV cop, without the slightest
trace of a laid-back RCMP officer. And yet, every once in a while he
could give me a look that said, "Gotcha, Kev! I know what yer
thinkin'."

I STEPPED INTO the elevator, motioning Spivic to join me
before slipping in the passkey, and pressing in my code. It was easy
to tell that Spivic, now bug-eyed, was intrigued.

In a few moments, the elevator opened into the Carrara-marbled
hall of the apartment. That sight stopped Spivic's breath in a gurgle.
"Hot shit! Yer the only person I know who has an elevator stop in his
own apartment." I kicked off my shoes and put on my slippers, then
picked up the phone, punched in the security code, and unlocked the
French doors to the apartment proper. The afternoon sun danced
through the Venetian blinds along the entire length of the living and
dining rooms, bringing life to the oil paintings in heavy gilt frames.
It never ceases to amaze me how the figures in Renoir's "The Dining
Room" evoke so many happy intrigues. I must confess all the

paintings are copies of originals. The height of *nouveau riche* decor. But only a trained eye would be able to tell our Monet from its original.

I turned to the open-mouthed sergeant. "Bear, we take off our shoes here. There's a basket of slippers in the hall for guests. Find a pair that fits you while I put on the coffee."

In a couple of minutes, Spivic padded into the kitchen, wearing a pair of poodle slippers. If they are worn just right, the poodles' heads will roll from side to side. A particular influential friend of mine, who will remain a nameless City Council member, loved prancing around in those slippers, and only last week had me, and his young lover in hysterics at his ability to give life to the poodles. Arf! Arf! Arf!

I stared at this affable, redneck RCMP Sergeant, decked out in poodle slippers, about to conduct a serious discussion regarding, I was sure, his first murder case. I shuddered as I set out two cups and saucers and a plate of cookies.

"Ya mind givin' me a mug?"

"No, not at all." I opened the cupboard door and took out a mug.

"Ya get more in a mug." He winked. "Mind if I look at the rest o' yer apartment before we git started?"

"Sure, be my guest. Only the upstairs master bedroom is off limits."

"Ya mean there's two floors?" He was nearly wetting himself. I could hear his thoughts: *When I retire, me and Mil will be livin' in a place jist like this joker has.* He asked casually, "What kind o' dishwashin' soap do ya use?"

"I don't know. Whatever's on special. What do you want to know that for?"

"I have my reasons." He walked to the living room. The poodles started swaying from side to side.

"Arf! Arf! Arf!"

"What?"

"I thought I was going to sneeze." For effect, I executed one of my Agatha Christie detective sneezes. They always brought down the house at the Metro Theatre.

"Bless ya. Jeez, git a load o' that view!"

I got a real charge out of showing off the impressive penthouse. The first night Brent had showed it to me, I ogled everything like a silver fox in a chicken coop. A little like Bear was doing at this moment.

Yes, I must confess, the penthouse isn't mine. It's Brent's. His mother owns real estate all over the world. Without setting foot in the city, she's built and sold at least a dozen towers in Vancouver. She developed this small eight-apartment unit with its two-story penthouse especially for Brent.

I wanted to catch up with Spivic, who had already gone out on the deck off the living room to admire the view. It wouldn't do for him to see the phallic ashtray that I kept on the patio table. Brent never allowed smoking in the apartment.

THK HAD FOLLOWED the two men to the corner of Dalmatian and Comox and was now watching them out on the deck. He could see them leaning against the rail in animated conversation. He wondered what they were talking about. *Me, probably. I spotted them both at the service, trying to case the crowd. Looking for me, were you, boys? Talk about the odd couple! One, over the hill; the other, a fat dimwit.* He laughed quietly, confidently. *O sweet Revenge, I'll come to thee both when thou least suspect.*

Chapter
Seven

"HI."

"Brent," I yelled. "Come on in. Sergeant Spivic's still here." I dashed to the elevator to intercept him, leaving Spivic in the living room, dunking his fifth Oreo cookie into his coffee.

I was surprised to see the Hendersons with Brent. "There's such a crowd over at the church, I thought it would be a good idea for Mr. and Mrs. Henderson to get away and have a little R&R before I take them to the airport."

"Good idea. My deepest sympathy, Mr. and Mrs. Hender—"

"Please. Call me Hilda. And my husband's name is Fred." Hilda was a big-boned woman, sophisticated, with beautiful snow-white hair styled short to accent her tall frame. She appeared a very determined woman who could handle any problem, any situation. She sucked in her cheeks. I could hear her spittle slip between her teeth. Then she swallowed. "I hope you don't mind if we take a half-hour rest stop. It's been quite a day." She leaned over to me and whispered. "Especially for Fred."

"Please, go in." Brent was already hanging up their coats. Fred appeared detached, his eyes not focusing on Brent or me; rather, they were glazed over under his thick horn-rimmed glasses.

Hilda's speech seemed normal, but her voice was hollow and it, too, was without expression, as if the words came out without thought. The grieving couple was coping with the death of their daughter. What would they do when they found out that her death had been so unnecessary? "Why don't you go on through?" They didn't move so I ushered them in the direction of the living room, trying to keep up a normal conversation. "Brent, would you like to get some cups for Fred and Hilda? Sergeant Spivic and I have been having a coffee. There's still lots in the pot. Or would you prefer tea?"

Walking towards the living room, Hilda answered, "No, coffee will be fine, thank you."

Once the Hendersons were out of sight, Brent grabbed my shoulder and whispered, "What the hell's Spivic doing here?" I'd already filled him in on Spivic Monday night after my frustrating time at the cabin and, without even meeting Bear, Brent couldn't stand him. Then Brent asked, "Is Spivic here because he knows for sure that Nancy has been murdered? Don't leave them alone with him."

I rushed into the living room and noticed there was only one Oreo left on the plate. "Brent," I called, "bring in some more cookies. Mr. and Mrs. Henderson, this is Sergeant Spivic."

"I'm investigatin' yer daughter's death." Spivic stood up, chocolate crumbs tumbling onto our white carpet.

"What are you talking about?" Fred became instantly alert. His eyes widened on Spivic. "Surely our daughter's death isn't a police matter?" The words *police matter* hung in the air. Both Hendersons grabbed each other's hands. I could hear their screams in my head as they both stood, staring at Spivic.

I jumped in. "Mr. Henderson...Fred...Hilda, any suspicious death requires—"

"An autopsy." Spivic interrupted. "Yesterday, our Forensic Identification Officer gave me his report."

"A Forensic Pathologist? They only work on—"

"Ya betcha, Mrs. H," Spivic broke in. "You're gonna hear it sooner or later, but it wuz murder all right." The moan from Fred tore at my heart. I gave Spivic a dirty look. He looked down sheepishly. This was not how I'd intended to break the news to the Hendersons.

Fred looked at Hilda and whispered, "Our baby girl was murdered? Who would want to harm a hair on her beautiful head?" He collapsed in the big blue lazyboy, his wife comforting him. He gripped Hilda's hands, holding on so hard that both their hands turned white. We were all quiet. Finally Hilda broke the silence, without taking her eyes off her husband. "How?" She sucked in her cheeks audibly and swallowed.

"I'm sorry, Mrs. H," Spivic spoke in hushed tones, "but I'm not at liberty t'talk about that."

"We have a right to know." Hilda released Fred. She gave Bear a withering look. "Nancy's our daughter."

"Mrs. H, ya hafta understand. When a murder's bin committed, police policy insists on a blackout."

"Even to the family? And please, don't use that word anymore," Hilda demanded.

"What word?"

I mouthed to Bear, "Mur-der."

"Oh, ya. Sorry, folks. Anyways, we don't want the media gittin' the details out to the public. That'd make our work a lot harder. D'ya see?"

"Do you honestly think that we're going to speak to the media?" Her stare demanded an answer. Her cheeks drew in again.

I interceded for Bear. "Hilda. Fred. We don't know how she died. I found her. When she didn't turn up for work, I..." I explained briefly and quietly all I knew. At last, I ended with, "Your daughter looked beautiful, like a sleeping princess, waiting to be kissed awake."

Fred and Hilda both nodded. This was what they needed to hear. Finally Fred asked, "Why Nancy? She was such a sweet darling woman. Kindness itself never breathed in a more beautiful body. She was my pride and joy." He removed his steamed-up glasses. He looked at Hilda and confided, "I-I will never be the same again, Hildie. Never. Do you understand?"

Hilda held out her arms and he entered her safe sanctuary. She looked at me with tears in her eyes. *See the tragedy that has befallen us!* We watched in sympathetic silence as she moved his head from off her chest and put her own forehead to his, whispering, "It'll be all right. I'll look after you."

They wept silently, foreheads touching, tears mingling. I could see that they were bonding in their own private way in order to help each other cope. We prepare our children for *our* deaths. Who prepares us for theirs?

Bear lowered his head. The reality of their grief had finally hit home to him.

Hilda opened her purse and took out some Kleenex. She gave a couple of pieces to Fred and then wiped her own eyes. "Have you got any leads, Sergeant?"

"Too early, Mrs. H. But we're right on top o' the case. I bin talkin' with Kev here and maybe he'll do a bit o' the leg work fer me." I gulped. *So he does want me to work with him.*

"Oh," said Hilda. "Have you found any clues around the cabin? A killer..." She bit her bottom lip, but with effort, recovered. She held her hand up and said, "I want to get this out even if it takes a while. A killer always leaves clues. Nowadays, even a single eyelash can be enough to make an arrest. So you're sure to find something there that will help. Isn't that right, Sergeant?"

"Yessiree, ma'am." Bear was feeling better now that Hilda was asking questions. "As I said, we're on top o' everythin', and us Mounties always gits their man."

Fred stared at this poodle-slippered RCMP officer dunking the last Oreo. Fred was the classic Mr. Peepers. His thick glasses made his eyes appear much larger than normal, so he looked curiously off balance with his thin face and sparse dyed brown hair atop his slight body. He looked as if he lived to read. "You're sure that Kevin will be working with you?"

"Off 'n' on," Barry smiled, "I haven't worked with a civvie before, but I'm sure he'll do as he's told." He knuckle-punched my left arm and guffawed at what he thought was a great joke. *The bugger.*

"How did you get assigned our daughter's case?" Hilda jumped in, squelching his laugh. She was a woman who expected to be obeyed. Her voice was stronger now. She wanted details.

"Would ya believe the luck? When Kev called the Detachment, Joan answered—Joan Riley's the Chief Inspector over in North Van. She took over Kev's job when he wuz..."

I coughed. Bear looked at me.

"Anyways, I wuz the only Sergeant 'round. So Joan says t'me, 'Barry, I want ya t'go to Swallow Lake and take charge of the investigation.' I wuz flabbergasted 'cause I'd bin workin' on them gangs that've sprung up all over North Van lately. Ya know, ya really hafta keep the lid on them slinkies and towel-heads. They'd jist as soon as slit yer throat than git rid o' their crack and pot and ecstasy junk. Anyways, she says, 'Kevin Porter will probably be there t'fill ya in.'"

Then he gave me a wink. "When this old bastard wuz on the Force, he had a knack of creepin' into a killer's mind. But more important, he gits into the skin of the victim too. You should see him at a murder scene, sniffin' around, talkin' to hisself, writin' notes. That's why this guy wuz known as Canada's super cop. He wuz that damn good, pardon my French. If anyone's gonna track this killer down, it's Kev here."

I was shocked by Spivic's generosity. And humbled. I looked at the Hendersons and could tell by their eyes that they felt more assured.

I didn't know what to say, and have learned at times like this, to remain quiet.

Thankfully, Brent walked in with coffee cups and a fresh plate of Oreos. I wondered where he had been. Probably overhearing enough that he didn't want to come in and face Bear.

"What're ya doin' here in Kev's place, creepin' 'round like ya owned the joint?" Bear grabbed a couple of cookies from the plate. Brent's mouth flew open.

It was quite obvious that this was not the time to tell the Hendersons or Spivic that we were sitting in *Brent's* living room. "Sergeant Spivic, you haven't met Brent, but he gave the eulogy at the service. Brent Barnes was Nancy's colleague. They shared the same office." I could tell by his relieved face that Brent approved of my tactic.

"I'm gonna be 'round t'see ya t'morra. Maybe one of her students had it out fer her because she gave him an F, and decided t'bump her off. Or maybe it wuz..."

Fred started to weep again. "Maybe we can change the subject, Barry." I said. "Let's talk about something more pleasant."

"Oh, yeah. I'm sorry, folks, to be talkin' shop 'n' all. In my job ya see stiffs every day and don't even think a thing about it. Ya should hear the jokes that go 'round the lab when they're sawin' through a..."

"Barry, would you like another cookie?"

"Don't mind if I do. They're damn good." We were all happy to see him dunk and slurp the Oreo, and immediately reach for another.

"Would you like to see the view from the patio?" I asked the Hendersons.

"Yeah, ya shouldn't miss it," munched Barry, as the Hendersons escaped to the deck. I followed them, leaving Bear and a disgruntled Brent.

Everyone who goes out on the deck for the first time *oohs* and *aahs* at the view. Fred and Hilda were no exception, but their enthusiasm was definitely not heartfelt. Hilda soon exhausted her praise of English Bay and the North Shore mountains. And when I pointed out Cypress and Grouse, she told me how lucky I was to live so close to two ski mountains. Then we stood in silence for a few minutes.

"I apologize for Sergeant Spivic. He's really a good cop, but he's been working with Asian gang members for too many years."

"Asian gangs?" Hilda enquired.

"There are a number of them in the Lower Mainland. Pretty tough lot. The Force needs hard-nosed, no-nonsense cops to deal with them. Spivic's great at keeping them in line. That job has toughened him, made him downright insensitive at times. I'm sure, though, that he's got a good heart, so I hope you can excuse him for talking with his paw in his mouth."

"Thank you for the explanation, Kevin," said Hilda. "I was wondering what on earth had happened to BC's laid-back, sensitive hospitality. I speak for Fred, too. Right, darling?"

Fred nodded. "Nova Scotian officers are gentlemen first; policemen second. I'm glad that you'll be working on the case."

"Thank you. I know you're still in shock, but we don't have much time before your flight. Would you mind if I ask you a few questions to help us in our investigation?"

"Not at all. Ask us anything," answered Hilda.

"When did you last see Nancy?"

"A month ago. Isn't that right, Fred? That's when we met Brent." He nodded while she hugged herself for warmth. "He's a lovely man. I don't know what we would have done without his help over the past two days."

Fred nodded solemnly. "We liked Brent the moment we met him last August."

I remembered that evening. I had a great time decking Brent out for his big date to meet Nancy's parents. When he returned home, he said, "Don't ever let me do that again."

"You were on good terms with your daughter?"

"Always. She is..." Fred stopped and rubbed his hands rapidly over his face.

"It's okay. You are bearing up remarkably well. I'm damned sure that if one of my kids was killed, I'd go off the deep end."

"Nancy *was* our only daughter and we loved each other unabashedly."

"What do you do?" I asked Fred.

"I am retired now, but I ran the English Department at Dalhousie."

"Ah." That explained the use of *unabashedly*. Once an English teacher...

Hilda added, "We were out the previous summer too. For three glorious weeks. That's when we bought the cabin at Swallow Lake. Spectacular beauty." She went on describing the different kinds of trees and rock formations around the cabin. I've seen hundreds of reactions to trauma, but spouting details as if she were a travel guide was a new one for me. But I let her continue talking for several minutes.

I finally broke in. "When did you and Fred meet?"

"Fred and I met at Dalhousie. I ran the geography department." *Ah!*

"I know that this may seem an unnecessary question, but do you know if Nancy had any enemies?"

"I can't think of a time in her life when she wasn't surrounded by friends. Nancy was the most outgoing young person I've ever met. And I'm not saying this because she's my daughter. I'm sure that you underst..." Fred convulsed. He looked tired and ashen as Hilda put her comforting arm around him. He kissed her hand. An unusual couple. She was definitely the tower of strength that he needed. I had the feeling that she sustained her strength by helping her husband grieve. I could picture her in the plane to Hawaii, sitting erect in her seat, patting Fred's brow, his head resting on a pillow on her lap.

Hilda continued where Fred left off. "After moving to Vancouver, Nancy devoted most of her time to her work. When she took on a job, you could always count on her to give it her best."

Fred continued, "And now...and now I know she's watching and feeling so sad that she is letting her students down."

Looking at my watch, I was amazed that we'd been out on the balcony for nearly half an hour. I was convinced I wasn't going to acquire any relevant information from the Hendersons and I knew that Brent was probably climbing the wall as he listened to Barry's scintillating conversation, so I suggested, "I think it may be time for Brent to take you back to the airport. You're doing the right thing. I know that Nancy would not want you to cancel your holiday."

"Yes, that's true." A forlorn smile crossed Fred's lips. "Our daughter would want us to go." Hilda nodded and shivered as she started to walk back into the living room, preparing to meet Bear again.

"By the way," I caught them as Fred's hand was on the patio door, "where in Hawaii will you be staying? In case I need to get hold of you."

"The Big Island. We'll be at the Waikoloa Hilton," Hilda stated.

"Nancy's favorite spot." Fred's lips trembled and his glasses steamed up again. We walked in.

We were surprised but relieved to see that Spivic had left. And there was no sign of Brent. I spotted a note on Bear's tray. It was in Bear's handwriting. I read it aloud: "Brent Barnes has went to get the car and yer to send the Henderson's downstairs when their ready. I got beeped and have to go and pick up the autopsy report."

"Didn't Sergeant Spivic say he'd already read it?" asked Hilda.

THOMAS HENRY KING smiled contentedly, having seen Nancy's parents on the penthouse balcony.

"Excuse me, miss," huffed Sergeant Barry Spivic. "Are ya lost or somethin'?"

"Oh, you startled me." THK lowered his head coyly, his long red hair covering part of his face. "I was admiring that beautiful apartment block."

"I wuz jist in there," Spivic bragged.

"Oh," he smiled. "Lucky you."

"Ya betcha. Ya should see that penthouse. It's a beaut." Bear whistled to make his point.

"One day maybe I might." He stifled a laugh.

"Gotta dash. Duty calls." Spivic strode down Dalmation Street to the car park. He sensed the woman's gaze on his back so he kept up a good pace to make an impression, both arms swinging out from his sides to propel his bulk forward. Whistling with his tongue pressed against his bottom teeth, Bear complimented himself on his good judge of women. "Now that's what I call a good-lookin' dame. Redheads are always hot stuff in bed, I hear." He attempted a little skip, to impress her, but nearly tripped.

The redhead wasn't even looking in his direction. THK was deep in thought.

Chapter
Eight

"HERE. READ IT 'n' weep." Spivic handed me the autopsy report. "This one's easy readin'. And you can thank me fer that."

"What do you mean?"

"The first one Frank Williams gave me I couldn't make head ner tail out o' all that anatomy crap. Why the hell can't doctors call a windpipe a windpipe instead o' sopho-what-you-call 'em? So I called Frank up and told him to write it again in plain English. He owes me one. It wuz him who beeped me yesterday while I wuz chattin' with that young teacher, Brent Barnes. I'm gonna be seein' him later this afternoon. Is he Chinese 'r Aussie?"

"Both."

"Ya don't say."

"Yes, his mother's Chinese; his father's Australian." Bear's eyebrows raised. I wanted to read the report instead of listening to Spivic, so I lowered my head.

"Kev?"

"Yeah."

"If ya wanna wade through the *official* report that Dr. Boyland sent me yesterday, I can pick it up from the office, but what we got here is a meat-'n'-potato readin'."

"Thanks, Bear. This'll be great for now." *How did Spivic ever get through high school, let alone that ball-breaking Mountie course in Saskatoon?*

I started to read the hefty report while Bear tore into a Triple O mushroom cheeseburger, a plate of fries, and a chocolate shake. We had met at Bear's favorite haunt, the Lonsdale White Spot Restaurant, close to the North Vancouver Detachment Office.

Sept. 29, 1998. Unofficial Autopsy Report, by Frank Williams, [written especially for Sergeant Barry Spivic's eyes only:]

I looked up. I could tell that Spivic was "jist as proud as punch" with that opening. I continued to read:

Victim: Nancy Jean Henderson, age 27 years, 3 months, 8 days.

Height: 5'7". Weight: 119 pounds.

Work was begun on the deceased on Monday, Sept. 28, 1998 at 1:14 pm in the morgue at the Lion's Gate Hospital. The autopsy was conducted by Dr. James Boyland, assisted by Frank Williams and Julie Smith of the RCMP.

The RCMP does not have forensic pathologists in the Force. Instead, they often use the medical examiners at nearby hospitals. Their own Forensic Identification Sections focus more on blood and urine testing, hair and fiber testing, and occasionally testing of body parts. Nancy's body, therefore, was taken to the nearest hospital to the Detachment. Dr. Boyland, however, was comfortable working with trained NCOs. Both Frank and Julie were experienced Non-Commissioned RCMP Officers.

I began reading the detailed "Preliminary Discovery," concentrating on Frank's concluding synopsis:

The killer probably applied Obsession perfume to the victim's pulse points so that the scent would be continuously activated during the last tortuous hours of her life.

I made a note and continued.

Her body showed no marks of trauma, no bruising, no needle pricks. We examined the entire body for latent prints. Unfortunately, we found none on her fingernails, toenails, eyes, or skin. While searching for any foreign material such as the killer's saliva, semen, hair, whiskers, blood, or skin particles, we noticed several minor traumas to various skin areas (especially around the pubic and anal areas, the armpits, and the scalp) where the skin was lifted in several minor puckers. This was a puzzle to us.

The victim was fully made up. NOTE: All makeup to be analyzed to obtain trade names of products.

I made a note, read the rest of this long section, and read Frank's conclusion:

The makeup was applied by an experienced cosmetician.

I looked up and watched Bear contentedly munching his burger, feigning complete indifference to my reading the report. *Devious son of a bitch!* I lowered my head.

The victim's hair contained a great deal of hair spray, to keep its stylized bouffant look. The hair reflected some burning as if a curling iron had been left in place too long... Conclusion: The killer, even though apparently distracted from time to time, knew exactly how to backcomb in order to create an attractive '60's hairstyle.

In examining her right hand, we noted that all her fingernails were carefully manicured and all except the one on the little finger were perfectly painted with dark-cherry polish. Conclusion: The killer had, in all probability, deliberately left this nail unpainted; all the other nails on both hands had at least two coats of enamel on them.

In attempting to remove her left thumb from her mouth, we noted that the lipstick on her lips had dried around the entire thumb... The procedure to remove the thumb took fourteen minutes. Upon removal, we discovered that she had bitten into her thumb. We had to pry her jaw open in order to extricate it. We noted that the victim had bitten down to the metacarpal [Spivic: that's the main bone of the thumb]. The entire mouth cavity was filled with congealed blood. In removing her thumb, we also removed the congealed blood that had adhered to it. After removing all the blood from the thumb, bagging it, and tagging it, we washed the thumb clean. The end of the thumb indicated heavy trauma and the skin was a deep purple. The nail was painted deep-cherry.

Conclusion: The victim must have bitten her right thumb to offset a greater agony. Question: Is it a coincidence that the color of nail polish is identical to the victim's gelatinized blood?

Overall Conclusions: We found no trace of foreign matter on the body. Nothing that wasn't the victim's own hair, skin, cells. Once we completed our search, Corporal Smith suggested that the killer might have vacuumed the victim's entire body. The minor skin puckers could have been caused by the suction of a heavy-duty, wet-dry vacuum cleaner. No other significant outward trauma, other than the self-imposed wounds to her left thumb, clearly indicates that the cause of death was internal. A full autopsy is required.

I picked up the manila envelope marked "Henderson: Photos of Preliminary Discovery." There were seven of them. Two interested me most. The one with the bag of congealed blood, conveniently photographed beside Nancy's right hand, showed that the color of the blood and nail polish were exactly alike. The other of her open mouth, still full of blood. It looked as though it was filled with several tablespoons of cherry jello. It puzzled me that so much coagulated blood was still in her mouth. I made a few notes.

"I'm gonna order a slice of boysenberry pie à la mode. Wanna piece?"

"Huh? Oh, no thank you, Bear, I'm still working my way through the report."

Bear flagged down the server. "Easy readin'. Right?"

I nodded, and began to read the Full Autopsy Discovery, the longest and most harrowing part of the report.

The mouth cavity was full of incrassate blood [thick, lumpy, caked]. After removing it all from around her teeth, cheek pockets, palate [roof of the mouth], and uvula [that's the little thing that hangs down at the back of the mouth that looks like a punching bag], we bagged and labeled approximately a cup and a half of blood.

As we suspected because of the large amount of coagulated blood in her mouth, the victim was missing her tongue. It had been removed by a precise cut deep in the back of her throat.

Conclusion: the tongue was removed immediately after death. The killer must have removed the thumb, cut out her tongue, and replaced her thumb between her clenched teeth while blood continued to seep out of the stump of her amputated tongue. Overall Observation: When you find this bastard, you'll probably find the victim's tongue in a deep freeze or pickled in a jar on his trophy shelf.

"Or he ate it!"

"Huh?"

I looked up at Bear, shoving the last piece of his hamburger into his mouth. I didn't realize I had spoken out loud. "Nothing." I lowered my head, as if to continue reading, and thought about the fact that many serial killers take a souvenir. And eat it. Eating part of the kill turns them on all over again. I made a note. *Do we have another Jeffrey Dahmer here?* I closed my eyes for a minute.

Sensing Bear's gaze, I looked up. He was contentedly chowing down his first bite of boysenberry pie. He stopped chewing. "We could have a serial killer on our hands, eh?"

I nodded and mumbled, "My thinking, too." Bear had read between the lines of Frank's report. "How many other women do you think he's killed?"

"We'll soon find out. I've got Abby workin' on PIRS."

"PIRS. That's an electronic retrieval system, isn't it?"

"Huh-huh, ya weren't around when we really got into this electronic snoopin' business. PIRS stands for Police Information Retrieval System. So, if we put an MO in the system, and if some other British Columbia police agency had a murder with a similar MO and has already put it into PIRS, then it'll come up on the screen as a match."

"That sounds too easy."

"It works."

"Well, okay, but I think we should still be concerned."

"Whatcha mean?"

"How many other women will he kill before we get him off the streets?"

"None," he said, filling his mouth with a piece of pie heaped with ice cream. "You'll see."

I gritted my teeth, lowered my head, and read on.

Both Corporal Smith and I were unsurprised to see that the throat cavity was also full of blood and, once we removed and bagged as much as we could, we noticed two other things that further disturbed us. 1. There was a great deal of tearing in the larynx [the cavity in the throat that contains the voice box]. The evidence seems clear that the killer made her fellate him. 2. We suspected that the congealed blood probably filled her entire trachea [windpipe] and maybe even throughout her entire alimentary canal [the parts of the body where food passes.]

Spivic was leaning in, looking at the report, trying his best to read it upside down. "Is that what I think it is?"

"What?"

He pointed to *fellate*. I nodded.

"In her larrie-inks?"

"Right. Deep into her larynx and trachea."

"Shit." Bear lowered his head and shoveled in a mouthful of pie.

"Is it okay that I continue reading?"

"Mmm."

I performed a Y cut to expose the entire torso of the victim from the larynx to the vagina. Through the sternum [breastbone], we opened the entire chest. [You'll have to come in next time we perform an autopsy, Spivic, so you can see how we do things.]

First, we removed the trachea from the larynx to the bronchi [the two main branches of the windpipe, one going to each lung]. We opened the trachea by...

As I continued reading, I was sickened by the sordid details. I stopped every few minutes to copy out his conclusions in my pad.

Conclusion: She had been repeatedly sodomized, probably at first by penile entry, then by a hose. We deduce that the killer used a black rubber hose to wash out any traces of his sperm. But this does not explain why the stomach and intestines were totally free of digested or undigested food. It would appear that the victim had somehow been sluiced out, pumped with air, and corked.

We proceeded to investigate her reproductive organs. Again, upon dissection, we discovered a perfectly clean...

I copied down Frank's Results of Tests:

The tests showed a small trace of alcohol, .02, but no evidence of sperm. Her liver and kidneys were healthy. Constable Smith indicated that the condition of her heart displayed evidence of a sudden, massive coronary attack. The pain had obviously been too much for her heart. In order to divert the pain from other parts of her body, the victim, while still alive, attempted to bite off her own thumb, as would an animal caught in a leg-hold trap. Her heart could not take the inhuman abuse that her killer was inflicting upon her.

I pinched my nose between my eyes. I'd been in the cabin with Nancy, feeling her pain. I forced myself to continue reading and made another note of Frank's Conclusion:

We have a killer with a cleanliness fixation who obviously brings along his own specialized equipment. In my 23 years as a forensic examiner, I've never encountered such a clean body as I have today. They usually come in here needing a good wash-up before we start to work; this one came in clean, outside and inside.

After her death and after removing his "souvenir," the killer had spent many hours transforming her into his theatrically beautiful fantasy.

We have a sicko beast here who I hope you can remove from society immediately. Corporal Smith calls him a "Clean Fiend."

[You're lucky I had some time on my hands today. Now *you* owe me, Spivic. How about a couple of jars of Mil's dill pickles?]

Having finished the report and putting a few last notes of my own into my pad, I looked over at Spivic. Our eyes spoke as one. *Let's get the bastard!*

"Thanks for letting me read the report, Bear. It answered most of my questions. And thanks, too, for asking Frank to rewrite it in layman's terms." Spivic grinned as he reached into his vest pocket and took out a folded piece of paper. "Here's a little surprise for you, Kev. You were right."

I opened the paper. It was a short report from Frank. I read it quickly.

Thank you, Barry, for your suggestion that we compare the makeup with Leichners. Results came in. All the makeup was definitely theatrical makeup. It's a perfect match to the Leichner brand. Very observant. Congratulations.

"Make ya happy?" I nodded. "Sorry about not givin' ya credit. But yer not really in the loop, are ya? You don't mind me gittin' a bit o' recognition, do ya?"

"Not at all. I'm here to help. Feel like a drive to Swallow Lake? Maybe you should take another look at the cottage."

"Can't. I gotta go to the college and start interrogatin' the staff and students." Bear looked at me and winked. "Are ya wantin' t'tag along?"

"Well, I haven't been doing much lately and thought I might do some of that leg work you wanted me to do. You know, make a suggestion or two. Here and there." *Damn! He's looking at me with his hooded, deadpan eyes.* "I could help, you know." *He's wanting me to beg, the crafty bugger. Okay, I'll grovel.* "I may be sixty, but there's still lots of muster in the old bod."

"Let me git this straight. Are ya wantin' t'be my assistant?"

"No, no....Well, yeah. Your silent partner. What do you think?" He stared at me. I decided to go for broke. "It'll be our little secret."

He pondered what I'd thrown to him. "Okay, Kev, I'll take yer bait. Ya hooked me."

"Great. You won't regret it. Now let's get out to Swallow Lake."

"I told ya, Kev. I gotta get to the college and talk to the teachers and..."

"They'll wait. You can call them and re-schedule. But some of the evidence around the cabin may not be there tomorrow."

"I already told Abby to go out there and arrange t'have the car towed away and then dust the cabin fer prints."

"Maybe it's not a good idea to have your subordinate poking around without you."

"Ya think?"

"Yeah. I think."

"Well, whatcha waitin' fer? Let's haul ass, partner."

AFTER HIS HUGE lunch, Bear was hibernating beside me in my Lincoln Continental. He wanted to take his cruiser but I didn't fancy traveling a hundred klicks an hour on the Upper Levels Highway and all the way to Swallow Lake, siren wailing. Spivic's philosophy: Why go slow when you're a cop?

I wanted to check on several things at the cabin, so I began to make a mental checklist: coat, purse, nail polish, makeup, brushes, combs, dishwashing soap, cleaning detergents, washer, dryer, vacuum cleaner... I looked in the rearview mirror. Paul Newman's eyes looked back at me.

Brent tells me—I'm sure to bug me—that my eyes look like Paul Newman's. I don't see that, but they *are* blue and pretty intense. On the morning of my sixtieth birthday, he asked me to go down to get some important papers out of his car, and there in *my* parking stall, instead of my little Honda, was a '60 Lincoln Continental, completely restored and painted blue, "to match my eyes." Around it was a huge red ribbon with a card on top. "Happy sixtieth, you drop-dead gorgeous hunk."

"Drop-dead gorgeous? Me? Hell, no."

"What?" Spivic awoke with a start.

"I was yelling at that dumb truck, cutting in on me like that." Then I rolled my window down and yelled, "Drop dead, buster!"

"Ya shoulda let me take my cruiser. But I appreciated the shut-eye. Last night wuz a late one, what with me havin' t'read through Frank's whole autopsy report. An' then havin' t'please Mil before I got my beauty sleep. That missus of mine can't git enough, if ya git my drift." He let out a bearish guffaw.

I shuddered at the thought and changed the subject. "We've got a number of things to check out at the cabin."

"Ya betcha. I got my pad all ready." Spivic leaned back in his seat to make a few notes. He was off to Bearland within a minute, filling the car with his wheezy snores and his...well I'm glad I kept my window open.

I tried to focus on the Clean Fiend, as Corporal Smith so accurately labeled him. I wanted to get a handle on the killer. What happened to this guy to make him such a monster? What kind of childhood did he live through? Was he born evil? I'd never come across such an MO as Nancy's and I had little hope that PIRS was going to turn up a slew of similar murders in BC. This killer was too clever. He covered his tracks too well. I had to figure out what made him tick. What kind of childhood he had to endure...

"THOMAS HENRY KING! What are you up to in there?" his mother screamed as she banged on the bathroom door. "Are you playing with yourself again?"

"No, Mommie! I'm going pottie." He was only four and he didn't understand what his mother meant. He wanted to surprise her.

"Open this door right now. Do you hear me?"

He jumped off the toilet and unlocked the door. His mother stormed in and slapped him across the face. "Don't you ever lock this door again."

"I promise, I won't," he sobbed. "I'm sorry, Mommie."

"Now let's have a look in that toilet." She peered into the empty bowl. "See, you haven't gone yet. You need Mommie to help you. Turn over."

"I want to try by myself. Please, Mommie."

"You know you can't. Now turn over." He did as he was told. He knew the position: on his knees with his head and right shoulder on the floor and with his little bare bum up in the air, ready for his mother. She turned on the hot water in the sink, put in the stopper, and put in a small amount of Ivory soap. He watched her open the drawer in the counter and take out a large red syringe with a hard six-inch black nozzle sticking in the end of it. She stuck the nozzle into the water and squeezed the globe. He could hear it filling with the hot soapy water. "I'm ready. Stick your ass in the air."

He knew it was going to hurt so he bit down on his thumb. He could feel her finger inserting a bit of Vaseline into his tiny rectum. Then he felt the pressure of the big black nozzle as it entered him. He groaned.

"Are you enjoying this?" she screamed.

"N'mmie. It huuus," he mumbled.

"What are you saying? You know I can't understand you with your fucking thumb in your mouth. Take it out or I'll cut it off." It was only eleven in the morning and his mother had already had two stiff shots of vodka and had listened to Wilson Pickett beat out "Midnight Hour" for the fifth time. She was an R&B woman. Always during his enemas, his mother played her favorite Rhythm and Blues or jazz records.

"No, Mommie," he said, "I don't like this. It hurts."

"That's right. It hurts. You remember that. Don't you ever let anyone but Mommie put anything into your bum hole. Do you understand? Now Mommie is going to let in the soapy water."

With his free hand, he grabbed his little penis and squeezed it. It helped lessen the pain. He moaned gently because he didn't want to upset his mother. He could feel the water entering him. He had a tremendous urge to push it out but he knew that his mother would get angry.

Suddenly she flipped him over. "What are you doing?" She stared at his penis. It was hard, like a little red pencil. "You dirty little masturbator. You are enjoying this, aren't you?" She flicked his penis with her little fingernail, painted cherry-red.

He cried, "That hurts, Mommie. I'm sorry. I won't touch it again."

"That's right, darling. Don't you touch your dirty little pee-pee. Only queers touch their pee-pees." She picked him up and plunked him on the toilet. "Now get rid of your shit. For Mommie."

He could hear the gush of water pour out of him. And then he heard the plink, plunk that he knew would make his mother happy. He looked up and smiled.

"That's my good little man," she said as she sailed out of the bathroom, a perfectly satisfied mother. She came back into the doorway and smiled sweetly. "Now you hop into the tub and get yourself nice and clean."

Chapter
Nine

"WE'RE HERE."

Spivic grunted and opened his eyes. "Already? That didn't take long. Ah, they're here." I did a double-take as I pulled into the driveway. Two squad cars were parked in front of the cabin. Two men jumped out of one of them.

Corporal Abby Davis was leaning against the other, smoking. She flicked her cigarette and ground it with her heel. Bear looked at me and winked. *The crafty bastard had no intention of going to the college. He was putting me in my place.* "You jist watch, Kev. Not a word. Got it!" I nodded.

Abby trotted over to us. The two men fell in behind her. She opened the passenger side for Bear. "Good afternoon, Sergeant Spivic." She nodded to me. "Mr. Porter." She was definitely a little more courteous to me, at least in her tone. I nodded, taking Bear at his word. She was expecting me to be with Bear. *Sly bugger. I'd better be on my guard.*

The security tape was still in position. "Looks like nothin's bin disturbed," said Spivic.

"Right, sir. We were waiting for you as instructed. I don't think anyone's been here since Monday, except the tow truck. As you requested, sir, I had them take the victim's car in for testing. They left about twenty minutes ago. I was having a fag while I waited for your arrival."

"Why don't we get started?" Bear hitched his pants and headed for the cabin.

"Good idea." I got out of the car. Bear turned. "Kev, you already know Abby. That there's Jeff Ferguson." I returned the nod of a trim, thirty-something Non-Com Officer. "He's from the Hair and Fiber lab, but he'll be looking for anything foreign around the place. And that there's Pete Springer. You remember Pete from the old days?"

"Great to see you again, Kev. Long time no see. How many years has it been?" I didn't recognize this six-foot, gaunt NCO in his late fifties. "I can tell you've forgotten me. I dusted many a murder scene for you, Kev."

"Pete. Of course," I broke the silence. "You got older! Where did all that wavy hair go?"

"Same place as yours, Kev. South! But I'm holding on to my fringe." He laughed as he pulled at the eight-inch gray mane that hung down his back.

"Well, if you two are through BS-in'," Bear interrupted, "maybe we can git some work done." Abby had removed the seal and Bear had unlocked the door. *Where'd he get the key from?*

Abby turned at the top of the small landing. "Put these on, gentlemen." She handed each of us a pair of cotton booties that we put over our own shoes before entering.

"It'll be a little like shuttin' the barn door once the horse flew the coop, but it's a good idea anyways," Bear said, looking at me. "We don't wanna contaminate the scene any more 'n it's already bin, do we?" He gave me a wink.

I was the last to walk into the common area.

Everything looked the same. Neat and clean with everything in its proper place. All except for a coat and purse on the maple chair next to the main entrance. "Why don'tcha check this here purse, Abby?" Bear ordered. "Jeff, the floor's yers. See what ya can find. And Pete, ya might as well start dustin' fer prints in here first. Kev, you stand over there." He pointed to the wall next to the sink. Obediently, I padded over and leaned against the wall. I noticed the picture on the calendar which hung there. It was of Nancy with her mom and dad.

Pete took out a bag of gloves from his case and held them out for us. "Everyone, here's some latex gloves. Put on a pair before you touch anything."

"Good, Pete, I wuz jist gonna say that."

"I am going to use my own." Abby frowned. "I like to wear my own. I'm allergic to latex." Everyone looked at Abby. "Hives," she snapped. "You got a problem with that?"

"No," said Pete quickly. "No problem. Take a pair for yourself, Kev."

"I don't need to wear gloves. I'm only observing. I'm not going to touch a thing." I took out my pen and pad and made a few notes.

Spivic reached in the bag for a pair. He ripped two gloves, chanting, "If the glove don't fit, ya must acquit." Abby let out a friendly groan; Jeff and Pete guffawed good-heartedly. Bear was in fine form. His staff liked him. Finally, he found a pair large enough to fit him.

"I'll jist check this here coat." Spotting the name tag inside, Spivic glowed. "It's definitely the victim's coat. Look here, 'Nancy Henderson.' Sewed right in. Imagine that. Jist like the way my Ma sewed my name in all my school duds."

Abby said, "She only had a tube of apricot lipstick and a wallet in her purse." She opened the wallet. "Well the motive of death certainly wasn't robbery. There's a hundred and thirty-five dollars here. All her credit cards are in place. Two photos of an older couple..." Pete was at her elbow. She dropped each item carefully into one of the plastic bags that he produced. As she dropped in an item, he sealed the bag and wrote something on the label.

"Fred and Hilda," Spivic said knowingly. He produced a small canister of pepper spray from the pocket of the London Fog trench coat. "Take a look-see at this. Our girl wuz prepared fer danger."

"Didn't do her any good, though," added Pete. "Did it?" He held out an empty bag for Bear, who dropped it in. Pete labeled the bag.

"Wonder if she used it? Or if she didn't, why not?" Abby chirped.

"We'll test to see if this pepper spray's been used." Pete added an additional comment on the label.

Bear pulled out some car keys. "Only other thing in her pockets are her keys." He gave them to Pete on the end of his pen, who was ready to bag them. "Fer yer information, I removed one of the keys the last time I wuz here." Pete wrote more on the label. "It wuz the key to the cabin."

Remembering that the autopsy report stated that there was evidence of soap in poor Nancy's intestines, I said, "Why not check out what soap she uses?"

"Good idea, Kev." Spivic walked over to the kitchen area and opened the door under the sink. He produced a bottle of Ivory and a bottle of Mr. Clean. Spivic made a note on his pad. There was very little else under the sink. Immediately, Pete began dusting both bottles for prints.

Spivic opened a closet door and noticed the vacuum. "Jeff. Ya finding anything?"

Jeff continued to peer at the nubbly carpet. "Nah. This is the cleanest carpet I've ever seen."

"Ya better take the vacuum cleaner in fer testin'. Ya never know what'll turn up in that bag."

I motioned Bear over to me. "Why don't you check it out now? I lay you odds that it's empty. Dead empty."

Jeff flipped the vacuum open and, sure enough, there was a brand new vacuum bag. "Nothing in this bag, that's for sure. I think I'll still take the vacuum in anyway. Never know what might be in the hose."

"You could be right," Bear said, rooting in the cleaning closet.

"But remember, Bear," I interjected, "Nancy was a bit of a neatness freak herself and probably had put in the new bag. I doubt whether that vacuum has been used in the last week."

"Look here, Kev." Spivic held up a package of vacuum bags.

"One's missin' from this three-pack."

"So what does that tell us?" I asked.

Abby answered, "The killer probably spent little to no time in this part of the cabin."

"Excellent observation, Corporal," stated Bear. "But we don't wanna miss nothin'. Let's do a last look 'round before we head into the murder room."

The room became a beehive again. They all checked around, trying to find something, anything that looked out of the ordinary. There didn't seem to be a thing in this part of the cabin that might lead us to the killer. I thought back to when I had been there on the Labor Day weekend and would have sworn there wasn't a thing — from that time to this — that was out of place. There were no glasses or cutlery in sight. As far as I was concerned, there wasn't a thing to check out. I looked again at the calendar; January was still showing. Nancy hadn't pulled off the months since then. *Suppose she's keeping it up because she likes the picture.* I casually flipped my trusty pen over to February. The photo for February was of Nancy and another young woman. The caption read, "Best Friends from Your Past." I continued flipping and saw several other pictures, all featuring Nancy with others. "Mother and Daughter" showed a couple of happy, smiling faces. "Dad and Nancy" depicted Fred sitting on a sofa with Nancy sound asleep on his lap. I continued flipping. I noticed something written in the August squares of the calendar. For August Eighth: "Dorothy Bovak spent the weekend, making me an offer I couldn't refuse." Puzzling. I knew that Dorothy was in the English Department at the college. Then written over three boxes for the Sixteenth to Eighteenth of August was: "Mom and Dad had a wonderful, laid-back weekend here." I flipped to September and closed it immediately. It was a picture of Brent and Nancy. I looked up, thinking that I was being observed, but everyone was still busy doing their own things.

"Pete, have ya dusted all the door handles, windows, backs of chairs, taps, all them glasses, whatever?"

"Not the glasses."

"Remember, Frank wrote, 'The blood tests found a small trace of alcohol, .02.' They probably had a drink t'gether before he showed her his hand. Among other things. So don't forget to dust the liquor bottles good."

"Right, Sarge."

Abby and Bear were busily taking out every dish and glass while Pete quickly dusted them. He kept shaking his head negatively after each dusting.

I took this opportunity to turn to September again. "Nancy's Beau" jumped out at me from under Brent and Nancy's happy smiles. *Christ Almighty. What is this all about?* Obviously this calendar with "special" photos from *last* year was a present Mrs. Henderson made especially for Nancy *this* year. Nancy must have sent her mother this picture of Brent and her. Where was it taken? There were trees, shrubs, and a lot of green grass in the background. She wore a smart casual pantsuit; he was in his blue slacks and matching paisley shirt that I bought him for his birthday. I recognized the golf course in the background. They were obviously out on one of their noon-hour walks on the path surrounding the college and golf course. I spotted two lots of writing in the September boxes.

"How ya doing, Kev?"

I looked up guiltily, dropping the pages. *Hell.* I realized I didn't have gloves on. "Fine. Amusing myself."

Bear went back to work.

I quickly flipped back to September. In the three boxes for the Labor Day weekend, she had written, "Brent and Kevin spent weekend. The reality of the situation was kind of weird. C'est la vie!" *How the Hell can I show this to Bear?*

I stared at the note in the September Twenty-Fifth box. Just last Friday. Nancy had filled the box with small print. "Unexpected guest. Nikki Henson. Had an accident. Poor kid. Lots of blood. Invited her in to clean up, have a bath, and a stiff drink. Could be an interesting evening!"

My heart stopped. A solid lead. The first. I heard a shot from a starter's pistol. It was a familiar sound. Every time in the past when I found my first lead, I'd hear the same shot in my head and knew that I was in a race to the finish. Then I had another thought: How come she wrote so much? What was going on? She sounded excited. Preparing drinks, looking forward to an interesting evening. My God! While she was out here writing this note, Nikki Henson was in the bathroom preparing to kill her!

"Kev!...Kev!"

"Huh?" I dropped the pages of the calendar.

"Ya look like ya seen a ghost. Y'okay?"

"Come over here, Bear." He was there in five strides. "Send the others in the bedroom. Or outside. Or any place but here. I've got to show you something." Bear stared at me. "Do it," I insisted.

"Pete and Abby, I want youse to go in the bedroom now and dust fer prints. Jeff, did ya find any fibers or hair in the washer or the lint trap in the dryer?"

"Nothing. Clean as everything else in here."

"Go outside and check the bushes and trees. See if any bit of fiber is hangin' on a branch. Ya never know. And check fer footprints, especially 'round the back. If ya see anythin' suspicious, take a mold. And Jeff. Look for any drops of blood out front."

They all left us alone.

"Take a look at this." I opened the September page hiding

Brent's picture and the Labor Day notation. Bear read the Sept. 25th entry. He looked up at me.

"Nikki Henson?"   Bear ruminated for a minute.   "Nancy Henderson identified her killer. That's a woman's name, ain't it? So, our killer's a woman."

"I doubt that very much. He probably disguised himself as a woman. For sure. You read Frank's report. Do you think a woman could do what he did to Nancy?"

"Ya! Yer right. Bet he wuz usin' an alias. Maybe his name is plain Nick. Whatcha think?"

"Could be."

So, now at least we know how the killer got inside. Invited in by his victim. Did ya git a load o' that last sentence of Nancy's?"

"Yeah. The understatement of the year."

"A good find, Kev." Bear picked off the calendar from the wall. "I'll take this in for further examination. Did she write anything else in here that's important?"

"Nothing that reflects on the killer."   I wondered how long it would take for my world to explode in my face, but I couldn't open the whole kettle of worms yet. *Why the hell don't I come right out and tell Bear that Brent and I are lovers and that we spent the Labor Day weekend here, in Nancy's cabin. Coward!* Maybe. Probably. Shit. Damn right. *When Bear finds out, I'll be off the case. For sure.*

"Let's go in the bedroom and see what they're up to." Bear walked over to the table and placed the calendar in a large plastic pouch, then strode into the bedroom. I followed.

Except for the crumpled duvet in the corner of the room — where the mop-up crew had dropped it on Monday — everything was as I remembered it. Abby and Pete had finished in the bedroom and were now in the small bathroom.

Spivic's indecision reared its head again. "So what should we do?" he asked.

I looked him in the eye, "You're in charge. I'll do your bidding."

Spivic cleared his throat, and blurted, "Frank's report stated that…" he frowned and then continued, " 'the makeup was applied by an experienced cosmetician.' Let's check out her makeup and see if there's any more of that dark-cherry fingernail polish. Good idea?"

"Great idea, Bear." He had quoted the report word for word. *Interesting.*

"Pete," he yelled, "have ya gone through the drawers in here?"

"Not yet."

Spivic looked through the dresser drawers. I didn't touch anything, but peered over his shoulder at the contents. After a few minutes, he said, "Definitely no makeup here." Then he yelled again,

"Pete, Abby, I wanna git in the bathroom."

They came out. Bear went in. He opened the only drawer there and found a few bars of soap, a package of bubble bath, baby powder, a brush and comb, and a small bottle of Obsession. Spivic lifted the perfume. "Git a load of this! In Frank's report he wrote that the perfume on Nancy wuz Obsession."

Spivic got down on his hands and knees to look on the shelf under the sink; no easy matter. I remained in the doorway of the bathroom to make room for him. The shelf contained a package of toilet tissue and a few towels, neatly folded. Getting up with great effort, he concluded, "Well, this lady doesn't have any Like-ner makeup. Do ya suppose the killer copped her makeup? What a..."

I could see that I was going to have to give Spivic a nudge. "Tell me again how she was made up."

He looked at me and then at Abby and Pete. "You two can continue dustin' in the john." They went in. Bear closed the door and turned. He pattered off the description Frank had written of Nancy's made-up face, virtually verbatim. Had he memorized the autopsy report?

As he was spouting the report, it came back to me. Spivic has this incredible ability to remember what he reads. That's how he must have aced his Sergeant exams. He doesn't always know what to do with the information he's memorized, but those RCMP exams ask for the facts rather than asking application questions, and Spivic could easily answer knowledge and comprehension questions with his near photographic memory.

"Well," I shrugged, "the only makeup that Nancy has here in the cabin is what Abby found in her purse."

"The lipstick. Apricot color, wasn't it? What kind o' color is apricot, exactly?"

"Kind of an orangey pink. Just like an apricot."

"A far cry from deep cherry. Right, Kev? What does that tell ya?"

"Well, I have a hunch that the killer brought his own makeup. After he killed her, he made her up. With his own makeup."

"Whatcha mean? This guy carries his own makeup?"

"Looks like it. Probably has his own makeup kit."

"Kev, are ya tryin' to tell me that he killed her 'n' then made her up?"

"Or before he killed her."

"So," Bear reflected, "this makeup thing is all part of the way he gits his rocks off. Rotten bastard."

"I'm sure you're on the right track, Bear. But to make sure, you better ask around the college whether or not anyone ever saw Nancy in heavy makeup." I knew that she had never worn much any of the times I met her, but I still wasn't ready to tell him that Brent and I had known Nancy socially.

"So, if our killer brings his own makeup into the cabin, he probably brings in other things, too." He grinned.

"I'm with you. Bet he brought in his own cleaning solution, catheter, hose, even a wet-dry vacuum cleaner."

Spivic smacked his hands together. "I bet that's exactly what that bastard did."

"You may have hit upon the most significant aspect of this case so far, Sergeant; our Clean Fiend brings in all his own equipment in his own car. He wants to make goddamn sure he isn't going to leave evidence or fingerprints by touching any of her stuff." Spivic was scribbling down notes. "And I'll lay you hundred-to-one Pete doesn't find a single fingerprint in the can."

Bear gave his belt a hitch and strode out of the bedroom. "Let's go see how Jeff is doin' outside." As Spivic and I left the cabin, I was confident in only one thing. The killer himself had left nothing for us to go on. He must have wiped down all the furniture, walls, doors, and the contents of every drawer and closet.

When we got to the back of the cabin, Bear asked, "So, Jeff, have ya found anything?"

"Not a thing. Not a single footprint. The ground is too spongy." Abby leaned her head out of the bathroom window and yelled excitedly, "Sergeant Spivic, we've found a perfect print."

We all rushed inside. Abby and Pete were all smiles. Spivic wheezed, "Where?"

"On the toilet flusher. It's a perfect sample. A thumb print. I bet it's our killer."

"Shit," I spat. They all looked at me. "It's my print. When I came to check on Nancy's whereabouts, I used the toilet and flushed it."

"Are you sure?" asked Abby, disappointed that the one piece of evidence they had found was worthless.

"Yeah, I'm sure. But you'd better check anyway. My fingerprints are probably still on file in the Detachment. Or do you want to print me now, Pete?" I felt terrible.

"Contaminated the scene, ya know," Bear said flatly.

"I know. I know."

"Well, it looks like we've done enough damage here," snarled Bear, giving me the evil eye. I felt like a naughty schoolboy. It wasn't so much the look on his face as my own awareness of guilt. Damn it, I had compromised the scene. I knew it. And I'd known it at the time.

Had I helped the killer? *God, no. I'm sorry, Nancy.*

Seeing Bear lumber out of the bedroom, I determined to make my presence felt. I needed to be needed, to be helpful. To prove my worth. "Jeff," I said with as much authority as I could muster, "I think you should vacuum the mattress. Go get your vacuum."

Bear stopped in the doorway and frowned at me, but I refused to wilt under his stare. I'd had it with brown-nosing. Jeff looked at Bear, who jerked his head toward the kitchen.

Jeff dashed to the other room for his equipment and was back before Abby and Pete began to strip the bed. As they unhooked the fitted sheet, the five of us stared in horror. Under a clear plastic mattress cover and directly under where Nancy's body had been lying, was a Polaroid of Nancy, nude from the waist up, obviously still very much alive in a sitting position, eyes straining in unmistakable agony, biting down on her thumb.

"His fucking calling card," I shouted.

Abby hugged herself. "The filthy bastard."

Spivic stood dumbly looking at the photo, shaking his head in sadness. His grief was touching. He quietly, reverently pulled the corner of the plastic sheet across the bed to expose the photo. God in heaven, it was already in a small Ziploc bag. With a similar pen to mine, Bear picked it up by one corner.

"What's that on the back?" asked Abby.

Spivic turned it over and read the typed label fixed to the back of the photo. "A souvenir for the RCMP for remembrance. I already have mine." I could tell that Bear was shaken, thinking of the killer's reference to Nancy's tongue. He roared, "That lowlife, mother-fuckin', slime-eatin', son-of-a-bitch monster! We'll get you, ya hear me. I promise, we'll get you." He placed the baggy inside a large plastic pouch that Pete held out to him. Pete lifted it and stared inside.

"What's this?" Pete pointed at the bottom of the plastic pouch.

"What?" Bear turned. He was trembling.

"In the bottom of the bag."

Bear held it up to the light. "It looks like hair."

Jeff opened his forensics kit. He carefully fished out the hair with a pair of tweezers and placed it in a glycine folder. He studied this find with a magnifying glass. We waited and waited for Jeff to finish his examination. Then, handing Bear the glass, he said, "Get a load of this, Sarge. It's a braid. Of three hairs."

Bear, peering through the magnifying glass, grumbled, "That's what it looks like, all right."

"And," said Jeff, "if I know my hairs, and I do, they all look like pubic hairs. Three different shades of brown to black. Braided in a neat plait."

"What the hell!" Bear said. "I want a lab analysis before you do anything else."

"Great. We'll be able to trace the DNA," I said confidently.

"Provided we find some others." Bear turned and started to walk out of the bedroom.

"Sergeant?" I stopped him. "That plastic sheet looks new. I bet the killer brought it with him. You better take it in for testing. Maybe he's left something on it."

"Think for a minute," snapped Bear. "If the creep cut out her bloodied tongue, there'd be blood all over the bed. It's plain t'see that he brought his own beddin' and his own plastic sheet and took the lot with him. We're not gonna find a drop of blood on this 'brand new' sheet which either he brought with him or was already on the bed when he got here. And it's gonna be a waste of time to vacuum the mattress."

"You're right. After he killed her, he probably carried her to the bathroom and put her in the tub. That would be a better place to perform his tongue amputation. That way he could wash away the blood, dry her off, and put her clean body on a newly made bed." I looked at the shocked expressions on the faces of Abby, Jeff, and Pete. This was all new information for them. Perhaps too much information.

Abby was the first to break the moment. "What makes you sexists think the killer is a man? Women commit murders too, if you haven't heard."

Bear attacked her. "The killer's a guy. Okay? Take it from me. Okay?" He looked at Abby's crushed expression. "I read the autopsy report, Corporal. I know our Clean Fiend is a guy."

"Right, sir."

Bear picked up the plastic mattress cover and struggled to fold it. Jeff ran over and took the other end to help. Bear would see to it that the sheet would be tested, to make certain. Both started to walk out of the bedroom.

"Pete," Bear ordered from the other room. "Print Kev's thumb to make certain it wuz his on the toilet."

"Right, Sarge." Pete looked at me. "Over here, sir." He took my right thumb and shoved it on his pad and pressed it on the paper. He didn't say another word.

I tried to ignore the process. "Abby? Did you come across a typewriter anywhere?"

Pete squirted a cleanser on a cloth and rubbed my black thumb semi-clean.

Abby answered, "No, sir."

Pete walked out without a word. I could tell that he didn't like printing his former Chief Inspector.

"That means the killer had already prepared his message for us before he entered the cabin," I said flatly. We walked outside without another word.

Bear and Jeff had finished putting all the samples in the backseat of the cruiser nearest the cabin. "Ah, Pete," ordered Bear, "you and Jeff git to yer labs right away. I want full reports out o' both of ya when I turn up later tonight." The two NCOs nodded, got into their car, and sped away.

Bear looked at me. "We're done here. We gotta git to the college 'n' ask a few questions. Kev, I'm gonna go back with Corporal Davis." Abby got into the driver's seat of her cruiser while Bear went up to the cabin, locked the door, and replaced the seal. As he opened the car door, he said, "I'll be in touch, Kev."

"I'd like to hang around a bit. Alone. Get the feel. Okay?"

"Suit yerself." Abby turned on the ignition before Spivic got into the passenger side. Once he snapped on his seatbelt and closed the door, she was kicking up dust and gravel as the cruiser sped out of the driveway. They were off to the college. I wondered when he'd ask her to turn on the siren.

Standing outside the cabin, I tried to relive Friday night. Whatever possessed Nancy, pepper spray in her pocket, to take her would-be killer into her remote cabin? Simple: she thought she was inviting a woman into her cabin. A woman with blood on her. A woman who'd been in an accident. A woman with her own car.

The killer needed a car. He had all his makeup and cleaning equipment with him. When he finished his weekend spree, he packed his car and disappeared.

Too bad we hadn't taken a closer look at the driveway on Monday, taken a mold of the tire markings, searched for drops of blood. It had rained hard the night before and there had been so much traffic in the driveway since the murder, a test now would be futile. I looked out to the main road. "What have we here?" I said out loud, looking at a broken florescent-painted log post near the end of the driveway.

I quickly walked over to the post. It had been at least three-quarters sawed through. I noticed traces of damp sawdust on the ground. Looking closely at the sawdust, I could tell instantly that the post had been sawn recently. "That's got to be it! The killer had been here before Friday to prepare for his weekend orgy. He had to know that Nancy was always here every weekend. He was probably here earlier in the week, sawed through the post, and then once he was sure she was in the cabin, he deliberately crashed into the post. She heard the crash and came out, full of concern and invited him in. Just like Nancy.

"Am I close, Nancy?"

Not yet. "Did you put on your overcoat before you went outside? No, you wouldn't take the time." Her purse had been on top of the overcoat. Besides, had she come in earlier, she'd have hung up her coat and put her purse someplace else other than on the chair. "So?"

It was obvious. He had already crashed his car into the post before Nancy arrived. When she came home, she saw the accident.

Being the careful woman that she was, she got out of her car, pepper spray in hand, to see if the driver was okay. She saw a woman and relaxed. "Nikki Henson" must have looked in bad shape, so Nancy pocketed the spray and took her inside to help clean her up. So how come we didn't find any trace of blood? Being a master at makeup, he probably used fake blood. Whatever he used, Nancy was fooled into a false sense of security.

"Is that the way it was, Nancy? You both walked into the cabin together. You may have even helped him in. Then he went to the bathroom to clean up and 'repair the damage.' And you? What did you do, Nancy? Make drinks? Yes! So what did you do while you were waiting? You sipped your drink and wrote on the calendar about your guest."

Goosebumps erupted on my legs. Someone was watching me. I could feel eyes on me. I casually turned round, but saw only the green cedars. I turned to the right, quickly. A branch was swaying ever so gently. And then nothing. No one was there. Maybe it was the breeze. *Maybe I'm hallucinating. Then why didn't the other branches move?* "Come on, Kev, get your mind back in the cabin that night." It took a moment for me to recall what I'd last said to myself. *Calendar. She'd written in her calendar.*

"Then did you take his drink in to him or did he come out to join you? Definitely the former. Had you seen him, you'd have run. There would have been evidence of a struggle. So you went into the bedroom with the drink. Or did you go into the bathroom with the drink? With him waiting for you? Nude and waiting. Erect and waiting."

Chapter
Ten

ON THE SET OF *The X-Files*, Harry, the makeup artist, powdered Agent Mulder down; the actor had complained that a few drops of rain had landed on his cheeks during the shoot. "Just a sec, DD. You've got an eyelash that's a bit out of whack. Look up." While Mulder sat in the chair, the makeup artist skillfully smoothed the offending eyelash with his pinky fingernail.

"Thanks, Harry. Nice to have you back on board. No one knows my face better than you." He was out of the chair and nearly out of the trailer when he turned. "Sorry to hear about your mother's death." And he was gone.

"Thanks, DD." DD was his pet name for the star of *The X-Files*. When he first met the actor, he was unable to get his tongue around his unpronounceable last name. The nickname stuck.

The Vancouver papers and radio and TV stations will do another dumb story about DD's ongoing hatred of BC's climate: "X-Files Star Holds up Filming because of Rain." Once their darling fair-haired boy, the citizens of Vancouver had become pissed off with DD.

Harry was pissed off with DD too, but for different reasons. He was consumed with his thoughts of this actor who was obviously on his way up, having completed a major Hollywood film that was receiving good reviews and reprising his role in the movie version of *The X-Files. Why should that little no-talent shit get all the press? Wait till the Mounties find my calling card at Swallow Lake. It's about time the media stopped talking about a monotone, expressionless two-bit actor and concentrate on someone with real talent. Me.*

Harry flew out of the makeup trailer, one of half a dozen other trailers parked along Broughton Street in the West End. During the last few years, Vancouverites had become used to lines of trailers blocking many streets. Good for the economy. And kind of fun bumping into a major star every once in a while. No doubt about it, BC had become Hollywood North. Since DD's brouhaha, though, the media had started calling Vancouver Brollywood.

When he got near the shoot, he slowed down. *Mustn't look like a brown-noser.* Strolling around the corner on Pendrell Street, he took out a cig from his smock pocket and lit it with a match. Better stay close to the action. *DD may get a few drops of rain on his precious, dumb-ass face.*

Today was Harry's first day back to work after a month's absence. Everyone on the show believed that he had been in England to nurse his ailing mother. During his busy month with Nancy Henderson, beginning with meeting her, stalking her, and finally being with her, he had requested extensions on his leave. He made very dramatic phone calls. "This is Henri le Roi. I'm a good friend of Harry's. Harry called me from London and asked me to let you know that his mother is gravely ill. He'll need another week." Then another call and another and another all made from different Vancouver pay phones. She rallied in the second week, fell into a coma and died in the third. He had to make all the funeral arrangements in the fourth week as well as act as his mother's executor. What a royal performance Henri gave to *The X-Files* producer. Real "O for a Muse of Fire" stuff. Academy award, anyone?

No one in Vancouver had spotted Harry during the past month. How could they? He had assumed at least a dozen disguises, many of them as women. *Now that's real acting, DD.*

But now he was back to work, a master at makeup. He was Harry again. A distinguished middle-aged man. Handsome, mustachioed, graying at the temples. After his month off, Harry felt refreshed and revitalized. Ready to tackle any makeup challenge that the powerful producer of *The X-Files* cared to throw at him: break-away skin filled with maggots, blood oozing out of an erupting eye. Anything!

He watched, following his script, as Agents Fox Mulder and Dana Scully huddled near a huge rhododendron in front of the red brick apartment block on Pendrell Street that served as Scully's Annapolis home. Mulder was mumbling on about some guy's ear.

```
MULDER:   Are  you  telling  me  that  her  ear
started to bleed when she answered the phone?

SCULLY:    The  blood  came  from  the  phone,
Mulder.  Not her ear.

MULDER: What?
```

No expression! Why the hell doesn't the director give that guy an acting lesson. Tell him to look horrified. Look right in the camera and gasp, "What?" That's how I'd do it.

```
SCULLY: The mother thought at first that her
ear was bleeding.  It filled with blood and
```

began pouring down her neck. But she felt no
pain. Then she looked at the phone. The
earpiece was bubbling over with blood. And,
Mulder?

MULDER: Yes?

It's a question, stupid. Don't you see the fucking question mark
in your script? Take your stupid-ass voice UP at the end of a
question!

SCULLY: The phone stopped bleeding the moment
her son walked into the room.

MULDER: No. How is that possible?

I give up. He's totally useless.

SCULLY: The paranormal response for such
occurrences is not as remote as you'd expect.
When the FBI planted that wire tap on her
line, they...

BLAH! BLAH! BLAH! Who the fuck writes this crap? Bleeding
phones! How the hell did this show become a TV hit? Why don't
they write about real horror stories. I could write a plot that'd grab
them by their short and curlies. Hell, my script would win me an
Emmy for sure, and it might even make an actor out of DD.

THK's temples were beginning to throb. This was only his third
day back to work since filming his own production. And he was
bottoming out. He'd been on the job for four and a half hours today
and he was getting antsy. He tried to concentrate on the scene, but
another voice was drowning out the actors' voices, screeching in his
head. *Stop thinking dirty thoughts, you filthy little brat. How many
times do I have to tell you? You're going to become one of them and bring
shame to your Mother. That's what you want, isn't it? That's what you're
trying to do, isn't it? Answer me when I'm talking to you? Do you hear
me?*

He threw back his head as if he'd been slapped across his face.
He gasped. *If I ever catch you playing with that dirty little cock of yours,
I am going to cut an inch off it every time you...* He groaned and gasped
for breath.

"Cut," shouted the director.

His eyes began to focus. Everyone was looking at him. Crew,
director, stars. He realized that Scully had asked him how he was.
He looked at her admiringly. "I was thinking about my mom! It's

been a hard month."

Everyone reacted; some with their heads down, others with concerned looks. But most were pissed off because he'd wrecked the scene. Maintaining her same mood and tone, Scully said kindly, "Death is always difficult for us to deal with, Harry. Time will heal. You'll see."

He mumbled a thank you and lit another cigarette.

"Let's do a pickup," shouted the director. Everyone got back into their spots and continued shooting the scene that Harry had interrupted.

He wanted to tell her that she acted rings around DD. Get into a meaningful conversation with her. Talk about why, during her acceptance speeches for her umpteen awards, she either gave her co-star a perfunctory mention or entirely left him out in the cold. He knew why, but he'd like her to tell him. So would the rest of the world. But she didn't invite him into her trailer. *She's never invited me in since I've been doing DD's makeup.*

Harry used to do Scully's makeup. Was her personal makeup artist. But one day the producer said, "Harry, Mulder wants you to do his makeup. Scully says she'll do her own. Her hair stylist will powder her down when necessary. She doesn't want to break in someone new. You understand? So after you make up the other actors, you're going to be his personal makeup artist ninety-five percent of the time. Gotta keep him happy. Know what I mean?"

"Sure, CC, I know what you mean." *And from that day on, I was responsible for making Mulder North America's heartthrob. You see his face on dozens of magazines now. And made up by me! It never ceases to amaze me that I can create so much out of so little.* He no longer felt any joy in his craft. He hated men. The feel of their faces. Even when they had shaved clean, he could still feel their stubble. The hairs stiffening out of their nostrils and ears. He wanted to get out his tweezers and pull out every goddamn hair from DD's ears.

He regretted no longer being the female star's makeup artist. Fuck. No more touchy-feelies with Scully. As he watched them drone on by the rhododendron, he felt a strain in his crotch. He imagined talking to the actress. "I always made you look gorgeous. Have you forgotten the wonderful neck rubs I used to give you before I made you up? If you had ever turned around in the makeup chair, you would have seen my ready invitation, standing at attention. Scully, you should have told CC that you needed me."

Finally, the scene was coming to an end. Scully walked up the steps of the Pendrell Street apartment and disappeared. "Cut," shouted the director. "Good work. It's a wrap."

Don't you mean "It's crap"? Harry threw his cigarette butt on the sidewalk and ground it to shreds.

"Dinner break," announced the assistant director. "We'll set up inside for scenes 47, 48, and 52 at seven fifteen. It's gonna be a long night, kids."

Harry watched the actress walk back to her dressing-room trailer with her coach and agent in tow. *Not even a "Hi" as you pass me, you bad girl. When I made you up during the first year, it was "Harry this" and "Harry that." Have you forgotten that I even did your hair back in the good old days? Once these unknown actors begin to see themselves on magazine covers and newspapers and start winning awards and getting interviewed on talk shows, they cast off the little people who made them successful. But I'm not a little person. I've never been a little person in the theatre world. Ask the National Theatre School. I won the fucking "Most Likely to Succeed" award, and don't you ever forget it.*

"I'll never get you alone anymore, will I? Because you're never alone anymore. Rest easy, Dana Scully. I'm content for another year. I've had Nancy Henderson in ways that I know you would have enjoyed."

The horn and screeching brakes stopped him in the middle of the street. He felt like a trapped animal, caught in the headlights. But he quickly refocused. No longer pinned by the glare, he looked at the vehicle. A sporty little car, with...*Can it be?* The driver was a handsome younger man. Brent Barnes.

Brent drove by slowly and lowered his window. He locked eyes with the older man, cocked his head, and smiled disarmingly. "Sorry."

Harry smiled back. "That's okay. I used to drive a car like that."

He could see the driver watching him through his rearview mirror until he turned down Pendrell Street. *I knew Brentie-boy liked older men.*

"Take this guck off me, will you?"

"Oh! Sure, DD. Let's go to makeup. You did a great job. That scene was really gripping." After a shoot, Harry had to scrub DD's skin clean. *Afraid you'll maybe leave a lipstick smear on a cup, for Christ's sake. Scared someone will call you a pansy-ass homo the way Larry Sanders did on national TV? Twice.*

"HI!"

It was Brent. He'd arrived home from the college. Much later than normal. *I could usually set my watch by Brent's homecoming.* After his "Hi," he'd slip out of his shoes and get into his waiting slippers, walk into the living room, and flop in his lazyboy. I'd appear from the kitchen with a martini, give him a welcome-home peck, and take my place in my lazyboy next to his. Then I'd say, "How's your day been?" We'd chat for about twenty minutes or so and head up to the master bedroom for an afternoon siesta.

I'd never napped in the afternoon before I met Brent. Now I

looked forward to his homecoming. Never discount afternoon naps. They make for wonderful evenings.

But today was different. Brent stormed into the kitchen, shoes still on. "Do you know what that dickhead is trying to do?"

"Who?"

"Spivic."

"No, what is Dickhead trying to do?"

"Put me at the top of his list of suspects. That's what he's trying to do!"

"That's crazy."

"I told him so," Brent bellowed, hands on hips. "How could I possibly have murdered Nancy?"

"Here." I handed him his martini. "Let's go into the living room."

He sat bolt upright in his lazyboy, looking uncomfortable. He took a gulp of his drink instead of his usual contented first sip. "How the hell can he accuse me of...?"

"Why don't you start from the beginning? What happened?"

"Well, at three o'clock, when he and his dyke sidekick banged on my office door, I —"

"Wait a minute. What makes you think that Abby Davis is a lesbian?"

"Duh!" He looked condescendingly at me. "It's so obvious. She's one big leather-lovin' mother dyke. You're losing your touch, Jessica." When Brent wants to test his acid level, he enjoys throwing *Jessica* at me. He tipped up his glass and drained his martini. "I gotta relax." He went upstairs. I followed.

The generation gap between us reared its head once more. Until recently, I'd always been interested in people's characters first, not their sexual orientation. But not so with Brent. Never with Brent. Even when he'd been frustrated or mad as hell, his gaydar antenna went up at the sight of a handsome older man, and even some not-so-handsome ones. When we'd been out together, he still played his amazing little game that he'd played all his adult life — or at least since he had turned seventeen.

Never giving women or young men more than a cursory glance, Brent focused his attention on older men, immediately classifying them as straight or gay. He dismissed the former; he undressed the latter. Figuratively, of course. Then he quickly determined whether or not this older, naked man would be worth getting to know more intimately. End of game. If he decided to cruise the man he'd just met instead of playing his mind game, he made a contact: a look, a smile, a where-have-you-been-all-my-life line. The same approach he had used when he met me. And believe me, it worked. After a first date, which always meant having sex, he determined whether it had been merely an interesting one-night stand, or whether it warranted further investigation. Sounds kind of callous, but it's common gay practice. So Brent told me. And during the '60s and '70s, that had been standard practice for the young hetero swingers, too; before the big A hit the fan.

To be honest, I always felt jealous when Brent played his game. I could tell when he'd entered phase one; he radiated an aura that was as palpable as a jungle animal in heat. Gaydar. He often reassured me that since we'd become lovers, he'd never gone beyond the imaginary undressing stage with any of the older men he'd been attracted to. But...I wondered. Every time I saw him look at another man, I'd wonder, the same tired litany running through my mind. *He's human. He's young. And he's very sexy. Can I really be enough for him?* The worry was exhausting.

"So, Abby's a lesbian?" I looked at Brent's outstretched, fully-clad body on top of our king-sized bed. He usually napped nude, under the covers. I got on the bed and cuddled beside him.

"Uh-huh."

"Enough of Abby. What happened at the college?"

"Let's rest first and then I'll tell you exactly what happened, step by step." He rolled over and was asleep in two minutes.

Damn. Another huge difference between Brent and me, and one that never failed to surprise. He could nod off within minutes of saying "I'm going to sleep," setting aside whatever issue should have kept him uneasily awake. I lay there bug-eyed, waiting. Waiting for him to wake up.

Forty-five minutes later Brent woke, fresh as if he'd slept for hours. He stripped and walked into the shower, as usual, inviting me in. After we dried and I crawled back into bed, he told me what had happened at the college, blow by dramatic blow. He began by acting out all the parts, beginning as himself, an innocent young man who had nothing to hide. "Spivic tossed his first order at me." I could tell that Brent was going to tell his story from his point of view so I was prepared to take most of it with a grain of salt.

Suddenly Brent adopted the stance of the overweight, lumbering Bear. "Bring all the English Department t'gether in that there classroom across that there hall. I wanna have a talk to 'em." Brent was laying on a thick back-woodsy Saskatchewan twang. "Have 'em there at three thirty sharp." He wheezed and puffed as he lumbered around the bed while I laughed in spite of myself. Stark naked, he still captured Bear's movements and vocal nuances to a T. My laughter encouraged him.

"And then Corporal Davis says—" Brent hesitated and shifted his stance, sticking out his naked tummy, narrowing his eyes, hardening his voice. "You heard Sergeant Spivic." And then he leaned in and hissed, "Hop to it, little man." Brent became an hysterically funny, over-the-top dyke as he stormed around the bed.

"While yer gatherin' the clan, we're gonna look through the desk 'n' file drawers of the deceased." He was Bear again, this time being ineptly officious.

"After twenty minutes, I completed my task and was back in my office." Now he was himself. "I noticed that they'd taken out some letters, papers, and a black notebook from Nancy's file cabinet and put them on her desk. They went out of the office and left me alone. And I started to look at what they'd left on Nancy's desk. I had just picked up an envelope, when the door burst open. "

BEAR: Hold yer horses there, Mr. Nosy Parker, whatcha think yer up to?

ABBY: Interfering with evidence, are we, Mr. Barnes?

BRENT: No, I just...wanted to...help...so...I...

ABBY: DROP IT!

Brent looked at me. "Bloody hell, I didn't have a fucking gun aimed at her! She scared the shit out of me. I dropped the envelope instantly and collapsed into Nancy's chair."

BEAR: Corporal, bring the evidence with ya before he has a chance t'tamper with it. We can't trust this Aussie t'keep his itchy fingers out o' police matters.

Brent looked at me again. "Davis reached over me to pick up the material one stack at a time, giving me an accusatory look as she picked up each pile. As she straightened up, holding all the evidence in her arms, she leaned in and whispered, 'Why don't you stay put, kiddo. Until we get back.'

"I was fuming but did as I was told and sat in my office for the next hour and forty minutes. Finally, Spivic opened the office door with a jerk. I jumped out of Nancy's chair, feeling guilty. But I hadn't done anything wrong. I hadn't moved since they'd left, too afraid to do anything."

BEAR: Mr. Barnes, what wuz yer relationship with the deceased?

BRENT: I was her mentor, Sergeant.

ABBY: Yes, that's what Jane Edwards told us. A striking-looking Department head, your Ms. Edwards.

BEAR: But she said that you 'n' Nancy were, as rumor has it, a number. Ain't that how Ms. Edwards put it, Abby?

ABBY: Yessiree-bob! That they were a number.

BRENT: (I tried to center myself.) What do you mean, a number? I had no interest whatsoever in Miss Henderson. That way. We were professional colleagues. Nothing more, I assure you.

ABBY: Are you telling us that you never spent any time with the deceased? Socially?

BRENT: (I just stood there.)

BEAR: Then explain this, Mr. Barnes. What were ya doin' over the Labor Day weekend? Are ya gonna tell us that ya didn't spend that weekend with Miss Henderson at her cabin at Swallow Lake?

"So, what did you say?" I interjected. Brent was silent for a whole minute. A dramatic pause!

THE LABOR DAY weekend had been great fun. On that Saturday, Brent and I had gone to Nancy's cabin with all our camping gear, tent, double sleeping bag, pillows, and enough food to feed Afghanistan. With Nancy's help we pitched our tent behind the cabin. For the next three days we had a ball—hiked, swam, ate like pigs, listened to music, told stories, and laughed like kids. Then, at night, we went out to our tent and slept like babies, enjoying the refreshing clean, crisp air that blew gently over us while Nancy slept, happily snuggled in her own bed in the cabin.

Brent had long ago confided in Nancy that he was gay and that he and I were lovers. He had sworn her to secrecy. She shook his hand to seal their agreement. "Your secret will die with me," she had promised in mock seriousness, then gave him a friendly hug. He was positively sure that she had never told a soul and, in her own satiric way, had added grist to the college rumor mill that she and Brent were a "number."

"SO WHAT DID you say?" I insisted. Brent continued his blow-by-blow playlet.

BEAR: After some careful questionin' by Abby 'n' I, a couple of yer colleagues told us that Nancy had invited ya t'spend Labor Day weekend with her at the cabin. And you went

there, din'tcha? All eight of yer colleagues said that you and
the deceased were gettin' it on, Barnes. Goin' fer romantic
walks every noon hour. In here with the door closed till all
hours. Come clean. Tell us the truth.

BRENT: That's preposterous, Sergeant. How can they say
such a...?

BEAR: Where were ya last Friday night?

ABBY: And all day Saturday?

BEAR: And all...day...Sunday?"

"Well, what did you say?" I shouted.
"I didn't know what to say. Would you have wanted me to tell
them that I was in Seattle aboard a yacht with a group of young
queers, planning next year's Chiron Rising Gathering?"
"So what did you say?"

BRENT: Sergeant Spivic, I can't remember where I was every
minute of the entire weekend... All of Nancy's students
meet on Fridays. You'll be able to see them next Friday at
9:00, 11:00, 3:00, and 4:00. Can you be here?

BEAR: Thanks. I'll be here at nine hundred hours sharp
t'meet with the students. That means don't leave town.

Lying there on our bed, we locked eyes. The jig was up, and we
both knew it. Brent would be outed at the college, maybe even
ousted. And Spivic would freak out and definitely not let me near
him. He'd see to it that I wouldn't get anywhere near the cabin or the
Detachment. I would receive no more inside information on the
Henderson case.

Chapter
Eleven

AT NOON ON Thursday, Spivic was only too pleased to meet with me at the White Spot restaurant. He listened intently to my summation of how the killer got into Nancy's cabin, the sawed post, the disguise, the entrapment of Nancy. He listened to my theories like an excited child hearing a good story. He punctuated parts of my story with laconic comments between mouthfuls. "Good point," chomp, "Right on, Kev," slurp, "Ya think?" gulp, "Smart bastard, our killer."

After a hearty belch at the end of his meal, Bear took his pad out of his uniform pocket, flipped it open, and wrote furiously for a few minutes. Then he flipped back a few pages and looked me straight in the eye. "There's somethin' I've bin meanin' t'ask ya."

"Yes?" I figured I'd met my Waterloo in this giant of a man with Triple-0 sauce lingering in the corners of his mouth. *Why the hell do gays have to go through this torture of hiding who they are? It's grossly unfair. I can say that with complete authority, having been raised — no, programmed — by the other side to look on homosexual activity with contempt.*

"So, tell me again, Kev. What took ya to the cabin last Monday?" *Relief! He wants to talk about the case.*

I thought through my options. Should I tell the truth, or should I continue the lie? Spivic kept his eager eyes on mine. "I got a call from Brent Barnes. We're good friends and longtime racquetball partners. He was worried about Nancy and asked me, if I had the time, to check up on her because she didn't make her first class."

"So ya went to her apartment 'n' kicked the door down?"

"Oh, you heard about that little incident. I was wondering when you'd find out. Nice bit of detective work, Sergeant."

Spivic was trying hard not to break into a grin. "When I found out it wuz you, I thought, 'Hey, this case ain't gonna be hard t'break.' Lots of things coulda happened to ya since ya left the Force. Ya mighta even become a murderer."

"Thank you for that vote of confidence, Sergeant."

"Well, you had the reputation, ya know. When ya wuz Chief."

"What reputation?" I was intrigued.

"That ya had a criminal mind. All us guys thought that ya'd

make a perfect crook. You were always a sneaky bastard, a lot sneakier than any of the creeps ya used to put away. You'll have to pay fer the damages, ya know."

"What?"

He flipped the page in his pad. "The apartment door's gonna cost ya three hundred twenty-five bucks. But I convinced the Vancouver Police not to press charges. I told 'em ya were doin' a bit o' leg work fer me and got a little overeager. The desk sergeant says, 'Kickin' down doors isn't my idea of leg work.' We both had a good laugh. Anyways, I told him that the manager wuz bein' kind o' an SOB. So ya had t'use force. They bought it."

Phew! Things may be looking up. "Thanks, Bear. I really appreciate that. Anyway, not finding Nancy there, I headed out to Swallow Lake."

"You shoulda waited fer me at the cabin. Leavin' the scene of a murder is a criminal offense. Surely ya know that, Kev. Or is it, leavin' the scene of an accident? I always git them two mixed up. Well anyways, Chief Inspector Riley wuz not amused that ya weren't there to meet me. So where were ya when I arrived?"

"At the college. Because I had to tell Brent about Nancy's death. You know, he had to cover her classes." Then I added lamely, "Besides, you thought that she died of natural causes."

He wasn't going to allow me to push the blame on him for my leaving the cabin. "Kev, have ya ever heard of phonin'?"

I hesitated, feeling strangely uncomfortable with his eyes still searching my face. I had misjudged Spivic. He was doing a damn fine job on me. *So what lie do I dream up now? I can't tell him that I had to be with Brent to break the news, to hold him, to comfort him.* "Well, I knew he was close to Nancy and thought it only proper to tell him of her death in person. He was her..." I hesitated.

"Her beau." Bear smiled. He'd looked at the calendar. He saw the picture of Brent and Nancy and he knew that Brent and I had spent the Labor Day weekend at the cabin. But nothing else.

"More like her mentor. That's the word I was trying to think of." I wasn't going to rise to his bait. If he wanted to bring it to a head, so be it. But I wasn't going to make it easy for him. *Besides, he still needs me. I can feel it. That's why he's being cagey.*

"Did ya tell him that ya thought she'd been murdered?"

"No," I lied again.

"So, let me get this straight. Ya went to her apartment, then to her cabin at Swallow Lake, then to the college, then back to Swallow Lake." I nodded. "That Brent Barnes must be some hot partner!"

I looked blankly at Bear's leer. "What do you mean?"

"Racquetball. He's your racquetball partner, ain't he?"

I relaxed again. "Oh, yeah. Racquetball. He's a hot partner, all right."

"Would ya like to join me tomorrow when me 'n' Abby interview some of the students at the college?"

I jumped at the chance. "Great. I'll be there at nine o'clock sharp."

"How d'ya know that Henderson's first class starts at nine?"

Shit. I put my foot in it again. "Brent must have mentioned it to me. He's quite concerned about the whole affair. He even thinks," I chuckled uneasily, "that you suspect him."

"He has told us several lies, Kev. Until he comes clean, he's definitely on my list." He leaned over to me. "If I were you, I wouldn't discuss this case with him any further. A deal?"

"A deal." Another lie.

Then he picked up a copy of *The Scoop* newspaper and handed it to me. "Seen this mornin's *Scoop*?"

"No."

"Look at page three."

The entire front cover of *The Scoop* was devoted to a sensational headline and photo. The parent newspaper of *The Scoop* had its birth when the reporters of both *The Vancouver Sun* and *The Province* went out on strike for some eight weeks. A few of the radical reporters decided to go it alone and start their own alternative paper. They even named it *The Alternative*. Everyone was reading it, frankly because there wasn't anything else to read. As soon as the strike settled and the mainline papers returned, no one read *The Alternative* any more, and the reporters became blacklisted. So *The Scoop* was born. Since its transformation to a tabloid style, its popularity has grown astonishingly. You'll find copies in all Starbucks, Denny's, and McDonald's where tired workers are busy waking themselves up with breakfast and digesting the morning's "hot" stories as they slurp their coffee. Page five always carries a nude beauty. Talk about wake-up titillation! The bus and Skytrain passengers too flip from one sensational story to another. Traditionalists who remained true to the *Sun* or *Province* either cast disgusted looks at *The Scoop* readers or long to "get the juicy details." Their papers follow a code of ethics.

So, there's only one way to describe Vancouver's latest newspaper: *The Scoop* is a rag.

Anyway, today's headline blared,

PROSTITUTES TAKE OVER SURREY CITY HALL.
Full story page two.

But I flipped to page three.
The caption beside Franny McGhie's pic read,

CLEAN FIEND VISITS SWALLOW LAKE.

I looked up at Bear, who beckoned me with his eyes to read on.

> Body of beloved Vancouver College
> instructor Nancy Henderson was brought into
> Lion's Gate Morgue Monday at 1:14 p.m. The
> trio who dissected Henderson are still in
> shock. "She'd been vacuumed out," one of them
> kept saying over and over. I'll report full
> details about this Murder Most Clean in next
> issue. Be prepared for shocking details
> guaranteed to give you nightmares like it did
> to at least one of the morticians. When
> contacted, North Vancouver RCMP Commissioner
> Sam Wheetley refused comment. Bad form, Sam.
> So, thanks to Sam, you will have to wait to
> find out exactly what the "CLEAN FIEND" killer
> did to Nancy Henderson.

To the right of the article was a picture of a fleeing Sam Wheetley, his hand covering his face as he darted into the North Van Detachment.

"Shit! Who leaked the story to McGhie? She's the most unscrupulous reporter on *The Scoop*."

"Ya. My sentiments exactly. Joan wants to see us. We got ten minutes to get there."

WHEN BEAR AND I walked into the conference room at the North Vancouver Detachment, I was surprised to see so many people. And the room was unusually quiet. No chitchat. Heads were down and everyone was reading. *What are they reading?*

The room had been transformed into a crime center. Four bulletin boards were up on the side wall. Each labeled. "The Victim Alive, The Murder, The Victim Dead, The Killer." Photos were pinned on the boards. On the last board I read several links to the killer, each on pieces of colored paper: TAUNTS, DISGUISES HIMSELF, PSYCHO, SERIAL KILLER. There was also an enlargement of the Polaroid that we had found, with Nancy alive and in obvious fear and pain. There was also a blowup of the killer's message from the back of the photo: "A souvenir for the RCMP for remembrance. I already have mine." Beside it was an enlargement of the braid of pubic hairs.

The silence in the room was broken when a smiling, overweight blonde bustled to greet us. She had a tray with two ecologically friendly paper cups of coffee and a plate of donuts. "Would you like some refreshments before we start?"

"Don't mind if I do," said Bear, taking a jelly donut and a coffee to the front of the room.

Where does that man put it all? I shook my head as she offered me the tray. "Just coffee. That'll be great." She returned to her place at the front of the room before I could ask her name.

Bear strode back and handed me a folder. "This is what everybody's readin'."

I sat down in the back row and opened the folder: the official autopsy report of Nancy Henderson. I gave it a quick scan and looked up. Heads shaking from side to side, hands rubbing foreheads or massaging necks, feet moving erratically, the readers displayed discomfort and revulsion.

Bear sat next to Joan Riley at the front table, watching her read. I hadn't seen Joan for twelve years. She'd aged; forehead furrowed, mouth drawn, eyes hardened behind her half glasses, the kind you get from a drug store. She glanced over her glasses for a moment in my direction, acknowledging my presence, nodding slightly. I nodded back. She lowered her head and continued reading. She'd cut her hair short. From this distance she looked remarkably like Helen Mirren's Chief Inspector Jane Tennison from the *Prime Suspect* TV series. Everything about her broadcast the look of power.

Jeff from Hair and Fiber, Pete from Latent Prints, and Abby sat to the right of the room. Frank Williams and a young woman sat a little ahead of me. They were not reading, but making notes in the folder. The refreshment woman sat at the left end of the table at the front. Her back was against the side wall; from there she could easily see everyone. In front of her was an open pad. She played with a pen, moving it from one hand to the other.

In the center of the first row, nearest the table, sat the Commissioner. From the back of his head, I recognized Sam, sitting rigid and tall. I was surprised to see him here. *Could be interesting when he realizes that I'm here.* I hadn't seen him in the twelve years since he bounced me out of the Force. *Shit!* He still has his imperial mane of silver hair, wearing it like a goddamn crown. I thought about my own, shedding more than fifty lost souls a day like a mangy dog. *But I simply love my shiny, balding pate. Not!*

I began to read the official report.

Ten minutes later, when everyone had finished reading, Joan whipped off her glasses and got to her feet. "I'm glad you all made it on such short notice." Joan did a quick perfunctory roll call to make sure that everyone there knew each other, leaving both Sam and me out. Then she looked at Sam. "Our Commissioner needs no introduction. I am very pleased that he has taken an interest in this case and has chosen to sit in on this meeting. Would you like to say anything to the team?"

Sam waved his hand, so Joan carried on. "As of today, you are

all part of the team assigned to finding the killer of Nancy
Henderson. Fast. I don't want to see Sergeant Spivic filling another
bulletin board with photos of another dead woman." *So, those boards
are Bear's handiwork.* "Before I turn the meeting over to Sergeant
Spivic, I want to thank Kevin Porter—at the back of the room—for
joining us today." Everyone but Sam turned and smiled at me. "I
realize that it's a bit unorthodox to bring in a civilian on an RCMP
case, but Mr. Porter found the body and, I understand, has been
retained as a private investigator to help us find the killer." *A
"civilian," for Christ's sake! Why didn't she tell the new recruits that I'm
a thirty-year RCMP veteran?* "I have decided that having him work
hand in hand with us will be beneficial to the case." She smiled at
me. "I really appreciate your coming in, Kev. I'm sure I speak for
everyone here. We all look forward to working with you." I nodded
and smiled back. Sam hugged his arms a little tighter. *Did he write
her speech? "Civilian." Shit!*

"Let's begin.   As you know, Sergeant Barry Spivic will be
heading this case. Take everything through him. Barry will report to
me. Sergeant Spivic, take it from here." Joan sat at the table.

Bear stood.   Even from where I sat, I could see the dusting of
icing sugar on his top lip and the residue raspberry jelly in the
corners of his mouth. I tried to catch his eye to get him to wipe his
mouth clean. He hitched up his pants three times before he opened
his mouth. Everyone knew that this was his first big case. And they
probably also knew that before this week, he'd always been a happy-
go-lucky follower. Now he was the lead investigator.

"Thanks, Joan. I mean Chief. First off, I wanna thank Margie
Connolly fer gettin' refreshments fer us.   Them donuts are great.
And thanks fer makin' copies of the autopsy report and puttin' them
all in those nifty folders.   Margie is here t'take notes of our meetin'
and will be yer official contact between you and I. So if you wanna
git in touch with me about anything and I'm not around, call Margie.
Margie, stand up and let them have a look-see."

Margie stood up and smiled. She casually handed Bear a napkin
and pointed to her own mouth. He quickly wiped his clean and gave
her a smile. "Thanks, Sergeant Spivic." She sat down quickly and
picked up her pad and Bic.

Clean-faced, Bear continued, "We are makin' good progress. The
team yesterday made several important discoveries and I already
have my suspicions as to who the killer is." I blanched. "The best
way to describe the killer is: he's a monster. What he did to that girl
wuz inhuman. Insane. You read Frank's report. So ya all know what
I'm talkin' about.   Right?   Anyways, he tricked the victim by
pretendin' to be in an accident and got hisself into the cabin."

"This is pure hypothesis. What proof have you?"

"Well, Mr. Commish," Bear didn't know how to address Sam,

"ya see, Kev and I think he disguised hisself as a woman, ya know, t'gain the victim's trust."

"Oh, really. Disguised *hisself*, eh?"

Sam's sarcasm shot over Bear's head. *What the hell's wrong with Sam? It's obvious he still hates my guts, but why isn't he supporting Bear instead of trying to humiliate him?*

"Anyways, Henderson invites her killer into her cabin on Friday, September Twenty-Fifth. We know this fer a fact because she placed this information on a calendar that we found in the kitchen there."

"What are you talking about, Spivic?" Wheetley interrupted. "Are you trying to tell us that the killer allowed Henderson an opportunity to write down details about him on a calendar?"

Bear became rattled again. "No, Commish sir, that's not what I meant t'say. The killer wuz in the bathroom, cleanin' up, ya see, from the accident."

"Pure supposition."

"We believe that Nancy wuz in the kitchen, preparin' drinks and all. While she wuz waitin', she wrote on the calendar. Looks like she sort o' used it like a guest book. Anyways, we're photocopying every page of the calendar and will be posting them on the bulletin board before the day's out." He looked at me for approval.

Sam snarled, "Carry on, Spivic."

Relieved, Bear continued with his agenda. "You've had a chance to read the official autopsy report that Frank Williams prepared. Frank, maybe you can answer any questions the team might have." Everyone except the Commissioner turned to face Frank.

"Certainly," said Frank. "First, let me introduce you to Officer Julie Smith. As you already know from your reading of my report, Julie officiated at the autopsy. I want to make one thing clear before I take questions. As usual, *The Scoop* got its facts wrong. I haven't had any nightmares. Have you, Julie?"

"Well, maybe I wouldn't call them nightmares, but I have kept the light on since the autopsy." I could tell that she was still traumatized by the experience of cutting up a young woman about her own age, size, and coloring. She tried to smile, but found it easier to sit and lower her head.

Frank continued, "Now, do any of you have any questions?" Hands shot up around the room. "Yes, Jeff."

"Why do you think she didn't have nail polish on her little finger? Do you think she was stopped before she completed her manicure or do you think she was starting to remove her nail polish?"

"I can't give you a definitive answer, Jeff. All I can say with any kind of accuracy is that the nail appeared to be deliberately left untouched. You see, the other nails had been painted with extreme care with at least two coats on each nail."

Bear jumped in. "I think ya'll find that her unpainted pinky is a trademark of the killer's. Kev thinks it probably holds some deep-seated message fer the creep." I was glad Bear was including me, giving me a bit of credit for my theories. Making me feel that I belonged at this meeting instead of making me feel redundant. "And besides," continued Bear, "the killer placed that pinky of hers in her..." He blushed. "You know, in her...privates."

"Privates?" hissed Sam.

"Yeah!" answered Bear. "When I uncovered her, that's what I seen."

Silence.

"Next?" Frank continued. "But let's keep the questions within my expertise. Address any others to Sergeant Spivic or Mr. Porter." He recognized Abby's waving hand.

"Can you really suck out all the contents of a body with a wet-dry vacuum cleaner?"

"The answer is *yes*. It would take a great deal of time, and apparently the killer had the time."

"But how?" Abby insisted.

"Well, the stomach can be pumped quite easily through the mouth. The intestines would be a more difficult matter. We did find three small bits of black rubber, indicating that — in all probability — the killer had inserted an extremely flexible hose via the victim's rectum. The hose undoubtedly was long enough to reach her duodenum, all the time sucking out the contents of her lower alimentary canal. The traces of some kind of cleaning compound also indicated that the killer pumped her full of soapy water to rinse out the canal, then re-vacuumed. Possibly several times, because, frankly, ladies and gentlemen, she was the cleanest corpse I've ever seen." During Frank's response, one by one we looked at the fourth bulletin board and stared into Nancy's eyes as she stared back at us in terror, biting down on her thumb. "We only pray that the victim was already dead before these despicable acts took place, but it is highly possible that she could have been alive during this terrible ordeal." Everyone recalled reading Frank's description of the condition of her thumb.

Frank had taken us into the crime scene with his direct, medical delivery. Everyone sat quietly, imagining the horror that poor Nancy had to endure. Everyone was imagining what was happening at the moment the killer took that picture. Was she being filled up with soapy water? Or was she being flushed out? Or was she...? Frank broke our thoughts. "Next question."

"Frank," Sam enquired, "I want to know exactly what killed Nancy Henderson. You skirt the issue in your report. Do you or do you not know?"

"This is the first autopsy I've done where I don't have conclusive data on cause of death. What he did to her was certainly unspeakable. We do know that she had a massive heart attack that was probably the climax of a series of atrocities performed on her. She may very well have brought on her own heart attack by allowing the agony to explode her heart. Biting her thumb nearly off wasn't painful enough. Does that answer your question, sir?" Sam nodded. "Next question."

There were none. The last answer was too graphic, even beyond our own imaginative powers.

Bear took the floor again. "Thank you Frank. And Julie. Your report was real helpful in bringin' us all up to date. If any of you think of another question you'd like to ask Frank, jot it down and pass it to Margie. She'll see that he gets it." Margie nodded. "By the way, Frank, before ya sit down, it looks as though you and Julie think the killer's some kind of crackerjack makeup artist or a hairdresser. That's mine and Kev's opinion too. We think that that's what the killer probably does fer a livin'."

"You could be right. That fact does give you a lead on where to start."

"Our thinkin' exactly."

The mutual admiration of the two was broken by Sam, who hadn't moved during Frank's answers. "I understand there's an unofficial autopsy report going around. Is that so?" Bear looked over at Frank uneasily.

Frank answered, "Yes, that's true. Sergeant Spivic asked me to elaborate on certain parts of the report in a strictly unofficial manner."

Bear chirped in, "And I appreciated it. Thanks again, Frank." *Good for you, guys.*

But the Commish wasn't going to lie down and play dead. "I assume that you showed it to Mr. Porter?"

"Yeah."

"Well, maybe it's time that the entire *official* team saw this *unofficial* report."

I couldn't hold my tongue any longer. "I've read both versions, Sam, and they're virtually the same. Just a little more detail in Sergeant Spivic's. I don't think the rest of the team would benefit one iota from reading it. In fact, in my opinion, it would be a waste of their very valuable time." Bear breathed a sign of relief.

"Really, Mr. Porter?" The voice came out of Sam's back. "I think I should be the judge of whether or not it would be a waste of time."

"Suit yourself, Sam."

He bristled. Bear jumped in. "We'll talk about this later, Commissioner. Sir. In private. Now, I wanna get on with our meetin' and introduce ya all to Corporal Abby Davis here. She's in charge of electronic surveillance. Abby, has anything turned up yet?"

Abby looked uneasy as she moved to the side of the room. The atmosphere had been quickly deteriorating and I expect she didn't want to be on the receiving end of one of Sam's lethal barbs. "Unfortunately, no similar MOs turned up on PIRS," she said softly. The woman was nervous. "So as far as PIRS is concerned, this stat is the killer's first in BC. Any questions?" She did not enjoy being in the limelight.

"Yeah. I have one," I said. I could see Sam's back tighten and Abby's eyes narrow. "Is it possible that a BC murder with a similar MO could have been missed and not got into the PIRS program?"

"Certainly not if it happened in the Lower Mainland or in Victoria." Abby rushed on, "Vancouver and Victoria police forces feed PIRS to keep it up to date. But it's possible in some of the more remote parts of BC that an MO might be overlooked. And it's also possible that cases before the introduction of PIRS could have been overlooked. An understaffed police district could easily be sitting on a similar MO to the one here that's still in a file drawer in Alert Bay or Fernie or some other remote Detachment. There could be a dozen other reasons why a similar MO hadn't found its way into PIRS."

Seeing no hands, I asked another question. "Would it be possible to send out a confidential description of the MO of Nancy Henderson to all RCMP Detachments throughout BC? Without naming names of course. You could ask them to check their files to see if they can come up with a match."

Before Abby could open her mouth, Sam's sarcasm filled the room. "Mr. Porter has been out of the Force for so many years that he doesn't realize that PIRS is perfectly adequate to trace all *modus operandi* in the province of British Columbia." He continued, while still facing the front, "If it's not in PIRS, a murder with a similar MO hasn't happened in BC. We don't have the resources to waste on *Mister* Porter's far-fetched idea."

I was ready to let the Commish have a taste of my temper. By now he was pissing me off royally. But both Abby and Joan gave me looks that told me to put a sock in it, or I was going to get kicked off the case.

I was amazed that Abby continued, "I'm going to get onto ViCLAS later today. And maybe VICAP." Sam sighed audibly. "These two programs should ferret out similar MOs outside BC," she said defensively.

I didn't know what she was talking about. I had been out of circulation so long that I really needed a course on current electronic surveillance.

Bear tried to center the meeting again. "Thanks, Abby." Relieved, she sat down. "Jeff Ferguson, do you have anything to report?"

"Yes, Sarge." Jeff walked over to the fourth bulletin board and pointed to the blowup of the hairs. "We found this braid of hairs, left by the killer under the mattress cover, in the same plastic bag as the Polaroid picture. This bugger is taunting us. The results of our microscopic analysis showed that all three hairs were from pubic areas." Jeff was on a roll. "We're doing mitochondrial DNA testing of the hair shafts on all of them as well. It'll take the forensic lab a month for the DNA results to become hard evidence. But, get this," he continued, "none of the hairs in the braid matched." He looked at all of us before continuing. " 'What does that mean?' I'm sure you're asking yourselves. Well, they've come from three different people. Each hair had its own follicle, which means that it was either plucked or had fallen out naturally. None of the hairs had been cut. One is a perfect match to the victim's. One is a lighter, finer texture. And one is coarse and black. Perhaps Native Indian or Asian." My stomach turned. "I suspect that one of the hairs belongs to the killer, but I haven't a clue as to the owner of the third hair. Or even the reason for a different third hair except to say that you need three hairs to make a braid. Any ideas?" Jeff was an eager young NCO and an asset to the team.

"Maybe." I raised my hand hesitantly. All eyes were on me or Sam. My nemesis sat, unmoving, facing front. "Maybe one of the hairs belonged to a former victim. Maybe the killer was fantasizing in his twisted mind a *ménage à trois*."

"Trust Mr. Porter to bring up abnormal sexual practices. That's the most ridiculous thing I've ever heard." The Commissioner's voice filled the room, but he still didn't turn around. "Didn't he hear Corporal Davis? There are no other MOs to match the Henderson case in British Columbia."

I wasn't going to be stifled any longer by this dinosaur. "Well, Sam, then we'll have to look further afield." He turned and glared. If eyes could stab, I'd be bleeding all over the conference room floor.

"Any other ideas?" asked Jeff, more timidly this time. No one spoke. Who would?

"Well, I have one," I put forth. Everybody was holding their breath. "Frank, in your inspection of the body, did you notice that a few of the victim's pubic hairs had been plucked out after death? I don't know what the skin would look like if hair is removed after death, but I'm sure you could tell."

"To be honest, Kev, we didn't examine the skin of her pubic area that closely. Did you, Julie?" He looked at his assistant, who shook her head. "We can go back. The body is still on ice."

"And why, pray tell," Sam was on the hunt again, "does Mr. Porter want to know whether the killer plucked out some of the victim's pubic hairs, before or after he killed her?"

"Sir," injected Jeff, "I think it is quite possible to suppose that one of the pubic hairs in the braid belonged to the killer's penultimate victim, and in all likelihood, he is preparing his next braid for his next kill. That kill will include a hair of Nancy's, one of his own, and one of his next victim." *Exactly.* Jeff was on my wave length.

"Very well. Check it out," said the Commish.

"As far as my other efforts were concerned," continued Jeff, "they all were negative. No fibers found in the hose of the vacuum cleaner I took in for inspection, no footprints outside the cabin that were significant, no blood or fiber on the trees or ground around the cabin. And in examining the canister of pepper spray, I can definitely say that it had never been used."

"Anything else, Jeff?" Bear asked.

"Only one thing. I haven't been able to find Henderson's immediate neighbor, up the road about half a mile toward Swallow Lake. I've been there three times and there's never been anyone home. An old lady owns the cottage." He referred to his notes. "A Mrs. Marigold Harcourt. The husband died several years ago. I thought she might have died too, but there's no record of her death. And there's no phone listed, so I'll keep hammering on her door."

"Good work, Jeff," said Bear. "Now, let me introduce Pete Springer. Anything to report from Latent Prints?"

"Not much, I'm afraid." Pete did not like the fact that he was the center of attention. He mumbled and looked at his feet most of the time. "I dusted the entire cabin and found only one foreign print. I didn't find any of the victim's prints. The killer must have done a thorough cleaning job."

"What foreign print did you find in the cabin?" Sam was on the scent again. *Why is he being such a prick?*

"We found one on the toilet tank lever," Pete murmured.

"Officer Springer, speak up, for God's sake. Nobody can hear you."

"I'm sorry, Commish, but I'm not good at public speaking. I said that we found one print on the plunger of the toilet." Pete looked directly at me, and gave a little shrug. I winced.

"The killer's?"

"I'm afraid not, sir."

"Whose?"

"Kevin Porter's. I have verified that the print came from Kev's right thumb."

"Wasn't he wearing gloves?" The old bastard was still talking about me as if I weren't in the room.

"I was there on Monday morning, Sam, doing someone a favor. I've already explained the details to Sergeant Spivic." I added, for effect, "To his satisfaction."

"That's right, sir." Spivic sprang into action. "Thanks, Pete. Anything else?"

"Just the calendar, Sarge."

"And you didn't find any prints on it, did you?" Remembering that I'd been pawing over it without gloves, Bear was sending a warning to Pete to shut up. He took the hint.

"No, Sarge. There were no prints, only a few smudges."

"Good work. Now I'd like Kevin Porter to address us. For you young guys, in case you dint know, he used to be the Chief Inspector here, before Joan, and he's now a PI. He's graciously agreed to work with us in this capacity." Graciously? Bear was really laying it on. He needs me. Bear continued heaping on the praise, "He has already assisted us in ways that I'd never of thought of. He's gonna be a real asset to the team. Over to you, Kev."

Sam folded his arms and I swear I saw the silver bristles of hair on the back of his head take aim at me.

"I think I've already said enough." I didn't want another confrontation. Then I surprised myself. "I lie. I would like to take this opportunity to say how glad I am to be back here. And working with you, Barry. Congratulations on picking such an efficient, concerned team. I look forward to helping you solve this case and bringing in this Clean Fiend."

"There, you hear that, Joan?" Sam jumped to his feet, pointing at me and shaking. "That's how that McGhie woman got hold of that god-awful handle. Porter's blabbed it to the media."

"What the hell are you talking about?"

Bear intercepted my tackle. I wanted to throttle Sam.

Joan slammed her hands on the table. "That's enough," she bellowed. "Gentlemen, please. I don't know what's gone on between the two of you in the past, but we've got a murder to solve. Can't you bury your differences?"

Without a word or a look, Sam stormed out of the conference room, slamming the door behind him.

"The pressure is on the Commissioner every time there's a murder in our district," said Joan. "He's already received twenty-five phone calls after this morning's article in The Scoop. Complaints from the Mayor right down to the usuals that are scared of their own shadows. And he's received five confessions. We're going to screen the calls from now on and not put them directly through to the Commish.

"Now, I want you to listen to me carefully. We've got to squelch this Clean Fiend crap. Sergeant Spivic will be in charge of what we say and don't say to the media. And I don't want to hear Clean Fiend or read Clean Fiend again. Understood? So in your inter-office memos, no mention of CF. Right? I don't care what you say to each other in private. You can call the monster anything you like, but say nothing officially. Have I made myself perfectly clear?" We all nodded, even Margie, who was busily shaking a bottle of Liquid Paper.

"For the record," I put in, "I want to make it clear that I did not in any way use that term to anyone. Not the media. Not friends. No one. I respected Nancy Henderson too much to link her name to such an ugly expression. But, Joan, I don't think we're going to be able to dry up the blister that Franny McGhie sucks on. Once she gets her beak in the jugular, there's no stopping her."

"I'm going to ring up Anne at the Vancouver Police. Maybe she can put some pressure on McGhie."

"I hope so."

"Well," said Bear. "Here's a list of yer duties." He called out everyone's name and handed each of them another folder. I was impressed. He called my name and I walked up to the front feeling like a school boy. He handed me a stack of material. "Here." It was Nancy's envelopes, papers, and black notebook. I recognized them from Brent's description. "I want ya to read these. Take a close look at all the highlighted bits. I had another long night last night." Then he whispered, "I'm buildin' a strong case against Brent Barnes. I know he's your friend, but he's as guilty as sin."

I was reeling. "Surely there's no proof in what you've given me?"

"I'll always remember what ya taught me."

"What was that, Bear?"

"Let the victim tell ya who the murderer is." And then he added, "You'll see that Nancy has done jist that. Thanks, Kev."

Chapter
Twelve

THOMAS HENRY KING cut out Franny McGhie's article from *The Scoop* and glued it on his Media Wall. But he was mad as hell, stomping around his small work room. He ranted, "No mention of *me*. Not a fucking word. Call that reporting, you stupid bitch? And that shithead Commissioner at the RCMP. It's all his fault. 'Refused to comment.' Refused to fucking comment! Why the hell not? Didn't they find my calling card? Dumb fuckers. Why hasn't my brilliant handiwork made front page news? Nobody relegates me to fucking page three! And why haven't I been the lead story on TV?" He was beside himself with frustration. And getting angrier by the minute. And dangerous. He flopped on his cot and pounded the sides. Over and over he recited, "Rogue, rogue, rogue! / I am sick of this false world." For him, murder held the same excitement and suspense as a good play. He chose his actors, selected the perfect set. Researched, rehearsed. The three-day kill built to a wild, thrilling, completely satisfying climax. "I've completed my finest production. So where are my sensational reviews?" As he lay on his cot, thrashing his fists against the mattress, he screamed, "No one knows what I've done. What I have accomplished so brilliantly!"

He had felt his energy level ebbing each day. Monday had been his first day back at work and he returned to sympathetic smiles and condolences from the crew and actors. But Monday night, not a fucking mention on the six o'clock news. Tuesday had been the memorial service, and luckily a short day for shooting *X-Files* for my poor old Harry. He had excitedly hurried home and made himself up, put on a slinky dress, pulled on a long red-haired wig, grabbed a shawl to cover his shoulders and small adam's apple. But the service had been a total letdown for him. He had wanted a funeral, a body. His creation. Instead, there was only the memory. He thought of leaving, but sat still, facing the altar.

If it hadn't been for his little run-in with the fat Mountie, there'd have been no thrills for him. Wednesday, nothing but work, work, work. Late into the night. *The only relief from boredom was that momentary look when Brentie-boy came on to my Harry.* Work was now back to routine. Standing around by the hour, always having to be ready to slap a bit more makeup on DD or powder him down because he'd discovered a drop of rain on his Neanderthal forehead. Dullsville.

He screeched, "And today only a lousy mention in *The Scoop.*"

THK closed his eyes and hugged himself. *I need a nightcap chaser. It's time I take out a fag...*

His mother dominated him over the years — mentally and physically. She regularly slapped him with her hand when he was younger, but as he matured, she used whatever was handy in order to inflict the most physical pain: a belt, a fly swatter, a broom handle, a hockey stick. And heaven help him if she broke anything in the process. "See what you made me do?" she'd scream. "You've broken my broom. I'll take it out of your allowance, Thomas Henry King."

Instead of playing outside with friends, he spent all his free time immersed in the classics. His best friends were Shakespearean characters. As a young child, he sat at his mother's knee while she read one classic after another. As he grew older, she forced him to read by himself. The characters became his constant companions. By the time he was twelve, he'd committed to memory many of Shakespeare's great speeches, knowing the exact phraseology.

His school life was filled with embarrassments. His mother took him to school every day and was always waiting for him at the end of his last class. Right up to the day she died. To hear her talk of Salmon Arm, anyone would think it was a metropolis instead of a small town in the interior of British Columbia. Soon, every teacher that Tommy had knew her. She wrote notes of concern for her son to them all. Year in, year out. He was never permitted to shower at the end of gym classes, but had to wait until he got home. "You're not going to let any of those other boys see your family jewels," she told him. "You never know which one of them might be a sodomite. They hide out in small towns, you know. They'll try to get you alone and cornhole you." He didn't find out what cornholing was until he was sixteen; after that, he knew that he'd never ever allow a faggot to sodomize him.

Always punctual, he followed a strict regime, governed by the clock. If he kept his mother waiting for a minute after school, he would gird himself as he ran to open the awaiting car door. Her suspicious eye and vituperative tongue were ready to blast him before he could do up his seatbelt. She would be waiting there, made up to the hilt, hair coiffed in a bouffant, and bleary-eyed drunk. He never understood exactly what she was accusing him of, but her sneering tone told him it was something hideous, something he'd never ever do. "Which one of your filthy old teachers gave you a blow job today?" He became so homophobic that when she took him shopping (an infrequent special treat), he walked with his head down, never daring to look at a man in case they made eye contact. He was always guarding against the possibility of another tirade of derision from his mother. She'd hiss into his ear, "You'd like to suck his cock, wouldn't you, you little homo?" The thought of doing so made him sick. As he grew older, her tongue became more vindictive. "When I die, you're going to become a cocksucker, aren't you? You're going to rim every faggoty ass you see. Aren't you, you miserable excuse for a man? You can't hide it from your mother. I know what you're thinking. I know what you're going to do when I die. You're going to become a fucking flaming h-o-m-o-s-e-x-u-a-l."

He was never allowed to go on any of the school outings unless she accompanied the group of students. He went once in his elementary days to the Kelowna Regatta, sixty miles to the south. And while in high school, he went to Kamloops, thirty miles to the west, to represent the high school in track and field. His mother was there to cheer him on and also to pick him up and take him to the hotel room she had rented. She wasn't going to let him stay in any of the billeted accommodations arranged by the school. "You could easily be raped in your sleep," she told him. "Those queers slip into your bed at night and cornhole you and you wouldn't even know what hit you until you woke up screaming your head off."

Every day after school, his increasingly drunk mother picked him up from school and drove the five blocks to their beautiful house on a hillside, overlooking a lovely view of the Shuswap Lakes and the whole town of Salmon Arm. On the way home, she'd always make some reference to "Daddy," who had disappeared before Tommy ever got a chance to know him. "You're my man now," she reminded him. "You'll take care of Mommie when I get old. Promise? Promise me, Tommy, that you will take care of me."

As the years passed, she was usually three sheets to the wind and she became more and more possessive of him. "Promise me you will please me tonight, Thomas. Promise me," she continued to slur, "that you'll be a good boy."

As soon as they came home, she'd pour herself a drink and run to her bedroom, sobbing. As always, he'd go to her, climb on the bed beside her, and comfort her. "Mommie, I promise I won't become one of them. I promise, Mommie." He'd pat her face. Tell her he loved her. Recite from memory several speeches from Shakespeare's tragedies. Then, when she fell asleep, he'd deliver one last speech to his snoring mother, usually adjusting Shakespeare's words to make what he thought a more appropriate speech for the situation. "Now cracks a noble heart. Good night, bitch cunt, / And flights of hellions sing thee to thy rest!"

Still on his cot, THK awoke in a frustration of angry sweat. *I got to get out of this fucking room.* He stripped and stepped into the shower next door. It felt good to let the cold water beat against his skin. He didn't shiver. He was a man and he enjoyed doing manly things. *A cold shower twice a day will make a man of you.*

After he dried, he left his sanctum to go into the bedroom next door, put on his favorite dressing gown, pick up a copy of one of the classics that lined the wall, read and relax on the king-sized bed, and wait for his wife to come home.

Chapter
Thirteen

BRENT WAS ALREADY taking his nap when I got home. I crept back down the steps and poured myself a stiff shot of scotch. I couldn't have slept to save my soul. I was still shaking with anger over good old Sam. Sam and I go back over forty years. He was one of my instructors at the RCMP academy in Saskatoon, and I was his fair-haired boy. When I got my first posting in Selkirk, fifty miles North of Winnipeg, and walked into the Detachment, Sam was there, grinning to greet me: he'd been made detective and was stationed there. We were like lost brothers, real buddies. When my son was born, I convinced Martha that we name him Sammy after my best friend, Sam Wheetley.

When Sam was posted to North Vancouver, he was directly responsible for bringing me out as his Chief Inspector. Life was good. We got along like a well-oiled team, cracking one case after another. And then, twelve years ago, everything ground to a halt. Smashed forever, if today's fiasco was any indication.

I finished my drink and went into my den with the material that Bear had given me to read. I had no idea what Nancy had written, but I had been feeling uneasy ever since Bear announced that "Brent wuz as guilty as hell" and that "Nancy will tell us who her murderer is."

Flipping through the whole stack, I quickly assessed that the envelopes contained copies of letters to her parents and to an MG, a girlfriend who was still living next door to the family home in Halifax. That would be Nancy's childhood girlfriend in the February photo on the calendar.

There were also two love letters to a B, telling him that she dies a little each time he leaves her, that he is the sunshine of her life, that a harsh word from him pierces her heart, yadda, yadda, yadda.

The seven sheets of loose paper contained copies of poems that Nancy had written. Spivic had highlighted a portion of this one, if indeed it was a poem:

Names
by Nancy Henderson
B
B
Barney
Bartholomew
No
No
B
Bill
Billy
No
No
B
Bob
Bobby
No
B
Brian
Brent
Yes
Yes
Brent
Brent and Nancy
My Brent

   I could see why Bear highlighted the last few lines. Her love
letters to B were obviously to Brent. And I was sure that Bear had
seen Nancy and Brent's picture on the September page of the
calendar and had no trouble putting two and two together and
making five.
   I glanced through the notebook, a journal. Reading a few of the
highlighted passages, I groaned at Nancy's style. Her diary read like
one of those cheap romance novels that cover supermarket shelves.
   Spivic had put a large NOTE in capital letters in the margin of
several patches and had written a date in the margin. Bear was

obviously building a time line for his case against Brent.

NOTE · August, 1997

> *Today I met the man I could easily spend the rest of my life with. B is my height (5'7"). When he greeted me, I looked directly into his eyes. They were pools of dark mysterious passion. He is slim but well-built. Even though he had his shirt on, I could tell that his abs were rippled like the old-fashioned washboard my grandmother used to use.*

NOTE · October 1997

> *Today, B told me that our friendship is special but must remain platonic. I understand. We teach at the same college, and we can't let our impressionable students know that we are having an affair. So, while we are at work, we must conduct ourselves professionally; but while at play, we can love each other with wild abandon.*

I continued skimming dozens of Nancy's saccharine entries and giving a little more attention to the ones that Bear highlighted. A few phrases caught my attention: "B helped me up and held my arm all the way back to the college. I could feel him tremble as his hand pressed against my full bosom...I invited B to meet my parents...I can't get that man of mine out of my heart."

When I read that last sentence, I whispered, "I know how you feel, Nancy. I can't get Brent out of my heart either." I continued reading her trashy style...

One sentence in her Labor Day Weekend entry caught my eye. "B slept outside in his tent with Karen."

"What's going on?" I said out loud. *Karen? Why hadn't Nancy simply continued using initials in her diary? Brent was at Nancy's cabin with me. Not a Karen.* Nancy knew that Brent and I were lovers.

She joked about it that weekend, for God's sake. "I'm having so much fun with you guys, I think I may be in danger of becoming a fag hag." We rolled around laughing.

Nancy was a sophisticated woman who accepted diversity with not so much as a raised eyebrow. So why include a distorted version of these events in her diary? Or was this a real diary? If not, what is the significance of this piece of trashy writing? I bet Nancy had her tongue firmly stuck in her cheek as she wrote this rot.

I continued reading. Long minutes passed. When I finally came to this, her last entry, I read it twice:

NOTE · Friday, Sept. 25, 1998

Today I twisted B's arm and he consented to walk around the golf course with me during our lunch hour. He agreed reluctantly. I suppose he felt guilty about our Labor Day weekend because we hadn't really spoken meaningfully to each other since. Actually, I was the one who didn't talk to him. A girl has to play hard to get, once in a while... During our walk, I stuck my courage to the sticking place and pressed him for the last time to give our relationship another try. He shouted at me, "There ain't no relationship. There's never been no relationship." He uses bad grammar for effect. I love him so, but I can't stop thinking that now he's enjoying someone else's touches every night. Not mine. Never mine... I'm back in my office now. B has left for his darn weekend. I made the most momentous decision of my virginal life. I am going to cancel my 4:00 class. I'm going to tell JE about B's secret. Then he'll know the lengths I'm prepared to go to keep him. And then maybe he'll see his big mistake and realize that a good woman, like yours truly, is hard to find...

Darn, I'm back at my desk. JE has gone for the day too. I will definitely tell her first thing Monday morning when I get back from the lake.

I tossed the diary aside. What a load of crap! What the hell had

Nancy been trying to do?

I crept up the steps and curled, spoon-like, into Brent's naked body. "Hmm. I missed you. Just get home?"

"Yeah. Missed you too, my manno." I kissed his hair. A fragrance of ambrosia filled my nostrils. I had missed the smell of my lover. *Yipes! I've caught Nancy's style.* I didn't believe it could be so contagious.

"Gotta shower. Coming in?"

"Sure thing. I've fallen into a honey vat."

"What?"

"Nothing."

Spivic was sniffing out the wrong man. This kind-hearted man was gay to the bone. I knew that for a fact. What a shower!

WE HAD A quiet evening. Prepared dinner together and watched the first-run episodes of our favorite shows. A three-hour Thursday night ritual.

Before the news came on, Brent said, "Have you found out yet how Nancy was killed?"

"Yes, but..."

"But what?"

"Well, I don't think you'd like to hear the details."

Brent looked at me for a moment. "Is it that bad?"

"Worse."

"Everyone around the college was talking about *The Scoop* article. Wondering why McGhie called the killer a Clean Fiend."

"So, do you want details?" I asked.

Brent shook his head and leaned down for a kiss. "I'm going to bed, love."

"Before you go, would you describe Nancy's writing style in a couple of words?"

Without hesitation he responded, "Crisp. Subtle. Perhaps a little obtuse. She enjoys...enjoyed... making her readers think for themselves."

"Thanks. Was she published?"

"She had a few articles published in English journals. You know, on classroom strategies."

"Can I ask you a few more questions about Nancy before you go upstairs?"

"Yes you 'may' ask me a few questions." English teachers are all the same: they love correcting someone's grammar.

"Whom was Nancy's bestest friend?" I thought I could take the mickey out of him. He ignored my lame attempt at bad grammar.

"Me."

I didn't want to hear that answer, even though I suspected it.

"No one else?"

"Not really. Maybe Dorothy Bovak. They've had lunch a few times and I think Dorothy spent a weekend with her at her cabin. But, Kev, we shared the same office and the same lunch hour. And you know we usually went for a walk around the golf course before our afternoon classes. We shared things."

"Like what?"

"Personal stuff."

"Did you talk to her about me? Us?"

"Sometimes."

"And?" *Come on, cough it up.*

"Well, she asked me about our age difference. I told her the truth. I'm attracted to older men. She really couldn't understand. But she liked you, Kev. I know that for a fact. Coming up?"

"I'm not very tired." My mind was going a hundred miles a minute.

"Night-night, then." He gave me one of his tongue-flicking kisses. "Love you."

"Love you, too."

Once in my den, I whispered, "Okay, Nancy. Talk to me. Tell me who killed you, darling."

I decided to read every goddamn schmaltzy word, not just the ones Bear had highlighted.

Well into her diary, nearly falling asleep, I stopped cold. A chill crossed my heart as I read,

You know, B, I haven't told you this before, but I have a secret admirer. I've seen him twice now. Once standing outside my class and once in Safeway when our carts collided. So why can't you find me desirable? I know he does.

I checked Spivic's dates nearest to this valuable piece of information. Nearly a month ago!

Now I was wide awake. I read on furiously to see what else Nancy wanted to tell me.

The last diary entry about the mystery man was the short statement Nancy made before her threat to see JE, obviously Jane Edwards, the English Department Head. Just last Friday.

When B walked to his car at 1:50, I accompanied him. I thought I saw someone sitting in the parking lot in one of those Japanese

imports. I'm sure he was looking at B, but I couldn't be certain because he whipped his newspaper over his head as B drove by. Could he have been my secret mystery man? But his hair was blond not brown. Long and blond.

"Thank you, Nancy. Your mystery man is a real sweetheart. He's now disguised as a blond. You were being stalked, and not by..." I stopped talking, realizing I was probably spouting pure nonsense.

But I wasn't going to stifle my optimistic feelings. I went up to bed feeling relieved, ready to convince Spivic that Brent was not his killer.

Chapter
Fourteen

THOMAS HENRY KING, closed his eyes, remembering it all. It was Springtime, 1997. *Eighteen months ago...*

Thomas Henry King walked along the path bordering English Bay to Second Beach. Instead of being the quiet, mature Harry he had been throughout that day, he was now convincingly disguised as an outgoing, handsome young man on the make in his skin-tight, crotch-cleaving, black leather pants and jean jacket. He knew that he looked delectable, irresistible, positively fuckable. He mused, "I will be found most cunning in my patience, / But (dost thou hear) most bloody." He walked along the path with his imaginary companion for the night: *Othello.*

Not seeing a single older man who looked suitable, he became disheartened. The night seemed to go on forever as he retraced his steps for the fourth time. He'd been home for three months and still had not had a chaser since his fun adventure in Hawaii with the strikingly beautiful Susan James who so resembled his mother. But on this balmy spring night, he was feeling antsy. He had to satisfy his unquenchable urge for a nightcap.

To pass the time and help calm himself, he communed with his companion: "My bloody thoughts, with violent pace, / Shall ne'er look back, ne'er ebb to humble love, / Till that a capable and wide revenge / Swallow them up." He was hungry for cock. Desperate.

On his fourth circuit along the path from English Bay to Second Beach, he picked up the pace and increased his stride as he spotted an older man walking a white Maltese pup. The man, well dressed in a trench coat and fedora, was in his fifties. *Undoubtedly a businessman.* They made eye contact as they passed, and both turned back at the same moment. Both grinned.

The man in the trench coat knelt and patted his puppy. "Are you getting sleepy, honey? You want me to take you home?"

"Nice puppy."

The older man looked up with an expression of mock surprise. "Hi. He is a cutie, isn't he?"

"Mind if I pat him?"

"Be my guest. My name's Dave."

"Call me Dick." He bent down to pat the pup. Both men continued stroking the little dog. Dick broke the silence. "Do you like to be touched, poochie? Do you like to feel my hands on your body? Hmm?" While THK's hands felt every part of the dog, his eyes devoured Dave. "You're enjoying my touch, aren't you, fella? Oh, you want to lick my fingers, do you? Hmm? That feels great." And then quite suddenly, he doctored one of Othello's lines. "Would you like to kiss the instrument of my pleasure?"

"This is your lucky day, Oscar," whispered Dave hoarsely. "It's not every day that a good-looking young man makes you an offer like that." He smiled. "Is Dick short for..."

"It's not short. I assure you." They both laughed.

Dave gave a little hoot. "Ooo! That sounds interesting."

Poofter! "Can I call you...?"

"What?"

"No, it's silly."

"Tell me."

"Well, I wondered whether I could call you Daddy."

Dave hesitated, looking at the expectant, smiling youth. "Sure, why not."

"Would you like to see me naked, Daddy?"

"Yes, indeed." He smiled eagerly.

"Would you like to taste me, Daddy?"

"Sounding better all the time."

"Why don't we hop off the sea wall?" Dick leapt down the side of the rock wall and landed silently on the sand five feet below. He stood between two large jagged rocks, looking up and grinning boyishly. "Out of sight, out of mind."

Dave stood on the edge of the wall and looked down nervously. "I don't think I can jump that far. Besides the tide's coming in. Why don't you come back up and we can go to my place? It's much more comfortable there. I live close by."

Ignoring his request, *Dick* coaxed, "Then sit on the edge here." He stood on the rock and patted a spot on the wall. "I want to help you get rid of any tension you're feeling, Daddy. You'll be in exactly the right position for my mouth if you sit right here. Hurry, I can hardly wait. You're killing me, Daddy." He licked his lips sensuously.

Excited, Dave crouched down and sat awkwardly on the edge of the sea wall.

"Better hand me Oscar. We don't want him to run away, do we? Besides, I bet he'd love to watch me give Daddy a blow job." He laughed gently, sexily.

Dave willingly handed him Oscar and started to unzip his fly.

Dick set the pup down on the sand with the command "Sit."

Without another word, he turned, grabbed Dave's feet, and yanked the unsuspecting man off the wall. The first thud of Dave's head against the edge of the wall was nothing compared with the crack against the jagged rock that split the back of his skull and ended his life. Thomas Henry King grinned in fiendish delight. He was positive that the last thing Dave would see was his moonlit smile as it faded to black.

"Put out the light..." he whispered in resonant Othellian tones; then he scooped up Oscar by his tiny hind legs and dashed his head against the same rock that was now dark red with his master's blood; "...and then put out the light." He relished in finding the exact Shakespearean quote for tonight's chaser. The Moor had always been one of his closest friends. He remembered the invigorating thrill he felt the first time his mother read the scene where Othello smothers Desdemona. Even at six years of age, he had wondered how it would feel to throttle his mother.

He knelt and tied the dog leash around his master's neck. "Now that's what I call a real nightcap."

He stood up, noticing his own bulging basket. He growled in disgust, "See what you made me do, Daddy. Murder's out of tune / And sweet revenge grows harsh. You gave me a hard-on, Daddy." He slowly, methodically removed all of his clothes, folding them neatly and placing them on a clean rock. Standing naked, he spoke menacingly. "Now I'm going to have to get rid of my load. Open your mouths, boys. I've got a surprise for you before Mother Nature drags you out to sea."

When he got home, he placed his trophies in a cooler and buried them in ice. Then he carried the cooler into his sanctuary, for later pleasures. He was elated.

Undressing and hanging up his fag-tease costume, he smiled at the garbage bags of costumes in his closet.

His mind filled with memories as he gazed at the sealed bags. I haven't killed a "furry creature" since I was a child. He laughed, while he looked at himself in the mirror near the closet. He liked looking at himself, especially while he laughed. He wanted to see whether there was any blood still on his teeth. He detected a trace. But he needed his trophies, and teeth work so much better than knives.

He stepped into the shower, making sure that not a drop of Dave's or Oscar's blood remained on his body. After he dried and felt squeaky clean, he slipped through his secret door and got into bed, waiting for his wife to return from her meeting. He laughed to himself. *Hurry up, woman. I really want to pump your hungry pussy tonight to consummate my nightcap chasers!*

Chapter
Fifteen

WE HEADED OUT of the car park in my Lincoln. Today, I was going to be around the college as long as Brent was, so one car would do us.

"Would you like me to turn on the heat, love?" I asked Brent. "I feel winter in the air and it's still only September. Or is it October already? I don't even know what month it is. I've lost all track of time."

Brent didn't answer. I turned up the heat anyway, to take off the morning chill. Today must be Friday. I figured out the date during the silence: Friday, October Second.

We'd eaten our breakfast in silence, quite unusual for us. Well, actually, unusual for me. I have a tendency to babble on in the morning. Brent preferred to be quiet. Another one of our differences. Brent was not a morning person.

But normally he tolerated my gabbing. "Yes, Chatty Cathy," he'd say between spoonfuls of his corn flakes as I carried on about one thing or another.

When Bear called me this morning to remind me to come to the college, he casually announced he'd been on TV last night and wondered whether or not I'd seen him. When I told him I hadn't, he said, "Well, ya can catch me on the seven o'clock news this mornin'." Brent and I watched in silence.

The Vancouver Police media officer interviewed Bear. "So do we have a serial killer on our hands, Sergeant Spivic?"

"That's jumpin' the gun a little, Annie, don'tcha think?"

It was obvious that she did not appreciate Bear's tone and cocksure attitude; she cut him off with her own statement: "Thank you, Sergeant Spivic." The camera zoomed in on her face. "As reported in one of Vancouver's papers this morning, the macabre murder of Nancy Henderson, one of the most popular instructors at the college, has devastated her colleagues and students. Interviews are being conducted by the RCMP with permission of the Vancouver Chief of Police. Over to you."

Brent continued to munch his corn flakes. I was relieved that Bear had obviously warned Anne Wyner not to refer to the killer as

the Clean Fiend. I breathed a sigh of relief after watching the rerun
of last night's interview.   And after I tore open *The Scoop* and
blessedly found nothing, I felt ready for the day. Was this the calm
before the storm?

As we headed out of the West End, my head filled with larger
events. I felt sure that I was going to have to out Brent today. To
save him.

"They're still filming *X-Files* around here," he announced with
surprising interest as we passed the crew setting up in the little park
near Roedde House. Those were the first words he'd spoken since a
grudging "Good morning," at six thirty.

"Yeah. Your favorite show, hon."

"Yeah!" Brent smiled. "Stop for a minute." He was now bright-
eyed, looking at all the action. The house looked as though it had
been plucked from some place in the deep south. Vancouver's
adaptable locations is one of a hundred reasons why British
Columbia has become Hollywood North. Brent was hooked on *The
X-Files*. David Duchovny was undoubtedly his favorite TV actor.
"Don't you love the way he underplays?" he'd say proudly half a
dozen times during each episode.

Because *The X-Files* had been regularly shooting in the West End,
Brent had been hoping to get a glimpse of the star. But in five years,
he'd never yet seen him in the flesh. And now with rumors that they
may move south, he knew he might never have a chance.

"Don't go yet, sweetie. Park for a minute," he yelled excitedly,
craning his neck one way and then the other.

"Okay." I put my foot on the brake.   *My goodness, such an
energized lover. And at eight a.m.*

Stepping out of one of the trailers was a distinguished-looking
man. Maybe one of the extras. Or a crew member. He wore a smock
and was carrying a jar of something red. He looked at us as we
passed. I caught a glimpse of Brent's giveaway expression. A dead
giveaway. He was playing his game. "Undressing him?" Brent's
face flushed. "I caught you in the act."

"No, you didn't. I thought he was David Duchovny."

"Hmm." I sped away to the college.

*THOSE TWO TOGETHER. And at eight in the morning! Very
interesting. Bet they're both off to the college to meet with the big, bad
RCMP officer. Brentie boy was definitely giving me the eye. Again.*

The X-Files' makeup artist headed for the shoot across the street,
his mind on what he had just seen.

DD was standing on the path. "Did you get a load of that
Lincoln, Harry? It looks brand new."

"Sure does. I gotta get this blood to the AD."

They were about to film the final shoot-out scene for the current episode. Harry was carrying a jar of his secret recipe for blood. He could already foresee the exact way the killer's throat would look when Mulder pulled the trigger. In self defense, of course. *Big hero man saves the day. He'd never kill in cold blood. Don't know what you're missing, Mulder.*

By the time they had set up for the shootout, Harry was in his own world. He was thinking back to his last chaser, an old fag called Dave, that he had sent off to la-la-land eighteen months ago. *Boy, did I surprise him! Now that was a chaser! I need another. Now!* He opened his pack of cigarettes and pulled one out. *I can hardly wait for this day to end. Then I can enjoy my first weekend alone, all by myself with my souvenirs from Swallow Lake.*

EVERY DAY AFTER school from the time he was eight years old, THK's mother would insist that he work out. "You have to be strong so that you can protect yourself against those pederasts out there, waiting to take advantage of you. You never know, Tommy, one of them could be your dad. He'd cornhole you just as soon as look at you. You got to be strong so you can beat the shit out of him."

By the time he was sixteen, he'd pump iron for twenty minutes, skip rope for fifteen, and end with mat work for thirty minutes. He could do a hundred non-stop pushups with ease, sit ups until he lost count, leg thrusts until he grew bored. His mother would sit close by, proudly watching him exercise as she sipped her cocktails and read him a classic. Always, at the end of the hour, she would close her book, turn on an R&B record, and say, "Come on in, Tommy. Your syringe is ready." Dutifully, he'd go into the bathroom and assume the position. Over the years, the syringe grew in size: the globe held a full pint of soapy water; the nozzle was over an inch in diameter and eight inches long. He continued to put his thumb in his mouth but, instead of biting down on it, he'd rhythmically suck on it. Occasionally he'd feel an erection so he'd flick his penis with his pinky until it went limp. He didn't want his mother to see that he was being turned on. He should have some secrets in his life. *Silence is the perfectest herald of joy.*

AFTER BRENT INTRODUCED Spivic, Abby, and me to Nancy's nine o'clock class, Spivic dismissed Brent. "We'll see ya back here at eleven for the second class."

Spivic tried valiantly to command respect. He hopped up on an empty desk at the front of the room for that casual paternal look he was so fond of projecting. All eyes watched as the supports between the seat and the desktop slowly spread apart. So engrossed in his own talk, Spivic wasn't aware that he was about to lose his dignity. The desk collapsed into two pieces under his weight.

Landing on his back, legs and arms flailing like a turtle stranded upside-down, Spivic took a minute to right himself. The students roared with laughter. They needed to laugh. Ten minutes ago the atmosphere had been funereal.

Spivic began again, laughing good-naturedly. "They don't make desks like they used to." To my surprise, the desk wasn't the only thing he broke. More important, Spivic broke the ice.

From then on, he had the students in his burly paw. "All of ya know about yer teacher's death. But I'm sorry to hafta tell ya that her death is now a police matter. Miss Henderson wuz murdered." I suspect that all the students knew this, but hearing it from a Mountie made it real. There were gasps. New tears. Shock. "I remember seein' some of ya at her memorial service when I wuz there doin' surveillance duty." He looked the class over. "Now, I know this is terrible news to hear first thing in the mornin', but *you all* can help me catch her killer. I want ya to set aside everythin' fer the next fifty minutes 'n help me. Will ya do that?" Affirmative nods all round.

Out came the pad. He went through a series of prepared questions. "Did she have any enemies? Did anyone see her bein' watched or followed? Did she say anythin' that might indicate that she wuz afraid o' someone?" Etc. etc.

Drawing no responses, he changed his approach. "Now I wanna talk to ya about her personal life. Did any of ya ever see her with a man?"

"What do you mean with a man?" asked the young woman sitting right in front of me.

"Romantically. You kids know what I mean. Wuz she gettin' it on with anyone?"

Hands went up. "Yeah?" Spivic pointed to the young woman in the second row.

"She was dating Mr. Barnes."

"Yes, everyone thought they were a perfect couple," the guy next to her confirmed. Several heads nodded.

I choked.

"Are you okay?" Abby leaned over.

"Yeah. No."

"Miss Henderson asked us to write a cinquain and..."

"How d'ya spell that?" Bear had his pen poised over his pad.

"C-I-N-Q-U-A-I-N. Miss Henderson read one that she wrote called 'Soul Mates,'" continued the student.

"What the hell's a sincwain? Pardon my French." The kids were turned on by Bear's prairie vernacular and were pleased that they were helping nail the killer of their wonderful teacher.

"A cinquain is a five-line poem invented by Adelaide Crapsey."

Spivic guffawed. The student smiled and continued, "The first line contains two syllables, the second four, the third six, the fourth eight, and the fifth two."

"Hell, ya gotta be good at math, too," Bear interrupted with a chortle.

The young woman continued, "Miss Henderson handed out copies of her cinquain."

"Anyone got one here?" asked Spivic.

Several students opened their notebooks and held up a copy of the poem.

"Who would like t' read it, so I can hear it?" asked Spivic.

The young woman in front of me stood:

"Soul Mates" by Nancy Henderson.

Soul mates
Found each other.
From down under he came,
Bringing insight and desire.
Sweet bliss."

Everyone in the room reflected on the subtext of that short poem. You could tell that they fully comprehended the fact that their teacher's dreams of pure bliss were now lost forever. Several young women wept openly; a number of the men lowered their heads. I choked again. Nancy had done a damn fine job of keeping Brent's gay life a secret. Everyone in that room was convinced that Brent had lost his one true love in Nancy Henderson. It was obvious to every student why this RCMP officer had asked Brent not to be present during the questioning: to protect the grieving lover.

"Are you okay?" Abby asked me again.

"I need a drink of water." I was out of my seat and out of the room in two strides. I needed to cool off and collect my thoughts.

I paced the halls.

DURING THE PAST years, Brent had taught me much, not only about the gay culture but life in general. Moving from high school, which is far from real life, to a career with the Mounties, which is even further from reality, I had a lot to learn. You'll notice I didn't mention family. Family for me was trying to keep ahead of the monthly bills.

But Brent taught me things that I had never before experienced. I remember each of our first dozen weeks after that first night we met. To me, each encounter was an adventure where my fantasies slowly, but miraculously, became realities. When he'd ring me up in his elevator, I never knew what to expect. And when he bid me farewell, he'd say, "See you next Wednesday. You ain't seen nothin' yet."

I would return to my little one-bedroom apartment and fantasize about Brent, living for the next Wednesday. And the next one. And the next. It never occurred to me to wonder what he was up to during the rest of the week. We'd occasionally phone each other, and he always seemed to be busy with his school work or doing the laundry or cleaning his apartment. We were free agents and respected each other's privacy.

Four months into our relationship I found out that he always got high before I visited. On this particular Wednesday when I walked in, I said, "I smell smoke."

He blushed. "I just had a toke. Makes love-making more sensuous. Want some?"

"Sure," I shrugged, not telling him that I'd never smoked pot in my life, "give me a tote."

He split a gut laughing. "A toke, not a tote. A tote is a purse — a *tote* bag! Get it? Where have you been all your life?" I shrugged, feeling as stupid as I probably looked. "You've got so much to learn, darl'. I'd love to teach you." That was the first time he called me darl', his abbreviation of darling.

"I'm yours," I smiled, embarrassed. He stuck the pipe in my mouth and winked. "Take a *tote*, love." Up to that time, neither of us had ever used the L-word. Spluttering and choking, I'm sure I swallowed more smoke than I breathed in. But it did the trick for me. The sex! A-Numero-Uno, for sure.

He smiled afterwards. "Lesson One. Most of the gay population smoke pot. Don't you feel like a heel, Mr. Big Bad Policeman, who spent so much of your time busting us marijuana junkies?" I laughed. "And, while I'm on a hot streak, Lesson Two: Throw away those running shoes. I will never go out with a man who has Velcro straps on his shoes." I looked down at my feet. My grungy white running shoes did look a bit ridiculous, but hell, they felt comfortable. He continued, "Hey, I'm on a roll. Lesson Three: The color of your socks should match the color of your shoes, not the color of your pants."

I pulled up my blue pant legs and looked at my black socks stuck in my white grungy runners. "So, I shouldn't wear black socks with white shoes?"

"Never!"

Not long after that, he took me to Dunn's Men's Wear and bought me a labeled wardrobe. "I think now you might be ready to move in with me, and become my senior toy." He gave me a sexy smile and slid his tongue over his lower lip.

It didn't take me long to move in with Brent. With Martha's

help, I rented my apartment, instead of selling it. That way, I had a steady income, walking around for the first time in my life with real folding money. And, if it didn't work out with Brent, I had a place to go.

AS I STUMBLED about the college halls, I couldn't stop contrary thoughts from tumbling around in my head. *Has Brent been using me, brainwashing me?* His senior toy! Ha! *Have I been a front for his extracurricular clandestine activities all along? He's been on his own an awful lot over the years.* Trips back home to Australia with stopovers in Hawaii; volleyball matches in Los Angeles, Dallas, New York, Miami, San Francisco, Winnipeg, Amsterdam, Berlin. His stories were always the same. "The team members wouldn't understand my liking older men. Besides, you'll be more comfortable at home." Probably true. I didn't feel like bunking in dorms with a platoon of muscular volleyball players, gay or not. And I did like puttering in my rooftop gardens.

I stopped in the middle of the college foyer, talking to myself. "Do I really know this man? Is he leading a double life? What does he do when he's not with me?"

I tried to suppress the question that kept rearing its ugly head. *Was he really in Seattle last weekend? Maybe I'm blinded by the love I have for him. Maybe I shouldn't have been trusting him so absolutely.*

"Stop!" I shouted. Several students gave me strange looks. I didn't give a shit what they thought. I kept mumbling. "Trust your lover, you silly old fart. He has nothing to do with this case. Remember what Brent taught you. "Trust each other, knowing that whatever we do, we'll always stand by each other."

But...but...

I headed for the cafeteria for a sugar fix before the eleven o'clock class.

BEAR'S HANDLING OF the eleven, three, and four o'clock classes was virtually the same as the nine o'clock one. Except that he didn't break any more desks.

Bear seemed convinced, more and more after each session, that Brent and Nancy were "havin' it on." I needed to distract him.

I wrote a note to Spivic during his talk with the four o'clock class. At the end of his agenda, he said, "My assistant, there in the back row, wants me t' ask ya this question. Did Miss Henderson cancel last Friday's class?"

"No," came the resounding answer.

Except for the introductions at the beginning of each of the classes, I hadn't seen Brent. Spivic's orders.

At five o'clock precisely, Spivic, Abby, and I walked to Brent's office. Spivic warned me, "When we get there, not a word out o' ya. Understand?"

He knocked on the door. Brent opened it. The poor darling was a wreck.

"Mr. Barnes. We're goin' fer a little drive. Chief Inspector Riley wants t' have a word with ya."

AN HOUR LATER I was standing with Joan Riley in the small viewing room of the RCMP North Vancouver Detachment. We were both looking through the two-way mirror at a nervous, young man sitting at a table, turning the pages of a black notebook, intently reading every highlighted passage. Not prone to perspiring, this young man was already flushed and glowing with sweat. I know for sure the RCMP deliberately turns the thermostat up in their interrogation rooms. I started the practice. When I used that room, I was never one to make interrogation a comfortable experience.

Many investigative techniques have changed since I retired. I've done a bit of reading about the different ways of tracking down serial killers using computers and feel that a whole world has passed me by. I needed to do more study. While I was humbled to see that Joan was still using the good old-fashioned method of turning up the heat to help wear down suspects, I was sick to death witnessing the scene before me. *That young man in there is my lover, and he is soon going to be roasted, grilled, and charred to a crisp.*

"So how are you enjoying your retirement years?" asked Joan.

My eyes were glued on Brent. I knew what he was thinking. "Why the hell didn't Kev ride with me in Spivic's cruiser? Or, "Why didn't Kev drive me in his Lincoln? The one I bought for him!" Or maybe, "Why the fuck did Kev let them shut me up in this hell hole, all alone? Why didn't Kev protect me, goddammit?"

And why didn't I? Because I'm a coward. I couldn't shake Raymond Chandler's description of an ideal private investigator: "Down these mean streets a man must go who is not himself mean, who is neither tarnished nor afraid." Well, he sure as hell wasn't describing me.

Truth time.

There are many things I've regretted doing in my life. But this one took the cake. Tarnished indeed. All I could do was hope this day would not be the worst of my life. Could today be any worse than letting Martha rape me in the front seat of her little Morris Minor back in '62? When it came to sex, she was seventeen, going on forty; I was twenty-four, going on twelve. After driving me home from a community center party, this very experienced teenager mounted me on the passenger seat, and two minutes later I realized I had had my first sexual experience. Okay, I'm not proud of it. Back then, I was a twenty-four-year-old virgin!

Three months later she phones me up and says, "You better get over here. I'm pregnant."

"Where do you live?" I hadn't seen her since that night.

So, my first sexual experience ended in a shotgun wedding five months later. Her parents had threatened they'd get me thrown out of the Force if I didn't marry their underaged daughter. How the hell could I tell them, let alone convince them, that she raped me? So naturally, coward that I was, I took my medicine. I married Martha. But to make the whole nightmare more disastrous, RCMP policy in the sixties clearly stated: no RCMP recruit is allowed to marry. So a very pregnant Martha and I married secretly with our two sets of parents and my best friend, Sam Wheetley, witnessing. We had our first child — Sammy — secretly. We didn't announce our marriage until nearly ten years, and three more kids, later, when the policy changed. In those days, being an RCMP cadet was as restrictive as entering the priesthood.

We kept living a charade for twenty-eight years. Settling into the routine of family life, I worked hard, bought a home, got saddled with a mortgage, and sired, in all, five wonderful kids. At least I always thought they were all mine until Martha ran off with Hank after I retired. Who knows how many previous lovers she'd had? But what does it matter? In my heart, my kids are mine, and I love them all with a passion.

I have many other regrets, but there is one other that'll rank right up there in the top three. After I became Chief Inspector, I found that I had more time on my hands; as a result, I began to examine my deepest feelings. I knew things weren't right between Martha and me, and I certainly knew it wasn't Martha's fault. I slowly began to give in to my "natural" inclinations. Anyway, one hot summer evening, I was driving home along my usual route: a quiet Upper Levels road. Suddenly, a red Porsche convertible sped by me. I hadn't given anyone a speeding ticket in years but I turned on my siren and gave chase. To this day, I regret not giving that hunky, twenty-something-year-old man — Rusty Towers his name was — a ticket. I remember walking up to his car, looking down at his bronzed, buffed, bare chest. I said, "Registration and license."

He wore mirrored sunglasses, but I was convinced his eyes were focused on my crotch. After a deliberate pause, he slowly tilted his head up to me and smiled broadly. I caught a glint of my own sexual excitement reflected in his sunglasses. He did a perfect Mae West imitation: "Well, hello, Officer. Is that a gun in your pocket, or are you just happy to see me?" I laughed. "Oh, you naughty Mr. Policeman," he chortled. I'd given myself away in more ways than one.

As I started to write the ticket, I noticed he was slowly rubbing his crotch. Then he spoke in a smooth southern accent. "Do you have any ideas of how you might like me to work that off?" He smiled. "The ticket, I mean."

"Well..." I was definitely turned on by this good-looking young man, but nervous as hell.

"Well, what?" he soothed. "Tell me what you would like me to do, sir, and I'll do it." He fairly purred sex appeal.

"You see those bushes over there?" I pointed toward a clump of trees.

"Uh huh," he grinned.

"How about you meet me over there? I'm sure we'll come up with something?" I wondered, at the time, whether he appreciated my limp pun.

"Sounds great," he said excitedly. "I'll come, all right. Why don't you go first. I'd like to see you walk across that field. I like a man in uniform. I'll pull off the road a bit ahead and meet you there."

I poked my pad in my hip pocket. (Another lesson I hadn't been taught way back then: Gay men never put anything in their hip pockets.)

"Go on, start walking," Rusty urged. I headed for the bushes, sensing that his eyes were following me. "Nice ass," he whistled. I felt excited, expectant.

Half way to the bushes, I heard the peeling of rubber and turned. I ran to the road and watched the Porsche disappear.

Standing there in the middle of the road, embarrassed by my gullibility, I decided not to pursue. I'd been taken in by a cock tease. As I tore up the ticket, I made a promise to myself to be ever vigilant.

That incident got me fired. Rusty Towers wrote Commissioner Sam Wheetley, describing the event in exaggerated detail. He threatened to out me through the media if Sam didn't take disciplinary action. My old friend handed me the letter and, without discussion, asked me to resign. Naturally, I protested. "What a load of crap! You believe what this guy says over my word? We've known each other for over twenty-eight years. We've been friends for most of those years. Hell, Sam, we named our first-born after you."

"You're not the same person anymore." Sam was adamant.

"You know me better than that, Wheetley. I would never do a thing like that."

Sam picked up a cassette tape. "He recorded your disgusting interlude. Would you like to hear it on CBC?" He added, to reinforce his repugnance towards me, "And to think, I'm little Sammy's godfather! He's going to need me when he finds out his father is a...a..."

"All right, Goddammit, you'll get my letter of resignation today." Coward that I was, I said nothing more to Sam. I left quietly. Ah, the Eighties! Nowadays, the Chief of Police walks down Beach Avenue in the Gay Pride parade.

And now I was living through another event that I was going to regret the rest of my life. I was allowing my lover to be interrogated, accused of murder, without my intervention. Even though I couldn't imagine he had anything to do with Nancy's death, there were still too many unanswered questions racing through my mind for me to intervene. And I was too afraid to ask Brent for direct answers because of what I imagined I might hear.

"Kev, where are you?"

"Uh?"

"You look as though you're miles away. I asked you," continued Joan, "how you were enjoying your retirement."

"Oh, fine. Just fine."

At that moment, Spivic and Davis walked into the interrogation room. Abby stood behind Brent. Bear pulled out the chair, turned it around and straddled it, facing the accused. "Do ya mind if we record this session?"

"No," Brent said quietly. "You are making a big mistake. I've got nothing to hide."

"You'll have to speak up." Spivic pushed the Record button. "Case Number 8909: the murder of Nancy Henderson, discovered Sept. 28, 1998. Today's date: October 2, 1998, 18:20 hours. Location: North Vancouver Detachment Office, Interrogation Room. Present: Sergeant Barry Spivic and Corporal Abby Davis. The subject Brent Barnes has agreed to have this interview taped." Bear was ready for action.

"What am I being accused of?" demanded Brent. "You said that I was going to have a chat with Chief Inspector Riley." He wasn't going to allow Spivic to get the upper hand. I was proud of him.

"I'll do the questionin', Mr. Barnes. *You* do the answerin'. Got that?"

"Yes," Brent replied too meekly.

Stand your ground, love. Don't let them push you around. You ain't seen nothin' yet. Remember? Why the hell was I putting my lover through this?

"So, you've read the bits of the victim's diary that I highlighted in yellow. What's yer reaction? Fer the record."

"The style is turgid, grandiloquent and tumid. But I'm sure you already realized that."

"That don't sound good, whatever all them words mean. But as far as I'm concerned, her style is great. That girl tore my heart apart, readin' what she wrote. "

Brent looked directly at Bear. "To each his own."

"Whatever."   Bear had no idea what Brent was referring to.
"You'll agree, however, that the B that she uses throughout her diary
is you, Brent Barnes."

"There are lots of different men's names beginning with B.
Barry, for example. And Bear, for another." Bear flashed a how-the-
hell-do-you-know-Mil-calls-me-Bear look.   "You shouldn't jump to
conclusions, Sergeant."

Good for you, lover, but watch your back.

"Read this."   Abby handed him Nancy's poem.   "It's called
'Names.' Take a look at the last five lines, 'Brent/Yes Yes/Brent/
Brent and Nancy/My Brent.' "

"So?"

Bear pounced. "You're supposed to be the English teacher, Mr.
Barnes. Surely ya can see that she is tellin' us that there B stands fer
Brent."

"Nonsense."

"Whatcha mean by that, Mr. Barnes? Are ya tellin' us that ya
weren't toyin' with this sweet woman's affections?   Makin' a
mockery of the love she wuz wastin' on ya? Ya led all her fellow
teachers and her students t'believe that you two wuz a number."

"That's pure fiction."

"That kind of evasive response isn't going to get us anywhere,
Sergeant Spivic," interrupted Abby. "Why don't we cut to the
chase?" She leaned over and shouted in Brent's ear. "Tell us why
you killed her?" Classic good cop/bad cop routine.

"I didn't kill her. And there's nothing more I can say."   Brent
folded his arms. His face became granite. His Roman nose rigid.

"Don't try that silent crap on us, Mister."   Abby looked over at
Spivic. "Let me have a go."

"Only for a minute. I gotta take a leak anyways." With sudden
alacrity Spivic was out of the room and standing beside Joan and me
in the viewing room.

"So, what's this big secret you're trying to hide, little man?"
Abby smelled blood.

"What do you mean?"

"You know damn well what I mean. What was Nancy going to
tell Jane Edwards on Monday morning? Was it so bad that you had
to silence Nancy for good?"

This was too much for Brent. Tears sprang from his eyes and
bounced on the table. Abby stared, astonished for a moment, then
savagely carried on. "Cut the tears, Barnes. You had motive and
opportunity."

"Where the hell did that come from?" I yelled at my lover's
inquisitor through the window in the viewing room.

Abby continued turning the screws. "And now you think that
this little-girl crying jag will make everything better? Not on your

keister, Mister! What was Nancy Henderson going to tell Jane Edwards?" Abby pounded her fist on the table so hard that Brent's tears stopped instantly.

"I am not going to answer any more of your questions. I want a lawyer."

Spivic was back in the room in a flash, pretending to do up his fly buttons. "So, how're things goin' Corporal? Got a confession yet?"

"He wants a lawyer."

"Do tell. We ain't arrested ya yet. We're jist havin' a friendly chat." Spivic sat down again on his chair and said calmly, "Brent, if yer innocent, then ya certainly don't need a lawyer. Now, why don'tcha prove to us that ya didn't kill Nancy. Prove that we're barkin' up the wrong post."

Abby softened her tone, too. "Where were you last weekend, Brent?"

Brent looked first at her, then at Spivic. "I was in Seattle."

"For the whole weekend?" enquired Spivic.

"Yes, from Friday night to Sunday night."

"Where'dya stay?"

"On a yacht." Eyebrows raised on the two Mounties. "I went on a short cruise."

"Who'dya go with?"

"I went by myself." Spivic and Abby looked at each other.

"I expect that you can substantiate this solitary trip," sniped Abby. "You've got receipts, for the cruise."

"No. It was a friend's yacht. I was attending a conference."

"A conference? On board a yacht? I don't believe ya, Mr. Barnes." Spivic looked at him sternly.

"It's true."

"Who owned this yacht?"

"A friend."

"What's his phone number?"

"He doesn't live in Seattle."

"Where the hell does he live?"

"On the Wanderlust. That's the name of his yacht. I don't know where the Wanderlust was heading after the weekend."

"Well then, what about the others who attended this so-called conference?" demanded Abby. "Don't you see, we need to corroborate your alibi."

"Is it necessary that I name names?"

"Don't you get it yet? If you don't soon get your act together, Sergeant Spivic is going to detain you regarding the murder of Nancy Henderson. Now name names, Barnes."

Bear smiled and looked at Abby. "Why don'tcha leave the two of us alone fer a while?"

"Good idea. I need to get some fresh air. It's getting hard to breathe in here." Within a few seconds, Abby was standing next to me in the viewing room. "We've nearly broken him. I can tell. Watch Sergeant Spivic finish him off."

"Do ya wanna glass of water, a smoke, anythin'?" Spivic asked.

"No, I want to get out of here."

"Well, then, let's make this fast. Tell me what Nancy had on you. We'll get back to your Seattle cruise later." Silence. "Come on. I'll turn off the tape and ya can tell me — man to man." He reached over and snapped off the tape recorder. "Now, whatcha tryin' to hide?"

More silence. Brent was not going to tell Spivic anything more.

"Mr. Brent Barnes, yer forcin' my hand." He stood up. I knew what was coming. Spivic leaned over and turned on the recorder. "I have to inform you that yer our prime suspect in the cold-blooded murder of Nancy Henderson. Anything ya say can and will be..."

"Stop!" I was in the interrogation room. Spivic and Brent stared at me. "You can't arrest Brent. Nancy and Brent weren't lovers. Brent and I are lovers."

Joan Riley hammered the intercom between the two rooms. "All of you, in my office," she roared. "*Now!*"

SILENTLY, THE FOUR of us sat facing Joan, who looked grim as she jotted down a few words on a pad.

"Let me try to explain..."

"Not another word out of you, Porter." She looked over her half-glasses, then took them off and flung them on the desk. She was pissed. She ran her fingers through her short-cropped hair and then took out her pack of cigarettes, tapped one out of the heap with her slender, nicotine-stained forefinger, and brought it to her lips. She flipped open her waiting lighter and, in an instant, was blowing smoke over our heads.

The silence became tangible as the smoke thickened. After every drag, she stared at each one of us. First Spivic, who was sitting on her extreme right, looking like he'd been caught with his hand in the cookie jar; then Brent, convinced that his world had collapsed around him; then Abby, sullenly waiting it out; and me, on the outer left, ready to face whatever lay in store. I damn well wasn't going to label myself "coward" any more.

"Now, what's this about you two being lovers?" She was now primed and aimed for the crotch.

"It's true," I answered.

Bear piped in, "Mr. Barnes, did Nancy Henderson know that yer a homo?"

"Sergeant!" Joan gave him a sharp look. "Mr. Barnes, did she know that you are homosexual?"

Brent looked at her and then blurted, "Yes. I told her in confidence. She said that she'd keep the information private."

"There's my case, Chief," beamed Spivic.

"Just a minute." Joan focused on me. "Kevin, how was your outburst in there supposed to help your...lover? If anything, it now gives Sergeant Spivic his motive. Could Mr. Barnes have any better reason for killing Nancy Henderson than his fear that she would reveal his sexual proclivities to the whole college? Right? Apparently your big announcement fizzled, Kevin. Are you so smitten with this young man that you no longer can see the trees for the forest?"

I nodded, marveling at Joan's ability to sum up the entire situation in such short order. I certainly had nothing more to say. I'd already said enough. I had got Brent in deep shit with my big mouth.

"Mr. Barnes, between you and me and the three gateposts in this room, I don't think you murdered your colleague." Bear growled as Joan continued, "But let's clear up a few things. Tell me, here and now, exactly what you were up to last weekend, or I will order Sergeant Spivic to book you on suspicion of murder and let him root through all your dirty linen."

Brent looked at me with such a sad little face that my heart went into low gear. His eyes told it all. "What should I do, Kev? What should I say?"

I helped. "Tell the truth, Brent."

"It'll all come out in the dish water anyways." Bear had to put in his two cents.

"As I explained, I was in Seattle from Friday night to Sunday night about ten o'clock. I am on the 2005 planning committee for the Chiron Rising Gathering."

"Which is?"

Brent gulped. "An organization of inter-generational gay men. We were planning the 2005 conference in Rio." Brent hoped that he'd said all he needed to say, but added, "Chiron plans their gatherings way ahead to ensure we get quality accommodations."

"And?"

"And what, Chief Inspector Riley?" Brent answered with a question.

"And who can substantiate that you were in Seattle?"

"I can," I interrupted. "Brent called me every night from Seattle."

"Is that true?"

Brent nodded.

"I do need to have harder evidence about your whereabouts last weekend than the word of your lover, Mr. Barnes. I need to have

names, addresses, and phone numbers of all those other men on the
planning committee. It won't take me long to arrange that Sergeant
Spivic visit Seattle to interview them." She looked at Bear.

He looked at her, with confused eyes. "Ya want me t'go to
Seattle?"

"That's right," answered Joan. Bear wrote furiously in his pad.

"I don't have their..." Brent tried to explain.

Joan ignored him. "And, Abby, I want you to check the phone
records to trace all calls that Kevin received between Friday and
Monday." She turned to Brent. "Which phone did you use when you
called Kevin? The ship's phone?"

"No, I used my cell phone."

"Convenient," said Abby. "In regards to the tractability of
cellular phones, according to Cantel, only outgoing calls are
traceable. In the case of long-distance calls, roaming charges would
appear on the billing invoices, but they wouldn't say where the calls
were made from. Very clever."

Both Joan and Bear made a note of what Abby had said. Joan
continued, "Just the same, get a record of all their phone bills."

"Sure, go ahead." Brent wasn't going to take this lying down
and he spoke with abandon. "And I don't know the addresses or
phone numbers of the other committee members. I don't even know
their last names. We just know each other by our first names. It's
kind of a...you know...a gay thing we do. 'Hi, my name's Bob.' 'I'm
Charley. It was great being with you, Phil.' "

I gave Brent a scowl to shut him up.

"I know one thing for sure," continued Brent. "None of the
committee lives in Seattle."

"Holy cow," yelled Spivic, "what kind of meetin' were you poofs
havin'?" Joan gave him a withering look. Bear gulped but
continued, "How the heck did all o' ya end up on that there
Wanderlust?"

"E-mail."

Abby put in, "Are you saying that all you guys communicate on
the Internet?"

"That's right. We arrange all our meetings that way. I'm in
charge of advertising the 2005 Mardi Gras Conference in Rio. It takes
a lot of organization and saves a lot of time to correspond through e-
mail. Sometimes we don't even use e-mail. We go directly into our
own private Internet chat room. So, when we have a..."

"All right, I get your point." I was thankful to Joan for stopping
Brent from babbling. "So, you're saying that you know only the first
names of these men and their e-mail addresses?"

"Not exactly."

"Whatcha mean, not exactly?" Spivic butted in.

Brent went on to explain, "Some of their first names are...you know...made-up names. Or maybe pet names."

"Meaning what?" Joan was ready to explode. She tapped out another cigarette.

"Well, for example, when Kevin goes on-line, he uses *Jessica*. No one knows his real name."

Christ, why did he say that?

"Jessica?" Bear looked at me with horror. Abby roared and slapped her leg. Joan swallowed a mouthful of smoke and nearly choked. *We've become the fucking comedy club.*

Mustering all the dignity I possessed, which was next to zilch, I stood up. "Okay. We'll get you the e-mail addresses of all the young men who attended the conference in Seattle from September Twenty-Fifth to the Twenty-Seventh and you can send them a form letter, worded anyway you damn well please. I'm sure when they realize that Brent is Sergeant Spivic's 'prime suspect,' they will all respond, confirming that he was with them on the Wanderlust for the *entire* weekend. They have nothing to hide. They are only having a bit of a lark, taking on assumed names. I'm sure that most of them will give you their real names if you insist on invading their privacy. These young men are all upright citizens who just happen to enjoy the company of older men. Got that, Spivic?" *I think I did rather well.* I sat down.

"Corporal Davis," ordered Joan, "you get the e-mail addresses from Barnes so that you'll be ready to send off a letter that I'll write as soon as we finish here."

"Certainly, Chief Inspector."

Joan turned to Brent. "You can go now. We know where we can reach you. At Kevin's place, right?"

"Well..."

"That's right, Brent." I didn't want him to tell them that I was his senior toy, living in *his* penthouse. "I'll take you home. Why don't you wait in my Lincoln while I have a word with Joan."

When Brent left the room, I continued. "I read through every word of Nancy's diary and found some interesting information that I'm sure you can use to nail the real killer. Perhaps we can get together and —"

Spivic stopped me. "Mr. Porter, I'll be handlin' this case by myself from now on. If I need any help, I'll take it up with my Chief." Joan nodded. I could see that it would be useless to force myself upon Spivic. "Besides, you could be an accomplice yerself."

Joan added, "Well, that might be stretching it a bit. But you definitely are in a conflict of interest."

I gave them a stunned nod and left the room. As I closed the door, I heard, "Jessica?" and hoots of laughter.

Chapter
Sixteen

"SO, HOW ARE you doing?" I said when I got into the car. Brent shut me up with "I don't want to talk." So we traveled in silence. Not our usual comfortable silence.

Once we were nearly home, Brent said through clenched teeth, "Thank you," and then added, "my knight in shining armor!"

It was nearly eight and the West End was gearing up for a party night. TGIF and all that. I answered Brent, "You're welcome." I ignored his sarcastic reference to my being his hero. Both of us knew bloody well I had botched it. But I wasn't going to rise to his bait and have a verbal battle that would end with one of his infrequent, yet familiar, Friday-night litanies: *"You know how I feel on Fridays. It's been a hard week. I'm miserable to be with. Why don't we have our own space tonight?"*

Most of the time I'd learned not to stand up to Brent when he was in a foul Friday mood. And the goings-on of today would probably be his best excuse ever to be alone.

"Let's put this behind us," I said quietly. "Okay? They're trying to make something out of nothing. You'll soon forget all about this day."

"I've been accused of murder, if you hadn't noticed, Ms. RCI!"

There was no stopping him tonight. He was determined to get me riled up enough to say something to justify his storming out to be on his own.

"Did you see Spivic's face when you called me 'Jessica'?" In spite of his black mood, I got a satisfying grunt out of him.

Recovering, he spat, "I didn't say that I *called* you 'Jessica,' I said you *used* 'Jessica' on the Internet." We pulled into my parking stall and got into the elevator to go up to our apartment. I wasn't going to get my usual elevator kiss. He wasn't finished haranguing me. "So, you let them think you were my sugar daddy." *Why did he want to be on his own so badly tonight? I wanted to comfort him. Hell, I didn't want to be on my own.*

"I wanted to get us the hell out of there. No more explanations." I punched the security code into the phone next to the elevator door in our hall. "Our private life is none of their business."

"Wake up, Jessica. Our private lives will sure the hell become their business. You watch."

While I slipped into my slippers, he stood still and yelled, "They thought I was your goddamn little boy-toy, living in *your* apartment, driving in *your* Lincoln."

"Love. Do you want to have some Brent time?"

He punched the elevator button. Instantly the door opened and closed. I was standing alone in the hall.

I went out on the kitchen balcony. He soon appeared outside the main door, passed through the security gate, and walked down Dalmation Street towards English Bay. Never once did he look back for a wave. I couldn't stop myself from wondering what he does when he goes out on his own. After all, before he met me, Brent had had a whole other life, filled with many sexual conquests. At least that's what he told me.

A DOWN-AT-THE-HEELS STREET woman, hidden between the two large shrubs, had just watched the Lincoln, with its two occupants, pull into the underground parking. "She" was now surprised to see the young man leave by the front gate. Looking up, she watched the older man waving from the upper balcony. But the young man ignored him. *A lover's tiff. Ah, how touching!*

When the older man went back inside the apartment, the dumpy old woman walked into the light. A sly smile crossed the frump's wizened lips as she quickly followed the young man towards English Bay, every so often stopping to adjust a trailing shawl around stooped shoulders.

"Double, double, toil and trouble."

AFTER CURSING AROUND the apartment for a few minutes, I cooled down enough to notice the red light blinking on the answering machine.

"Hi Kev. It's October, and you know what that means? Give me a call. But I may not be home yet."

It was Martha's voice.

I STOOD BY the answering machine, listening to Martha's short message. I'd forgotten that it was already October. Halloween month. I had murder on my mind. Not Halloween. Not Martha. Murder. A killer. But what could I do? I was off the case. My lover was out having some time alone. And I was working myself into a rage. Brent would call it a hissy fit.

I poured myself a stiff scotch and dropped in a couple of ice cubes. I walked into the living room, rattling the ice around in the scotch, and sat down in my lazyboy. I decided to give myself a present: some Kevin time. Forget the murder. Forget the killer. Think back to happier days.

For the past five years, Martha had been making Brent's and my Halloween costumes.

Depending on which night of the week Halloween fell, Davie Street was always a veritable hive of ghosts, goblins, and drag queens. Halloween will fall on a Saturday this year, so it's sure to be a big affair. The street will be filled with outrageous getups. The curious queer watchers will also come out in droves.

For the first Halloween party that Brent and I attended, we wore neither costumes nor masks. We stuck out like real party poopers, and Brent hates drawing attention to himself in public. So the next year he organized what we'd wear. "Kev, you'll go as Dame Edna, and I'll be Madge." Since Barry Humphrey is both an older man and a fellow Aussie, it wasn't a stretch for Brent to come up with his idea. We loved watching Dame Edna's wickedly smarmy talk show on TV.

He had kept everything secret from me, finding the right gown for Dame Edna at Valu Village and the right mousy, tea-stained sack dress for Madge. He created a huge Dame Edna wig out of pale blue feather boas and bought a mousy-gray page-boy wig for Madge. Then he designed and created an outlandish pair of rhinestone glasses that even Barry Humphrey might consider over the top for Edna.

I'll never forget that night six years ago. Brent insisted that I shave three times. When I stepped out of the bathroom, he had had everything laid out: a box of makeup, false nails, fingernail polish, mounds of junk jewelry. "Lie there," he ordered, pointing to the chaise lounge in the master bedroom, "and I'll make you up."

With the patience of Job, he applied layers of makeup on my smooth face, trying his best to soap-out, white-out, glue-out my moustache. I wasn't going to cut it off even though he pleaded, "It'll grow back quickly, darl'."

Watching him meticulously mix different colors of eye-shadow to get the right shade, I asked, "Where did you learn so much about makeup?"

"Duh! I'm a theatre major, too, remember?"

"Yeah, but..."

"I took makeup classes for two terms. We had to make each other up. So every time I walked into class, I was presented with a new challenge. You learn by doing, Kev." Then he said tartly, "Will you shut up, I've got a major challenge on my hands."

"What do you mean?"

"To make you beautiful."

An hour and a half later, he smiled at his artistry. "Let me take a look," I asked.

"No, Kev, you're not Dame Edna yet. Give me your hands." He made them up so that my dark hairs and age spots began to disappear under the peach foundation. Then he glued on long false nails and painted each one meticulously, a bright red.

"Stand up," he ordered. "You're ready for me to dress you." I felt like a total idiot, standing there as he helped me into black pantyhose and a padded bra. "Slip into your pumps." There on the floor was a pair of size ten and a half shoes that fit perfectly. He jumped up on the bed, holding the gown. "Come over here and slip into your frock." It fit fine. He connected the hooks and eyes and cinched in the waist. He picked up the edges of the gown where he'd sewn two loops. He placed the loops over my thumbs. "Lift your arms." As I did, the entire sides of my dress rose. I had butterfly wings. "Now your jewels, Dame Edna." Brent put mounds of gaudy necklaces around my neck and four huge glitzy rings on my fingers.

"Now, my *pièce de résistance*. Close your eyes." He put on the wig and slipped on the glasses, fussed a bit over both, and stood back. "Wow! Dame Edna, you look positively wisterious."

I felt excited. Me in drag! Never in my wildest imagination would I have even contemplated buying a bra, let alone wearing one, and here I was, all dolled up, and with someplace to go. "Let me see."

"Turn around and open your eyes."

I looked into the mirrored closet doors. There, gazing back at me was a startlingly larger-than-life Dame Edna. No one would recognize me. I didn't recognize me.

"Well?" Brent waited expectantly.

"You did great." I was in shock and needed fortification for the night.

"Now I'm going to create Madge for you to poke around, so why don't you go downstairs and play with yourself, Dame Edna." He smirked at his unsubtle *double entrendres*. As I tried to float downstairs, he yelled a warning, " Remember, Madge doesn't speak."

On the coffee table was a huge bouquet of gladioli, Dame Edna's favorite flowers. I yelled up, trying my best to assume Edna's brassy style, "Darling. You're too kind. My favorite flower. So long and firm. Hmmm." I howled with laughter.

By the time I'd slugged back a couple of healthy scotches, Dame Edna was ready to fly. I played with each gladiola spear, admiring myself in the mirrors as I danced around the living room. Then I tossed each gladiola to an imaginary admirer.

An hour later, mousy Madge walked haltingly down the stairs to a room strewn with glads. "Madge!" Dame Edna screamed. "I don't know why I keep you around." I slapped her with a glad and

giggled. I was already smashed. "It always takes you ages to come."
Edna smiled to the cameras sluttily. "Don't look so astonished, you
naughty old hag."

Hands flailing to the heavens, mouth grimacing disgust for
Madge, eyes sparkling at my *double entendres*, I rushed around the
room, picking up the blooms. With my arms laden with gladioli, I
was ready to go out on Davie Street. "Let's go to the Ball," I ordered.

Staggering, I screeched, "Where are you taking me, Madge?"
Madge pulled from her purse two tickets for Celebrities, a huge
dance club on Davie Street, and shoved them in my face.

"Merci hiccup," I bellowed, thinking I was the cat's meow.
"Freshen my drink, and have one yourself, Madge. You're too good
for me. Not!" I laughed lasciviously. "And get the pipe ready. I
want a tote before I'm seen on the street with the likes of you."
Madge kept a straight face, playing to the same imaginary camera
that I'd been playing to. We were in good form.

Halfway through the party, I had bestowed all of my gladiola
spears on any unsuspecting young stud I could find. "Would you
like a long, firm shaft of solid beauty?" I cackled mischievously as I
stuck a glad down his pants and whispered, "Make my glad happy."
Madge convulsed in silent laughter each time I poked a gladiola
down some sweet young hunk's pants. Neither of us were feeling
any pain, having fortified ourselves with more scotch and a few good
tokes. I laughed myself hoarse at things that really weren't that
funny. While dancing, I'd become fixated on my always-moving
hands. "Don't you wish you had such beautiful hands, Madge?" I
looked up at my camera, giving it a knowing wink. "Madge gave me
such a wonderful hand job, didn't she?"

Ever the straight man, Madge, with glazed eyes, turned away,
stifling a laugh.

I convulsed, tears of happiness streaming down my painted face.
At what? I'd no idea.

A handsome young man, dressed from the waist up in a tuxedo
and the waist down in a pink tutu, came up to us on the dance floor
and piped, "You look gorgeous, Dame Edna. I'm your biggest fan."

"You naughty possum. Are you trying to pick me up? Please." I
gave him a naughtier look. "Would you get a load of who I'm stuck
with?" Madge was looking blankly oblivious. "Why don't you take
me for a little spin on the dance floor, you darling man/woman and,"
right to the camera, "then maybe I'll see what you're itching to show
me under your tutu."

He had no intention of dancing with me and asked, "Has Madge
ever told you that you have Paul Newman's eyes?" I laughed so hard
I tripped through one of my butterfly wings, tearing it to shreds. I
hooted even harder at what I'd done. Brent, who'd been controlled
the entire night, glowed beet red through Madge's pallid makeup.

He finally broke. "Paul Newman's eyes!" he mimicked. He fell over laughing. Brent had completely lost it. Madge disappeared for the night. I staggered in fits and starts, trying to get up, but tripped again, this time shredding my other butterfly wing.

Over the din of music and my screams, I heard Brent yell, " I've created a drunken old queen." I cackled even harder.

At closing time, the music abruptly stopped and harsh white lights replaced the dancing rainbow colors of our fantasy world. My first Halloween party had come to an abrupt end.

"You look a mess," hooted Brent.

I looked in one of the many mirrors surrounding the dance floor, catching a dozen views of myself from all angles. There for all to see was this god-awful monster: ripped gown, butterfly wings torn, mascara dripping from under my glasses, pieces of moustache with bits of soap and glue poking out, wig askew, lipstick smeared down to my chin, a couple of nails missing. Dame Edna: the morning after. Not a pleasant sight. For once, Madge looked better than Edna. "I look like a miscarriage," I guffawed. Nothing was going to spoil this night.

Then, as we headed for the exit, I said in a serious tone, "Thank you, Brent, for another fantastic first."

Stepping outside into cold, rainy reality, I shivered. Brent put his arm around me and we prepared to hail a taxi.

"Kevin?" A familiar voice. "Is that you?" I turned and peered directly into the eyes of Little Bo Peep, her arm around a very well-endowed, black-nosed sheep. I recognized Martha; although we often spoke on the phone about our kids, this was the first time I'd seen my ex in nearly three years. She, and I assume the young man she left me for, had been to their own party. Looking as though they hadn't lost an ounce of sweat between them, they stood before me in their immaculate costumes. Smiling.

There was no place to hide. "Hi," I mumbled. I couldn't think of a damn thing to say. "Fancy bumping into you." Surprising how one sobers up under adversity.

"Love your costume. Don't tell me." She eyed me up and down. "The Wreck of the Hesperus. Right?"

"Yeah." I pointed a nail-less finger.

"Was it a good party?"

"The best. And yours?"

"Couldn't be better."

As we volleyed back and forth, our respective young men watched, in painful silence. I'm sure both were wondering what the hell they were doing with these two crazy seniors.

Finally, after bantering a couple of minutes, Martha said, "I'll call you tomorrow. Come on, Lambkins." She led her willing young man down Davie Street by his rhinestone leash, every inch a rutting ram.

WONDERFUL SEAMSTRESS THAT she is, Martha had made herself responsible for designing and sewing Brent's and my costumes every Halloween since that night. She'd always call October First, to make an appointment for our first fitting.

We'd go over, not knowing what she'd come up with. That was the deal. She'd provide the costumes. We'd have to accept them sight unseen. The first year I was the Spider to Brent's Little Miss Muffet. We won first prize, which totally changed Brent's attitude towards Martha. Always a happy winner, Brent would wait in anticipation for Martha's October call.

Chapter
Seventeen

THE OLD FRUMP followed Brent along the path that bordered English Bay, making sure to keep a safe distance between them. Brent sat down on one of the benches and stared out into the black waters, completely oblivious to the many passers-by. *Not going to go cruising tonight, Brentie boy?*

After ten minutes, Brent jumped up and jogged back towards the apartment on Dalmation Street.

"Fuck!" Inside his old frump disguise, THK fumed. He felt like ripping the wig and costume off right then and there and chucking the lot in one of the rubbish cans that lined the path. *Well, that was a fucking no-nothing walk before I even had a chance to get the little faggot alone.*

Earlier that evening, he'd been glued to his chair, waiting for the six o'clock news. He listened intently to a particular announcement: "Today the RCMP brought in an unidentified male for questioning regarding the murder of Nancy Henderson, the popular young college instructor. However, due to a lack of physical or corroborating evidence, the man has, as of this air date, been released." *Shit. No names. No mention of my calling card.*

The old frump, walking faster, with head down, thought of the reunion that was probably taking place in the penthouse on Dalmation Street and cursed.

There's only one thing I hate more than a faggot. And that's a pair of faggots. It's time to stir up a bit of shit.

ON HIS TWELFTH birthday, his mother told him that she had a surprise for him, but after he blew out the twelve candles and got some wax on the tablecloth, she became hysterical. "That filthy mouth of yours. Look what you've done, Thomas Henry King. You've ruined my best tablecloth. You'll pay for this, out of your allowance." She picked up the end of the tablecloth and yanked it off the table. Dishes, presents, cake flew off in all directions. "Look at the mess you've made," she sobbed as she staggered into her bedroom.

"I'll clean it up, Mommie. Don't worry. I'll do everything," he assured her, following her to her bedroom. He climbed on the bed. "Please don't cry any more. I'm sorry, Mommie." He patted her face. He stroked her arms. She grabbed his hand and, for the first time in his life, placed it on one of her breasts.

FOR THE NEXT four years, Tommy retreated more and more within himself. Hating himself. Hating his mother more. Desperate not to give her any opportunity to require consolation, he became more careful, more punctual.

It was during this time that he pleaded for and got several pets. Always one at a time. He grinned, remembering how once he got his mother pacified, he'd slip into the basement with his pet dog or cat or hamster. He enjoyed torturing the pets his mother bought for him. He loved killing them even more. And what a performance he used to give her the next day. "Mommie, Toby ran away last night. I can't find him anywhere." He and his mother would walk the neighborhood, calling for his little collie, or tabby, or runty hamster. He insisted on calling each of his pets Toby, male or female. "Mommie. I want another Toby. Please." He'd nearly gag with fits of laughter, hearing his mother, out on the street or in the backyard, yelling, "Toby! You come here this minute. Do you hear me?"

For four years his Tobys had been his salvation. When he had done something wrong to cause his mother distress, she forced him to be more and more creative to satisfy her. When he was thirteen, he stared, disbelieving, as his mother experienced multiple orgasms, screaming wildly in ecstasy. That year, during fellatio, he experienced his own first orgasm. He instantly became terrified and cried out, not knowing what was happening to his body. Afterwards, he sobbed, his head resting between his mother's breasts. He thought for sure that his mother was going to eat him up. Strip all his flesh off his bones and chew and chew and chew. But, she didn't. Instead, she hugged him gently, soothing his convulsing body and whispering lovingly, "My prince. You are my darling prince." Afterward, he left his snoring mother and went down to the basement to torture a Toby, mesmerized as he smiled at the convulsing body. "You deserved that cunt, you and your flapping tongue." Then he'd take a flash picture to add to his secret collection.

By his fourteenth birthday, he was able to reach two orgasms during one session. By sixteen, he too had learned how to enjoy multiple orgasms by achieving spasms in his spinal column. He would scream in ecstasy. His Mother would whisper in his ear during their all-day, all-night sessions, "You're the best fuck in the world, my prince. When I'm dead, you're going to break the hearts of thousands of women."

HAVING DUMPED THE old frump's costume and wig in a garbage bag and having removed his makeup and showered clean, THK stood in the center of his sanctum. He looked admiringly at the nineteen Polaroids of Nancy, propped here and there around the room. No matter which way he turned, he could see her staring at him, each of her poses clearly illustrating a different degree of pain. His enormous erection throbbed. He needed a nightcap soon or he'd go crazy. He reached for one of his favorite photos of Nancy. "I think Franny McGhie will get a bang out of this one."

He sat at his typewriter. "Dear Franny..."

Chapter
Eighteen

WHEN I FINISHED my scotch, I went into the kitchen and put some water on to boil. I dialed Martha's number. The message broke in on the second ring: "Sorry, Hank and I can't come to the phone right now. Leave your name and number at the beep. If this is Kevin, call me at Sammy's."

Sammy's? What's Martha doing in Frisco? This wasn't the time of year for her to visit our first-born. I started to dial my son's number in San Francisco. Martha and I had arranged a schedule of separate visits with our kids to avoid any embarrassing questions like, "When are you and Mom going to get back together again?" No matter how mature they are, kids always seem to feel responsible for their parents' breakup, and even when they know there is no hope, they still dream that eventually Mom and Dad will be reunited.

"Hi!"

I spun around. It was Brent. I put the phone down and glanced at the clock. He'd only been away twenty minutes. "Hi," I smiled.

"I'm sorry, sweetie." He came over and gave me a big hug. "Forgive me?"

"Sure. But it's me who should apologize. I was about to phone Martha. She left a message all the way from..."

"Oh, yes. It's costume time. I'd forgotten." A little smile crept over his face. "Give her a call."

"Will do. Then we can get on with our lives again."

"I've got to fax Dyke Davis those e-mail addresses." He went to the den.

As I dialed Sammy's number, I wondered whether Brent had come back early because he was really sorry or because he'd realized he had to fax off the addresses of the committee members.

"Hello. This is Samuel Porter's residence."

"Martha. This is Kevin. What's up?"

"Sammy's taken to his bed. Poor darling. I couldn't leave him."

"Is he still battling Debbie? How long can she prevent him from seeing his own kids?"

"Deborah and her lawyer are knocking all the gumption out of our boy. They've even persuaded the judge to serve him with a demand that he have a psychiatric evaluation before he's allowed to be with his kids again. He's not even allowed to phone them."

"Poor kid." For a thirty-nine-year-old man, Sammy still seems to act like a child who, when the chips are down, needs his mommie.

"Well, I've been here two weeks now and every day something new comes up. He needs my support, Kev. I worry about him. The custody case is set for the beginning of November."

"Will this never end?"

"Doesn't look like it. But I want to get home. I'm anxious to finish your costumes. Wait til you see them. I brought the material with me and I've cut them out and pinned them together. You and Brent are going to be blown away."

"So when are you returning?"

"By Thanksgiving for sure." Pause. "Are you okay, Kev? You don't sound yourself."

"Sure, I'm okay." Martha could always tell when something was bothering me. Living with someone for almost twenty-eight years does that. She detected my silence. "Are you keeping busy? How many chapters have you written on your novel?" I'd forgotten I told her that I was writing a novel. I didn't tell her the reason: More to please Brent than possessed by a great desire to write. I didn't really know where to begin, hoping I'd remember one of my cases that might interest a million readers and make John Grisham's publisher come banging on my door.

I finally answered Martha, "Well, actually, I'm working on a murder case."

"Ah. So that explains everything. I thought you gave up on crime. Finding lost puppies is more your speed, Mr. Senior Man." She laughed contentedly.

"Ha! Ha! Wash your mouth out." Martha and I could say anything to each other. We were the best of friends and always would be. "I talked myself into helping out Barry Spivic on a murder case."

"Bear? Is he still as sexy as ever? Don't answer. So," she took a breath, "who got murdered?"

"Nancy Henderson. She taught with Brent at the college. Actually, she was Brent's office mate. He asked me to help out."

"So you did. Nothing's too good for our young men. Right?"

"Right."

"So why are you so down? Can't get a handle on the case?"

Should I tell her? During all my life with the Force, I never brought home any work. *Hell, I have to talk to someone.* "They kicked me off the case today."

"What on earth for? You'd be an asset on any crime team. Surely they know that. You're not too old. You could sue them."

"It's a little more serious than that. Brent's their prime suspect."

Stunned silence. And then, "I don't believe it."

"Neither do I, but there it is. They kicked me out because they believe there could be..."

"...a conflict of interest. Understandable, but stupid. Don't worry, Kev. You'll prove that Brent had nothing to do with Nancy's death and you'll be back on the case."

"I hope so."

"Well, hon, I got to go. Don't overwork, now. Remember, you're not as young as you used to be and you have to save your energy for Brent." She chuckled. "Oh, I nearly forgot. Can you and Brent come for Thanksgiving dinner and try on your costumes?"

"Sure. I don't see a problem. So what are we wearing this year?"

"You know better than that. You'll know when you see them. October Twelfth. Bye, my Bi-Guy."

"Ha!" Since our divorce, Martha jokes about my sexuality and that she and I will probably end up together, sitting in rocking chairs in an old folk's home. She'd point out a randy old guy of a hundred and one and whisper, "Hey, Bi-Guy! Let's take him to our room and have some fun."

"DID MARTHA SAY what we were going as this year?" Brent walked into the kitchen.

"No," I answered, "you know it's always a big surprise. She's invited us over a week Monday for Thanksgiving dinner."

"That's a first."

"She said that we'll have the unveiling after we eat." I continued to stir the pesto sauce for our Italian dinner; I was making one of Brent's favorites.

"I'll put it on the calendar." He went into the den and was back again in a minute. "Read this. This just came in from Dyke Abby." He held a fax.

"You read it. I've got my hands full." I was straining the penne and I needed to put the finishing touches on the Caesar salad. Besides, I was still flying high on my scotch.

"The cover page says," Brent ran through the usual details and then read, "'Here's a copy of the letter that Chief Inspector Joan Riley wrote to your *friends.*' She italicized *friends.* The bitch! Now here's Riley's letter." He cleared his throat and read Joan's letter. "'I am investigating a murder that took place in Swallow Lake, north of Deep Cove, BC, and I would very much appreciate your help.

"'We believe you know the suspect, Brent (I will not use his last name because I understand from him that none of you use your real names. I will respect your desire for anonymity). For legal reasons, however, I must describe Brent so that both you and I are referring to the same man. Brent is an Australian/Asian man, 34, 5' 5", 140 lbs, straight black hair, clean shaven, dark brown eyes.'" He broke off to growl. "I'm not 5' 5". I'm 5' 7". I'm going to phone Abby right now before they send this out."

"Never mind, Brent. It's not that important. Keep reading." *Two extra inches are so important to him. He's such a size queen.*

"Okay." He grumbled and continued to read Joan's letter. "'Please reply ASAP with your answers to the following questions:

1. Was Brent present on the Wanderlust during your entire conference from Sept. 25 to Sept. 27 of this year?

2. Was there any possibility that he might have left the Wanderlust at any time during Sept. 25 to 27? (If yes, provide specific times that you did not see him on board.)

3. Are you willing to appear in a court of law, if I deem it necessary, to swear that your responses to the above are true?

If I do not hear from you by midnight, Oct. 9, which begins our Thanksgiving weekend in Canada, I will be forced to seek your identity and ask a member of your local police force to find you, so that you can make a formal statement. (For all you American readers, yes, in Canada, we celebrate Thanksgiving earlier than you do in the US.)

Thank you for your cooperation. JR'"

Brent had been following me from the kitchen to the dining room while I set the table and put out our dinners.

"Joan wrote a good letter," I said. "Don't you think? I'm confident they'll all respond favorably. I'm sure she'll call and apologize way before the ninth. Probably even tomorrow."

"You think so?"

"I know so. Now eat. I've been slavin' over a hot stove all day to feed my manno."

The phone rang on our first mouthful. Brent answered; he's always the one who answers the phone when we're both at home. He looked at the call display. "It's Jane Edwards. She's probably wondering whether I'm home or in jail." He punched the Talk button. "Hello...Yes, I'm here..." His eyes fixed on mine during the whole conversation and he threw me a kiss. "No, I didn't see the six o'clock news."

Brent's face hardened as he listened to the head of his department. He kept nodding and grunting what to me were non sequiturs: "Uh...Yeah... Huh...ooh... But they didn't mention me by name?... Good...Then this won't affect the good name of the college... Sure... Not to worry..." He listened intently for a minute and then raised his voice. "No, that won't be necessary...No, Jane, I don't need to take time off. I'll be in on Monday as usual. And Jane, I'd appreciate your not mentioning this to anyone. You don't want to have a suspect walking around the halls of the college, do you?" He laughed gently. "Yeah, you're right about that." He hung up.

He sat down, pierced a crisp piece of romaine with his fork, and stuffed it in his mouth. "Delicious."

THE RINGING WOKE us from a dead sleep. Brent reached for the phone and mumbled, "Yeah?"

"Baby, what's this murder shit about?" My ear was glued to the other side of the earpiece.

"Who the hell is this?"

"Wanker!"

"Do you know what time it is, Wanker?"

"Nine thirty in the morning. I like to get my beauty sleep, honey."

"Maybe in London," Brent explained. "It's one thirty *in the morning* here."

"I'm horrible at math. So sue me." Wanker was talking so loudly that Brent rested the phone between us.

"Sue yourself. Now what do you want?"

"Sorry, Brent, but when I got on-line, there was a letter from this Royal Canadian Mounted Police lady. What should I do?"

"Answer her questions truthfully, Wanker. And e-mail her right back."

"Rightie-o, but since you're already awake, give me the dirt, girl. Were you really arrested?"

Brent filled him in with a few details and after answering twenty more of Wanker's persistent questions, declared, "I'm dead tired. I got to get my zees. Thanks for your concern, Wanker."

"Ta ta. Keep your pecker up."

"You, too, Wanker."

"And I can hear that you've been keeping yours up, too, Jessica. I could hear your heavy breathing." Wanker hung up with a hoot. Brent put the phone in the cradle.

"How did he get your number?"

"We all exchanged phone numbers in case we needed to make a few conference calls." I gave his bicep a mock slug with my fist. "I know. I know. It's against the rules. But we thought it would make organizing the conference easier."

We snuggled together and were soon off to sleep.

Another ring woke us at two. Same story, but from Rude in Oslo. After he hung up, I tried unsuccessfully to convince Brent to turn off the ringer. When the bedroom door is closed, we were not able to hear the ringing of the other phones in the apartment downstairs. We couldn't even hear the security alarm being released or set. Brent asked, "What if my not taking the call will change their answers to Riley's questions?" Then he insisted on leaving the ringer on.

By four in the morning, we'd heard from five of the other

committee members. All clueless about the time in Vancouver; all deeply concerned about what was happening to poor Brent; all needing to be filled in on every detail.

Brent had had it by the time the five a.m. call came from Marydontask in Toronto. He began, "Brent! Why the fuck did you give the RCMP my e-mail address? The first thing I did was flush my stash down the john, thank you very much. You owe me, buddy. Now what's this stinky do-do about you committing murder? Did they take a look at you? How could someone so goddamn innocent-looking, and such a wimpy little bugger like you, commit murder? Only kidding. You're macho enough to stick it into anyone. Ooo! But seriously, you couldn't kill a fly. You know what I mean? But if you think I'm going to take the stand and run the risk of being outed in Toronto, you can think again, sweetie pie. You know those rednecks are waiting out there to get me into a corner and bash my little tush into a million..." Marydontask continued ranting on for five more minutes before Brent could break in and apologize. Then he demanded that Brent tell him the whole story. Who was killed? Why was he arrested? How come he was let loose? Forty minutes later he finally hung up.

I looked into Brent's bleary eyes. "I'm glad it was his nickel."

Brent ripped the plug out of the wall. "Let's get some sleep."

I LOOKED AT the clock radio. Eleven thirty. Brent was still puffing gently beside me. I leaned on my elbow, enjoying the look of his innocent face at peace. How could I have suspected that this sweet man had anything to do with murder. Shame on me!

He raised his right arm and began stroking it with his left hand. An idiosyncrasy that had intrigued me since the first morning I woke up beside him. He massages his arms while still sound asleep. I watched the familiar pattern, down the left side of the entire arm then down the right. Then change arms. I knew he'd be awake soon.

In a few minutes he opened his eyes. "Morning, sweetie," he leaned over and gave me a kiss on the cheek. "Dead-turtle breath." *Mine or his?* "Did you sleep well?"

"Yes, and I know you did."

"Watching me again, Jessica?"

"Uh huh." Saturday mornings were usually lazy affairs. I'd slip out of bed, get into my lounging outfit, de-activate the security system (because walking downstairs would set off the alarm: "Police have been notified. Identify yourself immediately!"), and go down to make breakfast. Breakfast would be waiting next to the bed, when Brent woke up. We'd eat and read the paper and luxuriate in not having to do anything till at least noon. Then shower, get dressed, and go to the courts to hammer a racquetball around for three or four hours. I introduced him to the game. For the first couple of years, I could wipe the floor with him, but now he whips me four out of five times. Brent's become a total "racquetball head." I wouldn't be a bit surprised if he gives up volleyball entirely.

"You relax and I'll bring up breakfast and the paper." I plugged in the phone and punched in the security code.

As I got to the bottom of the stairs, the phone rang. Brent answered it. I could hear him saying "Yes" and "Uh huh" as I walked to the kitchen. Then I heard a screaming cheer and footsteps banging down the stairs. "That was Abby. She's received ten answers already, and they all are the same. I'm a free man."

"Congratulations." I really meant it. As much for me as for Brent. I went over and hugged my excited, naked lover.

"That's an odd thing to say. Why did you say congratulations?"

"Because I'm so happy for you."

"Come on. Fess up. You actually thought I might have been a murderer. Didn't you?"

"No, of course not."

"The truth, Ms. RCI? You thought that I killed Nancy because I was afraid that she'd out me at the college. Right?"

"That's nonsense. You go up to bed and I'll bring our breakfast up."

"It was you who outed me to the police. And it was only through Dickhead's good conscience that he didn't out me on TV."

"I was rattled. I couldn't stand watching you being tortured like that. I wanted to share your pain."

"Whatever." He punched the elevator button. When the door opened, he picked up the *Sun* newspaper. As a decidedly more confident Brent walked back upstairs to read the morning news in bed, I knew I hadn't heard the last of my indiscretion. Brent's sixth sense was correct. It would have embarrassed me to admit it, but I had niggling doubts that Brent might have... *No, no. Get those thoughts out of your head.* "But admit it." I whispered, "You really don't know everything about your lover." As always, I shrugged those thoughts off and went into the kitchen.

ON MY LAST MOUTHFUL of breakfast, the phone rang. "Hello," said Brent. "Oh, hi, Abby. What can I do for you?...Good...We'll see. Thanks for calling. Bye."

"What did she want?" I asked.

"She got the last response from Zorro in Australia. It's unanimous." Then he smiled. "Abby said the RCMP has confirmed that I was on board the Wanderlust, floating around the San Juan Islands for the whole weekend. I'm no longer a suspect."

"Great. Let's celebrate."

"I've got a bone to pick with you first."

"I know. I know. But I needed to stay in Spivic's good books. A lot of good that did me. He won't let me near him now. I'm sorry that I put you through hell."

"Apology accepted. You could have shared your strategies with me, you know."

"I'm sorry already. But I didn't have any strategies."

"You're going to have to be punished, you bad boy. Turn over."

"CAN WE TALK about Nancy's diary?"

"Hm." Brent was still enjoying post-coital drowsiness.

"We'll talk later. When you're ready."

"No, it's okay. What about her diary?"

"Well, for one thing, it reads like a schoolgirl's first attempt at a lovesick novel."

"That's what she was trying to do. You know Dorothy Bovak's a literary agent."

"No, I didn't."

"Yeah, she is. She's been moonlighting as a literary agent for years. And she's always trying to build her stable of romantic novelists. She solicited everyone in the English department and nobody bit. Anyway, over the summer break, Dorothy stayed with Nancy at the cabin one weekend and convinced her to try her hand at the romantic genre. Nancy began her novel in the form of a diary six weeks ago and, as you saw, made me one of her main characters. She sure didn't conceal my real identity very well. I'm sure she was just having me on."

"You mean it's not a real diary at all? She didn't start it when she first met you over a year ago?"

"No. She wrote it for Dorothy. More for a lark than anything else."

"So, she'd only been writing this diary for a little more than a month. Did she ever talk to you about it? Let you read it?"

"Never. The only thing she said was that she'd have to state at the beginning 'Any resemblance to anyone living or dead is purely coincidental.' And then she winked at me."

"You can certainly see why she winked."

Brent knew nothing of her mystery man, since he'd only read Bear's highlighted passages in the interrogation room. So I continued my questioning. "While you were strolling around the golf course with Nancy during your lunch hours, did you ever notice anything strange?"

"Like?"

"Well, did you ever see someone watching you both? Following you? Hiding behind bushes? You know, anyone suspicious?"

"No.   We were always deep in conversation about literary criticism.   She'd want to share a student's interpretation of a particular poem or short story, and get my opinion. We usually only talked shop on our walks.   Those walks were really like work sessions for me.   I had to keep on my toes and concentrate on providing the right answers."

"How about on September Twenty-fifth?"   Brent looked inquisitively. "Before you left for Seattle.   Did you notice anything suspicious?   Did you notice anyone in a car watching you leave at one-fifty?"

"How did you know I left at ten to two?"

"It's in the diary.   Now think back.   What did you do while bidding Nancy goodbye?"

For a minute, Brent tried to place himself in the college car park. There he was, sitting in the bed with a faraway look in his eyes. "Well, we walked through the student lot on the east side of the college in order to get to the faculty parking."

"Close your eyes.   Imagine walking slowly.   Do you see anybody in any of the cars?"

Brent concentrated.   "I remember squeezing between two cars and sensing someone in one of them.   He or she had a newspaper over his head.   Or her head.   Probably a student catching some shut-eye instead of going to class."

"Or our killer. Spying on you and Nancy."

Brent opened his eyes. "That's stretching it a bit."

"Stand up," I ordered. I got out of the bed too, and dragged the lounge close to the bed.   "Imagine that the lounge is one car and the bed is the other.   Now walk slowly between them.   Close your eyes again.   You are in the student lot between the two cars."

After a moment of watching Brent taking small steps between bed and lounge, I said softly, "Tell me about the cars.   Describe them."

After more effort, Brent shouted, "Shit! I can't see one of them. I wasn't facing one of the cars.   I know the one I was facing was maroon. A beauty. A Mustang. But the one behind me? I can't tell you. I sense it was gray or tan. And small." He opened his eyes. "I'm sorry. That's all."

"You're doing fine.   Close your eyes and do it again.   Slowly. Keep your back to the small car." Brent turned to face the bed with his back to the lounge. He began to edge between the cars.   "Keep thinking about that walk to your car.   Any detail might be important."

Suddenly, he sneezed. And then again. And again. He plunked down on the chaise lounge. "What the hell was that all about?"

"I don't know," he yelled.

I stared in amazement as Brent continued sneezing.

Chapter
Nineteen

THK LOUNGED IN his sanctuary, reliving last weekend's triumphs. In full, living color. He blessed the inventor of the camcorder as he listened to Nancy's knock and stared at the closed bathroom door. He waited expectantly and then grinned when he heard her say, "I've got your G&T ready."

He was already fully aroused as he heard himself answer in his cultured feminine voice, "Would you mind bringing it in, Nancy?" He watched her open the door and hand the glass to him behind the shower curtain. "Thank you, Nancy."

"Call if you need anything." Then he watched her leave. She was totally unaware that she was on camera the entire time.

The suspense was killing him, as the screen froze for a full ten minutes on the door she had closed behind her. While he stood in his sanctum, watching the back of the door, he timed it just right so that he filled his hand at the exact moment his voice on the monitor called, "Nancy, can you help me?"

For fifteen glorious seconds, he massaged his chest and stomach while he waited. Then she opened the bathroom door. Oh, the look of shocking revelation on her face, captured forever, as she saw him standing in all his glory. *A priceless moment of film history.*

He pressed the Pause button and froze Nancy's face. He needed to have another thrilling wet orgasm immediately. Nothing or no one could bring him better than his own right hand. As he gazed into Nancy's eyes, he took his tumescent pride into his hand and began pumping life back into it. "Did you know that you have my mother's eyes, Nancy?" To ecstatic throbs, he cupped his left hand and filled it again, his back muscles spasming as he groaned in pleasure.

He pressed the Play button and began massaging his neck and face. His tongue yearned for a taste. *I should be a film director. My actress makes Janet Leigh's* Psycho *shower scene look tame. Nancy died for her art.*

From Friday night to Sunday night he had watched tape after tape. Every time a flash appeared on the video, he placed one of the nineteen Polaroids, he'd taken last weekend, around his sanctum.

He was so proud that he had been able to get his heroine to do whatever he wanted. He watched her undress, slowly, suggestively, hearing his own voice giving directions: "Slow down, Nancy. Tantalize me more. Oh. yes. Oh. yes. That's exactly the right speed. You don't want to bring me too soon, now do you?" When he threw the special harness he'd made on the bed, Nancy's reaction was one in a million. He could watch the detailed expressions on her face over and over. For years to come. "Put your left ankle in that one, Nancy. Not too fast, darling. Just slip it in. Yes, that's right. No, no, my dear, look more fearful. Don't forget, the audience has to believe that you are soon going to die. They will expect it. Good. That's it. That's the perfect expression. You're going to be my greatest star. Now the other ankle. Yes, in the same way. Beautiful. Now your left wrist. That's right, put it in and tighten it in place. Perfect. You are such a talented girl. Now slip your right hand in the last one and I'll give you a reward. *No, goddamn you to hell. Do you want a fucking bullet to explode in your head, Mommie?*" The scene went to black.

He remembered how Nancy had revolted against wearing the harness and ripped it off her wrist and both her ankles within seconds. He had to stop the camera and threaten her with his gun. He had some editing work to do before he watched the film a second time. He fast-forwarded to the part where Nancy was ready to slip her wrist into the last harness loop for the second time. "Good. Perfect. I'm going to have to tighten that one for you. You don't mind if I get into the camera shot with you do you? You deserve a handsome co-star, and who better than me? All eyes will be on you, though. After all, you are my leading lady and I am the world's greatest director. I'll make sure I give you the scene and not steal it from you." A hand came into view and laid down a small black .45. Then he watched his hands tighten the fur-lined cuff around Nancy's right wrist and check the others to make sure they were all secure. Then he spoke directly into the camera: "We wouldn't want to bruise your delicate wrists and ankles." He took a bite off a piece of jerky and chewed it, smiling and licking his lips. "Mmm. This jerky is so good Nancy. I know you want some." He held a piece within an inch of her mouth. "Open up, my darling. You must be very hungry. I know that you would love an *hors d'oeuvre* with your G&T before our main meal." She turned her head and held her mouth tightly shut. "Nancy! Pay attention. Open your fucking mouth and take a bit of my jerky or I'm going to blow your head off. Understand?"

He watched the screen, chuckling audibly, giggling convulsively, enjoying every minute of torment on Nancy's face. He could tell that she was assessing her options, nil though they were. *They all do that!* He filled his lair with a triumphant laugh when she faced the camera and opened her mouth.

"Good girl." He held the jerky and watched her bite off a piece. "Chew it well. Isn't it good? Lick your lips. It's okay to make lots of noise. That means you like my jerky." A flash filled the screen. He giggled. "You're so photogenic, Nancy. See?" A hand came into view, holding a Polaroid within six inches of her face. "Don't you look beautiful?" The hand and photo stayed in place for a moment. Then quickly pulled back. "Take a sip of your G&T, Nancy." A glass appeared, tilted so that she was forced to take a large mouthful of the liquid. "Maybe you'd like to dine with music, Nancy." Instantly the room filled with rhythm and blues. "Yes. That's it. Just the right ambiance for a romantic evening. Is your mouth empty yet, Nancy? Is it?" She nodded. Then he leaned into the frame and whispered with obscene intimacy into her ear. She let out an agonized scream and started to retch. He shrieked with laughter. "Very good. You've kept it down. I'm proud of you. Now, are you ready to fill your mouth again with my main course? I can tell by that wonderful expression in your eyes that you can hardly wait for my *big* surprise." The volume of the music became intense. Lit candles suddenly appeared as the camera pulled back for a wide-angle shot.

In his sanctum, he watched his film, mesmerized.

The head of his engorged pride slowly appeared at the right edge of the screen. The focus moved to Nancy's face. "Look over here, Nancy. Your entree is ready." Inch by inch, his erection dominated the screen, directly under Nancy's terrorized eyes. Then he slowly, deliberately mounted the bed so that only his lower back and ass filled the screen. Nancy's screams grew louder than the throbbing R&B, but soon they were drowned out.

In his sanctum now, he laughed hysterically at his epic film. "Was ever woman in this humor woo'd? / Was ever woman in this humor won?"

HE HAD RELIVED the entire weekend.

Satisfied with himself, he pressed the Pause button to freeze the last frame of his film. The picture on the screen was exactly the same as the one in the twentieth Polaroid. The same picture he had already sent to Franny McGhie. He gazed lovingly at the frozen frame: Nancy, thumb in her mouth, eyes full of terror. *What a performance you gave!* His body trembled in ecstatic joy throughout his ultimate orgasm. He was exhausted, but entirely gratified. He looked in his left hand. He had come clean.

Chapter
Twenty

SUNDAY MORNING BEGAN as always. Our routine was usually the same: sleep in and reminisce about our Saturday night, more often than not spent at Numbers. We'd shoot a few games of pool, then have a "tote," and dance ourselves silly for a couple of hours. On the way home, we'd always pick up a deliciously high-caloric dessert so we could pig out after enjoying a blissfully romantic love-making session. Sunday mornings were always the best. Lazy and hazy.

But when Brent opened the elevator door to pick up the Sunday *Scoop*, he let out a horrified scream. I ran from the kitchen to see what had happened. As I turned the corner, he was holding the paper up so that I was able to see the front page. The entire page was a full-color picture of Nancy's face, exactly as I'd seen it when I first entered her bedroom at the cabin. Eyes closed, thumb in mouth, duvet tucked under her chin. Under the photo in bold red type was:

WHO WILL DIE NEXT?

I grabbed the paper from Brent and laid it out on the dining room table. Flipping to page two, there was Franny McGhie's insipid smile. Brent and I read the article together.

Friday, after briefly interrogating their prime suspect on the Nancy Henderson murder case, North Van RCMP Commissioner, Sam Wheetley, was forced to let him go. The accused was seen to leave the Detachment with his "friend," an ex-Chief Inspector who 12 years ago was relieved of his position under mysterious circumstances.

When asked for a statement, Wheetley said, "No comment." Sound familiar? This whole affair is beginning to sound more than a wee bit incestuous! What are they covering up over in North Vancouver?

My source told me that the alleged suspect
was believed to be a colleague of the victim.
So, we seem to have a highly educated Clean
Fiend walking our streets. (See "Letters to
the Editor," page 8.)

When I looked up, Brent's face was chalk white. "What am I
going to do? This bitch is going to crucify me. I won't be able to
show my face at the college tomorrow."

"Sure you can. McGhie didn't name names. She's always careful
that way. And everyone knows that she makes up most of her so-
called facts." He didn't believe a word I said. I didn't either, but I
persisted. "If you don't go in tomorrow, people will definitely think
you've got something to hide. You'll be putting Jane Edwards in an
awkward position. You don't want her to have to make excuses for
you or the shit really will hit the good old College gossip-fan. So,
you're going to school and that's all there is to it." I turned to the
Letters to the Editor. The headline for one of the letters read:

CF TAUNTS

Open Letter to the Blockheads at the North Van
RCMP Detachment:

Up and down, up and down,
I will lead them up and down;
I am fear'd in field and town.
Goblin, lead them up and down.

Cowards, why com'st thou not?
(Exit pursued by a Bear)

Editor's Note (Written by Franny McGhie):
Accompanying the photo of murdered Nancy
Henderson was the above typewritten taunt,
presumably from the murderer. The message
seems perfectly clear. The Clean Fiend is
taunting Sam Wheetley and his team. Doubtless
he thinks they haven't enough know-how to stop
him, so he's provided a bit of help by sending
me a Polaroid of the victim and a message. Do
you hear that, Sam?
I think it's high time that the chaps at
ViCLAS (Violent Crime Linkage Analysis System)
get their act together. Or better still, our
Attorney-General should put the heat under the

police to search out and capture the Clean Fiend before he strikes again.

ViCLAS which is regarded as the finest computer search program in the world ironically isn't used in BC where it was developed. And why? Because the cops here are not putting the necessary details into the program. The Attorney-General should take a good look at Ontario's ViCLAS system. The government there passed a law requiring police officers to file all cases in ViCLAS. They had learned their lesson by allowing serial killer, Paul Bernardo, to move about the province, raping and killing, even though the MOs of his victims were all the same. No one noticed that Bernardo had simply switched cities.

Since then, Ontario's police officers report more than 90% of their cases to the system. By comparison, BC's police officers reported fewer than 30% last year. Shame!

By the way, readers, do you recognize the quotation? It's from William Shakespeare's *A Midsummer Night's Dream*. Puck, the speaker of these lines, is a mischievous fairy, who has great fun taunting the mortals. I can't figure out what he means by "Exit pursued by a Bear," except that my source tells me that one of the cops on the team is affectionately known as Bear. But clearly, the Clean Fiend not only had his way with his victim but is now having his way with the inept North Van RCMP unit and the Attorney-General of British Columbia.

Sam, I wonder why the Clean Fiend sent me the "scoop" and not you? Please call.

"The bitch!" I hurled *The Scoop*, pages just missing Brent as they flew all over the dining room.

"The killer or McGhie?"

"Both, I suppose. The killer for sending it. McGhie for printing it."

Brent stormed into the kitchen. I could hear him snap on the coffee grinder. He was needing some Brent time so I didn't follow. Instead, I got down on my hands and knees, gathering the offending pages of *The Scoop*. Sitting on the floor, I studied the picture on the front page. It was certainly different from the one that the killer had left at the cabin. In that photo Nancy was still alive.

In this one, the close-up of Nancy's face held my attention. She appeared beautifully peaceful in her eternal sleep. The color treatment of the photo replicated the colors of the makeup accurately. The eye shadow on both lids matched perfectly. Even the gloss on her top lip glistened in the photo. I suddenly noticed what appeared to be the corner of another photo near the headboard to the right of her head. I couldn't make out the details of this partial photo within the main photo. It looked as though some artist from *The Scoop* had attempted to airbrush it out. Or maybe the killer had. Or maybe the cover photo was only a portion of the original Polaroid. I had to get back on this case. I needed to see the original so that we could enlarge this partial photo near the headboard. I had a gut feeling this would be important.

I picked up the phone and dialed the North Van Detachment. "Sergeant Barry Spivic, please?"

"Who's speaking?"

"Kevin Porter."

"I'm sorry, Mr. Porter. This is Sergeant Spivic's day off. Do you wish to leave a message?"

His day off? Oh, yes. It's Sunday. "No, thanks. I'll call tomorrow."

I looked up Barry's number in the phone book and dialed. "May I speak to Barry?"

"Who's speakin'?" A woman's voice.

"Kevin Porter."

"Kev, this is Mil. Long time no see."

"Yes, it has been a long time. How've you been keeping?"

"Fine. Fine." I could hear whispering. "I'm sorry, Kev, but Bear isn't around right now. He's out with Andy and the girls." More whispering. "You can call him tomorrow at the office."

"Thanks, Mil, but maybe you could get him to call me when he gets in."

"I'll try. Bye, Kev."

I smelled coffee and turned. Brent handed me my morning brew. He gave me a weak smile. "I'll go to work tomorrow."

MONDAY MORNING WAS tense, to say the least. Brent went off to the college reluctantly. If I'd given in and suggested he not go, he'd have jumped at the chance to stay home. But I knew I was right. He had to show his innocent face around the campus for all to see.

While he waited for the elevator, I asked, "Would you walk through the parking lot at lunch?"

"Why?"

"To see if you can find that maroon Mustang. Remember? The one parked next to where you thought you saw a sleeping student. When you find it, get the license number. I'd like to talk to the owner to find out more details about the other car and see if the driver could identify that 'sleeping student.'"

"Sure, that will be easy. I'll take a stroll through the whole lot. If the Mustang is there, I'll find it." With a sense of purpose, he left for the college in a better frame of mind.

When he'd gone, I called the Detachment. Again, no success. I'm sure the receptionist had been told not to put me through to Spivic. Later I got the idea of speaking to Joan, but that, too, fizzled. The receptionist recognized my voice when I wouldn't leave my name. I hung up angrily. So I went into my den and wrote Spivic a fax, pretending I was a concerned citizen. I wrote: "If you haven't already, get original picture from McGhie and blow it up. You will find the small photo to the right of the victim's head interesting. Also get the letter that CF wrote to McGhie. Compare type with the one found at the murder scene."

I took my memo down to a little stationer's shop on Davie Street and had them fax it on their machine. I came home, feeling better that I'd done something. But I wanted to do more.

AS I CAME up in the elevator, I could hear the phone ringing. Hoping it was Bear, I grabbed the phone as soon as the elevator door opened. "Hello."

It was Brent. "Everything's okay, darl'. I wanted you to know that you were right. Everybody's pleasant and certainly no one indicated they thought that I was ever a suspect." He hung up before I could say a word.

I phoned his office immediately. "Brent, did you see that maroon Mustang anywhere?"

"No, not yet, Kev. I'll try again at lunch. See you." He hung up.

TUESDAY, WEDNESDAY, THURSDAY passed without any luck in finding the car. And no word from Bear. Not a word from anyone at the RCMP office. It seemed obvious I was in their bad books and officially off the case for good.

On Tuesday, I went to the Library and picked up several books on the latest additions to electronic surveillance, explaining how the police can link characteristics of one murder with others. ViCLAS, for example, sounded great, but my reading of past newspaper reports on ViCLAS didn't fill me with too much hope. Franny McGhie was right, bless her stone heart.

On Wednesday, I had lunch with Dorothy Bovak in the faculty

lunchroom at the college. Besides having one of the dullest meals I've ever eaten there, I had a fruitless interview with Dorothy. She offered no help whatsoever, except to say that she had encouraged Nancy to try her hand at writing a romantic novel.

On Thursday, I was going stir crazy and becoming as irritable as...what? A constipated grasshopper. I walked around the Stanley Park sea wall, kicking into the ocean every pebble I spotted. I kicked one particular stone the wrong way and felt a sharp pain in my toe. *Damn.* I didn't have my gout medication with me. I hobbled home, undressed, and crawled into bed, finally falling asleep after staring at the ceiling for an hour and a half.

Brent woke me up because I had been pounding the bed and shouting "Liar" over and over.

"Sweetie, wake up. Kev, that's enough now." I heard his words come from far away and then I felt his hands on my forehead. "You're dripping wet. Are you okay?"

"What?" I opened my eyes. He'd turned the light on. I felt clammy and immediately began to shiver. How long had I been sleeping? It was dark outside.

"Get up, love. I'm going to turn on the shower." He led me into the bathroom and stood me under a tepid shower. After five minutes, he led me out and dried me off. When I got back into the bed, he had changed it completely. It was fresh and dry. I crawled in and closed my eyes. "Now what the hell were you dreaming?"

"I can't remember," I lied.

"Whatever it was, it was pretty intense." He stroked my body gently with his fingertips and soon I was back off to dreamland. This time, no nightmares.

On Friday, by the time Brent had left for the college, I was becoming frustrated again. Not a goddamn word from Bear all week. Nothing more in *The Scoop.* Nothing on TV. Nothing. The case was stuck in low gear. We were going into the Thanksgiving weekend with nothing.

I tried one last time to phone the Detachment. I thought I'd try a new tactic, so I raised the pitch of my voice and asked for Margie.

"Margie Connolly here. How may I help you?"

At last! "Margie, this is —"

"I'm sorry, Mr. Porter. I truly am." She hung up.

Shit.

FEELING LIKE AN outcast, I resolved to spend all of Friday working the case on my own. On a hunch I decided to take another trip to Swallow Lake. This time, I didn't go over the Lion's Gate Bridge. I really hated the narrow three-lane span. It was all right for the horses and carriages and Model Ts of the '30s, but with today's traffic, the constricting lanes caused tension for most drivers. Certainly for me and my Lincoln. Instead, I drove through the West End, Gastown, and past the Pacific National Exhibition grounds to use the six-lane Second Narrow's Bridge. I was in Deep Cove in five more minutes.

Once I took the turnoff to Swallow Lake, I decided to drive for half a mile or so beyond Nancy's cabin. The road was primitive, a narrow gravel lane through the forest. It was probably once a logging trail. The forest was itching to take back what it owned. New saplings inched their way upwards through the packed gravel to repair the scar imposed by us humans. In most places, two approaching cars would have to slow down so that they could squeak past each other. There were occasional spots, here and there, designed for passing, but Nancy had told Brent and me that daredevil drivers didn't take advantage of these courtesy spots and often tore into the new saplings, keeping them at bay.

It was ten a.m. and I hadn't met a single car. So it was easy for me to keep an eye open for the cottage that Jeff Ferguson had said was Nancy's nearest neighbor. Getting no answer after his third visit, Jeff had deduced that the cottage had been abandoned. Up to the time I was kicked off the case, no one from the detachment had been able to find Mrs. Marigold Harcourt and interview her.

I spotted an opening in the forest where I assumed another car had turned off into the trees. I slowed down. Sure enough, I was sure Jeff's cruiser had left a few bent saplings, but the area certainly wasn't big enough for my car. Nonetheless, I pulled over and aimed toward it. There, twenty or so feet from the road and nestled under ancient trees, was a squat cottage, covered with mossy shingles on its walls and roof. Splendidly camouflaged from the prying eyes of passers-by. *So here's where Nancy's nearest neighbor lives.*

I drove off the road into the narrow, overgrown driveway. The lush undergrowth soon devoured my Lincoln. I turned off the engine and with great difficulty opened my door, forcing it against several eager young cedars. I squeezed out the small opening and walked up to the cottage. I knocked loudly, not really expecting anyone to answer.

From the other side of the door, I heard a muffled yapping, and then a whisper. "Hush, Sweetcakes. Mama's getting the door. Come into my arms." There was a peephole in the middle of the five-foot-high door. I sensed that I was being sized up. I could hear the chain being slid in place. "Be ready, Sweetcakes. You may have to protect me."

Within a few moments, the door opened a crack. Two pairs of eyes peered out, one set an inch above the chain; the other set, below the chain. "What do you want?"

"Hello, Mrs. Harcourt. I'm Kevin Porter and I'm a private

investigator. I'd like to talk with you and ask you a few questions about Nancy Henderson."

"Who?"

"Your neighbor. Down the road. She was murdered two weeks ago."

"Murdered? Nancy was murdered?" Her eyes widened. "Did you hear that, Sweetcakes? That lovely girl down the way got herself murdered." Sweetcakes' eyes widened, too.

"May I come in?"

"We weren't expecting visitors. You're not one of those RCMP chappies that keeps banging on my door, are you?"

"No. But I'd like to chat with you for a few minutes. About Nancy."

"Well," she said hesitantly, "perhaps. You're sure you're not with the RCMP?" I shook my head. "Okay. But first, we need to see your identification, don't we, Sweetcakes." Yap, yap.

"I'm here on my own. Here's my card." I slipped one of my cards through the crack. She snatched it and closed the door. I heard her whispering hoarsely: "It says Mr. Porter is a private detective. Should we let him in?" Yap, yap.

Sweetcakes must have liked me because I heard the chain being removed. The door opened wide. Standing there was a little lady no more than four feet and at least eighty. In her wee bonnet and long flannelette granny gown, she looked as though she'd stepped out of a Dickens' novel. Her feet were tucked into dirty carpet slippers. She held to her withered breast Sweetcakes, a god-awful ugly miniature bulldog as ancient as she in dog years. She looked frightened but managed a smile and a little wink, looking quite like one of those dried apple faces that are sold in tourist traps. "Nice automobile you're driving. 1960 Lincoln Continental."

I was amazed. "How did you know?"

"For years I've watched the intruders going to Swallow Lake. They used to come on horses and in buggies through my forest. And then they started driving automobiles. Oh, I know them all. From the Model T Ford to the latest 500SL Mercedes. I know all the makes of nearly everyone I see. I get books from the Deep Cove library so Sweetcakes and I can chat about the autos. Sometimes the librarian has to order books for me from the inter-library services. Libraries have improved over the years." She took a long breath. I could tell that cars were her passion. She chattered on, "I had to look yours up when you were here on the Labor Day weekend."

"You got me!" Now here was a real little cutie that might be very useful. "Tell me, how did you see my car? I didn't..."

"Come in, Mr. Porter." She turned and walked into the room. Ducking my head, I followed and closed the door behind me. Straightening up, I immediately hit my head on a model Volkswagen

Beetle that was hanging from the ceiling. It ricocheted and hit a Honda Accord, a Chevrolet Impala, and in turn they hit other mobiles in a domino effect. Soon the entire room was in motion with at least a hundred model cars on their strings colliding into each other, creating a dust storm. Sweetcakes went wild yapping. Mrs. Harcourt clapped her hands and giggled in delight. "You have made Sweetcakes' day, Mr. Porter. Thank Mr. Porter, Sweetcakes." Yap, yap. She pointed to a well-worn armchair. "Sit. Sit." I wondered if I should yap-yap!

I dodged swinging cars and plunked into the seat. An aura of urine engulfed me. Sweetcakes growled. Yipes! I had invaded his domain. Marigold chastised her dog. "What have I told you about sharing?"

While Sweetcakes beaded me with his popping eyes, I tried for a moment to take in my surroundings. As my eyes adjusted to the dusty gloom, I noticed that there wasn't a square inch of surface that was not covered with automobelia: more models, match-box cars, yellowed calendars of cars, on the walls faded photographs of cars, pics of cars from magazines or newspapers stuck here and there, piles of catalogues of model cars, stacks of brochures from car dealers. The tiny, one-room cottage represented a veritable history of the automobile.

The old lady watched me with satisfaction. "I can see you like my collection." She sat in another easy chair across from me and studied my card. "Shoot, Mr. Private Dick. We're ready for you to grill us. Aren't we, Sweetcakes?" She winked; he yapped.

"How long have you lived here?" I was fascinated.

"Herbert, my late husband built this cottage in 1929. Long before this terrible road was put through. Originally we were the only ones who knew that Swallow Lake existed, except for a few native Indians. I suppose you could call us squatters. We felt we owned the lake. Now it belongs to everyone and they aren't treating her with the respect that we and the Indians know she deserves. Right, Sweetcakes?" The dog had settled on her lap, twitching his tail and sniffing his large drooping balls. I wanted to learn how, way back in '29, the Harcourts had got through the dense cedars to build their little dream house. I wondered how tall Herbert was. "This cottage was my wedding present. Herbert was a successful businessman in Vancouver and cashed in all his assets and stocks before the big crash. He was such a clever man. He wrote to me that he was building me a beautiful home, if I'd come and marry him."

"What do you mean?"

"I was a mail-order bride. When I came out here from England, I was only fifteen. You can imagine my surprise when Herbert picked me up at the CPR station. He was nearly sixty. But I married him anyway because I had promised. Besides," she giggled, "he was rich.

He'd already given up his practice and was living here, finishing the cottage for me. He worked so hard getting it ready, what else could I do? We were married in Deep Cove and moved right in." She bowed her head shyly. "I was a virgin and I didn't know anything about...you know. But I soon caught on. Six months after our wedding night, poor Herbert died." A smile played on her withered lips. "I guess I was too much for him. I wanted him to make love every night."

"And you've lived here ever since?"

"Yes," she said whimsically. "He left me very well off. I put bags of money in an account in Deep Cove and it just keeps growing. He also left me with Sweetcakes' Great-Grandma. She was all I had for company. I buried her out back beside Herbert. And then I buried Sweetcakes' Granny and Mommy. And I'll be burying Sweetcakes out there, too. We're both the last of our line." Sweetcakes licked her gnarly fingers. "I don't know who's going to bury me. Mr. Porter, do you think that..."

I had to get the conversation back to why I came here in the first place. "Mrs. Harcourt."

"Call me Marigold." She twisted an already tight curl that protruded from under her bonnet. "How old are you, sir?"

"Sixty." I wasn't going to be deterred. "Marigold, where did you see my Lincoln? I've never driven down this road to Swallow Lake."

"Sweetcakes and I saw it on the Saturday, Sunday, and Monday of the Labor Day weekend you visited Nancy. You parked it in front of her cabin. Whenever we go grocery shopping, we walk the same path Herbert used to carry in the supplies for our home. The path goes a few feet from where you set up your tent with that young oriental man." She swallowed some saliva with a sound like a tsk tsk. Sweetcakes licked his balls. "I was so intrigued with your automobile that I had to go to the library when it opened on Tuesday morning. I knew it was a Lincoln, of course, but I didn't know the year. Your car looks brand new. I'd never seen a '60 Lincoln Continental before. But I have pictures, of course. Let me show you one." Dumping a startled Sweetcakes on the floor, she rushed to find a picture from a stack of dusty, yellowed clippings.

"That's okay, Marigold. I know how it looks."

"Of course. What could I be thinking? You own one." She laughed. "Maybe we could go for a ride after you finish interrogating us." She picked up her shivering dog and hugged him.

"We just might." *Depending on your next answer.* "Last weekend, did you see a car, beside Nancy's..."

"You mean her sandstone '97 Infiniti I30?"

"Yes, but did you see another car parked there between September Twenty-Fifth and -Seventh?"

"Yes, I certainly did."

Hallelujah! "What was the make? Can you describe it? The color? The condition? The..."

"Hold your horses, Kevin. I may call you Kevin, mayn't I?"

"You can call me anything you like, Marigold." *Paydirt.* "Now. The make?" I looked directly into her tiny dancing eyes.

"A Toyota Tercel. A '92. Beat up a bit. Had a small dent in the front right fender." My eyes grew as big as Sweetcakes'. "Repainted from its original Harvard blue to a muddy brown. Should have kept it blue. That's a nice color. Rich looking, if you know what..."

I held my breath and asked, "I don't suppose you know the license plate number."

"No. Numbers don't interest me. Seen one license plate; seen them all. I'm just interested in automobiles. Never had one myself."

I let my breath escape. "Did you happen to see who was with Nancy during that particular weekend?"

"I'm sorry, Kevin. I can't help you in that department either. Every day when Sweetcakes and I walked by, the only thing we ever saw from the back window was a flickering light. We heard music playing all the time. Jazz. Rhythm and Blues. Wilson Pickett. You know the kind. Good beat. When we were out on our Saturday morning walk, I thought there might be a fire. It was so bright I walked closer to the cabin to check. But when I looked inside through the branches, I saw movement. I figured everything was all right."

"Did you see who it was?"

"No. Just a shadow. I was surprised on our Sunday morning walk, the flickering was still going on and I decided that she must be having a romantic candlelight weekend. It happens, you know. In novels. I read a lot."

"Anything else?"

"Loud music. Very loud on Sunday. Sweetcakes didn't like it one bit. We went closer because — well, to tell you the truth, I was a little curious. Nosy me. I got ten feet or so from the window when suddenly there was a blinding flash. Sweetcakes had a bird. He ran back to the path with his tail between his legs and didn't stop until he got home. That flash frightened me, too, so I followed Sweetcakes, not having him to protect me. I wonder what that flash was."

"The killer took photographs."

"Ah!" She *tsk*ed.

"Did you see or hear anything else that may help us catch the killer?"

"No. I've told you everything. Nancy and I were a lot alike. We both loved our solitude. We only nodded and smiled when we met. I don't think I said a dozen words to her. I liked her, but I respected her privacy. Okay? I had to explain that to you. It's not that I wasn't neighborly, you understand. All I saw was your Lincoln again on the next Monday. And all the RCMP automobiles. That's why I thought you might be with the police. Anyway, we knew something was going on with all the commotion, but we never imagined Nancy got murdered. Isn't that right, Sweetcakes?" The dog had long been asleep and merely snored his response. "I like to keep my nose clean with the RCMP boys. Never been in trouble in my life, but they make me nervous, so I wasn't about to talk to any of them. We stayed out of sight for nearly an hour, watching. Then we got cold and had to come home for a wee nip." She winked. "He likes his wee nip, don't you Sweetcakes? Would you like some?"

"No. But thanks."

"Then let's go for a ride in your Lincoln."

We drove around Swallow Lake. I listened for another hour as Marigold vented her disgust at the build-up of the area. I agreed with her. Like so many resort places, this one was quickly losing the pristine beauty that had first attracted tourists. I was surprised that the lake was so small. Only about half a mile at its longest part and a quarter of a mile across. It was virtually surrounded by paved road with cabins on most of its shore. A few canoeists were already out on the lake. There was one little store with a sign: Open F/S/S/W: 10-2. I wondered how Swallow Lake would look ten years from now. Probably have its own McDonald's.

I headed back. Marigold was sad because the Thanksgiving weekenders were already filing into their cabins. I pulled out onto the narrow gravel road, to make my way back to her cottage. Cars were driving full speed past us. I pulled over several times to avoid an accident. "Maniacs!" screamed Marigold as each car zoomed by. Yap, yap, echoed Sweetcakes.

I dropped her off, promising that when I had time, I'd return for a "wee nip." I drove the next half mile fearing for my Lincoln. The *maniacs* came within a whisper of sideswiping my beauty.

I passed Nancy's cabin without stopping.

All the way home I was composing another fax to Bear, letting him know that we had a witness, describing exactly what Marigold had seen in the cabin on the Saturday and Sunday, and providing all the details of the killer's car. I felt excited, certain that Bear would invite me back on the case the moment he read my fax.

Chapter
Twenty-One

HERE IT IS Thanksgiving and still not a word from the RCMP. I had half hoped that I'd get a call from Bear after sending him the second fax about Marigold's find. She was able to confirm candlelight, Wilson Pickett's R&B music, flashes from a Polaroid, how long the killer was there. And a description of the car. *She is their only witness.* But I heard nothing out of any of them.

What else was there to do but enjoy Thanksgiving dinner?

"You're a brat, Martha. Stuffing us with your gorgeous dinner. And you know I love real whipped cream on my pumpkin pie."

Martha enjoyed a throaty laugh. "That was always how I could get him to do anything I wanted," she shared with Brent and Hank. "Bake him a pumpkin pie."

I grinned. "It became the family joke. Every time Martha made a pumpkin pie, all the kids knew she had a 'huge' favor to ask." I looked at Brent and Hank; they were distinctly uncomfortable hearing about the life that Martha and I had shared. But I continued. Hell, I wasn't going to ignore my past; it made me who I am today. "As they got older, the minute Martha brought a pumpkin pie to the table, one of the twins was sure to say in a sexy voice, 'I wonder what Mom wants Dad to do tonight?' And they'd all snicker."

Martha and I shared a good laugh at our family joke while Brent and Hank looked just plain grumpy. Our lovers were both about the same size. Slight, but well built, although Hank was a bit taller — which Brent was painfully aware of. Both were about the same age, although Brent looked younger. *Brent will be pleased tonight when we're cuddling in bed and I give him a good night kiss and whisper, "You're much more handsome than Hank and you look years younger, too." I know how to feed my lover's vanity.* It amused Martha and me to watch the two of them. They were both so obviously not the slightest bit interested in each other. They had eyes only for their older lovers.

That suited both Martha and me: she went for blond Nordic types; I loved the dark-haired hunks.

Martha and I launched into a discussion about our kids. When we got together or spoke on the phone, our kids filled our conversation. They were ours and we loved them all dearly, warts and all. We always organized our visits with them so that we wouldn't end up on one of our kid's doorsteps at the same time. Our children were our common denominator and we couldn't stop talking about their ups and downs, their achievements and defeats. "Did you send Sammy a birthday present?" Martha asked. "Remember, it's his thirty-ninth birthday next week."

"Yeah, I sent him a funny Jack Benny card I'd picked up at Little Sisters. I don't know if he'll get the joke; anyway, I put in a check and told him to go out on a date and have a fun night." I smiled over at the two young men's stony faces. Christ, they were both six or seven years younger than Sammy, probably neither of them had ever heard of Jack Benny. I wondered what they were thinking, besides being noticeably cheesed off with both Martha and me and our natural camaraderie. *Jealous, my manno?* If he was, he wasn't alone; Hank's shoulders had the same squared-off shape as Brent's. *That's natural, I suppose.* I was sure that if Brent started bringing around some of his ex-lovers and chatting up happy times they had spent together, I'd be as pissed off as these two young men were. "When are you going to Hawaii next?" I asked Martha. "I think it's my turn to visit Barbi, isn't it? I want to see my grandkids before they get too big."

Brent's nostrils flared. "So let's get on with the fitting before Kev asks for seconds of your pumpkin pie, Martha, or you'll have to make his costume two sizes larger."

"Bitch," I mouthed.

Hank shot a look of disgust. It was apparent from the first time I met him that he had never approved of Martha's continued friendship with me. From the beginning, he resented Martha's offer to make our Halloween costumes. And now, for Christ's sake, we were eating Thanksgiving dinner together. I could imagine his thoughts. *She'll probably suggest a menage à quatre next Thanksgiving. Over my dead body!* I caught his eye. He looked at me guiltily. I was right. That's exactly what he was thinking. Hank got up. "Okay, you guys. Why not go into Martha's sewing room?"

Once there, Martha ordered, "Strip down to your BVDs, boys. And close your eyes. Hank, you gotta help me. Fellas, make sure you don't peek." She was happy and excited.

We were poked and prodded like two babes being dressed. "Hey, your hands are cold!" Giggles aplenty. "Watch where you're putting that thing!" Laughs all around. "My, you have developed into an upstanding man." Roars galore. I recognized Martha's touch, so I couldn't help thinking how uncomfortable Brent must be feeling with Hank's probing, poking, youthful hands.

At last Martha proudly said, "Open your eyes."

Standing in the full mirror facing Brent and me were Batman and

Robin, in perfect replicas of the original comic-book outfits. Me in a skin-tight body suit; Brent in tights and jerkin. I admired my hood with stand-up bat ears, at least one was upstanding; the other was pinned on. Leather gloves and boots for both of us. Bat insignias all pinned on in the right positions. We looked sensational. Brent and I gasped in amazement. I could tell that Brent was sure the Dynamic Duo would win first prize at this year's Halloween ball.

"Move around a bit. But not too active," instructed Martha. "You don't want a pin to jab you."

"You've outdone yourself, Martha. They're wonderful." I swooped over to her and planted a kiss on her mouth.

"Sensational," added Brent, mimicking a Robin run. He kissed her on the cheek.

"I couldn't have done it without Hank's help." We both looked at Hank while Martha continued, "He's a big Batman fan and helped me with the design and making the patterns."

We both smiled at Hank. "Thanks."

Hank smiled back proudly and said, "Lift your arms." I did so and, to my delight, saw the entire cape rise. I did a spin or two. My huge cape floated regally. Hank looked at Martha and laughed. "I knew he'd like the cape."

Hey, a breakthrough. There's hope for Hank after all. I crossed my arms in front of me, noticing that the cape completely enveloped my whole body with lots of room for Robin under my cape. I whispered in Brent's ear.

Brent *oo-lah-lah*ed. Martha laughed. Hank snorted, but continued to smile happily, knowing full well what I'd whispered to Brent.

Martha looked at her desk calendar. She had one like mine. It covered the whole desk but I noticed that in several boxes, the entries were neatly printed, not scribbled in like mine. "Can you come back in two weeks for your final fitting? Let's say Sunday, October Twenty-fourth. For dinner?"

"We'll be here!" Brent was in heaven. He looked at me as an afterthought. "Okay, Kev?"

"HAPPY THANKSGIVIN', KEV."

I recognized Bear's voice. "Who is this?"

"Bear."

"Bear who? I know lots of Bears. There's Yogi, Paddington, Panda and...don't tell me...Is this Smokey Bear?"

"Kev. It's me. Barry Spivic."

"Oh, that Bear!"

"So how's things?"

"Fine." *He needs me.* I could tell. *Let him grovel.*

"So, ya think we might git t'gether t'morra sometime? Maybe?"

"I'll have to check my calendar. Just a minute, Bear." I looked at my watch. I stood there for two minutes watching the second hand. This was unreal. An RCMP Sergeant asking me for assistance. And on Thanksgiving evening. Something was definitely coming down. I had better watch my back. "Sorry, I'm getting my hair and nails done at nine and I'm picking up the Hendersons at the airport at eleven. They've got a four-hour layover before they head back to Halifax. I promised them we'd spend some time together and I wanted to look nice." I could hear Bear's raspy breath. "They'd like to pick up a few things from Nancy's apartment. I'm sure you and your team have gone over everything there with meticulous scrutiny."

He hesitated and said softly. "Ya betcha." I bet he would have another look at Nancy's apartment first thing in the morning. "When did ya say ya were pickin' them up?"

"At eleven. We'll be at the apartment about noon." Then I added a zinger. "They are sure to ask me if you've got the killer yet. What'll I tell them?"

"It's still early, Kev. Tell 'em it's still early."

"That's what you told them exactly two weeks ago." Another zinger. "You mean you haven't made any more *arrests*, Bear?"

"No," he replied meekly.

"Any leads?"

"Nope. I've been runnin' my ass off, checkin' a bunch of useless tips that come in. The crackpots are out." *Don't tell me he thinks my faxes were from a crackpot? Wouldn't that take the cake?* "We even have a couple of weirdos comin' in every day confessing to the murder. They're beggin' to be punished. But it's easy to see that they're too damn scared to jaywalk, let alone kill someone. This last week's bin a waste of time. Oh, except for a description of the killer's vehicle and the witness thing that you faxed Margie. And the one that you sent me about the picture. By the way, thanks."

"What makes you think that I sent you that fax?"

"Come on, Kev. Don't be a smart ass. Ya did, and that's all there is to it."

"Okay, I confess, Sherlock, but I was getting pretty pissed off with the cold-shoulder treatment from everyone on the Force."

"Orders from on high, Kev. Ya know who I mean? But, Kev," Bear spoke seriously, "Sam is in the hospital. He's bin headin' fer a breakdown for the last year, and I think that meetin' wuz the last straw that tipped the scale." I groaned at Bear's mixed metaphor, not for my one-time best friend. In the old days, I would have done anything for Sam; in fact, I had taken a bullet for him once, just north of Selkirk. A lunatic Indian had trapped us behind a woodpile and when I heard the shots, I leapt to push Sam to safety. But every time

I look at my miserable pension check my dander goes high sky, thinking of how that man turned his back on me.

I'd call Sam's wife later tonight, but right now, I couldn't let the opportunity slip away with Bear, my only tangible contact with the Force. "What about the clues in Nancy's diary? She's told you who her killer is."

"After that conference last week, I read that diary over until I can recite it by heart. Good piece of writin', that. Make a good book. Anyways, I don't see anywheres that she's pointin' her finger at her killer."

He needs my help. "Oh, it's there all right." I thought I'd rub in a bit of salt. "Maybe one day we can chat about it. By the way, did you get the original photo from the McGhie weasel?"

"Ya. And, Kev, you were right. That picture is a pip. Ya gotta see it."

"Did you get it in its original envelope?"

"Natch. The lab reports are already back. Pete couldn't find no fingerprints, but Jeff hit pay dirt on the stamp. He performed a PCR on the small amount of spit he found on the stamp."

"Good."

"In case ya don't know, PCR stands for Polymerase Chain Reaction," said Bear carefully as if he were reading it off the report that he had in front of him. "This test amplifies the small amount of DNA found in the saliva needed to lick a stamp. DNA is the new thing in makin' a conviction that'll stick. Well, in most cases, unless you're an OJ Simpson. Ya know what I mean?" He was becoming my old Bear again. This week, I had read everything I could get my hands on about modern detection, so I was completely up on DNA, but I let him continue. I wanted back on this case. "Anyways, DNA is found in blood, bone, saliva, skin, and mucus. The DNA in spit is concentrated in the yuppie-feel-ya cells which we slough off every day."

"Yuppie-feel-yal, you say. Interesting." Bear wasn't reading after all. He was reciting from memory from Jeff's report. He couldn't remember the pronunciation of the epithelial cells, and made up his own malapropism for them. *He'll never change.*

But I wanted him to ask me to come back on board. "Describe the picture to me."

"She's dead in this one. Jist like ya seen in *The Scoop*. Only this time there's five other Polaroids layin' around her head."

"Five?"

"Yep." He paused. "Would ya like to see it?"

You bet your big hairy ass I would. "Are you actually wanting me to help?"

Bear went quiet for several seconds. Then I heard a small, "Yep. Joan's given me a deadline. If I don't find the killer by the end of the month, I'm off the case. That's when Sam's due back."

"So you want to work with a poofter, do you?"

"Yep."

"I can't hear you."

"I said yep. I told Abby that there's no way I'd ever work with a queer and she announces, 'Well you'd better take me off the case.'"

"You mean you didn't know that Abby was a dyke? I recognized one of our kind the minute I saw her."

"How d'ya do that?"

"We gays can tell. It's a special scent we put out."

"Ya do? I don't smell nothin'."

"That's cause you're an ordinary heterosexual."

"So that's why there are so many of you gays around. Yer breedin' like rabbits."

I stifled a laugh. "Pretty soon we're going to take over the world, Bear. Then you better watch out."

"Holy shit!"

I burst.

"Yer kiddin', ain'tcha?"

I'd had enough fun. "I can see you Wednesday night. How be if you and your family invite my lover and me over for one of Mil's delicious dinners?"

I could imagine Bear turning purple. "Sure," he choked, "I'll ask her. I'm sure she'll agree."

He really needs me. "And have the Polaroid blowups there." I was about to hang up. "By the way, what kind of luck have you had in finding the car? Find the car and you find the killer."

"I assigned a corporal to that job on Friday. He's checkin' with ICBC. Got any ideas how many brown Toyotas there are out there?"

"Lots?"

"Thousands!"

Chapter
Twenty-Two

"DON'T YOU LOOK wonderfully tanned?" I waved to the leied Hendersons, his made with tei leaves, hers with plumeria. They wheeled their matching Samsonite luggage through the arrival gates at the Vancouver International airport. At first sight, I was convinced that their smiles indicated that they had found the best medicine to deal with their grief.

Once in my car, Hilda started to tell me about their stay on the Big Island, interrupted by Fred at strategic points so she could take a breath. No mention of the murder of their daughter. "I can certainly see why the Big Island was Nancy's favorite place to visit. Amid millions of hectares of black lava, you suddenly come upon an oasis with palm trees, flowering shrubs by the hundreds, birds of every plumage, and golden-sanded beaches."

Don't you want to know what's been happening here while you've been sunning yourselves on Hawaiian shores?

"When you drive to the Hilton," she continued her commentary, "you will laugh at a sign on the highway. Mule Crossing. Mule Crossing. Mule..." She sucked in her cheeks and swallowed audibly.

Fred broke the silence. "The Hilton has a golf course to test a master's skill."

Glancing over and seeing her wipe her eyes, I asked, "Are you all right, Hilda?" She was still grieving and in denial. Talking about her holiday was her way of coping. The travelogue continued until I parked in front of Nancy's apartment. "We're here."

"Already? But I didn't tell you about the mule crossing."

"On the way back to the airport. We'll have more time then."

I rang the manager. When he came to the door, he frowned. "Not you again."

"Yeah. The big bad wolf turns up again. These two nice people are Nancy's parents. Would you let them into the apartment?"

"Certainly. No problem. I have a key. Sergeant Spivic was just here and left me one for the *new* door." He looked directly at me. "He told me you'd be coming. Great Mountie, that Spivic."

"Yeah. Great."

Fred and Hilda walked apprehensively around their daughter's suite, pointing out the many little touches Nancy had thoughtfully introduced into the decor of each room.

They picked up a few small things and put them on the dining room table. A couple of photos of the three of them, a figurine of Pooh, a gold bracelet with "Today I am Six" engraved on it, a topaz ring, and a few other small items that obviously held important memories for them. All they had left of their daughter.

I gently interrupted their reverent search. "The police are having a difficult job tracing the killer. Could I ask you a few questions?"

"Most assuredly," answered Fred. Hilda sucked in her cheeks and nodded in agreement.

"Did Nancy write you often?"

"Not through the post," Hilda responded. "We phoned each other two or three times a week. And Fred and Nancy were always e-mailing each other."

"So, all those letters — written, but never mailed — were in preparation for her novel."

"Oh, those? Yes, she was trying her hand at writing a Harlequin novel," Fred interrupted. "She e-mailed most of her drafts to me. I had a good laugh at her style. I remember saying, 'Margaret Atwood needn't worry, darling.'" I could tell that father and daughter had a special bond. English and writing had been their glue. "Between you and me, she'd never have made a romantic writer. Couldn't shake her academe to save her sweet soul." He smiled.

"Did she ever confide in you about her love life?"

"Only minimally," Fred answered. "We always respected her privacy. She did, however, tell us about your Brent and how fond she was of him. But knowing that you were a happy, loving pair, she would never have come between you." I was surprised that Fred was speaking so openly about Brent and me. "So, she was content to keep her relationship with Brent purely platonic." Then Fred added with a twinkle, "She did tell me in an e-mail that she was having a lark, using Brent as her romantic hero. She knew full well the difference between reality and fantasy. But she was infatuated with him nonetheless. I accused her once of using her novel cathartically. She vociferously denied my claim. Who really knows, though? A writer can dissipate a plethora of guilt, rage, or jealousy by hiding in her characters." He looked at me and mused, "O, beware, my lord, of jealousy! / It is the green-eyed monster, which doth mock / The meat it feeds on."

Hilda smiled. It was clear she didn't want Fred to get too deeply into his lecture mode. "We wanted to meet Brent, his being Nancy's mentor and all. When he had dinner with us last summer, I couldn't help think that he and my daughter made a striking pair. I must confess, my first thought was 'What a loss to the female population!' But I bet you're glad he's yours?"

I smiled back, comfortable that the gay thing was out in the open.

"Did Nancy ever mention a mystery man to you?"

Fred jumped in. "Yes. She just used the diary as a prewriting exercise. You know, for accumulating ideas, dialogue, characterization."

"Oh, of course."

Fred continued, "She wanted to keep him an enigma until the penultimate chapter. During the story, she insisted, the heroine would catch only glimpses of him, and each time he would appear in a different guise. Sometimes young, sometimes middle-aged. Always handsome, though. She could recognize him only by his eyes. And at the end, she wanted to reveal him as someone whom she had known for years, but never truly appreciated." Fred waited a moment, then continued, "For that to work well in a story, however, I told her she'd have to introduce the man and the relationship he was having with the heroine early in the story. The reader will not accept an unknown character who is suddenly dropped in like a deus ex machina."

"A deus ex..."

"Machina." Hilda saw that I was confused. "God in the machine. The Greeks used this device in their plots to end their stories according to a particular established myth that all the audience knew and appreciated."

"Oh, I see." My head was reeling from too much academia.

"Wait a minute," interjected Fred. "Is there a connection between this mysterious man and Nancy's killer?"

"That's what I'm trying to determine."

"Kevin," said Hilda, "we've been talking and we think that we may stay here for a few days. I know we could be of help. We wouldn't feel right, leaving at this time."

Fred joined in. "We could stay right in this apartment, couldn't we, Hildie? We have so much to do anyway. Arrange to have our daughter cremated. We wish to take her ashes home with us. And we have to close down this apartment and put it on the market. And do the same with the cabin. We don't want to keep either of them. When this is all over, we'll live out our days on the East coast."

Hilda said, "As our minister told us when we called him from the Hilton, 'You've got to close the door and get on with your life.' "

"Well..." I was taken aback for a minute as the Hendersons divulged their well-thought-out agendas. *That's why they have their luggage in my trunk instead of having it shipped through to Halifax.* "I don't think the police will let you move into either place at this time. They may need to do another search, you never know. Sergeant Spivic was in here this morning with a team. I'm afraid you're going to have to come back to settle things. And if I need you, you're only a phone call away."

"But our daughter's remains?" Fred began. "We certainly don't want to leave without..."

"Actually, Fred, I've got a release form here for you to sign." I took out the form that I had picked up on my way to the airport. "I didn't know your wishes, but once you sign it, I'll make sure that everything you want is done for you here."

"Thank you," said Fred quietly. "I see you have an agenda, too. To put us on the plane back to Halifax as quickly as possible." He looked at Hilda. "It didn't work, sweetheart."

I looked at the couple, clutching onto their few mementos. "Believe me, it is best that you return home and get back to your many activities. Your minister is right." They nodded solemnly. "Are there any other questions you'd like to ask me?" Pause. "Most family members want to know how...well...all the details of..."

"We don't want to know," interrupted Hilda. "We want to remember Nancy as she was. See?" She held up a picture of a smiling Nancy standing between the two of them. "Isn't it better for us to remember our daughter this way than to know how a malicious killer destroyed all that was beautiful? I think so. Don't you, Fred?"

Their atypical behavior confused me. *Why aren't they shouting and screaming demands of every detail? I know I would.*

But Fred merely concurred with his wife. "Unequivocally. We are together on this, Kevin. Take us to the airport."

On the way out, there was no talk about the murder or their plans to stay on. I got another earful of information about the Big Island, Kilauea volcanoes, mule crossings, King Kam's glory, and Parker Ranch—the largest cattle ranch in the world. I knew the island well of course, so I didn't object. I enjoyed picturing everything through Hilda's eyes. I thought of my Barbi, happily enjoying her life in Hawaii. The thought of losing her, as Fred and Hilda had lost Nancy, brought tears to my eyes several times. I was still having flashes of seeing Nancy in bed, thumb in her mouth. All cleaned out.

"Good luck," the Hendersons chorused as they entered the gate to board their plane. "Find him," added Hilda and then sucked in her cheeks and swallowed hard.

Chapter
Twenty-Three

DINNER WITH THE Spivics and their three teen-aged kids was, I hope, a last-in-a-lifetime experience. In hungry anticipation, they moved mountains of food from huge bowls and platters onto their oversized plates. "You must have Mil's famous fried chicken," blurted Bear proudly. "And her famous creamed cauliflower casserole," added Andy, their eldest son. Not to be outdone, Iris and Ivy said we had to try their mother's famous garlic smashed potatoes and gravy.

After all the plates were heaped, Bear recited grace. "Good food, good meat. Good God, let's eat." They lowered their heads and attacked their food: chomping, slurping, stuffing their mouths as quickly as they could. "Can I have seconds when I finish?" Iris asked after she shoveled in her first mouthful of potatoes.

"Sure, honey-lumpkins." Mil smiled proudly.

Brent and I glanced at each other, devilry in our eyes. We watched, amazed, as the piles of food disappeared.

"This chicken is certainly delicious, Mil." I smiled, trying to bring some conversation into the meal.

"Mmm." She was sucking a neck bone clean. *Who eats chicken necks?*

"Mil's a great cook, isn't she, Bear?"

"Ya betcha. Sh...l...urp." Bear was sucking the marrow out of a chicken leg he'd just broken in half with his molars.

"So what grade are you in now, Andy?"

Andy smiled. He looked at me, then Brent, then me again. "Ten." *Hallelujah! A word!* Milk clung to the peach fuzz on his top lip as he smiled again at both of us. He gave me one of Bear's penetrating looks. *What had Bear told him about Brent and me?*

I tried to carry on a conversation with Iris and Ivy, but managed to get only a couple of giggles while watching bits of corn drop from their mouths onto their plates.

I decided to lower my head and dig in too, so that I wouldn't be the last to finish. I didn't think it would be safe to still have food on my plate if all the Spivics finished eating before me.

Belches all 'round signaled the end of their meal.

"Great dinner," put in Brent, giving my leg a nudge under the table.

"Ya betcha. She's a great cook, my Mil."

"Oh, go on with you guys," Mil cackled and ran to the kitchen. Iris and Ivy picked up the empty dishes and followed their mom. A second later Mil came out with a pecan pie and a pail of Lucerne Neopolitan ice cream. Bear clapped his hands. "Not yer famous pecan pie? You guys are in for the treat of yer lives." The girls ran in with bowls and spoons.

Mil cut the pie into seven equal pieces while we all watched. Iris said, "Mom, one of them pieces is smaller. I don't want that one."

"Neither do I," yelled Ivy. "Let Andy have it!"

"I'll take it," said Brent. He beat me to it. We never have dessert after dinner. We only pig out on Saturday nights. One dessert a week is our motto.

I looked over at Bear about to plop a huge dollop of Neopolitan ice cream on top of my pie and shouted, "Please, no ice cream for me."

"Suit yerself, but it slips down better with some chocolate, strawberry, and vanilla on it."

"None for me either," Brent said politely while he kicked my shin.

Try as we might, Brent and I couldn't finish our pie. "If yer not gonna finish, I'll eat yers, Mr. Barnes," said Iris hungrily.

"And I'll have yers," copied Ivy, giving me a hungry smile.

We gladly relinquished more than half our pieces to Bear's starving cubs. I hope I'm not giving the impression that Brent and I are a couple of snobby queers, looking down on the Spivics. But I'm not exaggerating. The meal reminded me of the one in Eddie Murphy's *The Nutty Professor*, but a lot funnier.

Another round of belches marked the end of the final course. "Now, let's retire to the sittin' room and let the ladies clean up," announced Bear.

"Can I come too, Dad?" Andy asked, following us in.

"It's business between Kev and I. Why don'tcha show Brent here yer baseball card collection?" Bear didn't want Brent in on our business meeting either.

"You want to see them?" Andy smiled.

"Why not?"

Andy led Brent upstairs to his room. Bear suddenly looked deeply troubled.

"What's the matter?" I asked, knowing exactly what had crossed Bear's homophobic brain.

"I wuz jist wonderin' if..."

"Brent only likes older men. Andy is safe."

"Ya think?"

"I know."

Bear wasn't totally convinced, but suggested that we go into the living room anyway. There, on the coffee table, was Nancy's "unfinished" novel and a brown manila envelope. I wanted to tear open the envelope and take a good look at the Polaroid that I knew was in there.

Once Bear had flopped in his armchair, he said, "Let's git somethin' straight right off the bat. I dunno much about this homo business, but I'm sorry I cracked up on ya in Joan's office."

"That's okay. It happens."

"But I nearly lost a muffin hearin' Brent call ya Jessica."

"Yeah. It's pretty funny. Between you and me, it was no doing of mine. I hate it when he calls me that."

"Really?"

"Honest Injun."

"So, ya know I ain't got nothin' against *you* personally. Ya know that, don'tcha?" He raised the furrows in his forehead and then gave me a big smile, slivers of chicken and corn still stuck between his teeth.

"I know. Thanks for clearing the air. Now. How can I help? Let me see the Polaroid."

Ignoring my request, Bear said, "I took yer advice and read the whole diary again. And I seen what ya meant. She had a mystery man, all right."

"Or she was telling us about her killer."

"Ya think?"

"I feel it in my gut. First, we have to separate fact from fiction. Nancy's parents and Brent confirmed that she was writing a romance novel. Since it's common knowledge that most writers dip into their real life for incidents, exaggerating them for effect, we must eliminate everything about the narrator's desire to have B for her own, and concentrate on this mystery man stalking Nancy. So, Bear, describe him to me."

"First he's grayin' at the temples, probably middle-aged. And then he's got long blond hair, and he's young. And then he's not described at all in some places." Bear scratched his chin. "I bin thinkin'. It seems like she's writin' about more 'an one guy. Maybe there's two killers?"

"No. I can't imagine Nancy letting two men into her cabin, disguised or otherwise. She was a careful girl."

"So whatcha make of all that stuff in the diary about this guy? First he's young. Then he's old."

"Piece things together, Bear. Think of the corpse. How she looked to you the first time you saw her. Then the autopsy report. What Frank wrote about her appearance. And now the mystery man. How he looks."

"I got it. Frank said in his report that Nancy was fully made up. Our guy is a master at makeup. He's probably an actor or somethin'. You know television or movies. He could disguise himself easily."

"You've got it. Or, as Frank suggested, he's a makeup artist."

"There must be dozens of them workin' in the Vancouver area."

"Well then, we had better get on it first thing in the morning. Interview every male makeup artist. Opera, theatre, night clubs, TV productions, film companies, the works. Pick me up at eight."

"I'll be there. I'm drivin'." He looked directly into my eyes. "Kev, this is between you and I. Okay? Yer my silent partner. Right? We can't let this get back to Sam, or it might kill him."

"How's he doing?" I asked.

"Much better. He's already gone home, but his doc won't let him come back to work until November." He got up to go. "We're through here. I'm sure Brent needs savin' from my Andy. He's probably borin' him silly with his baseball card collection." His face twitched. "Kev?"

"Hm."

"Ya think this was a random killin'?"

"Serial murderers are creatures of opportunity. Usually a victim is simply in the wrong place at the wrong time. The killer pounces on his good fortune. But they do select their victims as well. A killer will be attracted to a certain look, a particular voice, something that triggers a mental scream in his head: 'I want that one! Rape her. Kill her. She's the one.'"

"You mean..."

"Yes. He probably stalked Nancy for weeks. Planned the whole thing. Got into the cabin before that night. Sawed the post."

"To get the lay of the land."

"Right."

"Ya really think he's done it before?"

"There's little doubt. Now, let me see the Polaroid." I reached for the manila envelope on the table.

"Oh, it ain't there. That's Andy's report card. Joan is still workin' on the blowups. We wanna get a good look-see at those other pictures that were propped up around Nancy's head. Somethin' interestin' there, but the enlargements aren't sharp enough, so Joan's bringin' in an artist to do a few mock-ups."

"When will they be ready?"

"Any day now. Maybe even t'morra."

Damn, I wanted to see them tonight.

ON OUR WAY home from the Spivics, Brent asked, "Are you in Bear's good graces now?"

"Let's say, as long as he needs me, he'll do anything for me."

"Anything?"

"Get your mind out of the gutter. Can you imagine Bear and me that way?"

"Arrrgh! I don't want to think about that man."

"He's not a bad sort, really. Needs lots of coaching, that's all." I didn't tell Brent about the Polaroid and my concern that I was being shut out as to its content. *I'd bet anything that the artist has completed his job and the other photos are now under wraps.*

Brent smiled. "Sergeant Spivic is going to be in for the shock of his life one day."

"What do you mean?"

"After Andy showed me his card collection, all the time saying, 'I only collect these because Dad got me started,' he climbed on his chair to put them away on the top shelf of his closet. As he reached up, he lost his balance and grabbed at the shelf. Down came dozens of centerfolds, floating all over his room. He rushed to pick them up."

"The little devil. But that's nothing out of the ordinary for a sixteen-year-old kid. Sammy used to hide *Playboys* under his mattress. Martha and I knew, but we didn't make an issue of it."

"Yeah, but these were *Playgirl* centerfolds."

Brent, doing a perfect imitation of a raging, horrified Bear, kept us both in hysterics all the way home.

AT PRECISELY EIGHT o'clock a.m. the next morning the intercom buzzed. "Morning, Bear. Come on up."

"But I thought we'd push off right away."

"Let's discuss our plan of action first. Come on in and don't forget, just get into the elevator, and don't push anything," I reminded him over the intercom before I released the lock on the gate and the main door. I waited until I was sure he was in the elevator before punching the button to bring him up to the apartment.

I was alone. Brent had already gone to the college, quite upbeat. He always liked Thursdays. He had only two classes and could usually get home early. And he was really happy for me because I was "unofficially" back on the case. He was sure that a breakthrough was imminent. And he was quite confident by now that no one at the college thought he was a suspect. As far as everyone was concerned, he was keeping up a brave front, having just lost the woman of his dreams. Brent felt safe in his college closet.

The elevator door opened and Bear stepped out, in sock feet with his boots in his hands. "Where are my slippers?" he grinned.

"In the basket. No one has worn them since you were last here."

I left Bear looking in the slipper basket and waited for him in the living room. I had already prioritized our day's itinerary. But before I did another thing, I wanted to find out about that Polaroid.

"I bin thinking, Kev," he shouted from the hall. "How do you get up here if you lose your elevator key?"

"Well, if Brent has lost his as well, I call Martha. She lives down on Beach Avenue in a large apartment overlooking False Creek. She has a set of keys and knows the elevator code. Her name is registered with Alarmforce."

"Oh yeah. That's the security outfit who comes if there's an emergency. Right?" Bear padded into the living room, still in his socks. "Does she have keys too?"

"Yeah. They'd call her to get the keys and security codes."

"Sounds pretty complicated."

"Not really."

Why the great interest in my security?

"So you still see Martha, eh?" Bear looked at me quizzically.

"Sure. Once in a while. We still have lots in common, you know. Like five kids!" I wanted to get on with the day's agenda.

Bear stood with his hands behind his back. "So, what did ya want me up here fer anyways?"

"I want to see..."

Bear brought his right hand around and shoved a Polaroid in my face. "See whatcha make of this."

I looked intently at Nancy's dead face and recalled how she appeared when I saw her for the last time at the cabin: eyes closed as though in sleep.

"So, what d'ya see?" Around Nancy's head were five pictures. I studied them, but each was too small, too difficult to make out.

"My guess is that those pictures are different poses of Nancy. Do you have a magnifying glass?"

Bear whisked his left hand from behind his back, producing a floppy disk. "Put this in yer computer. Kev, since we're keepin' our partnership under wraps, so to speak, why don't we set up our own little operation center here? That's if ya don't mind."

"Come on." We both went to my den. Bear smiled when he saw that I'd put up a story board, just like the one he had in the RCMP Conference Room, titled: "Mini-Operations Room." I had divided the board into four, labeling each with the same titles Bear used.

"Great minds," he beamed.

"Thought you'd like it. Now let's get to work." I slipped the disk into the A drive and clicked a few buttons. The screen filled with an enlarged version of the Polaroid.

"Now whatcha make of that?"

I looked at this blowup, and could now see clearly the smaller pictures. They were Polaroids, each showing a progressively greater degree of terror in Nancy's eyes. My eyes lingered on one of them. "Wait a minute. This one." I pointed to the one on the extreme right.

"Thought you'd be interested in that one." Bear was standing behind me, puffing excitedly.

"My God!" I could feel the hair on the back of my neck prickle.

"Yeah. My God, all right. Click on that picture."

I did as Bear suggested. A dotted box formed around the image of the face and it enlarged before my eyes to fill the screen. It wasn't nearly as clear as Nancy's face in the original Polaroid, but it was unmistakably *not* a picture of Nancy. "Push F4," Bear huffed. Slowly, clarity came to the face, as if an invisible artist was filling in details. Within a minute, we were looking at a face that was incredibly clear and detailed.

This woman's head was in the same position as Nancy's was in the original Polaroid, her brown hair styled in a bouffant, her face identically made up, her thumb stuck in her mouth. "We're looking at another victim?"

"Ya betcha."

"And look at that shade of hair. I'll bet anything one of those pubic hairs in the braid we found belongs to this woman."

"I think you're right, Kev."

"We do have a serial killer. That's proof. And he sent the Polaroid to Franny McGhie himself. The bastard is bragging."

Bear prompted, "Click on her nose." I did so and watched the screen go black before this second woman's face came into fuzzy focus. It was not blown up, but the actual size of a Polaroid. "Look more closely around her head."

I stared at the screen. There was something like a halo around her entire head. I leaned closer. "Christ! There are more pictures around her head. Exactly as they were around Nancy's."

Bear nodded. "And?"

"No, don't tell me." I looked more closely at the unfocused picture to the right of this poor woman. "What the hell? Don't tell me that one is of another victim." I clicked on this small fuzzy picture.

"Sorry, nothin' will happen. Our photo and computer boys are still workin' on the next step. Do ya realize how hard it was to enlarge that tiny picture to the right of Nancy's head and get what we jist seen? Now they're tryin' to enlarge that speck of a picture beside this here woman. It's gonna take them time. But I'm bettin' on one thing fer sure. There's no tellin' how many women this guy has done in."

"How come we haven't heard about these other victims?"

"Abby's been doin' a search on CPIC today."

"Refresh my memory. What's CPIC?"

Bear was quick to explain. "That's another computer-generated retrieval system like PIRS. Stands for Canadian Police Information Centre. Abby had to get in touch with Ottawa to run through the MO on CPIC. That, too, apparently came up blank. She's gonna be visitin' the ViCLAS section this week. They're gettin' more personnel any day now."

"What the hell's the use in using a dumb machine to find a live killer who's obviously still lurking around Vancouver mocking us? Where was the photo posted from?"

"The main branch of the Vancouver Post Office on Georgia Street. Right downtown here."

"Well, let's do some legwork." I went over to the bulletin board and pulled off a sheet of names and addresses and handed it to Bear. "The first lot of makeup artists I want us to interview are those who work for all the TV series that are shooting here. They are generally local people. The film companies usually bring in their own makeup artists for a one-off and then they are out of here."

"What the heck is a 'one-off'?"

"Just film talk, Bear, a one-off is a single movie as opposed to a TV series. You know, Bear, Nancy's mystery man had to have been in Vancouver for the whole month prior to her murder."

So, Chief, where to first?"

Chief? I didn't correct Bear. *If it makes him comfortable thinking I am still his boss, who am I to stop him.* "I phoned a friend of mine at the IATSE office. There are twenty TV series currently being filmed in BC. She filled me in on the ones shooting today in and around Vancouver and which, to the best of her knowledge, have male makeup artists."

"Shouldn't we be lookin' at females too? After all, we're lookin' for a man who impersonates women."

"Of course. You're right."

"And," Bear was on a roll, "did ya ask her which of the productions were *not* shootin' during the murder weekend? We shouldn't be wastin' our time visitin' twenty productions."

"As a matter of fact, I did."

"And?" Bear gave me a piercing look.

"And, she said that only one was actually shooting that particular weekend."

"Which one?"

"*Viper*. But some of the shows might have two makeup artists and one of them was off on the weekend. So, I think that we should visit them all anyway. Is that okay with you?"

He nodded. "So which ones do you want us t'go t'today?"

OUR FIRST STOP was the *Poltergeist* location. By the time we got to the South-West Marine flats, Bear had changed his tune about visiting the shoots. He was filled with the anticipation of seeing a real live filming with real live actors.

When we parked across the way from half a dozen tell-tale trailers that so often monopolized many Vancouver streets, no one was in sight except a security guard.

"Where is everyone?" I asked.

"They're in full gear down on the flats. Who are you looking for?"

Bear interrupted, "We're on special assignment. RCMP business."

"There's the AD over there. Why not speak to him?"

"AD?"

"Assistant Director," I told Bear as we walked over to a young man with a walkie-talkie clipped on his head.

"RCMP," Bear flashed his badge, "we're here to interview yer makeup artists."

"Wait here and I'll get her for you," offered the AD.

"Her?" I was surprised. "Is there only one makeup artist working today?"

"That's right. Didi." I had been misinformed by my IATSE friend but union offices are busy places and people do move around from one job to another on short notice.

Curious about the whole scene, Bear whispered to me, "Since we're here, we might as well see how they make the spooks appear."

"Special effects," said the AD. "The smoke and spirits are all added down in LA by our computer technology department long after the scenes here have been shot."

"No kiddin'."

"It's true."

We stood for several minutes watching Derek Le Lint and Helen Shaver run over the peaceful flats as if they were being pursued by demons from hell. They repeated the same run three more times. "This is borin'," said Bear. "I'm gonna look fer this Didi gal. I'll see if she's a he. I kin tell."

I caught up to him going towards a canopy under which there were several canvas-backed chairs with the stars' names on them. One man was standing there, watching the shoot.

"Who's in charge here?" blurted Bear.

"The director. But no one disturbs Adolph while he's working." This man dripped contempt for us as well as for Adolph. "If you're the extras, you're supposed to be waiting under that tree over there."

"Police business." Bear flashed his badge.

"Oh, I'm sorry. I thought you were extras. I was going to say that you needed a new uniform. One that fits you."

By the look on his face, Bear was trying to figure out whether or not he'd been insulted.

"We wouldn't want to hold up the production," I whispered to Bear. Then I turned to the man. "When this scene is over, perhaps you might let us have a word with him. We're investigating a murder."

The man changed his attitude. "I'll get him for you." He walked over to the new setup and shadowed Adolph, trying to get his attention.

The two leads were now running into the arms of a motley crew of ghouls who were hanging in, around, and even under an enormous oak tree. The extras were all miked so that their screams, magnified for dramatic effect, helped Derek and Helen act terrified. Or at least, that seemed to be the idea. The scene wasn't working.

Adolph screamed, "Cut." He walked over to the two leads. "Darlings, do it again. You have to look as scared as squirty shit in this scene."

Two more takes and half an hour later, the director yelled, "Good job. Print it," and walked over to us. "My producer told me you're investigating a murder. How can I help you?"

"Besides givin' us a part in the next scene?" Bear laughed too long at his own joke. Adolph gave him a contemptuous look. "Jist kiddin'. I'm Sergeant Barry Spivic 'n this here's my assistant." I winced. "We have a few questions we'd like t'ask yer makeup person."

"My AD could have directed you to Didi. She's over there, powdering Derek." He pointed to the canopy. "Why don't you talk to her quickly so you can be on your way?" He disappeared among the extras.

As we walked over to the canopy, I whispered, "Bear, we're wasting our time here."

"Ya think?"

"Take a look at her." Didi was standing on a box, powdering the star of *Poltergeist*. Didi was no more than forty-five inches tall.

"I see what ya mean. She's a hot-lookin' chick but she certainly ain't no man no matter which way you cut it." Bear did an abrupt about-face. "Let's get to the *Madison* location. On the way, would ya mind if we pull into McDonald's for a couple of Big Macs and a coke?"

THE *MADISON* AD let us into the Lord Byng gym, saying, "Come on in. The more the merrier. I hope you don't mind if the camera catches you every once in a while."

"Not at all. Not at all," beamed Bear, trying hard to suss out the cameras.

The gym was a jumping place. Half of the high school's population was in the bleachers, screaming and cheering on two basketball teams who were going at it with ferocious intensity.

"We wanna see yer makeup person," shouted Bear over the din.

"You don't need to be made up for this show. Only the leads wear full makeup."

"No. No," I interjected. "We're investigating a murder and need to speak to your makeup artist."

"Oh." He looked more attentive. "He's under that set of bleachers." He pointed to the left.

When we finally squeezed through the network of pipes and grid-work holding up the stressed bleachers, we spotted the small makeup space. One of the leads, Sarah Strange, was being touched up by a burly, hairy man.

The din from the basketball game was deafening.

"Are you the only one doin' makeup for this show?" yelled Bear.

"That's right," an Italian accent, "and they *don't pay me enough*."

"What about for that gang on top of us?" Bear pointed above our heads.

"*No*. It's not necessary. I just do the leads."

"So you are the only makeup artist on *Madison*?" I yelled.

"That's right!"

"You've been *very helpful*. Thank you."

"There ain't any way that guy can pass as a woman. Did you see the hair on him?" Bear swaggered back to his cruiser.

"You're right, Bear. You'd make a better lookin' chick than he would." I chuckled at the thought of Bear in drag.

"What the hell are ya talkin' about?" Bear turned on the ignition.

After a few minutes of silence, Bear said, "Kev?"

"Huh?"

"We're not doin' so good, are we?"

"No." I was feeling a sense of panic that my suggestion of interviewing all the makeup artists working in Vancouver was ridiculous. *Damn it to hell.* Gumshoeing used to work well for me; now, in this computer age, it all seemed archaic.

"What?" Bear sensed my distress.

"We have a serial killer on our hands and we're pissing away valuable time trotting from one TV location to another. Maybe you should drop me off and work by yourself." I was feeling my age. *I should be home with my feet up instead of trying to track down a maniac.*

"Not to worry, Kev. We're eliminatin' suspects. That's all part of the process."

I smiled over to Bear. "I do have this gut feeling that we are on the right track."

"We should hurry to the *Millennium* set. North Van's a long way off 'n we should get there before the dinner break is over. We might as well chow down with'em while we're interviewin'. What d'ya say?" Bear gave me a wink.

"Might as well."

Siren screaming, we pulled up to the North Van studios at the start of the dinner break. We walked over to the crew's table in the commissary. Bear boomed, "Who's in charge here?"

"I suppose I am.   I'm the producer of *Millennium*."   The powerfully built woman in Ray Ban sunglasses extended her hand. Bear didn't take it.

"Step over here, will ya? My partner 'n me have bin visitin' TV shoots all day. We're checkin' out a few people in connection with a murder that took place not too far from here. You mighta seen me on the six o'clock news talkin' about the Henderson case at Swallow Lake."

"Yes. A horrible tragedy. What can I do for you?"

"I'd like ya to let us talk to yer makeup people."

"We only have one working our show, along with a hairstylist. That's the usual number most TV companies have under contract. The actors are brought in on a rotating schedule so that Mikey — he's our makeup man — can get them all ready for the shoot."

"Is that Mikey sittin' over there in the white smock?"   Bear pointed to the table.

"Yes, he's the one at the end of the table, across from the two empty chairs."

"Hm. To make our interrogation more natural-like, maybe we can git a plate of food 'n join him. What d'ya think?"

"Be my guest. I'll take you to the canteen."

We accompanied the very helpful producer. I picked up some salad and a roll. Bear went up to the two chefs in the canteen and proclaimed, "Gimme the works."

We took our food over to the table and sat across from Mikey.

"So, I understand you're the makeup guy." Bear got out the last word before he stuffed his mouth with half a pork chop.

"I thertainly am if you pleath." *Oh no.* Mikey was a lisping queen and instead of avoiding words that drew attention to his lisp, he enjoyed saying ever sibilant and fricative/s/.

Bear turned to me. "Why don't ya do the questionin'?"

"Great food they serve you guys, eh, Mikey?"

"Yeth. It'th alwayth thwell. Tho, what ith it you want to athk me."

I'm a good judge of character and I could tell this will-of-the-wisp was no killer. "We're having a little chat with all the makeup artists in the Lower Mainland." I added, "Just routine work. I know you're a busy man. Thanks for your help, but we won't need to delay you any longer."

Mikey minced out of the commissary.

Bear leaned over to me, sucking a large dollop of gravy from off his tie. "Now that's what gives homos a bad wrap."

"You think? I thought he wath rather thweet."

Bear gave me a dirty look, and I deserved it. But I must confess back in the old days when I was growing up, I thought that all effeminate men were homosexuals. How wrong I was. Hell, now I've seen muscle-bound, leather-and-chain gays that would make Spivic look like Pooh Bear.

A MARTINI WAS waiting for me when I got upstairs. Brent had been watching for my return from the kitchen balcony.

"Long day, darl?"

"Uh huh. I'm beat."

"Any leads?"

"A bust." I decided not to tell Brent that Nancy was now one of many victims of the same killer. I was too bushed to talk.

"Want a nap?"

"Thought you'd never ask."

Chapter
Twenty-Four

THK SAT GLUED to the six o'clock news, finger poised over the Record button. When the anchor said, "And now to Anne Wyner," he pushed the button. "So what's the latest on the Henderson case? We haven't heard much lately."

"Yes, that's right. The RCMP investigating team has been quiet recently. I just got off the phone with Sergeant Spivic and he said that there wasn't much to report."

"Not much to report!" THK screamed. "What the fuck are they waiting for? Another..." He stopped short and listened to the media officer.

"Sergeant Spivic told me that he visited three TV production companies today, to make enquiries."

"Which production companies?"

"I'm not at liberty to say, but he assured me that things are progressing exactly as planned."

"The lazy bastard probably didn't want to drive all the way out to the Fraser Valley to check out the *X-File* shooting." THK laughed loudly. *Now, when are we filming back in the Vancouver area? Monday, I think. Do I feel one of my terrible headaches coming on?* He stopped to listen to Anne Wyner.

"They do, however, have a witness—a neighbor—and a description of the killer's car."

"A witness!" he yelled at the screen.

"What's the make?" enquired the news anchor.

"You know I can't comment on that at this time. But I can say for the record: Sergeant Spivic believes he is now dealing with a serial killer. Over to you."

He snapped the Stop button and plunged the tape out of the VCR, throwing it on the fifth shelf of an already full bookcase. Paranoia consumed him. "Witness! What are they talking about? There was *no* neighbor. I checked!" he screamed. "I'll be revenged on the whole pack of you." Exhausted, he fell onto his cot.

He lay perfectly still, eyes darting around his sanctuary.

The room had no operative windows whatsoever. During his original renovations, he had carefully covered up the only window with drywall. From the outside, the window opening looked normal, filled with a tightly closed Venetian blind. The only ventilation in the room came from the adjoining bathroom vent, so the space was often uncomfortably hot and had a stench that reeked of his favorite smells. He always felt at home in his sanctum. Safe. Secure in the knowledge that no one would ever know where he was.

From his cot, he could see the contents of his entire room: his collection of memorabilia. He spotted a biography of his idol, Ed Gein. *Silence of the Lambs* didn't do justice to Ed's wonderful achievements, although he admired the performance of Anthony Hopkins in the movie version. He'd love to have had a juicy morsel of Jodi. *But she's spoiled herself for me.* There was a space left on the same shelf for another biography: Thomas Henry King. He smiled, thinking of what he wanted to appear on the cover of his bio: "Hannibal Lecter applauds Thomas Henry King's unique productions!" But today, even thinking that thought didn't turn him on. He still felt too ticked off. "What the hell are they talking about a witness for? There was no witness!"

He smiled. "I know. They're wanting me to go back to Swallow Lake and look for this non-existent witness. Well," he screamed, "you're not going to trap me with that trick!" His eyes wandered to the wall of his accomplishments: more than a hundred Polaroids of his victims.

His breathing became normal as he lay on his cot, his safe spot since childhood. His mother never came into his bed. He could do whatever he wanted there: dream dreams, make plans. Slowly his hands fell to the sides of his cot; he let his fingers run along the cold steel frame. It was refreshing. This bed offered him a sense of security that nothing or no one else in the world could ever give him. He had missed it when he was in Montreal, studying at the theatre school, and in England, working as a professional actor. He turned his head and let his cheek feel the smooth satin pillowcase.

The scent of his childhood emanated from the bedding. The warmth of his body released the essence of masculinity that surrounded him, like a rare perfume. His sense of smell was acute. He drank in memories of his youth from his multi-stained mattress, the pungent sweetness of his mid-teen sweat after a hard workout, the lifelong caviar of smells he splashed on his stained satin pillowcase. Who wouldn't find sanctuary in such a bed?

His eyes darted around his sanctum, stopping momentarily on the heavy Shakespearean tapestry hiding his closet. If he concentrated really hard, he could smell the blood that lingered within its depths. The delicious tingle in his nostrils conjured up death, killing, acting, brilliance. He looked at his desk to the immediate right of his bed. It was heaped with his editing equipment, video tapes, papers, notebooks, and his ancient typewriter. Reaching over to stroke his old Underwood upright, he recalled his fourth-grade science assignment. His mother had bought the typewriter for him when he "simply had to have it." He remembered how his teacher had allowed the class to choose an insect and write a report on it. He chose the praying mantis. It fascinated him that the female would eat the male after intercourse. He wrote his report as a little play and when he read it to the class, he took the parts of Mr. Praying Mantis and his wife, Mrs. Praying Mantis. He scared the living shit out of the wimpy kids who were watching him bug-eyed. But his happy memory soon soured. *I thought my bitch mother was going to eat me up the first time she sucked me off!*

After one particular school production when he was thirteen years old, she pretended to his teachers to be proud of her son's emerging talent, but he knew she hated every minute, watching her son sharing himself with others. On the way home, she talked nonstop and well into the night about the dangers lurking in theatres. "Theatre is filled with queers, Thomas. You don't want to be caught in a dressing room with one of them. They'll cornhole you the instant you bend over to tie your shoes. And, Tommy, now that you're thirteen, never wear tights. If a director asks you to wear tights, you tell me. I won't let you be in a play where you have to wear tights. All those deviants in the audience will be turned on just looking at your strong, athletic body. And that basket of yours. You make sure you keep your basket covered at all times when you are out in public. I don't want any of those lowlifes trying to touch you there." Then she looked at him and asked, "You know what I'm talking about, don't you, Thomas Henry King?"

"No, Mother."

She slapped his face hard, screaming, "Don't you ever call me *Mother*; I'm your Mommie." Then she reached out her hand and squeezed his testicles. "These are your family jewels." She then squeezed his penis as well. "That's part of your basket." He winced at the pain. She let go, but droned on. "Don't you ever allow any man to touch any part of your basket, you understand. When you meet a nice lady, you can let her touch your privates. And, Thomas?"

"Yes, Mommie."

"Come over here." He walked hesitantly to his kneeling mother. She undid his fly and took out his little penis. "I want to show you what faggots will do to you if they catch you alone."

Afterwards, the terrified boy ran to his room and crawled into his cot, pulling his blanket protectively around him.

Without lifting his head from the pillow, THK rolled his eyes to his Media Wall. *Look at those measly two articles that Franny McGhie wrote. And I had to help the bitch with the second one. Glad she printed my letter to the editor.* "Exit pursued by a Bear." *Ha!* He stared at the ceiling. It too was covered, but with photos of great British stage actors. "Faggots," he screamed. *Why the fuck do the queers get the best parts in theatre? Answer: They suck their way to the top.* He laughed disgustedly at his joke.

"I've got to get out of here. I need a chaser." But his thoughts consumed him...

In high school, the drama courses became his escape. He could get away from the sad, confused, schizophrenic life of Thomas Henry King, and enter into the life of whatever character he was asked to take on.

Shakespeare's great villains had become his only true companions: Macbeth, Iago, Richard III, Iachimo, Claudius — all became his best friends. He knew he would play all of them on the best stages in England. As well as the much wimpier heroes like Hamlet and Romeo. After all, he was destined to become the greatest actor in the world.

As a special treat for the cast of *The Tempest*, when he played Ferdinand, his high-school drama teacher, Mr. Goldman, arranged for a theatre outing to Vancouver to see the professional production of Shakespeare in the Tent's *As You Like It*. Tommy begged his mother to let him go. He told her that she was allowed to accompany the group. "Vancouver? I've never heard such a hideous suggestion in my life. You are never going to Vancouver. Even when I am dead, you are not going to Vancouver. Do you understand? Promise me that you will never go to Vancouver."

He stared intently at his mother's hissing tongue as she spewed out her venom. "Vancouver is homo town. The West End is filled with them. Thousands of queer men walk hand in hand there. Right on the streets. They'd take one look at a handsome boy like you and you'd be a goner. They'd make you one of them. That's what they do, you know. So you always have to be on your guard. There is no such thing as a good faggot. A good faggot is a dead faggot. Remember that, son. Promise me that you will never forget." He nodded. That night, she was almost inconsolable. He had to spend the entire night with her. This was a first; but not the last. Not the last by a long shot. For most of his last two years of high school, he would need to spend entire nights with his mother, away from his own cot, his safe place. *The cunt!*

THOMAS HENRY KING jumped up from his cot and stepped into his crotch-tight leather pants. "I need a chaser. Tonight. A fag, any fag, will stop my fucking headache."

Chapter
Twenty-Five

AFTER DOING NOTHING all weekend, I was frustrated as hell. At eight fifteen Monday morning, I stood by the intercom, waiting for Bear to buzz. *He said he'd be here at eight.* Today we were to visit *The X-Files* set, shooting conveniently nearby on Pendrell Street. Probably another waste of time.

The phone rang. "I'm sorry, Kev, but Joan wants to see me and Abby at nine. She wants a progress report, in writin'. I know I said I'd be at yer place first thing this mornin', but when Joan says jump, I say 'How high?'"

"Have you heard anything from the computer boys about the other blow-up?"

"They tell me that it wuzn't really clear enough to make much out. But there's no doubt. We're dealin' with a serial killer."

"Are you saying that the blow-up showed another new victim?"

"Ya betcha. They're sure of that. They can tell these things. Them lab guys had ta magnify that original tiny picture beside Nancy's head more and more and now they have a new one. It looked pretty blurred but when the artist got through with it, you know what we discovered?"

"To the right of that victim's head, I bet there was another photo of victim number three."

"Right again. We got an artist doin' a special whiz-bang drawin' of the third blow-up to help the computer boys. They're gonna have to blow that speck up even more and this artist is gonna fill in the details. I don't see how anyone's gonna make anything out o' that blur, but the artist says he's almost sure that there's enough color and shadows in that speck to indicate a fourth victim."

I yelled into the phone. "Why the hell haven't we heard about these other murders?"

"That's exactly what Joan will ask Abby and I in a few minutes. But Abby'll have an answer to satisfy her. I hope. She's been workin' at ViCLAS for the last three or four days. And she's linked up to VICAP."

"What the hell's VICAP?"

"The FBI uses VICAP, only it ain't as good as ViCLAS which

kind o' ticks them off. ViCLAS is winnin' world-wide attention. Australia, England, and lots of other European countries are hooked on Vancouver's system. I gotta run now. Chow."

"So when will you be here?"

"I'll give you a call when I'm leavin'."

"Do you want me to go over to *The X-Files* shoot and check things out? Unofficially, of course. It's only a few blocks away." I held my breath.

"Sure. Why not? Ya can hang out there. Pretend to be an eager fan 'r somethin'."

"Good idea, Bear. I'll do that."

"Good luck. I gotta git to that report or Joan'll have my neck."

IT WAS A soggy Vancouver day. The slow drizzle made life difficult for the technicians. They had covered the front of Scully's "Pendrell" apartment with yards of tarp to ensure that the steps out front would remain dry for the shoot. They'd laid hundreds of feet of electric cable from their generator to several key lights and two huge flood lights. They'd set up two enormous reflectors. The camera was set in place under its own tent.

When they snapped on the lights, the apartment glowed hot white. "Set and lights ready," someone yelled. "We're ready for the stand-ins." The cameraman and director took their positions for a placement rehearsal with the stand-ins to make sure the lighting and entire *mise en scène* worked. Surprisingly, when the stand-ins walked down the steps of the apartment, I thought they were the original leads. Amazing look-alikes. The director moved them up and down the steps. Sat the Mulder double down on one of the lower steps while the Scully double leaned against the railing.

The cameraman scowled. "Looks a bit hot on Scully. I need to use a couple of filters on her key light. Don't forget, the day is supposed to be drizzly."

In a few minutes, while everyone hung around waiting in the drizzle, the cameraman declared, "Yes. It looks good now. Bring in the smoke machine."

The best boy started to pump the area with smoke. Then they waited for it to settle a bit. When the atmosphere in front of the apartment looked like the same miserable atmosphere that surrounded their make-believe world, the AD announced, "We're ready." Show business is all illusion.

The director lifted his head from the eyepiece of the camera and smiled. "Congrats, guys." The crew beamed. You could tell that this company worked together like a well-oiled machine. And you could also tell that the local crew members were coming to terms with the fact that they were nearing the end of their contract with *The*

X-Files. The media was a buzz with stories about this award-winning series moving to Los Angeles. And the crew knew that their days were numbered, although nothing official had been said on the set.

"Bring on the talent."

The stand-ins disappeared along with a tall black girl who ran into the apartment with them. After a couple of minutes, she ran back out and huddled under someone's umbrella. Hugging herself to keep warm, this amazing beauty looked like an uprooted tropical flower.

The real Mulder and Scully opened the apartment door and walked out. *Brent will die of envy when I tell him who I saw today.* I hadn't noticed how extremely handsome Duchovny was in the flesh. *Even I could go for him.* The director put his actors through the same paces that he'd done with the stand-ins, but the stars made every move, every gesture appear natural. *That's why they're the stars.* They spoke their lines with the ease of pros, communicating each nuance. I could barely hear, but I was drawn into the scene. I could see why Brent was hooked on *The X-Files* and why he thought David Duchovny was such a great actor. He made it all look effortless.

"Let's shoot this thing now," the director announced. "You're both ready?"

The actors nodded and went into the apartment.

The director called, "Camera."

"Camera rolling," came the response.

"Sound."

"Sound rolling."

"Action."

Mulder and Scully walked out and, if possible, did an even better job than they had done a few minutes earlier in rehearsal.

The director yelled, "Cut. We got it in one take! Take a rest while we do the next set-up." The actors walked back into the apartment like the casual, confident stars they are.

The director asked to see the replay of the scene on the monitor. While the director watched the monitor intently, I sensed the make-up girl looking at me. Sure enough, her large black eyes were sizing me up. The director broke the moment. "What's that on Mulder's forehead?"

The cinematographer pushed the replay button. Everyone tried to see the monitor. Soon, the director groaned, "Shit! We need to reshoot the scene."

Mulder and Scully came out of the apartment. "What's up?" They spoke as one.

The director answered, "There's a tiny smudge on Mulder's forehead. Looks like hair dye." Then he shouted, "Makeup!" From under the umbrella, the young woman, long hair braided with gold beads, bounced into the action. She carried a small makeup kit.

"Let's go inside, hon," she said in a deep sexy voice to Mulder. "I'll repair de damage in a jiffee." She dashed into the apartment, two steps at a time.   Under her high-collared, multi-colored crocheted shawl, I noticed she was wearing a mini-skirt and high boots.

Mulder followed. He hit the door with the butt of his palm as he mouthed several expletives. "Dammit, Monique, where the hell is...?"

More waiting around. After a good fifteen minutes, Mulder appeared. "How's this?" The lights came on and the cameraman focused on his face. The director looked at the monitor.

"Great. Clean. Strong. You look fabulous. Now let's get this baby in the can."

Eight takes later, the scene was getting worse instead of better. The tension was electric. I wondered who would be the first to crack.

"Scene 146, Take 9." The clapper snapped.

The actors came out of the door for the ninth time and immediately Mulder muttered, "Damn. I've got water on my face."

"Makeup!" yelled the director.

Out bounded the makeup girl, hands covered in clear latex gloves, powder puff in hand. This was the sixth time she had powdered down the actor. He gave her a killer look and stormed into the apartment, leaving her stranded there, not knowing what to do. I sensed the girl would have been happy if the earth opened and swallowed her.

"Okay, everyone," the director announced, "let's have a coffee break." He went into the apartment, presumably to have a chat with his star. Everyone else under the canopy was obviously grateful. They popped open their umbrellas and trotted to the canteen trailer. Under the crowded canopy, keeping close to each other, they sipped their coffees and munched their donuts.

The makeup girl, wrapped in her shawl, collapsed on the apartment steps. She hugged her legs, buried her head between her knees, and began swaying back and forth. After a long minute, she lifted her head, beading me with her dark eyes. Giving me a little dejected smile, she buried her head once more. Obviously thinking that the whole unraveling of the shoot was her fault, she began chanting as she rocked back and forth again.

"Cheer up. It's only a TV show." I tried to lift her spirits.

Slowly she raised her head. I noticed a small gold nose ring through her left nostril. "Ya, but life's a beetch. Didja see de looks I got from off everee bodee?" She spoke with a strong Jamaican accent. "Dey cud be daggers stabbin' me heart."

"No, I think you're exaggerating."

"Yo' waz here. Watchin'. I seen yo' standin' under dat beeg brollee, keepin' yo'self warm. Yo' cud see dey all hate me fo' de delay."

"No, you mustn't think that. How long have you been doing makeup on this show?" I took out a piece of paper from my jacket and looked at it. "IATSE says that a Harry Le Roi is the makeup artist for *X-Files*."

"He used t'be. IATSE is allits behind in updatin' dere lists."

"My name is Kevin Porter. Yours is...?"

"Monique. Me Daddy loves dat name. He give me dat name on de night he made love to me Mommie. I dunno what he wudda called me if I turned out to be a boy baby."

"Monique, do you mind if I ask you a few questions?" I smiled, noticing three pierced ear rings through her right upper ear. She was startlingly memorable. Her thickly applied makeup enhanced her mahogany features perfectly. Her lips looked full but not large and contained specks of glitter that sparkled when she spoke.

"Whyd'ja wanna axt me questions, mon?" She reached into an inner pocket and pulled something that she started to chew. She gnawed on it savagely. Then waved it at me. "Wanna bite?"

"No, thanks."

"Yo' should try some. It's me daddy's jerkee." She took another bite and held out the remainder for me to take, shaking it in my face. To appease her I took the jerky and popped it in my mouth. It was surprisingly good. We chewed together for a few moments in silence, then, together, swallowed. "Whod'ja say yo' were again?"

"Well, to be honest, I'm an investigator and I'm looking for a man — probably an older man — who might be involved in a murder."

Monique shrieked and spat between her gloved fingers, bits of jerky flying. "Dat scares me, mistah. I dun't wanna talk about dat." She stood up, and stuck her hands in the deep pockets of her shawl. She hugged herself, wrapping the pockets tightly around her body. Then she began hopping from one foot to the other and moaning a kind of voodoo chant.

"It's okay. It's okay. Take it easy. I won't mention murder again."

She shrieked again, and again she spat between her gloved fingers, getting lipstick and spittle all over the latex glove, and resumed her chant. Some of the crew looked over at us, wondering what the hell I was saying to her.

"I promise, I won't mention that word again. But I must tell you, later today, you may have a visit from an RCMP officer who won't be so understanding. It might be better to answer my questions now and save yourself a lot of hassle."

She stood motionless. Looked directly into my eyes and purred, "Okay, mon. Axt all de questions yo' wanna." She sat on the steps again, leaning back on two of them and placing her left elbow on one of the steps.

"Who else does makeup for *The X-Files*?"

While looking at me with her large dark eyes, I could tell that—
under her shawl—she was slowly moving her right hand up and
down her thigh. "Dere iz jist me. I hafta do all de makeup. Usually
it's no problem. And it ain't nevah bin no problim, 'til t'day. Once't
dere made up, I jist hafta be ready t'powda dem down. Dat's why I
allits wear me gloves. I dun't wanna get powda on me hands." She
giggled.

"Makeup." The director was walking over to us with Mulder at
his side.

I quickly thanked Monique. "You've been very helpful."

"Maybe I kin see yo' afta we're finished shooting t'day, mon."
Eyes intently on mine, she whispered, "Follow me finger an' I'll
show yo' where t' meet me." Her long black finger poked through
one of the holes of her crocheted shawl. It pointed to the end trailer.
"Dat's me trailer ova dere," she cooed. "Six o'clock. Okay, mon?"

My face became hot. *She's propositioning me. Christ Almighty!* "I
don't think so, Monique, we have several more sets to visit today."
She licked her lips suggestively. Embarrassed as hell, I continued
babbling, "I think I'll be bushed by six o'clock. Ya, I think that will
be too late for..." The director and Mulder saved me.

"Monique, powder down Mr. Duchovny right away. This will be
the *last* take of this scene."

BEAR PICKED ME up at noon and we headed to the sets of *The
Outer Limits, Viper, Police Academy, The Sentinel,* and *Stargate,* all TV
productions that were being shot today in busy Vancouver.

"Any leads from *The X-Files?*" asked Bear.

"No. My contact at IATSE led me astray again. No male makeup
artist there. Only a sexy young chick. She kept coming on to me."

"No shit!"

"It's true."

"Maybe I better interrogate her. Sexy-lookin', ya say?"

"Very."

"How could *you* tell? You don't like women."

"Don't forget I was married for twenty-eight years. I can still
appreciate a woman with all the bits in the right places."

"She was stacked, eh?"

"You can say that again. You can't beat a beautiful Jamaican
woman." I caught Bear's reaction. It showed in the way he twitched
his nose in scorn. Bear grew up a bigot.

*I'll have to enlighten him one of these days. He's going to have to
recognize and appreciate diversity. For Andy's sake.* "And she wears a
nose ring."

"Christ Almighty. Why do these young people today hafta
humiliate their bodies?"

"It's a passing phase. In a few years it'll be something else. You'll see."

"I sure as hell hope so. So, where to first?" Bear no longer thought of meeting Monique. "*Outer Limits.*"

A useless visit. Totally non-productive. Same for our visit to the *Stargate* set. On the way to the next shoot, we babbled on, rehashing what we already knew about the case until we arrived at the gates of the Bridges Studios. I was sure we had been barking up our own arses and this visit was going to be another waste of time.

THE FIRST THING THK did when he got into his sanctuary was take out the black, shiny contact lenses and meticulously place them in their container. He took off the wig and threw it into the garbage bag that was on his cot. Then he unhooked the simulated pierced rings from his nose and ears and put them in his jewelry box. He sat on the bed and pulled off the high boots. Standing, he took off the bulky woolen shawl and threw the lot into the garbage bag.

He ran into his bathroom and looked in the mirror at his well-proportioned, buxom body and smiled. "Yo' really went fer me, din't yo', Kevvie. I cud see yo'r eyes tryin' t'get a good look at me bubbies an' I know yo' were itchin' to git a look at me black pom-pom, weren't yo'? Still swing both ways, mon?" He peeled off the mini-skirt and tight tank top and walked into his room to throw them into the bag. Then he squeezed out of the one-piece bustier. He did not throw this beautifully padded undergarment away but hung it up carefully in the closet. *I spent too much time and money on this little number.* Finally he ripped off a pair of sheer gold lamé pantyhose, then the chocolate-brown tights, exposing his white-clean, hairy legs. *No point in wasting makeup on my legs and there's no fuckin' way I'm gonna shave my legs!* He tossed them in the bag and tied a double knot with the plastic ends. He threw the bag deep in the closet. It landed on top of the other similar bags, each filled with special disguises. Some semen-stained. Some bloodied. All containing cherished memories.

The brown and white naked body walked into the bathroom. He looked at himself in the mirror. Face, neck, and hands up to elbows in lush chocolate brown, the exact shade of the smudge deliberately left on poor DD's forehead. Torso and legs, peaches-and-cream white.

He smiled. *My cock is a red hard poker.* Convulsing in laughter, he shouted, "Get it?" Then he made eye contact with his reflection in the mirror, "Poke *her!*" and dissolved into gales. He had lost all composure. He became relentlessly talkative as he relived his exciting day, changing voices and accents with ease.

"When I saw you in the crowd, Kevvie, I had to do something to keep you around. I wanted to get you alone. And it worked. I am really brilliant."

DD had been ready to kill little Monique when he found out he had to reshoot the scene, saying "Dammit, Monique. Where the hell is Harry?"

"He's got de headache, mon. I'm his sub for de day."

"Put on some gloves, then. You must have some dirt on your fingers. I don't want any smudges on my face again."

"Are yo' prejudiced against us Blacks? Do yo' tink us Blacks are dirty?"

He was engrossed in replaying his magnificent performance. *I looked so angry when I placed my hands on my hips and gave DD a threatening look that he wouldn't soon forget. That look shut him up good.*

And every time he opened his mouth to act the scene, I made a movement and gave him another killer look. I could tell he lost his concentration, which as far as I'm concerned ain't much.

"I jest loved disruptin' de whole shootin' schedule an' makin' it look like DD wuz t'blame." He hooted as Monique. Watched himself laugh. And suddenly stopped.

When the director finally called for a break, which I knew he'd do to protect the feelings of his no-talent star, I had my chance to be alone with Mr. Faggoty ex-Chief Inspector Kevin Porter. And when he ate a piece of me Daddy's jerkee, I nearly came in me panties. "Mm. Mm." He jist loved *dat jerkee.* He roared with laughter.

He stepped into the shower, delirious with thoughts of his day's achievements. After a few minutes of massaging his entire body with soap, he began to hum contentedly a slow Jamaican chant, occasionally interspersing it with, "Gudbye, Monique-ee. Luvlee Monique-ee." He was enjoying seeing the brown soapy water running clear. He was suddenly Lady Macbeth. "A little water clears us of this deed; / How easy is it then!" And then he convulsed, "Out damn spot!" His laughter stopped instantly.

A red light turned on in the bathroom and a buzzer activated. Straight away, he became subdued. He stared at himself in the mirror, his body still splotched with brown soapy makeup. Turning off the shower, he hissed, "Shit! She's home." Whenever his wife came home unexpectedly and he hadn't enough time to make it to their bedroom, he stayed in his sanctum until she left or, if it was late at night, fall asleep. He could always check her whereabouts. He'd lift up the stained picture of his mother, The Big C, which hung on the common wall of the bedroom. He had drilled two small holes through the wall so that he could see their bed and part of the living room through the doorway. When his wife fell asleep, he'd slip out of his sanctum and slide into bed beside her. She'd never know when he had arrived home. Lucky he had erratic work hours.

He sat down in the tub, hugging his knees and rocking slowly back and forth. To pass the time, he began to recite all of Edgar's lines from *King Lear* while he was naked on the heath. "Poor Tom is a cold."

Chapter
Twenty-Six

BY MONDAY NIGHT, after we left the last of five different TV shoots, I was totally disheartened. There was only one guy, who worked on *Viper*, that might have been a possibility. But after questioning him on his whereabouts at the time of the murder, he produced an iron-clad alibi. The director had had a special weekend shoot from September Twenty-fifth to Twenty-seventh. The crew received double time, and the makeup artist was on deck for the entire three days, freshening up a large cast, powdering them down throughout the shoots, and hanging around the rest of the time. The director, along with a dozen others, corroborated his story.

As far as all the other details of the case, Bear and everyone else in the North Van Detachment was leaving me out in the cold. Bear was tight-lipped when he picked me up, answering my questions with a laconic "yep" or "nope." Something was up.

"What did Joan and you talk about?"

"Nothin' much."

"Have you found the Toyota yet?"

"Nope."

"How are the blowups of the Polaroid coming along?"

"Slow."

All day, I tried to fish a little more info out of him, but I didn't get so much as a nibble. I was so tired of biting back insults that I was glad when he pulled up at the apartment.

When I got upstairs, I called, "Hi." I heard the TV. I got into my slippers and walked into the living room.

Brent was bolt upright in his lazyboy, engrossed in watching the six o'clock news. He held the remote control in his hand. "Hi." He looked ashen. "I've recorded a segment for you."

"What about?"

"A murder of one of our sisters." Brent often referred to gay men as "sisters." I always found that term hard to comprehend. It never really made sense to me. Another gay thing that hets don't understand. My god. I am using *hets* for heterosexuals. I'd heard it plenty of times, but never used it before.

"Anyone we know?"

"Bill Richmond." I looked blank. "You've met him before lots of times. At Numbers." I still couldn't place him. "About fifty-five. Six foot. Distinguished. Looked a lot like you. He beat you at pool about a month ago."

"Oh, yes. William." I looked keenly at Brent.

He looked down. A poignant pause. "Okay," he spoke quietly. "I fucked him."

"I remember. You told me. It's all right, sweetie. It was before we met."

"And it was only once. You know me and mature men, and..."

"...the opportunity came up and you took it." Another pause. "So...he's been killed."

"Horribly." Brent rewound the tape and pushed Play.

TWENTY-FOUR HOURS earlier and wearing his come-fuck-me leather pants, Thomas Henry King waited behind a tree in one of the favorite gay pick-up spots in Stanley Park. He watched for someone, anyone to pass by. *Sunday at dusk. Ah, I'll definitely find my chaser here.* He was in a dangerous mood because his last opportunity to kill a fag had failed miserably and he was frustrated because the media hadn't glorified him enough. He didn't want his name in the paper, of course, but he needed recognition. A chaser would help ease the pain in his head, the tension in his groin. As he waited behind the tree, he quoted the "Come, let me clutch thee" speech. He had invited his favorite murdering companion, Macbeth, to be with him tonight. To be a part of the kill. When THK sensed movement in the distance, he smiled in anticipation and stopped reciting. "Ah."

Down the path, he saw a cyclist, pedaling fast. An older man, in cycling gear. *One of those fucking tight fruity spandex outfits and a God Almighty rainbow helmet.* "Ah, my nightcap hath come."

Two seconds before the cyclist passed, THK bolted out onto the path. The cyclist swerved to avoid the young man who had just performed a forward flip and landed on his side.

THK had rehearsed the fall several times that afternoon and was convinced that it would look real to any passing cyclist. Timing is everything for an actor.

The older man came running back. "I'm sorry, buddy. Are you okay?"

Still on the ground, he groaned a little — for effect — and struggled up.

"Here. Give me your hand."

"No. I'm okay, Biker-Man. But you scared the shit out of me." He laughed good-naturedly.

"Ditto. You came out of nowhere." He looked more closely at the young man. "Are you sure you're okay?"

"Yeah. No harm done." He felt his groin, rubbing it gently,

which wasn't wasted on Biker-Man. "I better be on my way." THK walked a few paces and turned; as he expected, the older man was still looking at him. He let his gaze drop obviously, approvingly to the older man's crotch, then looked up suggestively. They both smiled. *He's the one!*

Walking deliberately off the path and into the trees, he could hear Biker-Man maneuvering his bike through a thicket and locking it to a small tree. *I knew that old queen would follow me.* He stood and watched him for a minute, taking off his helmet and strapping it to his handlebars and then taking out a comb from his pocket and combing his silver hair.

THK snapped a branch to catch Biker-Man's attention. *I knew the old fruit would follow a young, good-looking, raven-haired man like me. Now, let's go deeper into the woods.*

Every once in a while THK changed directions because there were other fags in the shadowy forest. Solitary wanderers or a couple *in flagrante delicto.*

He caught glimpses of the older man following slowly, carefully, excitedly. Now and again, Biker-Man seemed to lose the track but he found it again each time THK provided a deliberate movement. He had to make sure that his nightcap was convinced that this young stud really wanted him and was certain that he'd soon be in for a sensuous interlude.

Once THK found the exact spot he was looking for, away from any unexpected intruders, he stopped and waited in the small enclosure where three huge trees had co-existed for hundreds of years, creating a near-perfect place for an unobserved quickie.

When the older man finally came into the secluded hiding place, THK eyed him and said, "Hi, again." He flashed him one of his to-die-for smiles. "Welcome to my kingdom. My name's Dick."

"Is that short for..."

Christ, not that same tired response. Why can't any of these fags come up with something original? "It's not short, I assure you." *I assure you.* On cue, Biker-Man laughed lasciviously. THK grinned. "What's your name?"

He hesitated. THK knew that this answer would be one of his last words he'd ever speak — and it would be a lie. "Joseph."

"May I..."

"What?"

"You'll think I'm silly."

"No. Not at all. What were you going to ask me?"

"Well, I wondered if I could call you Daddy?"

Another hesitation. THK mouthed "Pleez." *Joseph* shrugged. "Why not? If it turns you on, you can call me Beulah."

"Thank you. Let's see what you've got to offer, Daddy." He knelt in front of the man, hooked his thumbs onto his bike shorts, and with one jerk, pulled them down to his ankles, then stood and stepped back a pace, feigning enthusiasm. "Ohhh. Yummy. Get it harder for me. Pump it for me, Daddy." Obliging, *Joseph* obeyed, slowly, rhythmically. He soon became iron hard and was obviously eager for some real action. "Is this a dagger I see before me? You're gorgeous. I really like you, Daddy. Come, let me clutch thee..."

"Let me see your cock, too," *Joseph* suggested. "You're as hard as me. I can see you're aching to get out of your tight pants."

Thomas Henry King looked down, disturbed to see his own erection. He raised his head slowly; dark, evil eyes stared into *Joseph's*. THK growled menacingly. "See what you made me do, Daddy." He grabbed the man's head and, with a sudden startling twist, broke his neck. THK released the head as if it were a poisonous snake. The body fell backwards, landing soundlessly on centuries of well-rotted pine needles. "Sweetness is my revenge, Daddy."

Looking at *Joseph's* open mouth, he took out his own bulging pride and started working it. "If it were done, when 'tis done, then 'twere well / It were done quickly." He kept repeating Macbeth's words as he intensified his manipulation. "Quickly...quickly...quickly..."

AS BRENT AND I listened in silence to the Vancouver Police media officer, we became more and more depressed. "Bill Richmond, well-known Vancouver social worker, was found dead this morning, in Stanley Park. He had been murdered. Because he did not come home last night, his partner of fifteen years notified the police. The Vancouver Police organized a search party at dawn and, after finding Richmond's bike locked to a tree near a cycling path, they soon found his body close to one of the known cruising areas frequented by members of the gay community.

"The victim's neck had been broken, and by the condition of his body, it has been established that Richmond's death will become the latest gay-bashing statistic.

"The last reported homicide of a gay man in the Lower Mainland was eighteen months ago. The gay community will recall David Bellamy's heinous murder. Bellamy, a retired teacher who volunteered for AIDS Vancouver, was found washed up on the shores of English Bay with his dog, Oscar. The dog's leash was tied around both their necks." Anne Wyner took a breath and continued, "That case remains unsolved."

"Do you see a connection between these two murders? asked the news anchor.

"That question is a bit premature," answered Wyner. "We're combing the area of the Stanley Park murder scene for evidence. So far, we have found nothing." She looked directly into the camera and said, "Anyone who was in that area last night is asked to come forward for questioning."

"Two gay killings? Surely there's a connection, Anne," asked the anchor.

"Yes, that's true. These two murders were definitely committed by a homophobic killer. Their bodies had been mutilated after death."

"Mutilated? How?"

"Sorry, but that's classified. Over to you."

Brent asked, "What did she mean about the condition of his body?" I had heard that bit of news too and wondered what the killer had done to the victim's body to clearly indicate a homophobic murder.

Chapter
Twenty-Seven

THOMAS HENRY KING couldn't have been happier. At last, recognition. Details.

He was gluing the cover of the morning's *Scoop* on his Chaser Wall next to his closet: a full-page picture composed partly of a photograph of three massive Douglas firs. Cleverly superimposed within the sanctuary of the trees was an artist's rendition of a man's body. He traced his pinky finger across the headline which discreetly covered a significant part of the body: "GAY MAN MURDERED IN STANLEY PARK." Anyone with half an eye could see that the man was nude from his ankles up to his chest hairs. *Why didn't they put the title on the bottom so everyone could see my wonderful handiwork? Why not show his crotch area? There's nothing to see there. Not anymore! Fuckers! The police photograph would have been more impressive.* He laughed spit.

He picked up Franny McGhie's page two article. Luckily he had taken two papers out of the news box after putting in three quarters. He hated cutting out the article because he knew he was destroying the picture on the other side, but anything for posterity. He began gluing the story next to the cover page, and read the article for the tenth time.

William Richmond Killed by Homophobe

The lying bastard said his name was Joseph. Can't trust anyone these days.

Well-known West End social worker "Bill" Richmond was killed literally with his pants down. His mutilated body was discovered after Silas Johnston (48), his partner of 15 years ordered the police to trace his lover's regular exercise route. Usually Silas and Bill cycle together, but Silas was coming down with the flu and insisted that Bill not miss out on his daily bike ride.

"I've always thought we needed better policing in Stanley Park," said Johnston in an interview yesterday. "Both Bill and I have been more and more concerned about gay-bashing and we've been doing all we can to combat it. I see very little support from the police." Johnston broke down, but then continued, "And now, it's too late. My dear, dear partner is no more."

There is no doubt that a homophobe committed this calculated, cold-blooded murder. Not only was Richmond's neck broken but Silas told me that "his penis was missing." The Vancouver Police Department was, as usual, close mouthed about the details.

The VPD did disclose one bit of relevant information: "We have reason to believe that the same killer murdered David Bellamy 18 months ago...again in Stanley Park." He and his dog's bodies were washed up in English Bay. At the time, the VPD wouldn't provide any more details. Since Richmond's murder, however, I have interviewed some of Bellamy's close friends who without prodding described his condition: when found, Bellamy's pants were around his ankles and he too was missing his penis.

There's a sicko out there boys! Silas's last words to me were "Sisters, beware. Stay in groups. There's safety in numbers."

THK heard the gentle buzz and then saw the red light flash. *She's back. Fuck! I wanted to jack off one more time.* He quickly slipped out through his private entrance to welcome his wife. He was, after all, the perfect husband, a role he had perfected above all others. "Hi, honey, I'm just stepping into the shower. Come on in. I'm so horny." *What woman could resist me?*

DURING THE REST of the week, we interviewed all of the remaining TV makeup artists who were working on shows in and around Vancouver. We also visited three mini-series production sites and three feature film productions. None of them produced a single bite. But Bear got the autographs of several of the leading actors. He had become a freaking star-struck movie fan.

Apparently Abby had got nowhere in her search for similar murders. Every time I asked Bear for a progress report, his answer was the same. "It's a slow job, but Abby assures me that she's gonna blow us away next week." Surely to god some computer program would have picked up such distinctive similarities: a victim who was beautifully made up with a bouffant hairdo, a victim who had nail polish on all her nails except her pinky, a victim who had a partially chewed-off thumb in her mouth, a victim who had her tongue cut out, for Christ's sake, a victim who had been hosed out, a victim who was found lying on a taunting calling card left by her killer, a victim whose pubic hair was braided together with two other pubic hairs, a victim who... I had a thought. "What if he changes the MO for every killing?" *No!* The Polaroids of the other women all showed some similarities.

Franny McGhie was having a field day with Richmond's murder because the gay community had not only come together but also had become shriekingly vocal. Two men had come forward to the Police, claiming they had seen Richmond pursuing a dark-haired young man. Richmond had even given a high-five to one of the men and whispered, "I've got a live one here." Silas Johnston was quoted in McGhie's Thursday's column. "Bill was always faithful. He never would have cheated on me. I don't know why the witness lied. I know that the killer must have forced Bill into that grotto." *Ha! Lots of gays fool around on the side, claiming that it doesn't affect their long-term relationship in the slightest. My own lover had Bill. Only once. I'm still hanging on to that bit of information Brent slipped me.* Unlike the body, the memory never ages. Deep in my gut as I listened to the denials of Silas, I couldn't shake the thought that Brent might still enjoy anonymous sex if the opportunity arose. He would never tell me; he knew I'd be devastated and wouldn't want the truth to jeopardize our love. And it would have. So I had lived, as Silas had lived, with my doubts, never daring to come right out and ask him directly, "Brent, have you been having sex on the side?"

It appeared that the media had all but forgotten Nancy. Hell, for a minute, I had. Her murder was so unlike the one that currently had the public's attention and sold papers.

A full spread in *Xtra-West* highlighted six murders of gay men during the past nine years. Each killing took place approximately eighteen months apart. The columnist had successfully unearthed a similar MO for all the murders that had taken place throughout the Lower Mainland. Even though each death was entirely different, they all had one shocking similarity. The columnist's thorough coverage gave the exact date of each murder and described, right up to the exact moment of death, every possible detail. Within a day of publication, it was impossible to find a single copy of *Xtra-West*.

Franny McGhie, naturally, got on the bandwagon too, and in

Friday's *Scoop*, she took all the details from the *Xtra-West* article and boiled it down succinctly. The cover of *The Scoop* was composed of six photos of the victims encircling the caption:

WHO'LL BE NUMBER SEVEN?

On page two was a photo of each man with a thumbnail profile. For all McGhie's pot-boiler phrasing, she did have some talent. I pored through her prose, and noted each victim's tragic fate. Stanley, strangled with his own belt, his body badly bitten. By animals? Or his killer? And Jerry's wreck of a body crumpled on Wreck Beach. Castrated, poor sod. And Herbert, victim three, found nude and lying prostrate, at the far side of the Par 3 Golf Course in Delta. His bitten-off penis was stuck in his mouth. Willie was found nude in the woods of Bear Creek Park with his penis in his anus. And the fifth and sixth victims, David and William, when discovered, were without their penises. *I bet the killer took them as souvenirs!* McGhie ended her sensational investigative report with:

> If the same killer is responsible for all these murders, and there is nothing to indicate that it is except that each victim had his member bitten off, gays had better be on their guard 18 months from now. If a homophobic maniac is, at that time, still on the loose in our city, the gay community will probably lose another of its *mature members*.

Low blow, McGhie, for that bad-tasting pun. She continued:

> But I have a bone to pick with the Vancouver Police as well as the Mounties. They've been spouting claims that ViCLAS will ferret out serial killers. But are they feeding the details of these deaths into the system, or is this a deliberate omission on their part because the victims are gay? Think about it! Now we have two fiends roaming the streets: a Clean Freak and a Dirty Freak.

My thoughts exactly. If a small newspaper columnist could dig up similar MOs on six murders, why the hell couldn't the staff on ViCLAS do the same? Perhaps they were deliberately holding back evidence from the media and maybe McGhie's "scoop" would make it more difficult for the police to trap this gay killer.
As I despaired that there were two serial predators loose in

Vancouver, I made a list of the names of the murdered men with the dates of their deaths, noting that all of them were between fifty and sixty-five. I was glad cruising had never been my thing.

BEAR AND I were about to enter another dead-end weekend, not really knowing what to do next in finding Nancy's killer.

On Friday, October Twenty-Third, we were sitting in Bear's favorite haunt on Lonsdale, both of us frustrated, both of us shoveling down a White Spot hamburger. "Okay, where are we?" I asked Bear between gulps.

"Nowheres, Chief." I watched him dip three French fries into the pool of ketchup on his napkin and shove them all at once into his mouth. He used his sleeve as his napkin.

"That's right. Nowhere. Four weeks ago tonight a beautiful woman was about to endure a weekend of terror, and we're no further ahead in finding her attacker than we were when we started. What the hell's Joan doing to help us solve this case?" I continued to vent my frustrations while Bear happily slurped his chocolate milkshake. "She's been significantly quiet. That's not like her." When I was Chief, I had my finger on all the cases, and if I saw no progress, I'd make it my business to find out what was going on. My corporals would be working around the clock. *All this PIRS, CPIC, and ViCLAS crap ain't worth diddly squat. But my gumshoe tactics ain't worth shit either.*

By now, I had got myself into a total snit. "Are you finished yet?" I snarled as Bear vacuumed the last remnants of his shake from the sides of his glass.

The belch that rose from his gut announced that he'd finished. "So tell me. What's Joan doing?"

"Abby's been in touch with the FBI. She's pretty excited. They're willin' to help. But they say it's a huge job. You should see the files she's received. Printed out every damn one of them she's gotten over the e-mail. There's stacks of papers every morning."

"How many similar MOs has she received?"

"I dunno. Too early to tell."

"How many times are you gonna say the same fucking thing?"

"Hold yer horses there, Kev. Abby's siftin' through hundreds of entries. And that's that." Bear had said all he intended to say. "Let's get out o' here. I'll drop you off home."

On our way to the West End, Bear scowled. "So much fer yer theory that a professional makeup person is our killer."

"Yeah. I sure as hell goofed on that one. But I've got a hunch our guy is in theatre one way or another. Probably an unsuccessful actor."

"Yer not suggestin' we start trackin' down actors, are ya? There must be hundreds or thousands of them around here. Who'da believed there's nearly thirty TV 'n' movie shoots goin' on in Vancouver right here? Now I know why they call us Hollywood North."

"Yeah." I was turning off his prattle.

"Ya know, I always thought that them big stars would be larger 'n life. Their mugs are always twenty feet high on the movie screen. They're just ordinary joes like me and you."

"Yeah."

"Except for that Leslie Nielsen. Now there's a funny guy and he's a Canadian, eh? Remember how I bust a gut when he pretended to fart every time I asked him a question?" Bear roared happily, reliving our interview with Neilson.

"Uh huh."

"My Andy's askin' me dozens of questions every night at dinner. I dunno what's got into him since you and Brent came over. He tells me now he wants to go into show biz. Can you imagine, my Andy a movie star?"

"Takes all types," I sighed.

"He was real disappointed I didn't get him autographs of those two *X-Files* characters: Moldy and Scoldy. Maybe I should pay 'em a visit."

"I already told you, the makeup artist on *The X-Files* doesn't even come close to our profile of the killer."

"Whatever."

Bear's car phone came to life. Spivic looked at his watch and then flicked on his phone.

"Sergeant Spivic." I could hear Abby's voice.

"Spivic here. What's on your mind, Abby?"

"Is Mr. Porter with you?"

"Yes, he's right beside me."

"Good," she said. "Chief Inspector Riley wants to see you both on Tuesday morning at ten."

"I'll be there," answered Bear. "Kev?"

"Count me in. What's up, Abby?"

"A couple of things. She wants you both to meet Dr. Fitzgerald Ormand."

"Who's he?" asked Bear.

"He's a visiting lecturer in the UBC medical department. A top-notch psychiatrist."

"A shrink? What do we need a shrink for?"

"He specializes in serial killers. With my assistance, he's prepared a profile of our killer. I think it'll be helpful," she continued with a large hint of pride in her voice. "And by Tuesday, I promised the Chief I'd have a list of victims with similar MOs to the Henderson murder. The FBI has assured me they'll have the last bit of their search ready for me on Monday. And the Winnipeg Police said that they have something of interest, too."

"About time," I mumbled.

"What's that?"

"I was congratulating you, Abby," I yelled.

"Thank you, Mr. Porter. I am still waiting on most of the Detachments to get back to me on my request that they look through old files with similar MOs but only a handful have replied so far, and they're all negative. Except for Winnipeg. I'm telling you, it's like pulling hens' teeth. When the hell will the whole world get on the same search system and we can stop these monsters sooner instead of later?"

We had just passed *The X-Files* location. I wondered if next year, they'd be a missed fixture in the West End. Bear's head craned in all directions as we passed the trailers and flood lights on Pendrell and Broughton.

"Keep the whole morning and afternoon free. The Chief wants to break the back on this case. See you Tuesday." Abby clicked off.

What's going on? How did Abby know that I'm with Spivic? And it sounds as though Joan has known all along that I've been assisting Bear.

I could tell that Bear was reading my mind. He pulled up outside my apartment, said, "See ya Tuesday," and disappeared as soon as I stepped out.

Chapter
Twenty-Eight

WHEN THK OPENED his eyes Friday morning, he was still enjoying the high he'd been on during the entire week. Monique had been a brilliant piece of acting on Monday. When he returned to the set of *The X-Files* the next day, no one had suspected that Monique had been their very own quiet Harry. He had given a masterful performance for Kevin Porter. He also had been the real director on the set, dictating exactly when the shoot was ready for the can.

And he'd had a chaser! Sweet revenge on Daddy. But best of all, the media had given him the acclaim he knew he deserved. He was ecstatic. He was satisfied.

For the time being.

"Now, who am I today?" He threw off the comfy duvet and looked down admiringly at his naked body in the queen-size bed. "Oh, yes. Good old Harry. I have to work today."

He didn't have to start till four. *The X-Files* was shooting night scenes on the Fraser River. He'd be on board one of those flat-bottomed tankers till midnight. He enjoyed location work, but he didn't look forward to being confined on the water.

After he shaved and showered, he applied a touch of highlight to bring out his bone structure. Then he put his well-made wig over his short, dyed hair. The graying-at-the-temples system added years to his face. Then he glued the small, refined salt-and-pepper moustache over his top lip. Finally, he slipped in a pair of hazel contacts. He could put on the disguise in his sleep. His wife had suggested that he make himself appear older in order to get the job in the first place. She had even picked up an "older man's" wardrobe for him. He'd scoffed at the idea, but she had been right. His distinguished appearance had landed him the job during his first interview.

He blinked and spoke to himself in the mirror, finding with ease the exact velvety intonation he had used for so many years: mid-Atlantic accent, rich radio-trained voice. "Hello, Harry."

He walked into the kitchen regally, newly transformed into a forty-six-year-old makeup artist. There on the table was his breakfast with his morning note: "Good morning, my Prince. You were sleeping so peacefully this morning I hadn't the heart to wake you.

But your Kate kissed your warm and inviting lips. Your breath smelled of ambrosia. Did you feel my arms around you as you slept? Have I told you lately that I love you? I'm already missing you and I haven't even left for work. Love and kisses, Your Queen." He crumpled the note and threw it in the garbage bag under the sink. *She dotes. She madly dotes on me.*

He sat down at the table and smiled as he broke apart the huge cinnamon bun that she'd set out for him before she left. As he poured steaming coffee into his favorite mug, he became lost in his thoughts of the night he first met his wife...

His futre wife attended the Langley Little Theatre production of *Henry V*. She had driven all the way out into the Fraser Valley with her girlfriend whose neighbor was playing the French princess, Katherine. Immediately, the young man in the title role attracted her attention. She couldn't keep her eyes off him. After the show, the two women went backstage to congratulate the actors. While her friend was busy bestowing compliments on her neighbor, she walked confidently up to the young star. "You were great!" she said boldly. He looked into her eyes and she melted. During the play she had thought he was one of the most attractive men she'd ever seen. Now, backstage, his charm seduced her.

He asked her name but before she could tell him, he declared, "You're a Kate. Queen Katherine. With a K. Oh, I wish that you were playing Henry's queen. My queen."

She laughed. "I can't act."

"I'll teach you. Want to go out for a coffee?"

She blushed. "I'm sorry, but I'm with a friend." She whispered, pointing to her friend, "Her neighbor played Katherine."

He whispered back, "And not very well." They both laughed conspiratorially.

"I'm sorry, but we really have to be going."

"Give me your hand." He took it before she could stop him and wrote his phone number on her palm with an eyeliner. Then he wrote:

Henry ♥ Kate

She looked at it and flushed again. "Don't you believe in love at first sight?"

When she got home, she copied his number into her phone pad, but she didn't wash his message off her hand. When she got into bed, she kissed her hand and dreamt of King Henry.

The next day she phoned him. And the next night she experienced two hours of the best sex of her life. And so did he.

With his Kate, he discovered a new satisfaction. Love sought is good, but given unsought is better. Would that it were enough to quench his unquenchable thirst.

He contentedly munched his cinnamon roll. *I am so brilliant. I've got a wife who adores me. My Kate tells me that I'm the only person on earth who makes her feel important. Hell, she was so grateful, she went out and had* **Henry ♥ Kate** *tattooed on her right shoulder. And now every time I'm pounding her pussy, she sings "Some day my Prince will come." But it works for me! I come, all right, but I cum when I'm good and ready!*

He began talking to himself as he finished his breakfast. "I'll never complain. I've got it made. I keep her indebted to me. And she spoils me like my fucking mother should have. She was a Catherine, too. Catherine with a C. Cunt! My Katherine never tires of praising her sweet King Henry. She's my Queen of Kindness. Of Keepsakes. Of Kisses. She leaves me little love notes and gifts everywhere in the apartment. 'Our last holiday was fantastic. You're my Prince among Men. Thank you for insisting that I take that night school course. You were right, I enjoyed that conference. I adore you. You inspire me to be myself.' I let her rant on. My Kate sure beats the hell out of the Big C. At least I get space to breathe. I let her go on as many trips as she wants. And then send her on more, if it suits me." He poured himself another half cup of coffee, contentedly reminiscing about his unsuspecting wife.

Maybe one day I'll tell her what her little Henry has been up to? She'll approve, because she loves me. He washed the final bite of cinnamon bun down with the last of his coffee and laughed.

IN TOM'S GRADUATION year, Mr. Goldman offered him the double role of Theseus and Oberon in *A Midsummer Night's Dream.* He loved the challenge of playing two roles in a single production. He knew that Oberon was the King of the Underworld, but after he read the dramatis personae and saw that Oberon was listed as the King of the Fairies, he knew that there was no way his mother would let him play this part. That night, he told her he was feeling sick. "I think I'd better sleep in my own room. I don't want you to get my cold." He read through the whole of *The Dream* and when he finished, he was determined to play both parts. The roles would show off his versatility and, besides, it was about time he did what he wanted. He was nearly eighteen. His life didn't belong to her. If she didn't like it, she could fly a kite.

On the way home from school the next day, after listening to her usual interrogation and warning to beware of homosexuals, he determined, for the first time in his life, to lie to his mother. "I've got a wonderful part in *The Dream*, Mom."

She gave him a dirty look. "Not one of those fairies, I hope. Why doesn't Goldman do a man's play for a change? He should do *Henry V*. You were born to play King Henry the Fifth." Then she added, "So what part do you have in that pansy-ass play?" He had no time to answer. "One of the lovers? Demetrius? Lysander? They're good parts." His mother knew her Shakespeare. Tommy was quiet. She looked at her son and said, "Don't tell me you're going to play Theseus." He nodded. "Wonderful. Duke Theseus, in love with the Amazon Hippolyta. You'll be wonderful. It's a small role, but you'll make him memorable. I shall be so proud of you. Congratulations, son." He smiled, but inside he felt a dreadful foreboding.

By opening night, he was a nervous wreck. He didn't think that he could perform with his mother in the audience. So, with well-rehearsed words, he said haltingly to her two hours before the premiere performance of the three-day run, "Mommie, I have never asked for very much from you. I've always loved you and obeyed you."

"Piss or get off the pot, Thomas Henry." She'd already had several shots of vodka, nervous about going to see her son act that evening. "What are you trying to get me to do now?"

"Nothing. I'm sorry. I shouldn't have spoken." He hoped this tactic would work. Let her pull it out of him.

"What? What do you want me to do?"

It worked. So easy. She's mine. "Well, I don't think I'm ready for you to see my performance quite yet. It'll be okay for the fuddle-duddle plebeians of Salmon Arm, but not for you. I want to be more confident when you see me."

"But I've always been there for your opening night," she slurred.

"This is the last time I'll be on stage in Salmon Arm and I think it would be great if you came to the final performance. On Saturday night."

"I don't think I can wait till Saturday to see my son..."

"When I come home tonight, I'll be by your side and I'll tell you all the details. I'll recite Theseus's lines, and you'll be my Hippolyta. Tonight when I'm on stage, I'll be thinking of you, preparing our bed for my return. I'll show you a performance tonight that you'll never forget, my Hippolyta. My Amazon Queen."

THAT NIGHT, CATHERINE King memorized Hippolyta's speeches while she prepared the bed with rose petals. Then she lay on the bed, expectantly waiting for the return of her conquering son.

He didn't disappoint her either night.

On the final night of *A Midsummer Night's Dream*, his mother — in a smartly tailored red suit, beautifully made up, hair stylishly bouffanted — walked to her reserved place in the third row. There on the seat was a box, attractively wrapped. She opened it expectantly and took out a pure-white orchid. Still standing, she pinned the corsage over her heart, making sure that everyone could see her. Then she picked up the accompanying card and read, "Thank you for everything, Mommie." She kissed it and held it to her breast and sat down with pride and anticipation as the first scene opened with Theseus.

Her son entered, in glorious Greek attire (a little too short in the tunic for her liking), with a tall blonde Hippolyta. He spoke manfully the first line in the play: "Now, fair Hippolyta, our nuptial hour / Draws on apace. Four happy days bring in / Another moon; but O, methinks, how slow / This old moon wanes!..." She felt he was speaking directly to her. When the actress spoke her lines, Catherine King mumbled Hippolyta's lines along with her.

Her son looked breathtakingly handsome; his strong, clear voice filled the theatre. His delivery of the lines was every bit as splendid as it had been for the last two nights in her bedroom. She reveled in the memory of their lovemaking. Any woman would be an idiot not to want him as her husband. *But I better keep him on a short leash. Why waste him on some young floozy when it would be so easy to keep him all to myself?* Thomas, with her at his side, would bring glory and recognition to the King family. Not like his no-good, son-of-a-bitch father who slunk out of town after she caught him entertaining one of his buddies in the rec room.

When Act Two began, the setting had changed to the Athenian forest. A fairy and Puck danced in. Automatically she tuned out as if someone had pulled the plug from her electrical circuits. She was there only to see her son. She listened as though through a fog to the voices of Puck and a vapid little fairy, expounding on the battle between Oberon and Titania. Suddenly the stage filled from both sides with a dozen fairies. Oberon and Titania, king and queen of the fairies, were instantly engaged in mortal combat. Oberon, his voice filled with menace, spoke. "Ill met by moonlight, proud Titania." Mrs. King shot to attention. She stared at the actor playing Oberon. Then she looked at her program. The part of Oberon was being played by Henri le Roi. She could have sworn that her son was standing in front of her, on stage, in pale blue tights with a very full basket for all to see, airy-fairy filmy cape floating from his shoulders and arms as he pranced around the stage, with an even airier-fairier goddamn faggoty headdress of feathers with little wire hoops that jiggled every time he moved his head. Flitter dust, covering the white makeup, was heaped on his lips, eyelids, and fingernails. The disguise didn't fool her. He might not have looked like Tom, he might not even have sounded like Tom, but she could tell that Oberon was her son. By her fucking faggot son! Henri Le Roi! *What kind of fucking affectation is that? Who do you think you are, Thomas Henry King? Wait until I get you home!* It was all she could do to sit in her seat. She wanted to go up on the stage and smash his face in. Drag him to his knees. *How could he do this to me? His own mother. Playing the King of the Fairies. Embarrassing me in front of the whole school. And by tomorrow, the whole town will know that my son is a fucking homosexual!*

Her son's performance soared. The audience ate it up. One minute he'd conjure fear in their hearts with his all-consuming anger for Titania and the next he'd fill the theatre with laughter at his wonderful sense of comic timing with Puck. When he uttered, "I am invisible," and became invisible with a magical gesture, the audience actually cheered. *None of your talented histrionics will soften my heart to the deception that you are so obviously enjoying at my expense.* Even the thunderous applause he received on his exit line, "And look thou meet me ere the first cock crow," refused to melt her heart.

At intermission, as she stormed down the aisle, she hissed, "I'll bite off your cock, you little shithead. I'll bite it off and stick it up your ass."

The director caught her at the exit. "Isn't Thomas great? I'm sure you are rightfully proud of your son."

"What?" she snapped. She wanted to get home.

"Do you like the surprise he planned for you? Imagine pulling off a double role with such quality in both parts! And he's only seventeen. He's going to be a big star," continued Mr. Goldman quickly. She was not listening to the drama teacher, but he kept talking and talking. *Get out of my face!* "Thomas dedicated this final school performance to you, you know. Did you see it in the program? He bought an ad, to honor his mother. He loves you a great deal." She still didn't seem to hear him. "And congratulations are in order, too. Did he tell you that he'd won the scholarship?"

She snapped to attention. "What?"

"To Canada's National Theatre School."

"What?" Her eyes looked icily through him.

"In Montreal. Your son was accepted by the NTS. Isn't that wonderful?"

She was gone. *The little tramp applied to a faggot acting school. I'll get him. Just like I got his old man. Faggot daddies tell no tales. And neither will his faggot son.*

AFTER THE SHOW, Tommy waited in the green room for his mother. He was the last to leave, wondering why she hadn't come backstage. Why she hadn't picked him up. To drive him home. What could have happened to her?

Making sure that everything was locked up, his director came backstage and was surprised to find Thomas still there. "I thought everyone had long gone. What are you doing here, Tom? It's eleven o'clock." He looked at the timid boy who was standing with an expectant look towards the door. "Tom! Are you okay?"

"Yeah. My mom will be picking me up soon."

The director looked at the boy. "She had to leave at intermission. I don't think she was feeling very well." Tom became tearful. "Would you like me to drive you home?" He nodded.

On the way to Thomas's home, the director talked a great deal about the wonderful job he had done in bringing the two characters to life, both so uniquely different. Tommy only grunted. When Goldman parked in front of Tom's home, he gave Tom's knee a reassuring pat. "Are you okay, son?" Tommy grabbed his hand and threw it aside as if it were a tarantula. All the venom that his mother had fed him over the years erupted. He grabbed Goldman by the throat and screamed into his face. "Keep your hands off me, you fucking faggot. You've been after my ass all year. No man will ever touch me again, do you hear me? Are you listening to me, slime bag? You keep your pansy-freaking, cock-sucking ass-face out of my sight or I'll squash you like the fruit fag you are. Do you understand, you pervert?" Goldman nodded. Tommy removed his hands in disgust. "If you ever come within six feet of me again, I will beat you into clamorous whining." He opened the car door and got out, horrified when he realized that he had a tremendous erection. He was now out of control, running blindly into the house.

TWO RCMP CORPORALS came to the house at one thirty a.m. Catherine King was dead in the bathtub. The shower was still spraying over her naked body. Her thumb was in her mouth. Later, they found that her tongue had been cut out.

Her son, Thomas, was sitting on the floor in the kitchen, the phone still in his hand. He was obviously in shock. He had an ugly discolored bulge on his forehead.

Looking at the police with wide tearful eyes, bits of flitter dust still on his lids, he began his third and certainly his best performance of the evening. "I can only describe what little I know that happened to my mother." He took a breath and asked for a drink of water. Then he began, slowly, to speak. "You see, I was in a play at school. My mum was there but she left the performance at intermission. I don't know why. Anyway, my drama teacher, Mr. Goldman, kindly drove me home after the play. I ran to the house because I was concerned about my mum. When I got to the bedroom I disturbed a man with a black hood over his face. He was in the process of fu... I can't say that word. I ran at him, screaming, 'Get off my mother!' I was ready to take him out. I knew he was hurting her because she was calling for me to help her." He started to weep, for effect. "I didn't even see what he hit me with. But whatever it was, he knocked me out cold." He felt his forehead and shuddered. "I don't know when I came to. I could hear water running. I didn't want to open my eyes in case he was still in the house.

"After a few minutes of not hearing a sound except the water, I slowly began to open my eyes. I was in my Mom's bedroom, in the same place where I had been when that man hit me. I bet he thought he killed me. Otherwise I'd be d..." He broke down again. "I got up and staggered into the bathroom and saw..." He sobbed so hard that the female corporal put her arm around him and told him that he could tell them about everything tomorrow. But he was unstoppable. He continued telling them about the hideous ordeal he had endured. Towards the end of his story, he became delirious, terrified, completely traumatized. He kept repeating, "What will I do? What will become of me? Who will look after me?" The police tried to console him but he was disconsolate. He was crying out a lifetime of torment in convulsive sobs. He ran to the kitchen sink and vomited. He was purging all responsibility for his actions.

When he finished his performance, he slid to the floor in silence as the male corporal examined his head. Thomas felt his breathing become more even. He felt more alive than he'd ever felt in his entire life. He suddenly sensed a surge of happiness take over his body. He was recasting himself as if he were about to take on a new role. He would play the part of Tommy no more. Little Tommy is dead. He would go to Montreal. Become the best actor in the world. He would forget his mother; just live off her money. And there was loads of that. He'd have the world by the tail. He gave the corporals a tiny hurt smile and said, "Thank you for helping me. I hope you find him." It was so easy to hoodwink these two morons.

When they take her carcass away, I'll eat her tongue. Fry it in butter. With a little pickle on the side. Then I'll digest it. And tomorrow I'll shit it away and flush it down the toilet. That will put a stop to her fucking flapping tongue.

THOMAS HENRY KING decided to continue to live in the house by himself till the fall, when the National School term began. No one in Salmon Arm objected or intervened. A few neighbors offered to help, but he assured them that he was fine. In fact they were amazed by his maturity for someone so young. In the past, they only had eyes for the mother; she was the gossip of the town, with her holier-than-thou appearance and mucky-muck attitude. They had barely noticed her mousy son who was always in her shadow. So now, they watched in nodding admiration as he drove to school, jogged around the neighborhood, bought his weekly groceries at the supermarket.

"He's such a happy outgoing teenager." "He'll be okay," they whispered to each other. "Isn't he a good-looking boy," one would smile at another.

The police never suspected him, convinced that a transient had committed the heinous crime. They interrogated Max Goldman, who, scared stiff of what might happen to him, corroborated Tommy's story. Goldman kept a wide berth from the boy after that night and never told anyone what he suspected might have happened inside the King home. The case was eventually forgotten, although never officially closed.

By graduation, Tom assumed a calmness that all mistook for bereavement. He turned eighteen the day after his grad and put his home up for sale. By the time he sold the house, he had a large bank account and plenty of investments. His mother's lawyer said, "Your mother certainly has taken care of you, Thomas. You are a wealthy man." He flew to Montreal to find digs near the National Theatre School. He found the ideal place and paid the rent till December. He had six weeks before classes began, so he decided to visit Vancouver. He decided to fly first class. *Hell, why not? I got the money and I'm a first-class kind of guy. And now I can see a production at Shakespeare in the Tent. The Big C owes it to me.* He saw *The Taming of the Shrew*. When he left the tent and hailed a taxi to go to his hotel in the West End, he said to himself, "What's the big deal about Shakespeare in the Tent? A bunch of amateurs! They need me to star in their shows. I'd show them what real acting is all about."

During the week in Vancouver, he bought an apartment in the West End, in spite of the fact that it was "swarming with faggots." His mother had been right, but no one accosted him and he did like Vancouver. After wining, dining, and charming the strata council, he spent two weeks renovating his new two-bathroom/two-bedroom apartment. He brought all his personal belongings from Salmon Arm and put them into his hidden room. And then he rented his one-bathroom/one-bedroom apartment to a nice older couple, knowing that they would never find his sanctuary.

LA next! First-class, of course. I've got to see a bit of the world before I submerge myself in acting. While in Los Angeles he stayed in the Hollywood Hilton. He was disappointed that the Hollywood of his imagination was not glamorous at all. In fact, it was filled with prostitutes. Male as well as female. He was disgusted. But one night he was determined to try one out. *I've only been with an old C. I think it's about time to see how a young fuck feels.* He stuck his mother's camcorder into his backpack.

New York beckoned. *I've got to have a taste of the Big Apple before I head up to Montreal.* He liked the Hilton chain so he stayed in the one right downtown near 42nd and Broadway. When he walked down 42nd Street he was horrified. It was far worse than Hollywood.

Male hookers licking their lips at him as he passed; prossies spreading their legs and wiggling their asses, brazenly asking, "Want some company?" But the theatre was exciting. He went to a different show nearly every night for three weeks, enjoying most of all Joseph Papp's Shakespeare productions in Central Park. *One day Joe will be knocking on my door, begging me to play Henry V.* On the night before he went to Montreal, he picked up his camcorder and went searching for an adventure.

THOMAS HENRY KING walked up the steps of Canada's National Theatre School in Montreal. It was the first day of classes and to fit into this predominantly French-speaking city, he decided to change his name, one more suitable for an eager thespian with dreams of fame. Henri le Roi was born. But Henri would be different; he would be the best acting student the National Theatre School had ever seen.

Chapter
Twenty-Nine

WHEN I OPENED my eyes Saturday morning, I realized I could do nothing more on the Henderson case. Except think. I'd reread every note I'd jotted down, examined the autopsy report for any small clue, studied Nancy's diary again. I turned on my computer and put in the disk that Bear had brought me of Nancy in death. I looked again at the enlargement of the fiend's other victims. I could see nothing new. I'd virtually exhausted my resources.

I set my hopes on next Tuesday when I would be officially invited to return to the North Van Detachment. I looked forward to being a member of the team again and to getting back on track.

But today, I had time to catch up on a few fatherly duties.

I slipped out of the bed, leaving my snoring lover to enjoy eighty more winks. Saturday was his day to sleep in.

I brought up the elevator to pick up the morning papers, but there were none. Sometimes they're late on Saturdays. So I went into the kitchen.

After my usual two glasses of water and my grapefruit and bran breakfast, I settled in my den to make a few necessary phone calls to my five kids: Tim and Jim in London, then Jeannie in Winnipeg. I took a few breaths and dialed Sammy in San Francisco. After his long-winded diatribe begging me to give up my sin of homosexuality, I hung up, exhausted. I looked at my watch, another gift from Brent. It was a New Year's Eve gift last year. I was reminded of that night every time I looked at my watch with its diamond in place of the 12. I dialed Barbi, even though it would be six in the morning in Hawaii. The answering machine kicked in. My three-year-old grandson's attempt at leaving a message, quite unintelligible, took up thirty seconds of tape. His message was followed by Barbi's clear, happy voice. "That was Kawika, and he said 'Sorry we're not able to answer your call but Barbi, Kai, Kawika and Leilani are all out. Probably at the beach.' "

"Sorry I missed you," I vocalized into their recording device. "Just checking in to see if all is well. Love you." I hung up.

I HAD DONE my duty and had to admit, I felt better. Working a case from the periphery is not my idea of having a good time. I was too much of a loner, too used to being in charge. Tagging along with Spivic was unbearable most of the time. Pun intended.

I had neglected Brent shamefully.

I checked to see if the papers had come. There in the elevator were *The Sun* and *The Scoop.*

There was nothing in *The Sun,* so I flipped past the cover of *The Scoop* with its headline: "HILLARY GOOFED AGAIN..." On page three was Franny McGhie's sneering smile. The byline read:

FORGOTTEN NANCY

I read her article.

> It's been four weeks since the murder of Nancy Henderson. Have you been aware of the silence from the North Shore? Their quietness alarms this reporter. Why are they being so tight-lipped? Are they waiting for the Clean Fiend to send them another clue?
>
> What if he doesn't? What if he's moved on to another city? Is that what they're hoping?
>
> In this humble reporter's opinion, it's time the North Van Detachment Commissioner banged a few heads together. Or better still, he should bring in some new blood.
>
> If you're reading this article, Mr. Clean Fiend, please send them another clue. They need help.

What a bitch! The only good use I can think of for that paper is to use it as a pooper scooper. But to be honest, I felt the same way as McGhie. It's only that nothing's gained by printing it in a newspaper. I marched into the kitchen to prepare Brent his favorite breakfast: pancakes, sausages, and eggs.

With a full tray, I tiptoed up the steps and walked through the open doorway of the bedroom. Brent was sitting in the middle of the bed, with two pillows at his back. "What kept you? I've been drooling for half an hour, smelling those magnificent aromas."

"I's sorry, massa. I bin workin' as fas' as me por ol' legs kin go."

His eyes sparkled as he downed freshly squeezed orange juice and bit off half a sausage. "Mmm. Delicious. I'll reward you later, Bag-a-Bones."

THOMAS HENRY KING woke up beside his sleeping Katherine and smiled over at her. She was radiant. She was his queen. He snuggled beside her. She instinctively put her arm around him. Such security his wife gave him, even in sleep. He whispered in a boyish voice, "I love you, Mommie. You're the best mommie in the world." Suddenly his whisper shifted to his normal voice, "And I'm the luckiest man because you're my wife.

"If thou would have such a one, take me!" He had long since memorized all of King Henry V's speeches and could recite them with ease. He continued reciting to his Katherine, his queen, "And take me, take a soldier, take a soldier, take a king, take a ki..." Suddenly his face changed and he thought of the night sixteen years ago that had altered his life irrevocably. He closed his eyes to clear his head. Slowly, he opened them again and continued whispering to his Queen Katherine. "And what say'st thou then to my love? Would you still love your king, knowing he is not a king but a kil.." He turned away under her protective arm. In sleep, she continued to hold him. He sobbed.

"Oh," she soothed, waking up. "My poor darling had a bad dream. Hush, my dearest. Hush." She held him tightly, pressing her naked body into his.

ON THE LAST night of *The Dream* after Mr. Goldman had dropped him off and he ran into his house, he knew he'd be in deep shit.

"Is that you, son?" She was in the bedroom. She sounded calm. Normal. Not drunk.

"Yes, Mother."

"Come in here, darling. I have a surprise for you."

He opened the bedroom door carefully, not knowing what might happen to him. In amazement he stared at the scene awaiting him. The drapes were closed on the windows. Candles flickered around the room. R & B was playing softly. His mother was lying on the bed nude under a filmy negligee. She smiled at him. "I'm so sorry I didn't see your whole performance. I had a sudden headache. Perhaps you will perform the second half of *The Dream* for me now. Will you be my Oberon? Just for me, Thomas?"

He gazed open-mouthed. What was going on? He'd never seen or heard his mother like this before. She looked beautiful. Fully made up, her brown hair newly backcombed and sprayed, she reached out her hands to him. Her pinky nail was painted cherry-red. "Please, for your Queen. For Titania." He stood bewildered.

He became transfixed on his mother's eyes, unable to remember a time when she was ever completely sober. Was she up to some new trick? She had been speaking with such controlled kindness; he was confused, yet expectant. "All right, Mother. Where do you want me to start?"

"I want my Oberon to awake his Titania with Cupid's flower. Go to your room and take off your clothes. I've laid out a costume for you. It's outside your door. And your Leichner makeup box is there, too. Hurry so that you can awaken me, my Prince, my King."

Thomas didn't know what to do. He sensed that something terrible was about to happen, but he was too afraid to run away, too dependent on his mother, and too excited. The evening wasn't going to be as bad as he had imagined, after all. He was already stimulated and he hadn't even seen his costume or his makeup. So, he went to his bedroom to prepare.

Twenty minutes later, a handsome, youthful Oberon entered the quiet bower scene. No music was playing. The flitter dust on his eyelids and lips over the chalky white makeup glistened from the light of the candles. Standing in the doorway, clad only in a vine-leaf wreath around his waist, he spied his Titania, asleep. Her left thumb was in her mouth; the little finger on her right hand was hidden within the heavy bush of her pubic hair. Her heavily made-up eyelids were closed. She looked beautiful enough to photograph.

He walked slowly to the bed. He was fully aroused, excited, expectant. Leaning over her head, he anointed her eyes with imaginary love juice. "Now, my Titania, wake you, my sweet queen."

His mother slowly opened her eyes and, smiling lovingly at her son, recited in regal tones, "My Oberon, what visions have I seen! / Methought I was enamor'd of an ass."

He turned to gesture to an imaginary Bottom, wearing an ass's head. "Here lies your love."

She sat up and looked. "How came these things to pass? / O, how mine eyes do loathe his visage now!" She turned her head in disgust.

Tommy continued his role, feeling more confident that all would be well. "Silence a while. Robin, take off this head. / Titania, music call..." His mother plunged the Play button of the cassette recorder on her bedside table. A piercing Miles Davis trumpet solo filled the room. The boy became startled at first; the music was all wrong — not like the sweet strains of Mendelssohn he'd been used to. He smiled bravely and continued, "...and strike more dead / Than common sleep of all these five the senses." Tommy gestured to the imaginary five sleeping characters who surrounded them. Then he spoke his next line, "Come, my queen, take hands with me, / And rock the ground whereon these sleepers be." His mother rose and took his hand as he attempted to guide her through the same graceful dance he performed with his stage Titania, where they had touched and separated and touched again. He managed to block out the loud jarring music and continue his lines. "Now thou and I are new in amity, / And will tomorrow midnight solemnly / Dance in..." He glanced admiringly at himself in the mirror over the dresser. A flash dazzled him. He turned to see his mother, grinning hideously and running towards him, her arm raised above her head, a butcher knife in her hand.

"Look at you admiring yourself, you fucking King of the Fairies," she screamed. "You're a queer. Prancing around like a goddamn nance." She lunged at him with the knife. He avoided her with ease. She continued screeching, "A good faggot is a dead faggot," and staggered at him again. He grabbed her wrist and knocked the knife to the floor.

"You're a gruesome excuse for a man. Cover your disgusting body. No real woman will ever want you near her. You don't know how to make love to a woman because you're a flaming queen. From now on I'm going to call you Queen Oberon. Get out of here!" She screamed, "Get out and never come back. I never want to see your..."

He grabbed her head with both his hands. She looked directly into his eyes and spat in his face. With one swift snap, he broke his mother's neck. Staring in disbelief, he felt the weight of her body between his hands. Staring into his mother's dead accusing eyes, he screamed non-stop. The intensity of his screams transcended the loud music. He was terrified. He had killed his own mother.

What should I do now?

After a long while, he couldn't tell how long, he had worked out a plan. He figured out a way to save himself. To enjoy the rest of his life and live it to the fullest. To go to acting school. To become the world's greatest Shakespearean actor.

He took time to rehearse the most significant role of his young life: a poor little orphan boy who caught a bad man in the act of killing his darling mother.

When he had his lines down pat, he went into his mother's bedroom to set the stage for the murder. As he moved various objects around the room to give a better effect for the police when they came, he was surprised to see a camcorder on the dresser. It was still on. He had been recorded with his mother. *The Big C was filming the murder of her own son.* The thought sent him berserk. "The bitch! Why did the cock-sucking cunt want to film us?" He stood stalk still. Then he screamed, "So she could watch herself kill me. Over and over and over." He turned off the recorder and threw himself on the floor, overcome with tears. "How could she hate me that much? Her own son!" He moaned like one of the animals that he used to torture. Suddenly he stopped howling. Drying his eyes, he stood up and said coldly, "You deserved to die, Bitch. I wish you were alive this minute so I could kill you again." A terrifying serenity overcame him as he picked up the butcher knife and pried open his mother's mouth.

Once everything was exactly to his liking, he recorded his mother. *Yes, yes. Very good. Excellent.* He zoomed in and out, focusing on different parts of her naked body. All the time he was fully aroused. "See, you're turning me on, Bitch."

Much later, he went into his bedroom and took off his costume and makeup. After placing the skimpy costume in the bottom of a garbage bag, he stepped into the shower. Using a bit of his own spittle, he massaged the blood on his face and hands onto his chest, then his stomach, then on his throbbing erection. He exploded within thirty seconds. Snapping on the shower, he watched contentedly as all the evidence poured down the drain. He stepped out a new man. Dried his body gently, lovingly, and dressed in the clothes he had come home in. He went into the kitchen for the *pièce de résistance.*

He placed the camcorder on top of the fridge to make sure that his performance would be captured for posterity.

He went to the kitchen sink, leaned over, and deliberately cracked his skull on the porcelain edge. *Nothing is too much for my art!* Then he staggered to the phone and picked it up. He crawled to the wall directly in front of the camera.

Hysterical and bleeding, he raised his face to the camera and yelled, "It's show time!"

He dialed 911.

Chapter
Thirty

BOTH SATURDAY AND Sunday were gorgeous gardening days. And I made the most of them, puttering around in my rooftop garden. The first time Brent showed me his thousand-square-foot deck that wrapped around the master bedroom, I couldn't believe my eyes. It was a space begging to be filled.

When I woke on the morning of my fiftieth birthday, Brent surprised me by saying, "Happy fiftieth, sweetie. Guess what I got you?"

I hadn't a clue.

"What do you miss most about living in the family home with Martha?"

I thought for a minute. Not Martha. Not the kids. "My garden?" I smiled.

"Go out on the deck for a minute, darl'." I got up and picked up my lounging pants. "Don't dress. Just go out."

So I walked out in my altogether. There, around the periphery of the entire deck were some thirty-five planters, varying in size from large to huge. A big sign read, "Happy Birthday, My Gardening Lover. Fill me, Plant me, Grow me, Eat me."

Overwhelmed by Brent's generosity and thoughtfulness, I hurried back into bed, shivering but excited. His smile was from here to Newfoundland. I showed my thanks by giving him all four of his own birthday messages. Use your imagination.

During the last five years I've made the deck into a garden worthy of a spread in *Better Homes and Gardens*, each season featuring a dazzling display of flowers. And we have fresh vegetables and fruit from early June to late October. My raspberries are mouth-watering.

Throughout this weekend, Brent poked his nose out on the deck every once in a while, bringing me a hot chocolate, an apple, a kiss. I enjoyed the interruptions from pruning the trees, filling garbage bags with dead or dying annuals, cutting back my biennials, trimming my perennials, mulching the soil, adding fertilizers, sweeping up. I had nearly got everything ship-shape. I had to put in a dozen bags of spring bulbs that I had bought mid-September.

I busily laid out the bags on twenty of the planters. Planting them would be tomorrow's job.

I reveled in the dirt all day Sunday, planting a variety of exotic tulips, daffodils, narcissi, hyacinths, anemones, snowdrops, nestling them all among winter pansies and wallflowers. In the afternoon, Brent came out on the deck and ordered, "Enough already, Mr. Gardening Man. You get in that shower now. We're due at Martha's in an hour."

"Ah, yes. Our final fitting."

"Your garden looks gorgeous. Happy?"

"Duh?" Over the years, I'd picked up a few of his favorite expressions and enjoyed dishing them back to him. He grinned.

MARTHA'S MEAL, AS always, was sumptuous. But the conversation gave me indigestion. We had finished our salad when Martha turned to Brent and said, "Well, how does it feel to be a grass widow?"

"A what?" Brent looked confused.

"Well, Kev is working that murder case. Right? Hasn't he been ignoring you a lot lately?"

Brent looked at me. I must have looked a little sheepish because he realized at that moment that I'd been talking to Martha about the case. "That's right, Martha, he has been ignoring me a great deal. And even when he is with me, he's not really there. He's always thinking of at least two things at the same time."

"Exactly. You're a grass widow. All of our married life was like that. Are you listening, Kev? You want Brent to leave you like I did?"

To my surprise, Hank said, "Is this supposed to be 'Get Kev Night?' "

Hear! Hear! I wondered where on earth Martha was coming from. I was glad I'd kept my mouth shut and let them air their grievances. I wanted to go over and give Hank a big hug of gratitude for standing up for me.

Martha and Brent looked at me and said in unison, "Sorry."

"No problem. You can't change a leopard's spots. When I get involved in a case, I lose part of myself."

"Uh huh," they nodded in unison.

"Okay, already. I lose a large part of myself. But to the case. To the victim. To the killer. Sometimes I feel there's not enough of me to go around, and yes, you're right. I ignore you much of the time. I'm sorry, I truly am. But I won't rest well until I've nailed that bastard."

"I totally understand," added Hank.

"Let's change the subject," said Martha as she passed me a plate of ribs.

"Martha, are those your *famous* barbecue ribs?" said Brent, looking at me and grinning. We both roared with laughter.

"What?" asked Hank. "What's so funny?" he said more loudly to shut us up. For the rest of our meal, we regaled them with stories of Mil's *famous* dinner. When Martha served us all a piece of her *famous* blueberry pie, and Brent asked if he could have some Neapolitan ice cream on it, I completely lost it. I know it wasn't fair to make fun of Bear and his family but I enjoyed the luxury of not thinking about murders and maniacs. I excused myself and doused my head in a sink full of cold water.

When I came out, Martha ordered Brent and me into her den-cum-sewing room to get into our costumes. "Hank and I will tidy up out here." We tore into the room like a couple of kids and got into our outfits in no time. We were both beaming. The costumes were magnificent.

After I kissed my Robin and he kissed his Batman, we bounded proudly into the living room. Martha and Hank, whom we caught in a clinch, applauded.

"Model them," ordered Hank. He had come around more tonight than ever before. In fact, he was my protector. One thing that Martha and I never did was talk about our respective lovers. Common courtesy. But I quite enjoyed watching Hank's obvious affection towards my ex. There was no doubt in my mind that he loved her as much as Brent loved me. So I was glad to see Hank relaxing more around us. I had suspected that he didn't like me, but tonight proved me wrong. When we'd met before, he probably had been nervous about meeting Martha's husband of so many years. Who wouldn't be? Anyway, he was much more comfortable tonight and I was quite sure that we'd now all become good friends.

Hank volunteered, "You look sensational. Which party are you guys going to on Halloween?"

"I've already got the tickets," put in Brent. "We're going to the Mars Ball."

"Mars?" queried Hank. "Mars is a straight club."

"Not every night. They have special gay nights."

"And Halloween's going to be a gay ball?"

"No, mixed. Everybody will be at Mars on Halloween." Brent was very excited. This was the first I'd heard about where we'd be spending next Saturday night. Brent always planned where we'd party, what movie we'd see, which friends we'd visit. In a relationship one partner usually gives in to the other. I was top dog in my marriage to Martha, at least I thought I was. I'm low dog in my relationship with Brent. Funny, though, I've never complained. I've always gone along for the ride, agreeing with Brent's suggestions—and most of the rides have been spectacular.

"Why are we going to Mars?" I asked Brent. "We've always gone to Celebrities for Halloween."

"Because at Mars, their first prize for the best couple's costumes is an all-expense week to next year's White Party in Palm Springs," answered Brent. "And we're gonna ace this baby." He pranced around the room, perfecting his Robin run. We all laughed. Hank joined in as we went into the den to get out of our costumes.

When we came back into the living room, I asked, "How about modeling *your* outfits?"

Hank and Martha looked at each other. "I don't think we're going partying this Halloween," Martha said.

"That's right." Hank added, "To tell you the truth, Martha's been working on yours every spare moment since she got back from Frisco."

I instantly felt guilty.

Martha said, "Don't worry, Kevin. I had no intention of staying so long with Sammy, but he's in a bad way." I felt even guiltier. Martha looked up at Brent and Hank. "Do you fellows mind? I'd like to have a chat with Kevin alone."

"Why don't the two of you go out for a drink?" I suggested.

"Sure," they both chimed in unison.

They got their jackets. "See you at home, Kev," Brent whispered as he kissed me goodbye. He scooped up the costumes and headed for the door.

Not to be outdone, Hank came over to Martha and planted a huge wet kiss on her lips. "Be in bed when I get home, woman."

She laughed contentedly and let her hand touch his blond hair and smooth face. " I will, my sweet..." Hank gave her another long kiss.

She whispered "Is that to remember me by?" He looked over to me and winked. Then Hank walked to the door where Brent was waiting.

I smiled contentedly.

The young men left the apartment together in animated conversation. Hank even put his arm around Brent's shoulder. "You're going to knock them dead at Mars." Martha and I smiled as they exited, and then looked at each other and grinned. "Youth," I said.

"Yeah. Ain't it grand?" We both had a good laugh.

AFTER MARTHA SHARED all of Sammy's latest dramatics with his Debbie, I left. When I got home, Brent was sound asleep. I smiled. Our costumes were carefully draped over the chaise lounge, or as Brent liked to call it, the fainting couch. The costumes would be there until Saturday, so we'd see them every morning and night, to get us in the mood to *be* Batman and Robin. To win first prize.

Brent loves to win. Nearly every time I picked him up at the airport after one of his meets, he'd exit the arrival gate with huge smiles, showing off the medal hanging around his neck.

I started to undress.

STANDING AMONG THE shrubs, Thomas Henry King, no costume, no wig, simply himself, had just watched Private Detective Kevin Porter enter his apartment block. He had waited until Porter got up to his penthouse and had watched the lights go out, one at a time on the main floor. Then he waited for several more minutes and spat as the light went out on the top floor, their master bedroom. "In the rank sweat of an enseamed bed, / Stew'd in corruption, honeying and making love / Over the nasty sty!" As disgusted as Hamlet, he turned away. *I'll be visiting you when you least suspect it. Just you wait!*

THK'S FIRST TERM at the National Theatre School in Montreal was idyllic. He moved into his attic flat in a beautiful old house two blocks away. He couldn't get used to the smell of his new bed, but said grudgingly, "I'll suffer anything for my art."

He enrolled in every course he could so that his time was completely taken up with classes in acting, speech, movement, singing, dance, French, makeup, set and lighting design, costumes, directing, stage managing. He was determined to become the world's greatest actor. And he wanted to be in command of all aspects of theatre. If Henri le Roi didn't like one of his costumes when he was starring at London's Old Vic Theatre then he'd be able to speak knowledgeably to the costume mistress on how to change an aspect of the design. And while playing at the Royal National Theatre Mr. Le Roi might need to suggest that the lighting designer use a different gel on his follow-spot because it wasn't flattering his makeup enough.

At night, when he returned to his attic room, he barely had the energy to do his exercises, but he never missed a night or morning workout.

By the end of his first year, he was head and shoulders above the others in all courses. His teachers were fond of him and the outgoing principal announced at the year-end assembly, "We have a new award this year and I would like to present it before giving out the awards to our grads. The new award is to the most promising newcomer in the first year. I hesitate to go out on a limb, but I wish to say something I've never said before in this assembly." She took a deep breath and said in clear, resonant tones, "In my opinion, Henri le Roi will be the next Laurence Olivier. Mark my words." The first-years went wild. The applause and cat whistles grew to such a degree that everything else, including the awards for the graduating students and the introduction of next year's new principal, were anti-climactic.

Dr. D. W. Cross took over as principal of the NTS. His specialty was Shakespearean and Restoration Acting. Henri was the first to enroll in his courses, determined to learn everything about Shakespearean acting that there was to learn. This class, that met for two hours four times a week, was the most challenging he'd ever taken, not because he wasn't already a superb actor, but because Cross singled him out. Not a class went by when he didn't pick on the lad. Cross's intent, it seemed, was to cut Henri down to size.

It was Cross's policy to team two students, assign them a scene, and give them a week to whip the scene into shape for his critique. Of course, in front of the rest of the class. For his first presentation Henri was assigned Macbeth and a strong dark-haired French-Canadian beauty, Fay Julian, was to play Lady Macbeth.

On the day of the presentations, *Macbeth* was last. Cross's praise of all the previous scenes was glowing. Henri was sure that he'd blow Cross away. "Now," announced Cross, "let's see the Macbeths." Henri and Fay walked to the stage, took their moment to get into character, and began.

MACBETH [Within] Who's there' what, ho!

LADY MACBETH Alack, I am afraid they have awaked
     And 'tis not done. The attempt and not the deed Confounds us. Hark! I laid their dagger ready; He could not miss 'em. Had he not resembled My father as he slept, I had done't. [Enter Macbeth.] My husband!

MACBETH I have done the deed. Didst thou not hear a noise?

Cross interrupted the scene. "Get into Macbeth, Henri le Roi. You're too busy looking at yourself. You're as phony as a three-dollar bill."

"Thank you, sir." Henri tried harder to concentrate.

LADY MACBETH I heard the owl scream and the crickets cry. Did not you speak?

MACBETH When?

LADY MACBETH Now.

MACBETH   As I descended?

LADY MACBETH Ay.

The scene continued without interruption until Henri began speaking the famous "Sleep no more" speech. Listening intently, Cross stood before Henri spoke.

MACBETH I heard a voice cry, 'Sleep no more!
     Macbeth does murther sleep' the innocent
sleep,
     Sleep that knits up the ravel'd sleeve of
care, The death...

Cross walked up on the small stage, knelt in front of Henri, and started pounding the young man's chest with both of his fists. "Recite it again." Henri looked down. *What the hell is this guy trying to do?* He looked out at his fellow students who were all convulsing in mimed laughter. Cross shouted, "What are you waiting for? Do it again." Henri began, all the time receiving blows to his chest with occasional expletives from Cross. "Get your bloody voice out of your crotch. Let me feel it in your chest!"

     I heard a voice cry, 'Sleep no more!
     Macbeth does murther sleep' the innocent
sleep,
     Sleep that knits up the ravel'd sleeve of
care,
     The death of each day's life, sore labor's
bath,
     Balm of hurt minds, great nature's second
course,
     Chief nourisher in life's feast

Henri grabbed Cross's hands and slowly lowered them. *Is this guy one of those pederasts Mother warned about?* "Mr. Cross, I'm sorry, but I can't continue. I've lost all my concentration." He sat down.
     "Get back up here," shouted Cross. "My technique is going to make you the best Shakespearean actor that ever trod the boards. When I get through with you, you'll be able to fill any theatre in the world with the power of your voice. But only if you can learn to become the character one hundred percent and forget yourself. For Christ's sake, Le Roi, stop standing outside yourself, telling yourself how gorgeous you look."

Henri got back up and allowed Cross to kneel in front of him and bang away. He looked out at his fellow students. *I bet they think the old fool is sucking my cock.* But he continued and, with insuperable strength, ignored Cross's pounding hands and a few of the students' indecent gestures. When he finally finished the scene, he knew he had entered a new level of delivery.

"Right. That's coming now. Remember my fists, Le Roi. Go beyond them."

Henri could tell, as the term continued, that Cross really knew his stuff and that he was making him into a strong Shakespearean actor. He still had problems with concentration, however, and worried that he'd never be able to completely lose himself in any character.

The final presentation scenes were announced. Henri and Jake Emery were assigned the roles of Demetrius and Chiron in Shakespeare's most obscure and difficult play, *Titus Andronicus.* Fay Julian was asked to stand in for the silent character of Lavinia. The scene was set in a forest. The Empress' sons, Demetrius and Chiron, enter with the daughter of Titus Andronicus, Lavinia, her hands cut off, and her tongue cut out, and ravish'd. Henri played Demetrius.

```
DEMETRIUS So, now go tell, an if thy tongue
can speak,
    Who 'twas that cut thy tongue and ravish'd
thee.

CHIRON Write down thy mind, bewray thy meaning
so,
    An if thy stumps will let thee play the
scribe
```

Silence. He had forgotten his next line. His concentration had crumbled.

"Do you want to begin again?" Cross asked.

"Yes, sir. Sorry, sir."

```
DEMETRIUS So, now go tell, an if thy tongue
can speak,
    Who 'twas that cut thy tongue and ravish'd
thee.
```

He was out of his body again, seeing Tommy, bending over the bathtub, knife in one hand, his Mother's tongue in the other.

With all the energy he possessed, he dredged up Demetrius's next line.

DEMETRIUS   See how with signs and tokens she can
scrowl

CHIRON   Go home, call for sweet water, wash thy
hands

DEMETRIUS She hath no...

Henri froze. Cross shouted, "Tongue! She has no fucking
tongue!"
"Fuck you, Cross." He exploded. "Who needs to be stuck in this
hell-hole school with you. I'm out of here." Reeling, he stormed out
of the electrified classroom. He ran down the steps of the school and
didn't stop until he got to his apartment.   He threw his few
belongings into a suitcase and hailed a cab to the airport.
Disappointed that he had missed the last flight to London, he stayed
all night in the airport.   The next morning he bought a first-class
open-ended ticket with cash that he had drawn out of the airport
bank machine. He left Montreal for London.
As he sat curled up in his comfortable seat, he smiled. *I'll make it
big in England and show Cross what real acting is all about. Ya hear that,
you no-talent has-been?*

Chapter
Thirty-One

"KEV, I GOTTA see ya right away."
"Bear? Is that you?"
"Ya."
"What's up?" I looked at the bedside clock radio. Eight forty-five. Where was Brent?
"I received a cassette this mornin'. Ya gotta hear it." Carrying the phone with me, I wandered downstairs looking for Brent. Monday morning and I'd slept in. A first for me. And Brent was nowhere in the apartment. I picked up a note from the kitchen table. "Is it from the killer?" I asked Bear as I read Brent's note.

Good morning sleepy-head,

You looked so gorgeous, puffing away, that I didn't have the heart to wake you. I got my own breakfast and I'll pick up a bowl of noodles for lunch. You'll be punished tonight, so get plenty of ZZZs. You'll need them.

Love you, B

x x x x x

"Damn tootin'," answered Bear.
"What does he say?"
"It's not what *he* says. It's a tape of Nancy."
"Nancy?" *What the hell is going on?* I was freezing my balls off, standing on the cold tiles of the kitchen floor. "As soon as I get dressed, I'll come to the office."

"No, you're not invited there until tomorrow. I'll bring the tape to you."

"Okay. When will you be here?" The intercom buzzed. I went over to it and picked up the receiver.

I heard a booming "Now!" in both ears. The bugger was downstairs. "Buzz me in." I waited long enough to hear him call the elevator down to the first floor and then I pushed the button to bring him up. Flapping in the breeze, I dashed upstairs, jumped into my lounge outfit, and raced downstairs.

I turned the corner to the hall and there stood Bear, slippered, thank heaven in a subdued pair. He handed me a tape. "Put this on."

Picking sleep out of my eyes, I walked over to the stereo system and slipped in the tape. We both sat down in the living room and listened.

"My name is Nancy Henderson." Definitely Nancy's voice. I recognized her instantly even though her voice was tremulous and hesitant. "I have been chosen by the world's greatest director to audition for his film. And to appear opposite him. I am terribly...honored, to have been...chosen." *He's a goddamn director!* I listened intently; Bear's and my eyes locked. "Now I would like to recite my audition piece." I leaned forward to listen. "O, stand up blest! Whilst with no softer cushion than the flint I kneel before thee, and unproperly show duty, as mistaken all this while between the son and parent."

The tape ran silent for ten seconds. "Is that it?" I asked. "Is there anything on the rest of the tape?"

"Nothing. That's the works. Front and back. What the hell was all that about?"

"I don't know. I've got to hear it again. Can you leave it with me?"

"Sure. This one's a copy. Before I touched it and the note that came with it, I called in Pete, ya know, from Latent Prints? He dusted. Clean, as usual. And Jeff tested the envelope and note. Same manila envelope as last time. And the typed note was done on the same typewriter as the message on back of that Polaroid we picked up at the cabin and that there Letter to *The Scoop* Editor."

"How did you receive the envelope? In the mail?"

"No. Fed Ex. The envelope was inside a pouch. Jeff is testing the handwritin' on the weigh bill. But we know that it was a drop-off in a box in the Bentall Four building downtown. The exact money was attached to the bill."

"Did you bring the note?"

"Ya betcha."

"Well, let me read it." Bear was hesitant. Then he reached into his inside pocket and pulled out a folded piece of paper. "This is a photocopy."

I looked at the note. I recognized the stationery immediately, even though it was a photocopy, and I could see the mauve color of the stationery in my mind's eye. Down the left margin was a motif of Greek satyrs in various lewd poses. I stared at the lower right-hand corner, reading the fancy embossed inscription:

"From the Desk of [   ] written especially for you."

It was Brent's stationery. His name had been cut out.

I didn't want to read what the note said; rather my eyes lingered on the cutout portion. My lover was being framed. Quite obviously. But by whom? And for what reason?

"Well, what d'ya think?"

I could feel Bear's eyes on me and wondered whether he was hearing my thoughts. I read the letter.

```
To Spivic: Up and down, up and down
I will lead you up and down

To Daddy Porter, my last chaser, at Hallowmas:
In YOUR rank sweat of YOUR enseamed bed,
Stew'd in YOUR own corruption, honeying and
making love
Over the nasty sty with YOUR flaming faggot!

Exit pursued by Bear!
```

I looked up at Bear. "What color was the stationery?"

"Purple. What's that got to do with the price of tea in India?"

"Everything this killer has left behind or sent us has something to do with the case."

"Well I can't make head ner tail out o' what he's writin' here. What d'ya make of it?"

"He's quoting Shakespeare. The one to you is from *A Midsummer Night's Dream*. I don't recognize the quotation to me."

"It sounds like the killer's wantin' us to catch him. Keepin' in contact and all."

"You saw the crime scene. This guy is careful. Some serials are careless. They accidentally leave clues behind that make it easy for us to find them. This fiend cleaned up after himself, deliberately leaving us things as taunts. And I don't think for one hot minute that he's trying to help us find him. Or that he wants to get caught. He's a taunter. Pure and simple."

"Ya think?"

"I'm going to do a bit of searching today. I'll be in the library, thumbing through an anthology or two."

"A what? Don't answer. I got my own list of things to do. I'm out o' here."

Once Bear left, I shaved, showered, and dressed, all the time thinking out loud. "I should call Brent. He'd recognize all those quotations. He could tell me exactly which plays they're from. After all, he is a theatre and English lit major." By the time I'd finished my breakfast, I had decided I wasn't going to call Brent. What would I say to him? "Bear brought over a note from the killer. Written on *your* stationery. Now, can you explain to me how the hell that is possible?" I strolled up Robson Street to the library, with my Walkman, earphones clamped on my ears, listening to the tape of Nancy. "Have you left me a clue, darling?" I whispered over and over.

LAUGHTER ECHOED WITHIN the hidden room. If anyone were in the rest of the apartment, they would surely hear him. He had another late shoot for *The X-Files* so he had plenty of time to enjoy his videos during the day. He was watching the episode of his "magnificent six-part film of Georgina MacIntyre." He hadn't seen Georgina's film for months. Now that he'd had Nancy's chaser, he had grown tired of seeing her, thinking about her. What was left but to taunt the cops a bit, and look at his past achievements?

He continued to watch Georgina, a handsome, robust, healthy, beautifully tanned woman. He loved to revisit, reliving how she so enjoyed his performance. *You surprised me, Georgie-girl. You can still turn me on.* And now, three hours later, he had cum clean. He laughed uproariously at his own thoughts and then, with full dramatic flare, he crouched in the middle of the room. He was Poor Tom from *King Lear*, naked, hugging himself. "Poor Tom, thy horn is dry." He roared again with laughter, thinking how Porter and Spivic would be standing there scratching their balls as they stared at his note and listened to Nancy's audition tape. *The stupid buggers don't know I'm having them on. They'll never catch me. I'm too brilliant.*

I HAD NO trouble finding the sources of the two quotations. The librarian immediately recognized the "Up and down" line. "That's from *A Midsummer Night's Dream*," she said confidently. I knew that already, but I let her continue telling me about Puck, the merry wanderer of the night, as she thumbed through a copy of the play. "Puck is such a little devil. He plays many parts. Here, look at this." She opened to Act III and read, "I'll follow you, I'll lead you about a round, / Through bog, through bush, through brake, through brier; / Sometimes a horse I'll be, sometimes a hound, / A hog, a headless bear, sometimes a fire, / And neigh, and bark, and grunt, and roar, and burn, / Like horse, hound, hog, bear, fire, at every turn."

My God. That's what the fiend is doing...leading us by the nose.
"This 'Exit pursued by Bear' line is from the same play, I suppose."

The librarian laughed. "No. That's a stage direction. One of Shakespeare's few directions and certainly his most famous." She continued clucking.

"So what play is that from?"

"*A Winter's Tale.* Here." She walked over to a stack and pulled out a copy of the play. It took her only a minute to flip to the quotation. This lady knew her Shakespeare. "When Antigonus runs off stage, he is 'pursued by a bear.' The audience always laughs at that scene."

"Let me see." She turned the copy to me and pointed. I read Antigonus's line, "This is the chase; / I am gone for ever." Then I read "Exit pursued by a bear." *This fucking fiend is having a field day with us.*

Unhappily not recognizing Nancy's audition speech, the librarian taught me how to use a concordance. "Look up the word 'cushion.'" I did so, and there was a list of every time Shakespeare used the word "cushion." Five times in five different plays. The first play was *A Midsummer Night's Dream*, but the "audition" piece wasn't from it. I looked through the other three others with no luck and there, in the fifth beside *Coriolanus* was "Whilst with no softer *** than the flint" with the act, scene, and line number. The "***" replaces the word "cushion."

The librarian continued, "Ah, yes. *Coriolanus.* One of the Bard's lesser produced plays. A great play, mind, but it can be heavy going." She brought me a copy of *The Riverside Shakespeare* and said, "Go to it."

"Huh?"

"Find *Coriolanus* and then the act, scene, and line. I've got to attend to another request. Good luck."

"Thanks. You've been most helpful." I found the quotation easily, and decided to read *Coriolanus* in its entirety. Not exactly the easiest reading for a Monday morning, but I hoped I might unearth a clue or two.

As I read, I wrote pages of notes, trying hard to get a handle on this latest bit of "help" from the Clean Fiend. The fucker was leading me "Up and Down"!

The speech that Nancy read on the tape is one of Volumnia's, Coriolanus's mother. I had listened to Nancy's audition piece so many times that I knew it by heart, so when I read the original speech, one word jumped out at me.

O, stand up blest!
Whilst with no softer cushion than the flint
I kneel before thee, and unproperly

Show duty, as mistaken all this while
Between the child and parent.

Nancy had changed "child" to "son." I sought the librarian. I pointed to the line. "Could this be a misprint?"

"What do you mean?" She read the line out loud: "Between the child and parent."

"Shouldn't it be, 'Between the son and parent?' "

"Why don't you check other editions of *Coriolanus*?" She led me to one of the stacks. "It's all yours."

I looked through a dozen copies. Each one read "child and parent." Poor tortured darling Nancy was still perceptive enough to identify her would-be killer. He was definitely a man, a son. And not the woman she tried to help. Nancy must have realized that she wasn't going to live long and took this chance to help the police find her killer in case they ever found the tape of her audition.

When I finished reading, just before noon, I sat and pondered my notes. Now, why did he want Nancy to quote *Coriolanus*, one of Shakespeare's lesser-known plays? Coriolanus had real hang-ups with his mother, but here she kneels before him. Improperly. What had he made Nancy do after she read this speech? I didn't want to imagine, although my mind boggled at the possibilities.

Could it be that the fiend had troubles with his mother? It would certainly fit the scenario of most serials. Examine a serial killer, look to his parents.

I had copied out a few of Coriolanus's speeches. One required closer examination. "O mother, mother! / What have you done? Behold, the heavens do ope, The gods look down, on this unnatural scene / They laugh at. O my mother, mother! O!" His mother was having him. *That's it? And I'll bet my bottom dollar that Nancy looked like his mommy, all made up, hair bouffanted.* He was killing his mother. Again? Yes, definitely. Again and again.

There's no doubt that Coriolanus had a mother fixation, a love/hate relationship. In the same way, the killer probably had a similar relationship with his mother, but iced with incest. And every time he killed again, he repeated the process, but with a new mother. Nancy became the fiend's latest mother. *Damn, I'm good. But I could as easily be talking out my ass.*

I was zonked out. And I still had another quotation to look up and another play to read. I took a lunch break. Walked across the quad and ordered Chinese. Then hauled myself up to the stacks again.

"Still not finished?" the librarian cooed with a smile.

"Not quite, but I'm quickly becoming an authority on Shakespeare." I winked. She clucked good-naturedly.

I looked over the fiend's taunt, directed specifically at me, telling me that I would be his last chaser at Hallowmas, whatever the hell that meant:

> In YOUR rank sweat of YOUR enseamed bed,
> Stew'd in YOUR own corruption, honeying and making love
> Over the nasty sty with YOUR flaming faggot!

I couldn't imagine that this was a direct quote from the Bard. Anyway, I looked up "enseamed bed." There was only one reference in the concordance: *Hamlet*. The fiend had clearly doctored it to taunt me:

> In the rank sweat of an enseamed bed,
> Stew'd in corruption, honeying and making love
> Over the nasty sty!

I knew the story of *Hamlet* fairly well so I didn't read the whole play, only a few scenes, especially the scenes between Hamlet and his mother, Gertrude. Throughout the play Hamlet slams Gertrude for marrying his uncle. In the killer's corrupted version, he is clearly referring to Brent and me. And on stationery exactly like Brent's. *He's homophobic. That's clear enough. Taunt all you want, asshole! We'll see who taunts last.*

I had a sudden thought. Maybe Bear was right. *Maybe he wants to be caught. Yes, he's tired of the chase, but can't stop on his own. His last chase!* I will be his *last* chaser. That's what he said. *He knows he must be stopped. So this note and tape...yes...it's his plea for help. Begging me to stop him.*

If you believe that Kevin Porter, you're as crazy as the killer.

I closed the books and returned them to the shelves. Thanked my helpful mother-hen librarian, and walked down the steps toward the exit. "Didn't you wear a coat?"

"Huh?" I looked around at the librarian leaning over the balcony's steel railing.

"It's pouring."

"It wasn't when I got here. The sun was shining."

"Are you new to Vancouver? Never leave home without your umbrella," she scolded.

I looked up at the huge sloped skylight over the stairs. The rain was cascading down it like a waterfall. And I had no coat, no umbrella. Shit!

"Thanks. I'll be okay." I continued walking down the stairs toward the exit. *So, what's he telling us, this director/actor killer who knows his Shakespeare?* My head was reeling as I poked my nose outside the library. I had entered on a beautiful sunny morning. I exited at four in a dark, pouring-cold-rainy afternoon. Zigzagging through the streets of the West End, I padded home, leaping puddles all the way. My feet were sopping. My hair was dripping. Icy water trickled down my neck. If anyone followed me trudging home that stormy day, they would have heard me raging at the storm.

I wanted a long hot soak. And an afternoon nap. I deserved it. I railed at the weather until I reached home.

I SENSED SOMETHING pressing down on my mouth, hard, unyielding. I couldn't breathe. Someone was smothering me. But I wasn't me any more. I was Nancy. Nancy on her death bed. I tried to scream. I gasped and opened my eyes. Two dark eyes stared back into mine.

"Wake up, sleeping beauty."

I stifled a scream of terror. "Ahhh?"

"What's the matter with you?"

The eyes pulled back. Brent's mouth left mine. He stood beside the bed, looking down on me with a smile. "Still in bed, darl'?" I stared, uncertain that reality had indeed replaced my nightmare. "Haven't you roused yourself all day? I phoned you five times, sleepy head."

"Brent," I whispered.

He bent over to give me another kiss. And his eyes came at me again.

I rolled over, still unsure of where I was. Who I was. Brent jumped on the bed. "Is my lover playing hard to get?" *Oh no. He* was going to whisker kiss me, a favorite game of his. Brent started rubbing me with his five-o'clock shadow. I could feel my body tingling as his face darted everywhere. He kept repeating, "I'm going to eat you up." I was awake. I wasn't dreaming. I started to laugh, not because whisker burns had ever turned me on, but relieved that I was no longer asleep. I was no longer Nancy. On her bed of torture.

Brent nuzzled me and whispered, "Are you awake now, my sweet love?"

My nightmare flashed back into my brain, as real as Brent's whisker burns and mischievous school-boy giggles. There had been three in my dream. Me, Brent, and the killer. I was making love to Brent, listening to his moans of pleasure, when suddenly I heard his voice from the other side of the room. I turned and saw...Brent...sitting on the dresser, aiming a camcorder at me. "Look at yourself, you disgusting whore." Then I heard his voice to the right. I looked over and a new Brent was standing on the lounge filming me and shouting, "You call yourself a porn star? You think anyone's going to pay to see you trying to look sexy?" Then another voice from the hallway and yet another Brent. "Get with it, old man.

Enjoy him."

"Yes. Enjoy me!" Brent's voice was now coming from in front of me. A dark, voluminous laugh erupted from deep inside him. I was surrounded by a huge ethereal white cloud that was enveloping me. I could no longer move a muscle. Slowly his head turned but I could see only his eyes through the mist, eyes of ever-changing colors becoming larger and larger. Bright green. Shiny blue. Laughing brown. I tried to get up, to run, to escape, but I was bound to the bed. I was Nancy again. Nancy on her death bed. The eyes came closer and closer. Then disappeared altogether in the white fog. I was being suffocated with my own pillow. My mouth, my nose, my lungs were bursting. I was filled with terror. Then silence. My life was being snuffed out. I stopped breathing.

Then I heard Brent's voice, pulling me back to reality once more. I opened my eyes. I tried to focus on my lover's smiling face. "How are you, sweetie?" he asked, now concerned. I stared into his eyes, his dark brown eyes holding mine. *Am I still dreaming?* "What's happening to you, Kev? Wake up, Jessica." I inhaled deeply and let the air out slowly, evenly. I could feel Brent's face next to mine. His bristly five-o'clock shadow pressed into my cheek. He whispered softly into my ear... I was back again, in my nightmare.

Chapter
Thirty-Two

TUESDAY MORNING, I was sitting uncomfortably in the North Van conference room with Spivic, Joan, and Dr. Ormand. We had finished listening to the tape that Bear received yesterday and had read the accompanying note. Bear had asked me to fill them in on my library search, so that was now all behind us. I sat quietly, looking at the bulletin boards. Many more memoranda, newspaper clippings, and the latest Polaroid had been tacked up.

I had a rip-roaring headache. All night I'd had repeated flashbacks of my nightmare, whether I was asleep or awake. Even during my presentation this morning, I had two trips back into Nancy's body. We were both being smothered by Brent. Filmed by Brent. I couldn't shake the nightmare. I felt the six pressure points on the back of my head with my fingertips. *Take this headache away. Empty my head.* I still hadn't determined why I had been invited to this meeting, but refused to ask; better to keep quiet and listen. I'd put my foot in my mouth the last time I was here; I wasn't about to contract permanent foot and mouth disease.

Dr. Ormand, an old-world European psychiatrist, was a rambler, but pretty much on the mark. "Very interesting, Mr. Porter. A good piece of deductive reasoning. Your serial killer is, in all probability, a sociopath," he sucked on his pipe, "a homicidal sociopath. It's highly possible in cases like this that no one knows the real killer except his victim. And, of course, himself." He looked at Joan. "You say he wears disguises."

"Yes, that's our theory. We have no real proof of that other than the entry on the victim's calendar, indicating that she invited a woman in to freshen up."

"Yes, I read that calendar entry." He pointed to the bulletin board that contained a photocopy of all of the calendar pages. I squirmed. There, smiling at us, was the picture of Brent and Nancy.

"And of course we have her diary, which you've already read, Dr. Ormand," reminded Joan.

"Yes. Yes, but that was merely the ramblings of a lovesick girl."

I opened my mouth to explain about Nancy's writing a novel but, before I had a chance to make my point, Ormand dismissed my story as "clutching at straws." Maybe he was right. I'd stay zipped up.

"Kev believes that Nancy *identified* her killer in that diary," emphasized Bear, "so, let's go along with that theory fer a while, eh?"

"All right, Sergeant Spivic." Ormand fixed his beady eyes on me. "Let's say your killer was stalking his victim. It's logical that he would keep hidden, but if he was particularly brazen, he might disguise himself and meet her face to face. Such confrontations stimulate many predators in the human and animal kingdom. The cat loves to confront the mouse and then move away. Several times will the cat do this, and then—" Ormand banged his hand on Joan's desk so hard, she jumped. He then mimed eating the mouse.

"The killer, in disguise, probably came into close proximity to Nancy four or five times during the month," Joan added. "Her diary indicates this."

"If we accept the diary as substantive evidence, your killer was getting braver and braver each time he met her, probably planning exactly what he would do and how he would look, making sure that his disguise would never give him away." Ormand stuffed more tobacco into his pipe and lit up. I could tell that he was coming around, believing that there just might be some relevance in the diary entries.

"And on the night of September Twenty-Fifth, Nancy invited him into her cabin, thinking he was an injured woman," Joan offered.

"Yes, I can see that your killer would enjoy doing that. Think of the thrill he would feel, knowing that his mouse had no notion that a killer cat was ready to pounce." Ormand smiled at his strained analogy.

"And then," Bear declared, "he showed his true colors to Nancy."

"But, by that time, it was too late for her," Joan stated softly.

"He must have overpowered her with fear," I added, unable to contain myself. "Probably he had a gun, because she had no bruises."

"Whatcha mean?" asked Bear.

"With a gun pointed at her, she probably obeyed his demands until she was in no position to fight back, gun or no gun."

"That's right, Mr. Porter, serial killers enjoy power." Ormand continued, "And never tire of reliving the immediate events leading up to the murder."

"Ever since I went to the cabin, I have wondered what I would have done if such a maniac confronted me." There was no shutting me up now. I was describing my nightmare. "I've crawled into Nancy's skin. That night. I'm looking forward to a quiet weekend. And then an accident victim bangs on my door. A woman in distress. Bleeding. Of course I would take her in. Try to help her. But then, she becomes a he? And *he* intends to kill me? Film me and kill me."

I looked up. Everyone in the room was quietly staring at me. I was lost in the daze of my nightmare. I coughed and rubbed my head. "If I were Nancy and realized my life was in jeopardy, I'd kick him in the balls and run outside into the forest. I know the forest. The paths. I'd escape. I'm strong, athletic, clever. So why didn't I get the hell out of there?...I was surprised? Tricked?...I knew who he was? Or...he had a gun?"

I stopped again, on the verge of being drawn back into my nightmare. "That's a possibility. What can a victim do when her life depends on the caprice of a monster who retains the power of life and death? Simple: she holds on. And on and on and..."

"The killer took Polaroids," interjected Joan. From the look she was giving me, she obviously wanted to shut me up and give the meeting back to Ormand. I took the hint.

"Yes, I know. Corporal Davis showed me a copy of the one you found at the scene of the murder as well as the one the killer sent to the newspaper. The computer blowups, I understand, indicated that the killer has murdered at least four other women." Ormand looked at us all and pointed to the bulletin boards. "There are probably a lot more photos like those two that he would look at while masturbating in the security of his safe place. It's classic serial-killer behavior. And may I be so bold as to conclude that your killer probably made a sniff film of Nancy Henderson?"

"Snuff film, I believe it's called," Joan asserted.

"Ah, yes. Snuff film. The big moment for your killer would be to capture on film the last breath of his victim as he snuffed out her life."

Bear butted in, "I hear such films are sold for hundreds of bucks on the black market."

"No, no, no," insisted Ormand, "I am using *snuff film* in its narrower sense. I.E. someone being murdered while involved in a sexual scenario, not someone merely dying on film. The police used the snuff films of Bernardo and Charles Ng as evidence in their trials. You will never see these for sale."

I had another flashback. *I was in a snuff film. I know exactly how it feels.*

"Kev, are you okay?" I looked up. Joan was giving me a concerned look.

"Sure. No problem. Only a slight headache. Think I got a chill yesterday."

"Ya know, the creep's probably in the damn thing," scowled Bear. "I bet his ugly puss is on film somewheres. If his snuff film ever turns up, we'd have our hard proof."

"I don't think he would sell his film," Ormand said. "I don't think he'd ever want anyone but himself to see it. He probably is still — how do you put it? — getting his rockets off on it. Right?"

"Yeah, ya got it right, Doc. Do ya think the killer lives alone?" asked Bear.

"Quite probably. But you would be surprised how many women never know that their mates are leading double lives. These husbands may have families and be exemplary citizens. And then, one day, one of these paragons of virtue cracks and becomes a Mr. Hyde."

"Yer paintin' a picture of a killer who could be jist about anybody." Bear shook his head. "He could be any Tom, Dick, or Harry."

"Yes, unfortunately, you have no hard evidence as to your killer's profession or personality, other than his fixation for cleanliness."

"Maybe he's a cleaner," suggested Bear, "or a window washer, or a..."

"Or anything, Sergeant Spivic," replied Ormand. "Your killer could work in any profession. His fixation on cleanliness could reasonably be attributed to the killer's attempts at removing evidence, rather than any deeper psychological motivation."

"Ya think? Anyways, we've also been checkin' all the makeup artists in the greater Vancouver area," Bear announced brightly.

"That's a good idea. And I think you should continue," conceded Ormand. "Your killer could very well be a qualified makeup artist, and if he passes himself off as a beautiful woman, he must be an accomplished actor. And one who is devoted to Shakespeare. To be a successful female impersonator, he most likely has a slight physique."

"But still have muscles. Our man is strong." Everyone looked at me. I forged ahead. "He probably works out a lot. When we finish with the TV and film studios, we should visit the..."

"What makes you think he's still here, Mr. Porter?" asked Ormand.

"It's a feeling I can't shake. And don't forget the taunts we've been receiving have all been sent locally. That tells me that our guy, whether he lives here permanently or he's only visiting, needs gratification."

Bear asked, "Why does that tell ya he needs gratification?"

Ormand answered. "Your killer must be — how do you put it — mounting the walls...because you're all keeping quiet. He wants to hear you talk about him. He wants to read things that you are saying about him. He wants to fill his scrapbook with clippings about his latest big kill."

"So," Bear nodded, "he decides to help us a bit."

"Exactly," I said, "And, Joan, I think you're dead right in keeping silent. Can you imagine how he was feeling, having to send his second calling card to Franny McGhie, from Vancouver I might add, and no one from the Detachment here breathes a word to the media." I had their attention so I continued, "And with the brouhaha surrounding the gay murders, our killer probably felt neglected. He had to make another statement. So he sends us a tape of his victim and a taunting note. Our guy is probably as jealous as hell that another killer is in the spotlight, receiving the attention that should rightly be his. We've established that he has a huge ego. I bet he listens to the news every night, hoping to catch a glimpse of you, Bear. It would give him a thrill to be close to you, even talk to you. All the while he'd be laughing at you because you didn't realize who he was."

"That's very correct, Mr. Porter," puffed Ormand. "Your killer could disguise himself as a man or a woman and talk directly to you or Sergeant Spivic."

"Sergeant Spivic, has any stranger made a point of talking to you?" asked Joan. "Since the murder, I mean."

"I don't think so." Bear scratched his belly.

"How about at the college or at the funeral or when you were being interviewed on television?" Joan pushed him. "Think, Sergeant, any unusually striking woman try to come on to you?"

"Hey, wait a minute. One did. When I was comin' out of Kev's apartment block on the day of Nancy Henderson's funeral." He looked at me. "When you wuz out on the deck with the Hendersons. I nearly bumped into this gorgeous redhead. I'm kind o' partial to redheads, so I noticed. Anyways, she wuz lookin' up at yer penthouse."

Everyone in the room suddenly tensed. "What did she look like?" I insisted, "Describe her."

"She was a knockout. All in black. A suit with a skirt. Long black gloves and a filmy kind o' scarf around her neck that she kept playin' with when she wuzn't showin' off her legs to me."

"A scarf hides an Adam's apple," Joan interjected.

"Ya think?" Bear answered.

Ormand chimed in, "Was she wearing a lot of makeup?" All eyes were on Bear, who was becoming rattled by the unexpected focus on him. He nodded his answer.

"Did she say anything to you?" I asked.

"Well," he said hesitantly, "at first I thought she wuz lost, so I asked her if she needed any help. But she said that she wuz jist admirin' the penthouse. I looked up and saw you and the Hendersons jist walkin' inside. I told her I'd jist come from there. 'You should see it,' I said." He looked at everyone in the room. "Kev has got the greatest-looking apartment I ever seen."

"Anything else?" Joan scowled.

"Ya betcha. I remember exactly what she said."

"What?" I raised my voice.

" 'One day maybe I might.' "

"I would like to make a wager. I wager you five dollars, each, that was your killer." Ormand stood up and shouted, "Sergeant Spivic, you were looking into the eyes of your killer on the day of his victim's funeral."

Joan added, "He probably followed you both to the apartment. He knows you both by sight and name."

The silence was thick. We all immediately understood the significance of what Joan had said.

She continued, "Neither of you is safe anymore."

"Hell," I put in, "none of us is ever safe in this business. Barry, is it possible that redhead could have been..."

Abby rushed into Joan's office with an armful of reports. She was flushed. Frothing with excitement. Ready to burst. Joan said, "Ah, Corporal Davis."

Abby exploded, "I've got a match. Dates. Names. Places. Autopsy reports." We all stared at her. Instead of saying anything more, she started throwing down copies of her report in front of each of us. Then she said, "Read 'em and weep." She sat down and wiped the spittle from the corners of her mouth.

Trying to play down the melodrama of her young corporal, yet pleased and excited herself, Joan said, "Would you like to stay for the rest of our meeting, Dr. Ormand?"

"Wild water buffalo couldn't pull me away," replied Ormand, his eyes sparkling as he opened the report.

I noted that Abby had assembled a list of unsolved North American cases of women murdered over the past six years. There were well over two hundred. "Before you all start to read," Abby broke in, "I want to point out that the cases I've selected for you to look over are only a handful of the hundreds of unsolved female murders that have been reported on ViCLAS and VICAP over the last six years. Each has at least one similar MO to Nancy Henderson's murder.

"What I thought would be helpful is if you put one to five beside each case, one representing those we should not waste time investigating further; five representing those cases we should find out more about." She looked at each of us, licking her lips. "One is an exact match to Nancy's murder, to which you will certainly assign a five. But I'm not going to tell you which case it is. I don't want to influence you." She looked like the proverbial cat, trying to hide the canary feathers from the corners of her mouth.

"Then we can pool our findings and go from there," added Joan, still trying to be a calming influence in the room.

"By the way," continued Abby, "I've ignored all domestic murders, all gunshot and stabbing murders, all murders of known prostitutes...."

"Why eliminate prostitutes?" interrupted Ormand. "If their deaths follow your killer's pattern, we should study them."

"You may be right," I interjected before Abby could respond, "but I think that our killer enjoys the more virginal victims so that he can stalk them over a long period of time. Remember the blow-ups. All of the women looked glamorous, yet innocent, after he had bouffanted their hair and made them up. Probably to look like his mother," I emphasized. "I think he would consider prostitutes beneath him." Bear sniggered.

"A good observation, Mr. Porter. But humor me for a moment. Maybe your killer has moved up in the world of murder. Now, he stalks the virgin. Before, when he was learning his craft, he apprenticed on prostitutes. They would be easy prey for your killer."

Abby took note of Dr. Ormand's theory, as we all did. "I will do another search for unsolved murders of prostitutes who have at least one of the same Henderson MO characteristics. It'll take me till tomorrow to get on ViCLAS and VICAP."

Joan nodded. "Thank you, Dr. Ormand, for your suggestion." I was impressed. Ormand could well be right.

He sat back, filled his pipe, and enjoyed playing sleuth. "Now, let's snare our killer."

Our killer? Ormand had become one of us.

We read in silence, each of us making notes in the margins of Abby's thorough reports.

TWO HOURS LATER, everyone but Bear had finished reading. As each of us finished, it was obvious from our looks that we were excited. Anxious to discuss what we'd read, we waited, watching Bear turn the pages slowly, meticulously write in a "mark" for the report he was reading as if he were a conscientious grade-school teacher correcting his students' papers. Finishing one, he'd inhale deeply and take another from the unread pile.

Joan smiled. "Okay. Let's have a little break. I'm sure we can all do with a stretch. I'll get us some coffee and send out for donuts. It looks like Sergeant Spivic is doing a more thorough job of reading than the rest of us." He looked up and grinned.

We all went off in different directions, leaving Bear to finish. Joan had a nice way of making Corporal Spivic feel important.

"Make sure you get some chocolate donuts," Bear said offhandedly, as we abandoned him.

I found Abby and asked her to make me a copy of her computer disk, containing the ViCLAS and VICAP information about the murders.

"EAT SLOWER, LOVE," prompted Brent.

"Huh?" I looked up, having bolted down a mouthful of the delicious dinner that Brent had prepared, but I couldn't have told him what I'd swallowed to save my soul. I continued shoveling in the food, munching and scribbling notes on the pad I'd laid beside my plate. "Sorry, hon, but I've got to hole up in the den tonight. I have to study the two murder cases that we unanimously assigned a five. They both had identical MOs. I also want to study one that I think is important enough to include, even though no one else considered it significant."

Brent had no idea what I was babbling about. But he could tell that I was wired. I could also tell that he was not impressed with me. Pissed off would better describe his feelings towards me. For the past couple of weeks I'd neglected him terribly and here it was, another Tuesday night, our regular movie night, and we were staying in.

He had always loved watching thrillers with me. He never stopped holding my hand while munching his popcorn or sipping his drink with the other. When the tension ever started to build, he would begin to squeeze my hand and, when really scary bits leapt out of the screen, he would nearly break off my fingers. Once he actually pulled my arm right out of its socket.

"Aren't we going to a movie tonight? There's a great double bill at the Denman."

"What's on?" I muttered, jotting down another note.

"Don't sound too interested."

"What?"

"Ah, what the hell. I'm going by myself."

"Yeah. That'll be nice. I've got my work cut out for me tonight." I flipped over a page. "Hope to meet Bear tomorrow morning at eleven at the Detachment. We're finally onto something." While I was talking shop, Brent got up from his unfinished dinner, put his shoes and coat on, and called up the elevator.

"Where are you going?"

"Oh, you noticed?"

"Of course I noticed."

"I don't want to interfere with your work. See ya." Brent got into the elevator and disappeared. I ran to the balcony.

He didn't look up. He was in a right smart huff, and had every right to be. "Have a nice time, Grass Widow," I called after him.

He turned around and looked at me. Then he blew me a kiss. I caught it. I knew I'd get lots of apologies later tonight, but there was no way Brent was going to come back now.

I didn't waste any time getting to my den and turning on the computer. I wanted to read the two cases that everyone had given a five to again and add my own observations in caps. That's the way I used to work to make what someone else wrote totally mine. But I used to do it in longhand.

The screen sprang to life. There, in my WordPerfect document, was an e-mail letter to Brent. He'd probably moved it from Eudora to WP and had forgotten to close the file. I knew I shouldn't be reading his personal mail, but there it was:

Hi, Brent,

Why the hell haven't you written? You know what I mean? Ever since I answered that Chief Inspector's questionnaire about you, I haven't heard an effing word from you. Come on now, girl. What's going on? As far as I'm concerned, the only excuse for you not writing is that they've finally nabbed you for murder. So if you don't answer, I'm assuming the worst.

I'm dying. You know what I mean? Ever since you made me throw my stash down the john, I've been scared s***less to buy any more. You owe me, girl. You know what I mean?

Remember our motto, one for all and all for one. "Us criminals" have to stick together. You know what I mean? Ha. Ha. But seriously, I don't see how they could lay that murder on you. All us girls told Joan Riley that you were on the Wanderlust with us for the whole weekend. I talked to them all and we've agreed to help you. Sisters stick together.

So write already.

Keep your pecker up — Marydontask

I bounced the letter back to Brent's documents. But I couldn't help wondering what that letter was all about. And how could I ask Brent about the contents without divulging that I'd "accidentally" read Marydontask's letter? What did he mean by "Remember our motto, one for all and all for one"? I tried to get into Brent's e-mail to read his reply, but I didn't know his password. I couldn't shake one resounding question: Is it possible that they were all covering for Brent that weekend?

Stop it. That's plain stinkin' thinkin'. Get on with the facts of the case.

I slipped in the computer disk that Abby had given me. Apprehensively, I began my task of entering my own observations into the document. I started by typing in some details that I alone thought significant.

I'd been blown away ever since I discovered the locations of the three murders: Winnipeg, San Francisco, and Hawaii. Each was where one of my kids lived. Each was where Brent and I visited at least once a year.

Chapter
Thirty-Three

HARRY WAS NEARLY home after a grueling six hours on the Fraser River. The shoot had gone well. Like clockwork. No hitches. Loads of compliments all round. Even DD had done surprisingly well.

And then the producer called an emergency meeting. As the cast and crew listened to him read an official statement from the big boys to the south, all his compliments became hollow lies.

"After five seasons of producing *The X-Files* in Vancouver, Twentieth Century Fox Television has reached a decision to move the series production to Southern California for the beginning of the show's next season."

Everyone in the crowd groaned, knowing now that the rumors had been correct. Harry looked around for DD, but he had disappeared. *Coward.*

The director continued, "Vancouver has been home to *The X-Files* for five years, and the support of the city and its citizens and the superlative work of the film community have been invaluable to the show's incredible success..."

Blah! Blah! Blah! *What the hell am I going to do now? DD wouldn't want me as his personal makeup artist down there in Hollywood. Besides, I couldn't get a green card. I don't want anybody investigating me.*

Driving home, he could only think of getting out of Harry's clothes and taking off Harry's makeup. He was agitated, not himself, pissed off. He needed to get up to his apartment and cuddle into the back of his Kate, his Queen Katherine, his Mother.

He stepped on his brakes. "Who the hell is that, walking the streets at this time of night?" he cursed. "Brentie-boy. Now what are you doing walking along English Bay at eleven thirty? Cruising? Yeah. That's what I bet you're up to. On the make without your 'Daddy.' Bet he's home snoring while you're sniffing around for cock. Well, you ain't getting a look at my family jewels, you little fruit. It's too fucking limp tonight."

He couldn't resist lowering his window as he drove slowly by Brent, and giving him a looking-for-company stare.

Brent stopped walking and glanced over. His eyes told

everything. Sudden interest. *Ah! Sweet vengeance will soon be mine.*

He pressed his foot on the gas and the dark blue Toyota sped down Beach Avenue. "Oh, I love being a cock-tease," he laughed himself silly all the way home, feeling a little bit better. "I'll get you, Brentie-boy. But only when I'm good and ready."

"HI, DARL'."

I jumped. Brent was standing in the doorway of the den. I hadn't heard him come in. He came over and gave me a peck on the top of my head. "Were the movies good?"

"Yeah, but I had no one to hold hands with. One was really scary."

"I'm sorry." I looked up at Brent's sad face. "You know I wouldn't stand you up if there was any way to get out of this huge job."

"I know. I'm going to bed."

"What time is it?"

He looked at his watch. "Twelve thirty."

"I'll be up soon."

"Don't hurry. Finish the job. It'll be worth it if you nail Nancy's killer up by his balls." He walked upstairs. No hug, no goodnight kiss.

"Where's Brent been for the last hour and a half?" I thought. "The movie got out at eleven and the theatre's five minutes away."

I heard the shower running. Brent showers at least three times a day. Another difference between us. I grew up with Saturday-night baths in a metal tub that my whole family shared. The same water grew grayer as each of us slipped out: first Dad, then my sister, me, and finally Mom who had spent all day heating the water on the back of the wood stove. "Don't you pee in there Kevin," she'd warn.

And here I am now, sixty years later, sitting in a lush two-floor penthouse, living with the man of my dreams, who happens to be half my age, staring at a computer screen that is telling me that page one of my personal document has been printed.

And I still don't feel completely content. An uneasiness has been creeping over my heart ever since Nancy's murder. *Will my world collapse?* I whispered, "Will I lose my lover?"

There, I finally said it. I hadn't discussed my suspicions with anyone, but there it was. I still suspected Brent. *He may be the killer. Or an accomplice. Fuck. How do I shake these negative thoughts?* But what the hell had he been up to tonight?

I realized I had tears in my eyes. "Smarten up, you old fart," I spat and forced myself to pick up the first few pages of my forty-page report. I wanted to give the whole thing another read before I attached it to my e-mail to Bear.

CERTAIN SECTIONS OF the report I will dream about for years to come...

The four victims: Nancy Henderson Murdered in BC Sept. 27, 1998; Susan James Murdered in Kona, Hawaii 1 1/2 years ago; Dorothy Parkinson Murdered in San Francisco 3 years ago; Georgina MacIntyre Murdered in Winnipeg 4 1/2 years ago.

Similarities: All victims were in their twenties, Caucasian, brunette, healthy, athletic, attractive; all were respected citizens in good jobs; all lived alone; all owned cars; all were killed within approximately 18 months of each other; all were savagely and repeatedly raped and had endured fellatio–Dorothy's rape was more savage and of a different nature.

There were many other similarities I'd committed to memory: all hair — sixty's bouffant; all fingernails — painted, except for their right pinkies; all had something cut out or cut off; all left thumbs in their mouths.

And calling cards left in Ziploc bags with Polaroids of the victims with typed messages. Plus braids of three pubic hairs.

In my e-mail I made a note to Bear to request original photos of victims so we could blow them up and compare them to each other.

I made a note to myself to check out the messages on the back of the photos. I remembered only too well the message on the back of Nancy's "A souvenir for the RCMP for remembrance. I already have mine." On Susan James's: "A souvenir for the State Patrol to make your remembrance dear. I already have mine." There was no message on the back of Dorothy's hateful picture. But Georgina's read: "A souvenir for the police to burden your remembrances with a heaviness that's gone. I already have mine."

I'm going to check my trusty Shakespeare concordance to find the sources of the killer's taunts on the backs of the Polaroids.

I sent Bear a list of my observations that went on for six pages. Most important: We are definitely dealing with a serial killer.

I provided him with a profile of the killer: Our Clean Fiend is devoid of conscience. Self assured. Thinks he's brilliant. Shakespearean scholar. Probably a theatre actor or director. Accomplished makeup artist and hairdresser. Mother fixation. Probably involved incestuously with her. Feels superior to police. Confident that he commits perfect crimes. Has murdered at least four women. Definitely a clean freak. Probably homophobic. Has killed at least one transvestite, Dorothy Parkinson.

I read over the profile again. *These heinous details couldn't possibly apply to Brent. Unless...unless I have been entirely hoodwinked.* "Stupid old man," I hissed. "Get those thoughts out of your one-track brain."

I looked at the stack of pages sitting in the print tray. They contained Forensic Pathology and Police reports on Susan, Dorothy, and Georgina. All with my own personal observations included in caps.

I was too tired, too depressed, and felt too dirty to read anymore. I e-mailed Bear a quick note:

Bear,
　　First, congratulate Abby on her search of victims throughout North America. She did a splendid job, very thorough. My respect for ViCLAS and VICAP has gone way up. They may be the death of gumshoes like you and me before we know it. Beware the future! Private Detectives will be standing in the unemployment line.
　　Ask Abby to call Inspector Archie Hall at Scotland Yard. I want him to search for any murder that took place in London six or more years ago with a similar MO to Nancy's. Tell Abby to send my regards to Archie.
　　I have attached my report. You can pick it up in your "Receive" file. Look for C:/receive/cleanfiend.wpc.

See you about nine at the Detachment.
Kev

I highlighted the second paragraph, intent on deleting it before I sent it to Bear. I had felt like a traitor as I typed it, but, hell, I'm a cop. I sent the letter *with* that paragraph. I switched off my computer and left the den.

I didn't want to wake Brent, so I took a shower in the downstairs bathroom off the guest room. This area was set off from the rest of the penthouse in its own wing. It was nice because guests could feel independent and come and go as they wished without disturbing us beyond the French doors.

While showering, I came to a devastating realization. During my life, I'd given more attention to strangers than to those nearest and dearest to me. Hell, I thought I knew Martha really well, having lived with her for twenty-eight years. I hadn't a clue she was having an affair with another man during the last two years of our marriage. I was too concerned with myself and my work to sense what my own wife needed. There are evil people in the world and, all too often, those closest to them are the last to know the truth. Dr. Ormand's words came into my mind: "The killer could be someone's husband (or *lover*) and appear to all intents and purposes perfectly normal. And then, one day, he's a Mr. Hyde."

How could I possibly suspect Brent? *But then, how much do I really know about him? What goes on behind those gorgeous almond eyes? What secrets lurk in his past? Where does he go when he heads out on his own? And what exactly does he do? What does anyone truly know about another? They say we all have a dark side.* Was my imagination getting the better of me? Or were my insecurities overriding my common sense? Could my kind, sweet lover be the clean fiend?

I remember all too well the first night I met Brent at English Bay. He took me to his home, this penthouse, and we made sensational love. When he put me in the elevator, he kissed me passionately and asked, "What's your name?" That's another gay thing. After having sex, exchange names. Go figure.

Anyway, I said, "Kevin. Kevin J. Porter."

"What's the J stand for?"

"That's for me to know and you to find out." I grinned. "What's your name?"

He hesitated. "Brent," he said.

"And," I prodded. He hesitated again.

"Have you forgotten?" I laughed, a little uneasily.

He looked into my eyes and said, "Barnes." I wondered, at the time, why he really didn't want to share his name with me. Curious.

And as I stood near the elevator, I was still wondering: *Maybe I should crawl into bed down here in the guest room. But how would I explain my not sleeping with my lover? In the morning, Brent would give me the third degree.*

I punched in the security code and slipped upstairs, crawling in beside my lover's warm, naked, sweet-smelling body. So clean. I leaned over and kissed his delicate skin. A Judas kiss!

Chapter
Thirty-Four

"DID YOU GET my report, Bear?" It was eight a.m. and I'd just walked into the North Van RCMP interrogation room where Bear was organizing stacks of paper.

"Sure did, Kev. I wuz in here at six this mornin'. Abby wuz here before me and she's already bin in contact with Scotland Yard. Yer Inspector friend, Archie Hall, said he'd get right on it. Pip pip 'n' all that rot!"

"Great." After nearly four weeks, we were finally onto something. But I was growing more and more afraid of the results.

"I got a lot of questions about yer report, Kev."

"Thought you would."

"Naturally, I already read over all them autopsies and police reports and made my own notes, but I really appreciated readin' yer comments. Thanks fer the notes to me. I already got on to 'em all. I know now why you wuz made chief."

"Thanks. I wanted to bring you into my thought processes. We've got to crack this case together."

"Ya betcha." Bear smiled a little nervously. "Now to my questions." He turned to my Observations section, coming right to the point. "Why should we look to London? What makes ya think the killer started his handiwork over there?"

"Just a hunch."

"A hunch?"

"Yeah."

"Come on, Kev, cough up." He stared me down, not saying another word.

"Well, I..."

"What?

I took a deep breath. "I don't know where to start."

"Ya suspect Brent, don'tcha?"

I was astounded by Bear's keen insight. "How did you know?"

"Elementary, my dear Kevin," he laughed. "Barbi lives in Kona, Sammy lives in San Fran, Jean's in Winnipeg, *and* Tim 'n' Jim's in London."

I kept staring at Bear. He was getting ready for a loaded

question, I could feel it coming. "Do you 'n Brent visit yer kids regularly? T'gether?"

"Yes." I lowered my head. And then like a little kid, I spat, "Martha visits them, too."

"Hey, calm down, Kev. I'm not gonna arrest yer boyfriend again. Yer forgettin' somethin'. Eleven of his 'friends' all swore that he wuz with him from September Twenty-fifth to -seventh. The guy can't be in two places at once."

"Yeah. You're right, b..."

"But? You were gonna say 'but,' weren't ya?" I was. My suspicions of Brent were screaming in my brain. I'd barely slept the whole night, doubting my whole life with him. The pickup, moving in, accepting his generous gifts, being his senior toy.

I exploded. "It's possible that he got everyone on that bloody yacht to provide him with an alibi. 'Birds of a feather.' You know what I mean?" I stopped, realizing that tears were flowing down my cheeks. Bear continued to look directly at me. I tried to laugh. "I don't know what I'm saying. Hell, I'm too upset to think straight."

"No pun intended," smirked Bear.

That old bugger! He pretends to be stupid to get dopes like me to spill our guts. I suddenly had a new respect for Sergeant Barry "Bear" Spivic, but—if I was right—this wasn't the time to break his cover. I continued as if not hearing him, because, frankly, I wanted to air all my dirty suspicions.

"Brent and I were in those exact cities where those murders took place."

"So?"

"So," I gulped, "there were lots of times he was on his own. We never stayed with my kids. That would be too much for them. You know, to see their dad and his young lover going off to the same bedroom at night. They'd be up all night, listening to see what we were up to. So we stayed in apartment hotels where we'd cook and have them over for an occasional dinner. As well as have our own friends over, too. You know what I mean?

"I think I get the picture."

"Anyway, I often visited my kids and their families on my own. I even spent a few nights with them. Brent, of course, was on his own. He had opportunity, damn it. I never questioned him when I returned, and he never offered much other than to tell me about what he'd been reading. Brent's an avid reader. And at times, a non-communicator."

"Let's cut the stonewalling. Were you both in these places during the exact times of the murders?"

"No. Never."

"Well, there you are. Your boy can't be in two places at once. Right?"

"But he travels a lot. He belongs to a volleyball team that's competed in the gay games for several years. Even before we met. The games are held all over the world. Last night I checked our itinerary calendars for the past seven years. I record all our trips: mine and his. During Susan James's murder in Kona, Brent and his team played in Sydney, with a stopover in Hawaii for a few days. And during Dorothy Parkinson's, Brent was in San Francisco with his team."

"But Dorothy was a he. Brent doesn't hate homos, so he'd never kill one."

I ignored Bear and continued, "And during Georgina MacIntyre's murder, Brent was in Winnipeg with his team."

"Bingo!" It was Abby. She opened the door of the small interrogation office without knocking and plunked a five-page report on the table in front of me. "Read this MO from London, taken from Scotland Yard files. They're fast. See the date of the murder. Seven years ago."

I read the MO of Christine Perkins, twenty-two, Caucasian, prostitute, raped, fully made up, dark red nail polish on all nails but the right baby finger. Cleaned out with bleach. Found in a basement flat in Brixton. A photo had been found under her body. It was a picture of her mouth with the killer's dick in it. A typed message had been fixed on the back of the photo: "Whore! The ignominy sleep with thee in the grave, / But not remembered in thy epitaph!"

"What the hell," I said to Abby and Bear, "it sounds like our killer's an English major." I continued to read. "And get this," I read aloud, "no finger prints were found, but several black pubic hairs were discovered on the victim's body. Our prossy was a natural blonde. All over." The case was still open, but little attention had been given to it. Probably because of the heavy incidence of prostitute murders in London.

I put down the report and looked up at Bear. Reaching into my back pocket, I took out a piece of paper and looked at it. I said gravely, "When Christine Perkins got herself killed, Brent and his team were competing in Amsterdam, with a layover in London!"

At that instant, Bear pressed a tape recorder. I heard Brent's voice: "Hi, Nancy. I'm sorry I left you standing in the parking lot. But you know I had to hurry off to my big weekend. I'm really looking forward to it. I bet I'll enjoy my weekend more than you'll enjoy yours. Ha! Ha!"

As I listened to Brent's laugh, tears welled up in my eyes. Everything seemed to fall into place. Brent was guilty. The recording was the ultimate taunt to Nancy, to the Police, *to me*.

"Okay, I've heard and seen enough!" It was Joan's voice over the intercom. "Kevin, I want to see you in my office."

I looked at the two-way mirror and shouted at it, "What the fuck do you think you're up to, spying on me like that?" There was no answer. Maybe Joan had already left, feeling pretty shitty. I looked at Abby. "Were you in there, waiting to drop the Scotland Yard report on my lap right on cue?" I stopped my tirade, looking at both Bear and Abby's guilty faces. "Christ Almighty! Did you know all along there was a London connection?" Abby looked down and picked at her dirty thumbnail. I grabbed the report on Christine Perkins, and waved it at her. "You had this all along, didn't you? You had it yesterday. Didn't you?" I screamed. She wouldn't look up. I turned on Spivic. "Bear, I'm right. You set me up. Holy shit! I confided in you. Did you know that Joan was in there all the time? Eavesdropping?"

"You'd better go to Joan's office. She's waitin'." Bear and Abby left me alone.

As I waited alone, I felt old and worn out. I'd come in this morning feeling like Judas and now all I wanted to do was hang myself. *Shit!* I'd been taken in by a variation of the classic good cop/bad cop routine.

I'd experienced an excruciating twenty minutes, spilling my guts out like the snitch I was. Bear played the good cop to perfection, sucking me into his confidence. Joan was the silent bad cop, waiting her turn to pounce. I told them things I shouldn't have mentioned. Christ, I had confided in Bear. I thought we'd become friends! "Never trust a cop," I yelled, banging my clenched fist against the wall.

My hand hurt like hell. I looked at the mirror and saw a traitor. I could hear Brent saying the same words to me. "I thought we were *lovers*! Never trust a cop." I rubbed my fist with my other hand and groaned. I stormed out of the interrogation room and practically ran down the hall. I kicked Joan's door.

"Come in."

"Hi." I smiled at Joan as I walked into her smoke-filled office. "Is this the office of the bad cop?"

"You recognized the routine." Her eyes lowered as she stabbed out her cigarette in the butt-filled ashtray. "In a way, take it as a compliment. I was following the master's plan. Remember what a good team we used to be?"

"You did a good job on me. I never dreamt..."

She raised her head. Our eyes met. I saw sympathy there, felt her compassion. "We had to know whether or not you were protecting Barnes and whether or not you were in danger." I sat and listened to Joan in disbelief. "I've already been in touch with police stations all over the world. The gay committee members are probably being interviewed as we speak. I want to make sure that they were not lying in their responses to my questionnaire." I shuddered, remembering what Marydontask wrote: *we have to stick together.* Joan continued. "You're off the case as of now. Do you understand?"

"Yes."

"I have two requests to make of you. First, we need a sample of Brent's DNA, and perhaps a couple of his pubic hairs. Can you do this for me? It shouldn't be too hard. You probably have received several love letters from him. He'd probably have licked the stamp. We already have an example of the killer's DNA from the envelope he sent us with the second Polaroid." Joan continued as my head reeled, "And I'm sure you can find a pubic hair on the bottom sheet or..."

"I know how to find a goddamn pubic hair," I snapped.

"Okay, then. Sergeant Spivic will go home with you and be a witness to your finding the samples. He won't leave until he's got what I need. Those are his orders."

"And your other request?"

"That you disappear for a few days. Go visit one of your kids. I don't want you living in Barnes's penthouse anymore."

"What makes you think it's his..."

"His penthouse? Actually it's in his mother's name. But certainly not yours. Have you ever met his mother?"

"No. I don't think she's ever been to Vancouver." I stopped short. *Is she even alive? Did Brent...? No, stop thinking that way. Brent is innocent. He's my darling lover. My whole world, damn-it-to-hell.*

"You're a guest." I looked up at Joan. "A long-term guest of eight years, but still a guest."

I was smarting. "I'm not going to leave him."

"Why?"

"Because my gut tells me he's innocent. And I love him. He's done so much for me. More than I can ever explain to you. We've built a life together, filled with our own traditions, our own special memories." I smiled, probably pitifully. "We still exchange cards every month to celebrate the night we met. Tonight is our ninety-seventh month. As trite as it may sound, I only feel truly alive when I'm with him." Those damn tears again. They wouldn't stop.

"And I want you to remain alive."

"That's not what I meant."

"I know," soothed Joan. "I noticed a huge change in you when I saw you three weeks ago. You looked younger, more confident than you were twelve years ago. Your eyes had a sparkle that I don't remember ever having seen when we were working together."

"Well, I'm not leaving Brent, so you can forget that request."

"I didn't think you would. So I have another request. No, not a request, an order."

"What's that?"

"That you tell Brent nothing about the case. That mean's

nothing, Kevin. You understand?"

I nodded. "Uh huh."

"Tell him that we are taking over the case, which is a fact. You are not to contact anyone in the Force. And we will not contact you, until we are sure that we have enough hard evidence to make an arrest. Will you follow my orders?"

"Yes." I looked into Joan's eyes. "I promise." I got up to leave.

"By the way, I understand that Sergeant Spivic has seen every room in the penthouse except the master bedroom."

"That's right. What's the point?"

"Does Barnes have access to any of the other apartments in the complex? Or does he have another apartment close by?"

I hadn't a clue what Brent owned. But I knew exactly to what Joan was referring. "Not to my knowledge."

BEAR WALKED INTO our master bedroom, his mouth agape from the moment he entered.

A stunning nude of Brent and me hung on the wall facing our bed. The portrait was in excellent taste. I was in a sitting position; Brent was standing beside me, his arm on my shoulder. We both looked happy as kids, although we certainly didn't look like kids. The artist (an older friend of Brent's) was overly generous in painting certain parts of our anatomy. Not saying a word, Bear stared for a moment, then averted his eyes to the entertainment center.

The open door of the huge armoire revealed a thirty-nine-inch TV screen and a shelf of tapes. Bear turned his head sideways to read the spine titles on a series of Jeff Stryker videos, another gift from Brent. "Who's this Jeff Streeker?" Bear was trying to be blasé. "Sure a busy actor, starrin' in all them movies."

"Yes, you could say that. But I could give you twelve good reasons why you wouldn't enjoy any of Jeff Stryker's videos." As I was speaking, Bear pulled out *Powertool* and looked at the illustrated cover, showing, in full color, Jeff's claim to fame.

He shoved the video back into its place as if it were a hot potato. "Shit. Let's get on with what I'm here fer." He turned and faced the bed. Seeing himself, from the stomach down, reflected in the full mirror, tilted over the headboard, he grunted his disapproval. Our duvet cover and pillow shams were patterned from a design on a Greek vase, depicting satyrs. Bear again shook his head in disgust. I'm sure he thought he was in a sin pit.

"Hell," I finally yelled, my frustration getting the better of me, "this room isn't open to the public. So keep your redneck thoughts to yourself." I yanked back the duvet and top sheet on Brent's side. "There. Find your damn samples."

With difficulty, Bear searched the black satin bottom sheet for a black pubic hair. I could imagine his thoughts. He finally found three hairs and put them into a plastic Ziploc bag. He tried to sound officious, "These might be yours. Can you prove they're Brent's?"

"You could be right, I do spend a lot of time on his side of the bed." He looked blankly into my eyes. "Bear, most of mine are white. I do have a few black ones, though. They're still hanging in." I started to undo my belt. "Do you want one of mine? I'll let you pluck it out."

Bear ignored my histrionics. "How be if we check the dirty laundry? Where do you keep it?"

"In the bathroom." We walked down the spacious hallway. There were three doors: two on either side to walk-in closets and one at the end to the bathroom. The bathroom was very large. In the center was a large shower stall that you could access from either side. At the end of each walkway were individual toilets. As Bear walked down the second corridor, he whistled. "What the hell do ya need two johns fer?"

I pounced. "You know what they say about fags and toilets." The instant the words left my mouth, Bear's look of disdain filled me with regret. I hated Bear. I hated Brent. But most of all, I hated myself. Bear curled his lip but decided not to growl. He looked at the large double-sink area to the left and then walked to the right where a large Jacuzzi tub dominated a third of the bathroom area. The only thing that Bear really focused on, though, was a large phallic candle that a friend had given us. It was sitting on the side of the tub, waiting for a night of bubble-bathing fun. *Would that night ever come?* I was seething. "Not one word out of you." I gave Bear a look that could kill.

I reached into Brent's laundry hamper and found a pair of his jockeys. "Here." I tossed them to Bear who immediately began to look for pubic hairs.

"Hell, these look cleaner than mine before I put 'em on."

"Brent changes often." *Damn, why did I say that?* I tossed Bear another pair. It was one of the first things I learned about Brent, how very particular he was about doing his own laundry. Hell, he insisted that we even have separate hampers. From the start of our life together, he insisted, "I do my own laundry." Two evenings a week he made a production of washing his clothes, turning his jeans and shirts inside out, making sure colors never go in with whites, drying some clothes outside on the deck, others in the dryer...

"I got one!" hollered Bear excitedly.

"Well you can push off now," I snarled. "You got your sample."

Walking back into the bedroom, he pointed to the door to the outside. "What's through there?"

"The upper deck," I answered grudgingly.

"Better take a look."

"Orders from Joan? Case the joint?"

"It'd make her feel better."

I opened the door and Bear walked out on the deck that always takes people's breath away. At least the few who got the chance to be on the upper deck. "You got acreage up here," whistled Bear. "Five floors up." He stared in disbelief at the bank of eight-foot cypresses, the magnolia tree, peach tree, rhododendrons, lily of the valley shrubs, azaleas. "This deck's really somethin'," exclaimed Bear. "You've even got ripe raspberries and strawberries and it's nearly Halloween." He was like a kid in a candy store. "And look at those carrots and what's them?" he pointed.

"Parsnips." And then I stupidly added, "They need a touch of frost to make them sweet."

"Wow!"

"You should have seen it in the summer..." I caught myself in time. "Now get the hell out of here."

"The envelope. Joan says I gotta get a sample of Brent's spit."

"Come with me." We marched down the stairs and into the guest quarters. The room served a dual purpose. It was a bedroom when needed. The wall unit contained a murphy bed. It also contained Brent's desk. I opened it up and found, as I knew I would, several envelopes with stamps on them. After Brent purchases special commemorative stamps, he always comes home and sits at his desk, fixing each of the stamps on the envelopes in his correspondence file. When I first discovered this idiosyncrasy of his, I chuckled to myself. Only Brent would be so organized. Everything had to be in its place. Another difference between us. I buy stamps but can never find one when I want one.

I picked up an envelope that I knew would contain a sample of his saliva. "Here. Now get the hell out."

"What's them?"

"What?"

"Them purple sheets in that there holder. Let me see one of 'em." I took out a sheet of Brent's personalized mauve stationery, with the motif of Greek satyrs down the left margin and "*From the Desk of Brent, written especially for you*" inscribed in the right-hand corner.

Grabbing it from me, Bear said, "Now that looks familiar!" He walked out into the hall and punched the elevator button.

Chapter
Thirty-Five

THE ENTIRE CREW of *The X-Files* was still in shock. Rumors of a big move are one thing; reality is another. During the last several days on the set, the crew members were all whispering among themselves between takes, during coffee breaks, during meals. "Get your résumés up to date and out there, boys and girls. They'll be climbing all over you to pick you up." When Harry walked by, they'd shut up. Since he was DD's personal makeup man, they didn't trust him, assuming he'd be emigrating south with the star.

At the end of the day, he'd watch the crew walk to the parking lots in twos or threes, discussing their latest negotiations for future work. "I sent my résumé to Viatron Monday and the producer got back to me this morning. 'You got the job,' he says. 'If you've worked *X-Files* for five years, you're hired. Congrats!'"

Harry'd sent his résumé out to all the producers in Vancouver, but so far he'd only been contacted by *Madison. Would you believe that idiot? He offered me assistant makeup to Roberto Landro.* "You'd be in charge of making up some of the extras."

"Extras?" he screamed. I've been the personal makeup artist for both the stars of *X-Files*, for Christ's sake. Do you think I'm going to make up a bunch of snot-nosed teenagers?"

"Suit yourself."

He received no other nibbles, so he phoned around. "We're not hiring makeup people at this time. Sorry. We'll keep you in mind." Shit! Although he was no stranger to rejection in his acting career, he didn't know how to handle this latest blow to his ego. That was why he had become a makeup artist. So that he could act in parts of his own choosing without ever being rejected. *A plague on all your houses!*

AFTER LEAVING THE National Theatre School, taking the plane to London, and finding a furnished flat in Chelsea, THK looked in the telephone book for acting agents. He was ready to make it big in England. He finally got an appointment with one agent, a Sydney Hamilton. All the others that he called, asked, "Where are you from?" When he told them Canada, they all said, "Sorry, we have all the Americans we need," and hung up.

He buzzed the entrance system of Sydney Hamilton's office, a stone's throw from Piccadilly Circus. "Come up," a tinny voice told him. "I'm at the top of the last staircase." He heard the lock release so he pushed open the heavy oak door. He started to walk up the long narrow staircase. When he arrived on the landing, he looked up and saw another staircase, even narrower, and then another, and another. By the time he tapped on the door of Sydney Hamilton, Agent for Actors of all Accents, he was less than enthusiastic about whether or not he'd sign up with him. "Enter."

He opened the door. "Good afternoon, Mr. Hamilton. My name is Henri le Roi. It was good of you to see me on such short notice." He knew how to conduct an interview with a potential agent. The National Theatre School taught their students thoroughly.

"No problem. Sit. Do you have your résumé, son?"

He opened his briefcase and handed him his short, but what he considered impressive résumé.

Hamilton read it within fifteen seconds. "Is that it? You're completely inexperienced. What made you think that we're waiting over here with open arms to greet an amateur actor from the colonies?"

Henri didn't know what to say. So he stood up and recited the entire opening Chorus from *Henry V*.

O for a Muse of fire, that would ascend
The brightest heaven of invention...

After delivering an impressive reading, he sat down quietly, and gave Hamilton a boyish grin.

"You're very good son. I must say, you surprised me. I'll take you on."

I knew I was good. I could tell that he was impressed with me. And now he dares to say that he'll take me on. "I'll let you know. I am seeing a few other agents and then I'll make my decision."

He bounded down the flights of stairs, leaving Sydney Hamilton flabbergasted. *Why the hell do I need an agent? I'll go to auditions and they'll cast me in all the leading roles.*

He experienced a frustrating week. Every casting director he called told him the same story, "We only see actors represented by agents." He picked up a copy of *The Stage* and looked at the Auditions column. The same wording appeared at the end of each ad, "Equity members only." He went to the Equity offices to join.

"You must have appeared in five professional productions before you can apply for an Equity card," explained the receptionist.

"But no professional company will hire me unless I'm Equity."

"Try the Fringe theatres. You have to build up your professional résumé. When you've done five Fringe shows, come see us. But not until. Those are the rules."

I don't live by rules; I make the rules. "So how do I get in to audition, then?"

"My dear young man. You need an agent, even for the Fringe Theatres."

Once more he spent an entire day on the phone to all the agents he hadn't already contacted. None would see him. *Time to eat a little crow.*

He buzzed Sydney Hamilton. The tin voice said, "Yes?"

"It's me, Mr. Hamilton, Henri le Roi."

"Come on up. I thought you might be back. Your contract is waiting for you to sign."

Months passed and Henri had not acted on any London stage. He had demanded that he work only in a Shakespearean production. When Hamilton put his name forward to casting directors for upcoming productions of modern plays, they were interested. Several wanted to see him. Hamilton had to convince him to audition. "Go for the experience. It won't hurt. You'll get seen. That's the most important thing you can do in this town. Be seen. Remember, lad, you're only as good as your last role."

But he blew every audition. He began each one by condemning the script. "Well, this certainly isn't Shakespeare. Do you really think people are going to pay money to see this trash?" They'd be on the phone to Hamilton before the end of the day, saying, "I don't want to see that Henri le Roi ever again. Send him again and it'll be the last time I see a single one your clients. Ever."

When Hamilton confronted him with these tales, he said simply, "I told you I'm a Shakespearean actor. Get me an audition with the Royal Shakespeare Company, or the National Theatre, or the Old Vic. Or the Chichester Festival. Or the Birmingham Old Vic."

MORE MONTHS PASSED and he had still not acted anywhere in England. He did see a lot of theatre, though. Nearly every night he went to a different play. But he walked out of most of them. *Not up to my standard.* He waited anxiously for a Shakespearean production. He was totally bowled over after seeing Antony Sher in *Richard the Third* at the Barbican Theatre. And then he saw Ian McKellan do *Macbeth* to Judi Dench's Lady Macbeth. And Derek Jacobi's marvelous *Hamlet* at the Old Vic. What a thrill it was for him to see John Gielgud, in the title role of *Julius Caesar* at the National Theatre. He was sitting in the front row and after the senators stabbed Caesar, Gielgud gurgled "Et tu, Brute?" and fell dead at his feet. He was so impressed that he couldn't resist whispering, "Well done, John," and smiled when he saw dead Caesar's eyelids flicker a *Thank You, son*. He couldn't believe his luck when he went to Stratford one weekend. The Royal Shakespeare Company presented three Shakespearean productions: *Much Ado About Nothing, Othello,* and *Coriolanus*. He didn't recognize any big names, but he sat mesmerized, dreaming that he would soon be up on that same stage. *Everyone will recognize my brilliance.*

A few of the Fringe theatres also tackled Shakespeare. Even though the productions were not as lavish as the big shows, they held his attention. "Let me put your name up for a part in one of the Fringe shows?" Hamilton pleaded. "You've got to be seen. And reviewed." Finally he agreed. He auditioned for the Orange Tree Theatre production of *Romeo and Juliet*. Hamilton phoned him excitedly with the news. "They were most impressed with you, lad. They're offering you a contract."

"Yes!" His right arm flew up towards the ceiling. *I will conquer London.*

"They've offered you the parts of Sampson and the Apothecary."

"What? I read for Romeo. Is the director trying to insult me? I hope you told him that I wouldn't be caught dead acting in those no-nothing parts."

"You have to start somewhere, son. This is a good offer. The Orange Tree is reviewed by all the London critics. You'll be up, up and away from then on. So...I said you'd accept."

That doesn't even dignify a fucking thank-you. He hung up the phone and flipped on his VCR to continue watching a production of *Richard II* with Ian Richardson. He admired the ease with which Richardson spoke his lines. So natural. So clear.

By the time he had finished viewing *The Tempest,* he mused, "I've seen all thirty-seven of Shakespeare's plays." And he had. He had seen every stage production of Shakespeare that played anywhere in England. At least twice. And for those that were not playing on stage, he bought the BBC videos and watched them whenever he could, even when he was doing his morning and evening exercises. He became obsessed with Shakespeare's words. His villainous companions had now taken palpable shape for him. No longer were they words on a page, no longer were they his imaginary playmates, they were now real.

He sat in his room and thought out loud about the Orange Tree offer. "Sampson is a servant to one of the Capulets in a little scene at the beginning of the play. And the Apothecary is only in a tiny scene at the end of the play when he sells Romeo poison." *It's a start!* "Yeah, but I won't be playing Romeo." Then he had a brilliant idea. "Maybe I could be Romeo's understudy. I'll ask Hamilton to sweeten the offer for me." *And then when I sell Romeo the poison...*

The next day, he heard his agent tell him: "They bought it, lad.

You're to play Sampson and the Apothecary. And, son, you're to understudy Romeo."

He danced around his flat like a happy child. "I got the part of Romeo. My first role in England and I'll be playing a lead."

The rehearsal period was a month. He went to the first rehearsal word-perfect. But boredom soon set in as he watched the other actors struggling with their lines, calling "Prompt" every few minutes. The actor playing Romeo was good but too old. He was probably thirty, and he played the part more like a young fruity Gielgud than a fiery Olivier. Every day on his way to rehearsals, Harry would listen to the tapes of the famous production where one night Gielgud had played Romeo and Olivier played Mercutio. Then the next night they'd reverse roles. He identified much more with Olivier's interpretation than Gielgud's pansy-assed romantic interpretation. But he was confident that his interpretation of Romeo would transcend both of theirs.

The moment he left the stage as Sampson, he'd sit in a corner and listen to his tapes. With disgust in his eyes, he would occasionally watch the director of the Orange at work. *An obvious old queen. Can't you keep your dewy auntie eyes off your darling Romeo and see what else is going on? Bet he got the fucking part by sleeping with the old fart.*

The dress rehearsal played like silk off a spool. The costumes were rich Elizabethan brocade. The set a stylized version of the Globe Theatre. The lighting atmospheric. He was excited to be a part of a first-rate professional show, albeit a Fringe production. The first preview audience of twofers applauded politely at the end of the play for the curtain call. For him, it felt good to hear the applause. *This is where I belong, but I shouldn't be stuck at the end of the line, I should be in the center where all eyes are fixed on me.*

The director gave one note after the preview: "The production needs more zip, more life. Rest up tonight so that tomorrow you can bowl over our last preview audience." He looked over at Romeo. "I'd like a word with you, if you don't mind." They walked out together.

Romeo'll probably have to shag the old fruit tonight. So that's how you rise to the top! Well, enjoy tomorrow's performance, "darling." It'll be your last.

That night he opened a copy of *The Poisoner's Handbook* he had picked up at the local library.

"PLACES, EVERYONE." Electricity filled the air backstage.

On stage, the Chorus introduced the play. In his role as Sampson, he and Gregory appeared in their first scene. He had already worked privately with the actor who was playing Gregory to make the scene a little gem of comedy. The audience got all the off-color jokes.

He flew to his dressing room and transformed his makeup into that of the Apothecary. After he changed into his tattered costume, he flew upstairs and remained in the wings, watching the rest of the play. Well into the performance, he observed Juliet pick up the vial she received from Friar Lawrence and drink the contents. Then he waited for Romeo to make his entrance down left and call for him: "What, ho! apothecary!"

He entered in shadows, his face covered with a hood. He used deep guttural tones in his delivery.

APOTHECARY Who calls so loud?

ROMEO   Come hither, man. I see that thou art poor.
    Hold, there is forty ducats. Let me have
    A dram of poison, such soon-speeding gear
    As will disperse itself through all the veins
    That the life-weary taker may fall dead.

APOTHECARY Such mortal drugs I have. [*As soon you will find out.*]
    Put this in any liquid thing you will
    And drink it off, and if you had the strength
    Of twenty men, it would dispatch you.

ROMEO   Farewell. Buy food and get thyself in flesh.
    Come, cordial and not poison, go with me
    To Juliet's grave; for there must I use thee.

He stepped out of the shadows to count his forty ducats. The audience gasped. He looked exactly as Romeo's lines describe the Apothecary: "Famine is in thy cheeks, / Need and oppression starveth in thy eyes, / Contempt and beggary hangs upon thy back; / The world is not thy friend."

He walked into the shadows to watch the rest of the play. He had done this every night, so no one would suspect that tonight was any different from any other.

In a later scene, Romeo entered and saw his Juliet, dead on the bier. He pulled the stopper out of the vial and recited, "Here's to my love." Then Romeo drained the contents.

From the shadows, THK smiled at the actor's reaction. *It's not just orange juice, is it, "darling"?*

Romeo continued, "O true apothecary! / Thy drugs are quick." He was gasping, but he managed to get out his last line. "Thus with a kiss I die." He fell in the exact place he was directed to fall: Across Juliet's lap with his hand tightly clasping the vial.

Standing deep in the shadows, THK relaxed. The rest of the play was anticlimactic, although he did have the slightest buzz when Juliet picked the vial out from Romeo's hand and tried to drink from it. "O churl, drunk all, and left no friendly drop / To help me after?" *You don't know how lucky you are, my dear. Tomorrow night. Opening night. You'll be my Juliet. And it will be me, lying across your snatch.*

The curtain call surprised him. Though extremely pale under his makeup, Romeo took his bow with Juliet. *What the hell went wrong? I followed the recipe exactly.*

All the way home, he cursed. During his nightly exercise session, he cursed. During his shower in his poor-excuse for a bathtub, he cursed. He cursed in his "uncomforting" bed until he fell asleep. He could hear Romeo's line ringing in his ears: "The world is not thy friend."

He was awakened at two a.m. "Henri, this is Stuart. I'm at the hospital. Gary has been taken ill. He was staying over at my place because he didn't feel up to the long journey home and woke up with stomach cramps." *O true Apothecary!* "They have him on intravenous. They pumped his stomach and filled him up with something black. It's dreadful."

"I'm so sorry. What can I do?"

"Well, for one thing, dear boy, you can learn Romeo's lines. The doctors said that under no circumstances would they let Gary out of the hospital tomorrow. Stupid boy. He went to an Indian restaurant before last night's preview. What an inconvenience! I'll see you at the theatre at nine a.m. We have a sold out house tomorrow night and all the reviewers will be there. Do you think you're up to it? I know I haven't rehearsed you, but you are technically Gary's understudy. You better start memorizing the..."

"No problem." He banged down the receiver and danced around the room.

THE MORNING RUN-THROUGH went like a dream. Not only did he astound Stuart with his performance as Romeo, but the rest of the cast hung in the wings, watching his fiery, original delivery. He followed the exact moves that the director had set, but he commanded everyone's attention because he exuded a charisma that few possess; certainly they had never seen Gary's Romeo in this light. The fight scenes were filled with electric energy, although he never deviated from the choreography that had been carefully set.

When Tybalt slew Mercutio, Romeo flew into a rage. He roared towards the actor who played Tybalt. *I'm scaring him shitless.*

STUART CALLED THE cast together at noon. "My darlings, you are all ready for tonight. Thanks to Mr. Le Roi. Thank you, Henri. Your Romeo will dazzle our audience." The director gave him a look that spoke volumes, and the company's new Romeo felt he could hear the faggot director's thoughts: *Why the hell didn't I cast this boy in the first place? And look at that basket! Silly-billy me. He's perfect!*

I'll soon be on the top without having to sleep with this cocksucker.

Stuart continued to drone on. "Yes, your Romeo will dazzle our audiences. Mark my words." Then he announced, "There'll be no rehearsal this afternoon. I've got to learn Sampson's and the Apothecary's lines. As you all saw, I was the weakest member of the cast." Everyone laughed.

AND THAT EVENING, the audience *did* go wild. The next morning, the reviews followed suit. "A new Olivier is in our midst" wrote the *Daily Telegraph* critic. The *London Times* gushed, "RSC, Grab Henri le Roi. Put him in anything and it'll be a hit." The *Guardian* praised the entire production: "Mr. Le Roi's youth and charm drove this production to its inevitable conclusion by infusing the entire cast with energy. A must see!" *The Standard's* critic, usually hard to please, praised his performance. "Seldom, if ever, can an understudy in a Fringe production step into a leading part and make it work. Twenty-one-year-old Le Roi is the exception to this rule. He dazzled, he took risks that amazed me. Do I see a Best Actor Trophy for our Evening Standard Awards? This actor will go places."

THE NEXT DAY the box office phone never stopped ringing. Before the second performance curtain, the entire run was sold out.

An hour before the curtain, Gary walked into his dressing room. Henri was already in costume and makeup and was arranging Romeo's black locks neatly over his short hair. "I'm back," Gary said, smiling but seeming nervous. Had he read the reviews? "Thanks for taking my place last night."

"What?" Henri looked at Gary in horror.

"I'm back to take my rightful place in this production. Take off my costume and hang it up. And then get out of my dressing room. I'll be back in five minutes."

Within two minutes, Stuart knocked on the door. "I'm not ready yet," came the reply.

"It's Stuart." He opened the door and walked in. He looked at Henri, who had taken off his tights and was unbuttoning his doublet. "Oh my. I've caught you with your pants off." He smiled. Henri ignored him and continued stripping down while Stuart sat and watched the youth's every move, his flexed muscles, his well-defined abs, his strong calves, his tight ass. Henri hung up Romeo's costume. Stuart asked, "Would you like to continue playing Romeo?"

"That's a stupid question. What the fuck do you think? Of course, I want to continue in the role. I was born to play Romeo, Hamlet, Hotspur, Macbeth, Henry V, Antony, the whole fucking folio."

"Well then," smirked Stuart, "maybe we can work something out. Come over here."

Henri walked over to him. He stood close to Stuart, his full basket covered only by his skimpy dance belt. "What did you have in mind?" He thrust his hips forward so that his bulge was within six inches of his director's face.

Rheumy eyes oozing lust, fingers twitching, Stuart licked his lips. "Well, maybe you could come over to my place tonight after the show. I'm sure I'll come up with something."

"You mean I won't play Romeo tonight?"

"Not until we've..." Pause.

"We've what?"

"Come, come, dear boy. Haven't you ever heard of...?"

"So you want me to cornhole you. Is that what you want?"

"Cornhole," roared Stuart. "How positively colonial. Cornhole! Wait till I tell *that* story at my next dinner party." He stopped laughing and looked at the young actor. Then he said in a perfectly business-like tone, "Tonight you cornhole me and for the rest of the run you'll play Romeo. Deal?"

"Deal." Henri dressed quickly, all the time feeling Stuart's eyes, defining each movement. He walked out of the star dressing room, down the hall, and past the dressing room where his two costumes hung. He walked out the stage door and past the long queue of people hoping for return tickets. They had come especially to see him. He stepped into the underground train and was home, packing his bags before the curtain rose to a standing-room-only second-night house. He ignored the ringing phone. He imagined that by the time the curtain dropped, with an hysterical Apothecary requiring two prompts for his little scene, Henri le Roi would be on his way to Vancouver on an all-night flight. *Mother, I promised you that no faggot would ever touch my basket.*

IN HIS RECLINED first-class seat, he snuggled under a blanket and sucked his thumb. He started giggling, reveling in the fact that the Orange Tree's future audiences who'd paid to see his Romeo would be demanding their money back. Revenge felt good. He drifted contentedly to dreamland with one thought: Vancouver. "Are you ready for me?"

Chapter
Thirty-Six

I'D SPENT A hellish three days. I hung around the apartment, waiting by the phone, for a call from Bear, or Joan, or Abby, or someone from the RCMP. I even took the phone into the bathroom with me for fear I'd not hear it ring. When Brent came home from teaching all day, I felt like a spy. I caught myself watching his every move, judging his every word. I was tired of living a double life with Brent, wanting desperately to tell him exactly what was coming down.

But, still the coward, I lied again, telling Brent that Joan had things finally under control and that the RCMP didn't need me any more. He bought it. "I'm glad," he smiled. "Now I can give up my grass-widowhood. I was getting tired of doing all the cooking." I nodded. "Welcome home, lover. I've missed you."

On the surface, life became almost normal for the rest of the week. I made his breakfast and packed his lunch and stepped out on the kitchen balcony to wave him goodbye as he drove off to work. "Try to get a look at Duchovny," I yelled each morning. I didn't know whether they were shooting around the corner or not, but I had to yell something. Brent was so depressed when he heard that X-Files was leaving Vancouver, he said, "I've got to see my favorite actor once before he leaves for good."

For him, life at the college had settled down. The staff and the students were concentrating on midterms and had no time to think of Brent's loss or whether or not he was a suspect.

I tried to get on with the editing of Chapter Two of my limp attempt at becoming a published author. As I picked and pecked and changed and deleted most of what I'd written, I waited expectantly for my usual calls from Brent, half hoping Bear would call instead, to tell me that he'd been "barkin' up the wrong bush." Brent had resumed his habit of a couple of calls a day, between classes. Then I waited for his homecoming, martinis, and naps. I had convinced myself that my suspicions of Brent were the result of my vivid imagination, and was trying very hard to get our lives back to the way they were before Nancy's murder. We even strolled down to the Denman to see *Scream III*. I reveled in the welcome return to normalcy, trying to ignore the fact that the whole charade could fall apart at any moment when the RCMP came knocking.

When Saturday morning came, I woke to Brent's whispering in my ear. "Today's the big day!" I opened my eyes with a start.

"Huh?"

"Bad dream?"

"No, I don't think so," I lied. I had starred in another snuff film during the night, with twenty Brents yelling directions and obscenities at me, ordering me to perform acts that I would never tell a living soul.

"Today is the big day."

"What do you mean?"

"Duh! Halloween, my silly lover."

"Is it really?" *Where had October gone?*

"Yes. Saturday, October Thirty-First. Halloween." He got up on the bed and jumped up and down like a kid. "We're going to the Ball. We're going to the Ball." He had no idea what I had been going through.

I looked up at his smiling, dancing face. There was no way on God's green earth that this beautiful man could kill anyone.

"Brent?"

"Yes?" He stopped jumping. I think hearing his name from my lips jolted him. We rarely used our names when we addressed each other. It was always sweetie, darl, lover. Only in public did we resort to the more formal salutations.

"Brent, I have to talk."

"About what?"

Here goes. I was not going to be a coward anymore. It was time to tell Brent what was going on. He deserved to hear the truth. And from me. To hell with Joan. "You remember I told you that the RCMP didn't need my services anymore?"

"Yeah. So?"

"Well, that wasn't exactly true." Brent's smile disappeared. "Joan Riley warned me to keep my nose out of their investigation because I was personally involved with their leading suspect."

He looked at me hard. "You mean me?"

"Yes, Brent."

"Will you stop calling me Brent!" he shouted. Then he resumed calmly, "My alibi is foolproof. You yourself heard eight of the committee say that I never left the Wanderlust on the weekend that Nancy was killed."

"I know." I blushed to remember that I had read his e-mail and what I had told Bear: *Birds of a feather.* "But there's more."

"What do you mean *more*?"

"There have been four other unsolved murders with similar MOs, in Kailua-Kona, San Francisco, Winnipeg, and London."

"Christ. Are you saying that a murder has taken place in each of the cities where your kids live?"

"Yes."

"And...don't tell me. All these killings took place when you and I visited. We have visited each of them at least three or four times since we became partners."

"No. None of the murders took place on any of our holidays."

"Well, what's the big concern?"

"They all took place when *you* were on one of your volleyball tournaments."

He was silent for a while, getting up and walking around the bed. His thoughts raced. I watched him intently. What was he thinking? Finally he came back to his side of the bed and sat down. He looked directly into my eyes. "How did the RCMP discover that bit of information?"

I looked into his accusing, full-almond eyes. "I told them when they interrogated me."

His Roman nose instantly became rigid. The skin around his eyes and his entire forehead tightened. "*You* told them!"

"Yes. I looked through our itinerary calendars for the past seven years. You were at a tournament at the time of each of the four murders. Over the past seven years, and ending in Nancy's murder, each killing took place approximately eighteen months apart." And then the zinger, "While we were separated."

"And you suspect me?"

"No. Never."

"You do," he yelled. "I can tell by your eyes that you're lying. Why else would you give them those dates?" He didn't wait for an answer. He stormed into the bathroom and slammed the door. "Shit!" I heard him yell as he turned on the shower. I followed. For a minute I stood and watched him from my side of the shower stall, as he held his face directly under the spray.

"I'm sorry," I yelled. "Forgive me." He didn't move. "Please." I got down on my knees and begged. "Please forgive me."

Brent looked through the steamed glass door and wiped a small eye-hole clean. I gave him one of my little trembly-chin looks that always melted him.

He said nothing, but turned on the other shower. Slowly the door opened. I got off my knees and walked into the shower stall.

We stood facing each other, eyes searching eyes, water splashing backs. Brent handed me a bar of Tone. We soaped each other in silence. Suddenly he dropped his soap and reached his two hands up and put them on either side of my face. I automatically lifted my arms in defense and then lowered them slowly, deliberately. With his strong hands, he slowly forced my head down to his and I closed my eyes. His lips enveloped mine. We kissed while the steaming water massaged our bodies.

This was Brent's way of saying, "I forgive you."

After drying, he led me to the bedroom. "Get in bed." He crawled in with me. "Okay, Jessica. Now that you've eliminated me from your list of suspects, once and for all, who is the fucking killer? Don't you remember your code?"

"What one is that, love?"

"There are no coincidences."

The phone rang before I could respond, and even if I could, I didn't know what Brent was getting at.

"Hello," said Brent into the phone. "Yes, Sergeant Spivic, he's right here. Beside me. In bed!" He handed me the phone.

"What's up, Bear?"

"Kev, we've got the results on the pubic hairs. I received the Polaroids and braids from the victims in Kona, Winnipeg, and London. All them forensic boys wuz pleased as punch to think that I wuz gonna close their cases for them. Kev?"

"Yeah?"

"Ya think I'm gonna be some kind o' goddamn hero or somethin'?"

"Probably," I said nervously. Brent had moved his head next to the earpiece so that he could hear Bear. I looked up and saw in the mirror our two heads, separated by a phone. *Bear? Be careful what you say.*

"Jist as ya thought, each victim's hair is similar but it's gonna take a month fer Jeff to work up that mono-something-or-other DNA. But as far as he's concerned right now, the braid from Nancy's cabin wuz made up of hers, Susan's, and the killer's." Brent's face broke into a smile. He winked at me in the mirror.

I tried to ignore his enthusiasm. "And at Susan's murder scene?"

"The braid wuz made of Susan's, Georgina's, and the killer's." Brent mouthed *yes!* "And jist like we talked about, the Frisco police didn't find no pubic hairs on or anywheres near Dorothy's body."

"What about Georgina's?"

"The same crazy braid that wuz at Nancy's and Susan's. But this time, Jeff says the pubic hairs were from Georgina, Christine Perkins—she wuz the London prostitute—and the killer."

"And Christine's? Another braid?"

"Kev, there wuz no braid left at Christine's murder scene. Remember? Scotland Yard found several black pubic hairs. We received one from them by FedEx last night and Jeff tested the color, core size, scale count." I could feel Brent stop breathing.

"And?"

"Jeff says 'between me, you, and the bedpost,' they'll all match the ones I picked up on Wednesday." Brent gave me a high-five. I made eye-contact in the mirror with Brent's happy face. Then his forehead furrowed as his eyes locked mine. "Are you still there?" Bear asked.

"Yeah."

"And... Are ya listenin'?"

"Yes. *I* am listening."

"We got the DNA results back from the stamp on that envelope. You know... the one I picked up...on Wednesday." I breathed easier because I had the feeling that Bear now realized our conversation was being overheard by Brent. He was choosing his words carefully. I was relieved that he didn't say that he had picked up the envelope from Brent's desk. "The DNA is a perfect match with the stamp on the envelope that Franny McGhie received two weeks ago. We'll talk later." He hung up. I stopped breathing.

"What was that last bit all about?" Brent asked. "He sure hung up fast."

MY BRAIN WENT into a seesaw mode. He's guilty. He's not guilty. He's guilty. He can't be guilty.

"What was that all about?" Brent demanded.

"What?"

"Duh? The phone call."

"Oh. It sounds as if Spivic has finally found some hard evidence." I looked intently into my lover's face, searching for some guilty tic, some giveaway flicker in his eyes, something. Anything that might suggest a killer had heard that his days were numbered. Nothing. Only a deep look of concern.

"You mean the envelope and stamp?"

"Yeah."

"That's good. Right? Why don't you sound overjoyed? That killer murdered five women for God's sake. You should be happy that you've got samples of pubic hairs and a DNA match." I let him go on. "I don't know that much about DNA tests and police procedures, but Spivic must have enough evidence now to make an arrest."

"All he's got are some pubic hairs that are similar to the ones found at the murder scenes. And a DNA match of saliva taken from a couple of stamps."

"So?"

"So, what?"

"Why the hell doesn't he make an arrest?" .

"Because he doesn't know whose pubic hairs and spit he's got," I lied.

"What? That doesn't make sense." Brent startled me with "Are you telling me the truth?"

"Of course I am." *Another lie. God damn it to hell.*

"What are you hiding from me? Come on, cough it up. Spivic knows who the killer is. Right?"

"Well..." I had to come up with a more convincing lie. "The RCMP confidentiality code has been in effect on this case from the very beginning. Bear is simply following police procedure. No names before an arrest. Not until he picks up the suspect and he either gets an outright confession from him or, during interrogation, the guy trips up and incriminates himself. Then, the whole world will know the identity of this maniac." I could tell that my story about keeping crime details under wrap was having an effect on Brent.

"You mean if the killer finds out that you have samples of his pubic hair, he could do something to avoid being trapped? Yeah. He could shave off all his hair, couldn't he? And he could say that he lost the envelopes with his spit on them. When you hear about killers getting off on technicalities smaller than that, it's a good idea to keep things hush-hush." I was surprised by Brent's understanding of the importance of withholding key information from the public.

"We'll wait for Bear to make an arrest. Okay?" Brent visibly relaxed. "He has two matches now, so with a little more sleuthing he'll be able to track him down." I looked directly into Brent's eyes. "It's the first real break in this case. And the evidence will be bad news for the killer, when Bear gets him."

"You don't sound overjoyed."

"I'll be happy when they have him behind bars."

"Me too. It's only a matter of time, then?" I nodded. "It's out of your hands now. Right?" I nodded again. "Okay, then. We can go to the party tonight and have a ball. You won't have to worry about a thing any more. Right? So, let's get up and get dressed."

I started breathing normally again. Talk about an inquisition! Brent's grilling of me was high-quality interrogation. *Or maybe that's my guilty conscience talking. So, what now?* I had a couple of ideas I wanted to check out before the party. *Today is the day that I prove that Brent is not guilty. He's not guilty. I know he's not guilty. I pray he's not guilty.*

As soon as we finished our very late breakfast, Brent said, "My God. It's nearly two o'clock. I need to go out to do some errands."

"No problem." I wanted to be by myself anyway. To think. He flew up to the bathroom to brush and floss his teeth and in a couple of minutes he returned wearing his small backpack.

"Won't be more than a couple of hours, darl'." He pressed the elevator button.

"Where are you off to?"

"It's a secret," he winked. "Come here." He gave me a lingering, passionate kiss while waiting for the elevator to come up.

When the door opened he said, "That's to remember me by."

Staring at the closed door, I stood dead still. I hadn't even the strength to go out onto the balcony and wave goodbye. *Remember, Kevin Porter. Remember, ex-Chief Inspector of the Royal Canadian Mounted Police. Remember, Private Dick. Put two and two together. The killer used the word "remember" or one of its derivations on the back of every victim's Polaroid.* My mind was whirring as things began clicking into place. I needed to go to the library. I flew around getting my shoes and jacket on, picked up my notebook and police reports, and rushed to the elevator.

All the way down, I felt heady. Was it the result of Brent's kiss? Or from what he had just said? Did he slip up, or was it just a coincidence? There are no coincidences in police work, besides I had never shared with Brent any of the killer's taunts. On my way to the library, I looked over my notes and each time I saw a key word from one of the taunts, I said it out loud. "Remember... remembering...remembered... remembrances."

He's not guilty, he's not guilty, please God, he's not guilty.

THE MOMENT HIS eyes popped open, after a satisfying full night's sleep, Thomas Henry King realized that today was going to be the most important day of his life.

His eyes widened. "Today is Reckoning Day!" He turned his head to look at his wife, sleeping peacefully beside him. Connected to him. Her little finger still resting between his cheeks. He always went to sleep contentedly when her pinky was plugged in. Big C had started the practice years ago when he began sleeping with her and he had taught his Kate to do the same, but he had never felt violated like he had with his mother. His wife's connection was one of love. He continued smiling at his Kate, remembering last night. He'd quoted volumes of Shakespeare while he made love to her. Over and over and over. *She couldn't get enough of me!* He knew how to satisfy a woman, physically and intellectually.

His performance had been magnificent. He remembered last night so clearly. During his final orgasm, he had howled when he came clean, "I am the king of kings."

Today he would produce his crowning achievement: Sweet Revenge, by Thomas Henry King. He shouldn't linger. *I am very proud, revengeful, ambitious; with more offences at my beck than I have thoughts to put them in.*

He bent over his wife and yelled, "Wake up my sweet Kate. My Kate of Kates." He laughed hysterically.

Her eyes flew open. "What..."

He filled her mouth with his flicking tongue, mingling his breath with hers. Then he pulled away. She tried to hold him but he jumped up on the bed.

He spoke excitedly, getting louder and louder. "I have much to do today. And I have a surprise for you. Get up. I'm going to drop you off at the Waldorf Hotel this morning."

"Why do...?"

He cut her off. "You'll have work to do." He jumped off the bed, and strutted to the bathroom. "I have to piss."

Standing at the toilet he looked down, and roared, "Vengeance is in my heart, death in my hand, / Blood and revenge are hammering in my head." He tore open the shower curtain and stepped into a cold shower. He raved, "I will revenge these bitter woes of mine."

THK was not aware that his Kate lay quietly, listening to her husband's rantings. Tears began to fall from her bewildered eyes.

USING MY NOTES and the trusty Shakespeare concordance so efficiently that I didn't have to ask a librarian for help, I became elated with each discovery. I was definitely on the right track. The old bloodhound had finally caught the scent of the real killer. Not Brent. Not Brent at all.

After an hour, I happily zigzagged my way back home through a sunny West End. I wasn't howling at the rain and wind this time; I whistled a happier tune. I was an inch away from identifying the fiend.

In front of me several trailers were pulling into place. Getting ready for another shoot. "When are they filming *The X-Files* again?" I inquired from one of the drivers, thinking that Brent might get his last chance to see the star.

"They're shooting the last episode Monday. In Vancouver, that is. Before they move to LA."

I suddenly had an image of an older man stepping out between two of the trailers. Graying at the temples, wearing a moustache. He was carrying a jar of something red and wearing a white smock. "Shit," I yelled. "A makeup artist!" *So, who the hell is Monique?* Monique with the thick Jamaican accent. Monique with the rich chocolate skin? Monique with the plastic gloves on her hands? "Yes, of course!"

I jogged all the way home.

"WHERE HAVE YOU been?"

"Sorry, my manno, but I needed a bit of exercise. My mind and body needed a stretch."

"Well get your hunky ass in the shower. We've got a Ball to go to, Batman."

"I'll be up in a few minutes, I promise. I have to do a couple of little things in the den. Then I'll be yours for the whole evening. Hell, I'll be yours for the rest of my life. Nothing can go wrong now."

I got down on my hands and knees and dragged out from under my love seat all the calendar pages I'd never thrown away for the last nine years. I checked our itineraries, reading everything I'd written in the immediate weeks prior to and after each of the murders. I froze! Several notations on the calendars took on a life of their own and entered my nose, my mouth, my lungs. I found it difficult to breathe. I whispered, "Martha!"

I picked up the phone and dialed.

"Ya?"

"Bear! Here's what I want you to do..."

Chapter
Thirty-Seven

BATMAN AND ROBIN stepped out of the black limousine in front of Mars. "Thank you, Albert," I said to the chauffeur, who gave me a dumb look. "Pick us up after our mission is accomplished."

"Be here at two-oh-five." ordered Robin. He turned to me and said, "Put this on! I bought it for you this afternoon." I opened his gift and smiled at an authentic Bat Watch. My lover had been searching all afternoon for the perfect gift to make our Halloween Ball memorable. I gave him a big hug.

We bounded into Mars convinced our acolytes were ready to cheer our entrance.

The elaborately costumed crowd was already in action, not paying any attention to our arrival. "Register here for the Costume Contest," screamed a mustachioed queen sitting near the door. "You two look wonderful. Confidentially, you'll see two or three imposters tonight, but between you and me, you're the best Dynamic Duo here." We grinned like kids under our masks. "Now write down your introduction so the MC will know what to say when she presents you on stage."

All contestants were to be introduced to the crowd at midnight and all had to make up their own intros. Brent completed the form. He'd worked on his few lines all week, changing words and phrases daily. I'm sure he was revising as he wrote right now. I felt confident that tonight would be perfect. If Bear followed Plan A, and he assured me he would, the Clean Fiend was probably already behind bars. I could now relax and enjoy the party. And I was confident that Brent and I were a shoo-in for first prize. Life was good again.

After a scotch on the rocks, we moved onto the dance floor, gyrating with Flintstones, cheerleaders, Frankensteins, Cowardly Lions, Star Wars characters, poor imitations of Batman and Robin — although there was one interesting Robin that caught my eye who later joined us for a dance set which turned into a sensuous *ménage à trois*. Use your imagination.

Throughout the night, my Robin was high on several "totes," but I kept my head clear. Time flew by.

We were surprised when the lighting changed and the music stopped. The MC, a bearded Dolly Parton in a billowy pink-and-purple number, swept out on stage and yelled into the mike, "Okay, pipe down. Pipe down, I say." The noise level was still deafening. Dolly took out a police whistle from her ample décolletage. She blew it right in the mike. That shut everybody up. "Well, good. Now you're listening... Ladies and gentlemen, and all you others..." Roars of approval came from the crowd. She lifted her arms and everyone became quiet. "It's a pleasure to see you all tonight. Who says that a Halloween bash couldn't work with a mix of breeders and queers?" Another roar of approval from behind masks, makeup, and loads of facial hair. "We're getting ready for the Pair's Costume Parade, so drag your asses over there." Shrieking with laughter, she pointed to the right of the stage. "Chop chop."

After twenty minutes in the line, we got ready to make our entrance on stage. The MC introduced us loudly and dramatically: "Batman and Robin. Are they or aren't they? Only Robin knows for sure." We bounded on stage. Performed a dynamic run with capes flying. I stopped mid-stage and posed, my cape held high. Robin ran to me and knelt, pointing at my crotch. I had padded my trunks with my cell phone, in case Bear needed to call me. From the roar of the crowd, I must have looked very well endowed. I enclosed Robin in my cape, turned to the audience and grinned. The crowd went wild.

When we bounded off stage, the MC bellowed, "And now the nemeses of Batman and Robin. Ladies and gentlemen: Catwoman and the Riddler." Out danced a pair in spectacular costumes. "Riddle me full and riddle me hollow. Robin will die, and Batman will follow."

I stared in disbelief. This Riddler made Jim Carrey's histrionics look tame. He flew, tumbled, flipped, and darted around Catwoman as she meowed and clawed the air. The crowd ate them up.

"Our competition," grumbled Brent.

After all the other pairs paraded across the stage, the MC announced, "The big prize will be presented in one hour." The music started up again. We took to the dance floor. After a few minutes, Catwoman and the Riddler cut in. She whirled me away, clawing, meowing, purring, and feeling me up and down. I went along with her, chuckling to myself, convinced that Catwoman was Martha. But my eyes never left Riddler as he danced around Robin, whispering in his ear, then laughing fiendishly. I could tell that Brent, even though he was still high and giggling a lot, wasn't enjoying himself. I could tell he was going along with the charade just to be sociable.

When the set ended, Brent pulled out four tickets from his utility belt. "Let me get us a round of drinks. What would you like?"

The Riddler simpered, "Buy me a gin, and Kitty a shooter. I

gotta piss, take care of my kitty." Leaving a startled Catwoman behind, he darted through the crowd. With a shrug, Brent headed over to the long drink line.

Catwoman and I were alone. I watched her for a moment in her incredible costume. I dropped out of character to say, "Martha, your costume looks great. Did you make it yourself?"

She stared through intriguing cat-eye contacts. "Meow." She began licking her fingers and brushing her ears. She wasn't going to let me know whether or not she was Martha.

"You and Riddler make a great pair."

"Purrfect."

Seeing my Robin still in the line-up miles from the bar, playing with his drink tickets, I asked, "Would you like another dance?"

"Purrfect."

A minute into the dance, we heard ringing. Startled, Catwoman looked down at my crotch. I blurted, "Excuse me," and bolted to the nearest john. Once there, I put my hand down my trunks and pulled out my cell phone.

"I've been admiring your basket all night," a Princess leered. "Fraud!" She hoisted up her skirt and stood before the urinal.

"Bear," I yelled into the phone. The john was full of loud laughs, loud jokes, loud partygoers. I couldn't hear a thing. I yelled, "Hang on" as I ran to the exit. "If I go out, can I get back in?"

"Sure. Let me stamp your hand." I was out and down the street in a flash, huffing and wheezing like the little train that *couldn't*. "Can you hear me now, Bear?"

"Yes, I can hear you, but I'm not a bear."

I didn't recognize the voice. "Who is this?"

"Hank. Is this Kevin?"

"Yes. How did you get my number?"

"Martha told me to call you on the off chance you took your cell phone with you. Thank heaven you did. You're at Mars. Right?"

"Yeah. I thought *you* were here."

"No. We didn't go out tonight. Martha didn't have time to finish our costumes. Too busy working on yours. But she needs you. Now. She wants you to come over here right away."

"Why?"

"Kevin, I'm sorry to be the one to tell you this, but Sammy's overdosed."

"What?"

"He's in a Frisco hospital and Martha's freaked out. She's here packing like crazy. Can you come over now? She's arranging a flight for both of you. You must come over right away. She needs you badly, I don't know how to help her. She just keeps repeating, 'I need Kev. Tell him to...'"

"Hank!" I interrupted. "Let me talk to Martha."

I heard the phone drop and listened to Martha, crying uncontrollably, in the distance. Between sobs, I heard, "Kev, come...*now*."

Still from a distance, I heard Hank yell, "Do you hear her, Kevin?" Then I heard him run to the phone and pick it up. He hollered, "Get the hell over here, man!"

I looked at my Bat Watch. It was five to one. I had to see Martha. "I'll be right there." But first I dialed Bear.

"Yeah?"

"What the hell's going on? Give me the Plan A status report."

"I went by to check out the Toyota, just like you told me to. It wuzn't brown. It wuz blue. So, I couldn't make the arrest."

"Shit. Haven't you ever heard of paint?"

"Ya. That dawned on the old noggin' as soon as I left, so I turned around and went back."

"Well?" I shouted impatiently.

"The Toyota wuz gone. It wuz nowheres in sight."

"Did you get into the apartment?"

"I rang, but there was no answer."

"Shit!"

"Go to Plan B. *Now!* Join Abby immediately." *Have I gone crazy?* I trusted Bear to save the day. There was no Plan C. *Shit!* I hung up and ran back to the entrance of Mars and strode to the head of a long line. "Hey, get to the back of the line."

"I've been in before. I have my hand stamped." Everybody held up their stamped hands, pointing their thumbs to the back of the line.

I yelled, "This is an emergency police matter. I must get in immediately. The welfare of Gotham City depends on my getting back in now." They all laughed loudly and one shouted, "All right, Batman." Soon others joined in. "Anything you say, Batman." "You gotta protect our City." "Go get him, Batman!" I ran to the head of the line and was inside Mars again. The noise from the music hit me sickeningly. I needed a pee. *Christ Almighty, why does everything have to stop when I get the urge?* If I didn't relieve myself instantly, I wouldn't be worth squat. I dashed to the john.

I walked to the front of another line ignoring the hecklers by saying, "Prostate, prostate, sorry, prostate, sorry..." and marched up to the first available urinal. *How the hell do I get my dink out of these tights?* I lifted, shifted, stood on tip toes, and finally found my John Henry. "Ahhh!" During my groan of relief a voice next to me ogled and *oo*'d. I looked over. The same Princess was still standing there, a real tea-room queen. I didn't care. *Take a good look, honey.*

I left the john in search of Brent. He was no longer in the drink line. I peered into the sea of a thousand grinding costumed bodies. A strobe light-show had been added to the already dizzying colored lights. My chances of finding Brent in this crowd were next to zilch. I ran back to where I had left Catwoman. I wanted her to tell Robin I'd be back and not to worry. I was convinced that Catwoman was Martha. But that was impossible. I had just heard her on the phone, for God's sake. *And now I can't find Catwoman anyplace.* I dashed to the exit.

I left Mars and vainly tried to break into the long line of costumed party-goers waiting at the taxi stand. They were probably heading for other parties. I looked at my watch: one-thirteen. Giving up, I ran as fast as I could to Martha and Hank's. If my son had indeed overdosed, how could I ever face Martha and say, "The party at Mars was more important than the life of our first born"?

THK STOOD IN the sound-proof lighting and music booth, high above the dance floor, his face pressed against the window. His grin widened as he watched Batman make his quick getaway. He smiled contentedly at Catwoman, with four drink tickets in her hand, inching her way to the bar. He had a perfect view. Directly under him, he watched Robin, standing in a shadowed corner, fishing for his pipe and matches. He hissed, "Yes. Light up. Get high, you little poofter."

Everything was working out better than he had dreamed possible. At that moment, he could think of only one thing: *Tonight I'll have a double chaser!* As he left the booth, he stepped over the technician's body.

BRENT WAS TICKED off that Kevin had disappeared. He had given Catwoman the drink tickets and said, "I got to take a leak." He really wanted another toke. A good long puff. Or two. Or three. He was going to fly tonight, confident they would pick up first prize.

"Hey, Boy Wonder. Can that stuff be good for you?"

Brent turned around guiltily. No one was there. Then he heard, "I've got a message for you." Brent looked up and stared hazily. An evil upside-down green grin hung in mid air. The shape freaked him out as it slowly slithered down a rope from the catwalk.

"Huh?" Brent staggered back, hypnotized as he watched the Riddler's grin grow in size as he descended.

"Batman had to leave his little Robin and he asked me to drive you home." Suddenly the grin began to spin around Brent. He tried to follow the swirling vision.

"What?" Robin tried hard to concentrate on what he was seeing, convinced this was the most bizarre trip he'd ever experienced. "I'm not leaving. The party is just getting good."

"It'll get a lot better. Believe me." The Riddler let go of the rope and dropped to the floor. He gripped Brent's arm.

Pulling away, Brent shouted over the loud music. "Hey, who the hell do you think you are?" With a sudden jerk, he was pushed into a dark corner. Bang! He felt something hard hit his head. Then he was pinned against the wall, a strong forearm across his throat.

Brent stared into a pair of wicked green eyes. "Who the fuck are you?"

"Your adversary, Boy Wonder," The Riddler hissed, sticking his tongue out and rapidly trilling it between his teeth. "I'm going to make you my Queen for a Day!" He laughed mirthlessly, spittle flying from his mouth. "I'll have you, but I'll not keep you long."

Brent's eyes bulged through Robin's mask. His mellow buzz had disappeared. This was not a trip. This was real.

With all the effort he could muster, Brent tried to free himself from the vise at his throat. He tried to kick his tormentor in the groin but suddenly found himself flipped around with his face plastering the wall. He felt a sudden pressure against his spine. "If you're not a good boy and come with me this second, I'll blow your heart out." Brent could feel a gun, pressing into his back. "Do you understand, bum boy?"

Brent nodded, terrified.

"My gun is under your cape. Pointed at your faggot heart! Feel it?" Brent nodded. "And now, we're going to walk out of here like two buddies. Understand?" Terrified, Brent nodded as he felt the gun's pressure. "And if you make one false move, I'll shoot you instantly and run. No one will ever catch me in this crowd. Now let's get the hell out of here, you pansy ass-wipe."

They walked towards the entrance. If anyone had cared to take notice, they would have seen Riddler, laughing and joking, holding tight to Robin's arm. What they wouldn't see was a petrified man, his heart pounding against the cold metal pressed into his back.

They left without incident.

"Good boy," the Riddler cooed. "Now, get into my car." He led the way to the shiny blue Toyota Tercel parked across the street. Brent frowned; hadn't Kevin said something about a Toyota? But no, that had been brown. The Riddler unlocked the passenger side and opened the door. "Get in and put your hands behind your head." He slipped into the backseat and within seconds Brent realized that he had been handcuffed to the headrest.

Sitting next to Brent, the killer taunted, "Now let's go and have some fun, Wonder Boy."

Brent fought the effects of the marijuana surging through his veins. At times he still imagined that he was having a bad trip. Then moments of reality darted into his dope-distorted brain, telling him that he was with a madman. And then, in the next instant, he'd think, "When I come down, everything will be okay."

Within a minute — or was it twenty minutes? — or an hour? — he realized that he was standing outside his own apartment block. He stared in disbelief as the gate opened, then the door into the apartment foyer. He tried hard to concentrate on what was happening as they stood in the elevator. A hand appeared out of nowhere. *That's not my hand! My God, who is pressing in the code to my penthouse?*

When the door opened, he felt himself being pushed out into his own foyer. *How did I get this suitcase? Why am I carrying it?* He watched in disbelief as a green finger punched in the security code and he heard the familiar sound of the system being deactivated. Then a key unlocked the French doors.

"Upstairs, queenie."

Brent felt the pressure of the gun in the middle of his back as he walked slowly up the stairs, suitcase in hand.

I STOOD IN front of Martha and Hank's apartment, pressing the intercom code for the fourth time. I took out my phone and dialed Martha's number. No answer.

There I was, a shivering sixty-year-old Batman, standing in front of the intercom board, realizing I'd been sent on a wild goose chase. *Why?* I looked at my watch: 01:32. Then I noticed an envelope stuck in the top of the intercom panel. A Batman insignia was glued on the envelope. I tore it open. My heart froze.

Up and down, up and down,
I have lead you up and down;
I am fear'd in field and town.
The Clean Fiend has led you
Up and down.

Happy Hallowmas, you poor excuse for a Private Dick.
Dickhead would be more appropriate.

Have you already forgotten? Idiot!
Robin will die and Batman will follow.
"Where? Where? Where?" I can hear you say,
Scratching your disgusting, geriatric balls.

For Christ's sake, wake up!
In YOUR sweat-enseamed bed, you old ponce!

Run, you stupid ass-rimming queer.
I'm cleaning out Brentie Boy right now.
What the fuck are you waiting there for?

Don't be late for the R E A L L Y Big Shew
Like you were for Nancy's!!!

"Oh my God, Hank knows I'm on to him. He's flipped out.
He's capable of anything now."

I felt out of control as I ran headlong as fast as my legs would go.
Cape flying, breath condensing in the cold night air, I had to save my
lover. He was four blocks away. *I'm coming, Brent. Hold on. I won't
be late. I pray to God I won't be late.*

Chapter
Thirty-Eight

THE BEDROOM FLICKERED in candlelight. A camcorder sat on top of the armoire, its red light a glowing ember. A suitcase lay open on the chaise lounge. Loud R&B music blared from the open entertainment center. Riddler flew around the room like a mini-tornado, dancing, performing a flip, biting off bits of jerky, chewing it, giggling, smacking his lips, and shouting curses at Brent, who lay naked, spread-eagled on top of the king-sized bed. There was no sign of Robin the Boy Wonder or even his costume. Brent's cries of distress had become the bleating of a lamb waiting to be sacrificed.

The green shape picked up a gun from his suitcase and took aim. "Bang-bang, you're dead."

Face up, his wrists and ankles secured to the bedposts by the too-often-used harness, his eyes staring in horror at the antics of his captor, Brent held his breath.

Riddler aimed his gun from several places in the room. "Bang. Bang."

Then he stopped his fun and walked to the bed. "You're wearing the same harness Nancy wore, Brentie boy," he yelled as he placed the .45 between his victim's trembling legs. He crawled on the bed and grabbed Brent's hair. Yanking his head off the bed, he stuffed a pillow under it and threw his head back down. He then crawled above Brent's head and sat, straddle-legged. "Are you ready for your close-up, Mr. Barnes? Smile! You're on camera. And you're going to give the performance of your miserable pathetic life." His head leaned over Brent's as he spewed his venom.

Terrified, Brent stared into the upside-down grin.

Leaping off the bed, Riddler danced around the room. "'Up and down, up and down, / I have lead them up and down.' Bet you don't know what that's from."

"Puck." Brent answered automatically. "A 'fairy' in *A Midsummer Night's Dream*."

"Well, aren't we the smarmy pants. But I bet you don't know what I did to Nancy. Bet your old senior toy kept that little secret from his itty-bitty crybaby. You want me to tell you? Bet you're dying to know how I killed Nancy, aren't you? Or, better still, let me

show you, Brentie Boy Wonder."   Laughing uncontrollably, he
jumped up on the lounge. "I'm such a brilliant man. And you're
such a wisp!   A bed-wetting wisp.   Smile for the camera,
cocksucker."

The flash startled Brent, still trying to control his hazy brain. He
watched, fascinated, as the camera belched out the photo.

Grabbing it before it dropped on the floor, the killer jumped off
the lounge and leapt up on the bed, straddling Brent. He bent down
and lovingly propped the photo on the pillow near Brent's head.
"That's exactly where I placed Nancy's first Polaroid," he mocked,
"just four inches from her left cheek."   He stared down at it for a
minute, watching the image come to life. Suddenly he lay on top of
Brent, nearly every part of their bodies connecting. He stared hard
into Brent's eyes, breathing hard into Brent's mouth. "You're not
doing good enough, fruitcake. This is a lousy picture." His nose
touched Brent's nose. "Nancy was a much better actor than you. But
maybe that was because I was naked, just as you are now."

In one motion, he leapt to his feet and bounded onto the floor.
He snapped off the music. Then he ran to the suitcase and took out a
piece of paper. He held it in front of Brent's eyes. "Here's your
audition piece. I'm going to let you rehearse it *once* before I record it
for posterity. Read." He screamed, "Now!"

Brent struggled to see the print in the flickering gloom. He read
quietly, hesitantly, through a haze of confusion. "I have been chosen
by the world's greatest director to audition for his film."

"Louder! Damn this *amateur* to Hell! Why do I always get stuck
with fucking incompetents? If you don't speak louder, I'll bite off
your cock." He leaned down so that his face was within inches of
Brent's limp penis. He banged his jaws together so that his teeth
sounded like castanets.

Petrified, Brent started again. Somehow he summoned enough
energy to speak louder. "I have been chosen by the world's greatest
director to audition for his film. And to appear opposite him. I am
terribly...honored, to have been...chosen. Now I would like to recite
my audition piece." He took an audible breath and tried to do his
best. Brent recognized Volumnia's speech to Coriolanus and,
incredibly, managed to deliver a precise interpretation.

The killer was impressed. He instantly became Coriolanus,
seeing, not Brent lying on the bed, but his mother kneeling before
him. He spoke in the solemn tones of Richard Burton. "Your knees to
me? To your corrected son?" He crawled up on the bed, peering at
Brent, but seeing Volumnia, seeing his mother. He gasped. Shook
his head. He was now peering into Brent's questioning face; his
mother had disappeared from his vision. He jumped onto the floor.
Clawing at his tight Riddler costume, he began ripping at it
viciously, splitting it open in several places. With parts of his

nakedness appearing through huge gaping tears, he laughed uncontrollably. "Good, Boy Wonder. Very good." He became calm. "Between you and me, you passed your audition piece better than Nancy. You got me answering you. Now, where was I?" He flew over to the stereo and hit the Play button. Loud rock filled the room. "Did I tell you how I distracted Nancy while she was auditioning for me?" he screamed over the music. "I have such an inquisitive little pinky. Maybe that's why Nancy didn't recite as well as you. He wanted to go a-traveling, didn't you, darling?" He kissed his cherry-red pinky fingernail. "Now, let's record it."

Again, he ran over to the stereo and turned off the music. Then he flew back to the suitcase.

He reached in and pulled out a recorder and set it on the bed. He held the mike near Brent's mouth and snapped on the Record button. He whispered, "Begin. And do it perfectly or chomp chomp."

Brent did as he was told, reciting the speech in a daze, not knowing whether or not he'd please his captor who held him at his mercy.

"Good boy. It's recorded for all time. Reward time. I'm going to share my jerky." Brent held his breath as the maniac flew to the suitcase, throwing in the tape recorder and taking out a piece of jerky. "Open up."

"No." Brent shook his head. "I don't want anything in my mouth."

"Is that so? I thought homos *always* wanted meat in their mouths." He held the piece of jerky in front of Brent's mouth and ordered, "Open up, Boy Wonder, and take a big bite."

Brent turned his head away.

The killer shrieked, "Take a bite, do you hear me? Nancy took a bite. You take a bite. It's part of the script. Now eat or say goodbye to your silly willy." He was down on all fours; his teeth gripped Brent's limp penis.

"Okay, okay," Brent yelled. "Give me your damn jerky."

The green-shadowed face looked up. "I knew you'd see it my way. I'll feed it to you." His face was now inches from Brent's. "First, it's my turn." He took a bite. "Now, it's your turn. Open up." He stuffed the rest of the jerky into Brent's mouth. "Good boy. Now chew." Their heads were six inches apart. They watched each other chew the smoked meat in silence for several seconds. Then, the killer jumped up. "I want a picture of you chewing. Lick your lips. Enjoy the taste. Mm-mmm."

The flash startled Brent and he swallowed the contents in his mouth.

"Wonderful!" Lovingly, the killer placed the Polaroid to the right side of Brent's head and jumped over to his left side. He lay down beside Brent, resting his head on the pillow so that his mouth was an inch from Brent's ear. He whispered, "Let me tell you a little secret, Brentie-boy. You know that Nancy was always trying to get her tongue into your mouth when she was alive. Right? Wasn't she?" He jumped up and grabbed the camera.

"And now she's done it! How did it feel to have Nancy's tongue in your mouth and down in your throat? And how does it feel to know that you have Nancy's tongue in your guts?"

Instantly, Brent understood the significance of the madman's words. His stomach erupted and he heaved. At that exact moment, another flash filled the room.

"Oh, that was wonderful acting. Not everyone can puke on cue. Nancy didn't vomit up Susan's tongue jerky. So I had to clean her out." He jumped up on the bed and placed the new Polaroid above Brent's head. "Congratulations." Then he sniffed. He made a disgusted noise from deep within his chest. "*Ooaarrggg!* You smell, you filthy boy. You made a dirty mess. Puke all over your cheeks and chest. You stinking, naughty little boy." He stood up, straddling Brent. He looked down and wailed, "And look what you've done! You've pissed yourself too. You've goddamned pissed all over your buggering bedspread. I'm going to have to clean you out before you mess up the bed any more than you've already done." He flew over to the stereo and punched the PLAY button. A trumpet solo blared out of the sensurround speakers. He dashed to the suitcase and brought out a large syringe and a jar of soapy water. He poked the large black dildo-like nozzle into the jar and squeezed the globe in order to fill it. "Assume position!" he ordered in a severe female voice. Suddenly, he stopped short and looked down at the bulge in his torn costume. "See what you made me do?" he howled. "You made me get a hard-on!" He threw the syringe into the suitcase and picked up the gun and walked deliberately to the side of the bed and aimed it at Brent's temple.

"Your party's over, Hank."

Chapter
Thirty-Nine

THE MANIAC'S HEAD darted up. Then he smiled confidently. I was standing in the doorway, breathing heavily, my Batman costume stained with sweat. *Why the hell didn't I keep my gun when I left the Force?* But I was ready to meet my nemesis face to face, taunt for taunt. Gun or no gun.

Riddler erupted in gales of laughter. "Great welcome makes a merry feast! Welcome, Batman. You certainly took your sweet time. Happy Hallowmas!" He mugged ferociously. "What kept you? A wild goose chase?" He chuckled and aimed the gun directly at the bat insignia on my chest. I took a step into the room. "Don't move one goddamn inch. Stand perfectly still. Move closer and I'll put a bullet between your little Robin's eyes. Look at this pathetic excuse for a human being." The voice was cruel, unfeeling. I didn't recognize Hank's voice at all. Had I been wrong? *If this isn't Hank, who is this maniac? It's got to be Hank. Martha's Hank!*

I looked at each of the sickening Polaroids around Brent's head. His wet body writhed in the shimmering candlelight. The room smelled of sour bile and urine. But I detected something far worse. A stench of evil had invaded our bedroom, palling everything good.

"Darl'," Brent whimpered.

"Shut up," the fiend roared. "You've had your turn." I tried to pin down the voice. There was something familiar about it, but I couldn't put a face to the voice. *It has to be Hank!* "You would have been proud of your little fruitcake. He did a splendid audition piece for me."

"Why not? Brent could act you under the table any day!"

"Oooh! A taunt! Mr. Ex-Chief Inspector of the RCMP is trying to badger me." He laughed wickedly. "But that won't work on me! How can a feeble senior toy like you possibly stand up to the world's best actor?"

"You're kidding yourself. If you're such a great actor, what the hell are you doing here? In this room. Terrorizing my lover. Who the fuck are you anyway? A nobody, that's who you are."

"I was a hit in London," he screamed. Suddenly a bluster of laughs filled the room. "I see what you're trying to do, Batman.

You're deliberately baiting me, but it won't work." He picked up a piece of jerky from the suitcase and threw it to me. It landed on the bed. "Have a piece of jerky."

"No," shouted Brent. "It's Nancy's tongue."

"What?" I stared in horror, looking at the jerky. Remembering...

"He made me eat some."

A rich, velvety voice filled the room. "Dat's not Nancy's tongue jerkee, mon." The Fiend spoke in a perfect Jamaican accent. "Dat be de rest of Bill's cock jerkee. Yo' loved it, din't yo', Kevvie?"

"Monique!"

"Yo' wanted to git a look at me pom-pom, dint yo'?" He grabbed his crotch and went into more gales of laughter. "Now," he said in a normal voice that sounded more like Hank's, but wasn't Hank's, "that's called acting. You didn't have a fucking clue that I was Monique."

I leaned against the doorway. I felt like I'd been kicked in the balls.

"Ah, poor Kevvie. You're such a klutzy old queer," he snarled. He changed CDs. "Now get out of that fucking costume. Strip for the camera, Batman." Jazzy striptease music filled the room. "Grind your ass, big boy. Your public wants to see the real Ex-Chief Inspector Kevin J. Porter. One time good husband and father, one time respected RCMP officer, now a flaming *faggot*."

I didn't move. "You strip, you son of a bitch, or I'll put a hole right between the little chink's eyes." He drew aim on Brent's head.

"Okay," I shouted. I slowly took off the Bat Watch Brent had given me earlier in the evening and placed it with care on the dresser. Then, hesitantly, I took off the cape. Then the gloves and boots. Then the utility belt. I undressed as slowly as possible, piece by piece while trying to collect my wits. I wanted to know who the killer really was.

"Oh, yes, Batman." He licked his lips, suggestively, liquidly. "Continue taking them off slowly." He groaned sexily, pretending he was near orgasm. "Yes. Yes. Tease me. Tease your audience." I removed my trunks quickly and threw them on the floor, then my mask and headpiece. All that remained now was the skin-tight spandex body suit.

"That, too. Every last stitch."

He wanted me as vulnerable as Brent. I shouted, "Damn you to hell!"

"Shut your trap and take it off slowly. Invite your audience into your filthy secret thoughts. They're all waiting to see what you're hiding in your basket." I ripped off the last of my costume as fast as I could. I'd give the maniac no satisfaction.

Standing naked and defenseless in front of this creature from hell, I faced the broad, evil grin of my antagonist. "My-oh-my! What have we there, dangling between your bony legs? So that's why your little pansy playmate always has such a stupid grin on his face. You're hung like a horse, you fucking senior toy!" And then he recited in exaggerated Shakepearean tones, "A horse, A horse, my kingdom for a horse." He convulsed in fits. "Thank you, Ex-Chief Inspector Porter. I've waited all my life for the opportune moment to quote *that* line."

My mind whirled. *Let the bastard revel in his own madness, it gives me more time. Damn it to Hell. Something about him is familiar. But what?*

"Perfect. Now get on the bed with your nancy lover. Don't you love my pun!" A high-pitched cackle filled the room. Gun still in hand, he jumped on the side of the bed across from me.

I sat on the bed next to Brent. "On top of him, you old fart," he ordered, "you know exactly what to do, you disgusting old fudge packer. My Mommie told me what you faggots get up to in bed. Bet you'd like to plough the Hershey highway one last time."

I wanted to beat the brains out of this foul-minded tormentor. Instead, I lay on top of Brent, holding his trembling body.

"You make me sick, Porter. I've always hated your guts, even *before* I met you." He jumped off the bed and ran to the foot of it. Then, in a perfect Mae West voice, he cooed, "You're not as excited to see me this time, are ya, honey."

I looked up and saw the killer's reflection in the mirror above the headboard. He was in the process of removing his makeup and costume. "Don't you look at me," he shrieked. "You've jumped your cue. You're supposed to say your goodbyes now. The curtain is about to fall on your miserable lives and the audience knows that you have only one minute to live." He articulated slowly and deliberately, "Give Brentie-boy his farewell kiss." Then he bellowed, "Now!"

I immediately kissed my terrified lover, believing that this would be our last. The killer rumbled disgusting slurping sounds as he watched us. As my own tears mingled with Brent's, I had a sudden idea. I lifted my head. "Congratulations."

"What?" the killer spat.

"Your plan was brilliant. You really *are* a superb actor."

"You think so?"

"I *know* so," I said with all the sense of truth that I could muster.

"Then you know who I am?"

"Yes, of course. More than that. I know why you planted Brent's pubic hairs next to Christine Perkin's body six years ago."

Brent stirred.

"In London," giggled the killer. He was hooked.

"Yes. And what a brilliant idea to braid Brent's hairs with Nancy's and Susan's, and Georgina's."

"I'm impressed. I'm so pleased you liked that touch of genius."

"And sending Franny McGhie that Polaroid of Nancy in one of Brent's self-stamped envelopes was sheer genius." I was on a roll, my mind racing. *I must get control.*

"Brentie-boy was my insurance..."

"You mean your patsy." Brent's body stiffened under me.

"So you figured it out! Good for you, Ex-Chief Inspector."

"Thank you. That's a real compliment coming from a man who has committed at least five perfect murders."

"Fourteen."

I stopped breathing. The killer was silent, enjoying the stunned reaction.

"Fourteen?" I gagged.

"You probably missed the two prossies before Christine. Too busy picking up innocent young men, you filthy old cornholer."

I ignored him, wanting to bring him back to my agenda. "So that makes seven, counting your mother."

Screaming in terror, he ran from one side of the hallway to the other, pounding the walls with the gun. Screaming obscenities.

Bingo! My confidence increased. "You killed your mother, didn't you? Admit it. You can't ever forget you killed her. You'll always remember that you...killed...your...own...*mother!*"

"Shut your fucking mouth."

"You killed her because she wasn't a fit mother. She abused you. Night and day. Day and night. She made you perform unnatural..."

"Shut your face."

Nothing was going to stop me now. "You were fucking your own mother, for Christ's sake!"

His voice deepened as if it came from the depths of his black soul. "She deserved to die, the bitch."

He stood still in the depths of the hallway. "She wouldn't let me become an actor. She wouldn't let me go to the National Theatre School. I didn't want to kill her." I was fascinated by his self-pitying intensity. "I had to kill her. Don't you see?" Suddenly he stopped short, realizing he had gone too far. He turned his back to the bedroom and, howling like a tortured animal, he began to inch his way towards the bathroom. "Poor Tom is cold."

I watched the dark reflection in the mirror above the bed, only occasionally catching a glimpse of what looked like a phantom shadow. Convinced that I was in the presence of a psychotic madman, I nonetheless began to ease myself off Brent for a better view.

"Don't you move your goddamn ass, you old queer."

"You hate older men, don't you? I bet you killed your father too. Did he molest you, as well?"

"Idiot. I never touched the old fairy. He ran away before I knew him. I don't even know what he looked like." He sounded busy, distracted.

"So, *that's* why you butcher older gay men. Trying to track down and kill your daddy. You mutilated those six men in the same way you mutilated Dorothy. My God, all those deaths to prove a point!" I waited for a reaction.

"And you two queers will make the total a glorious, sweet sixteen. But there could be more," he taunted.

Intent on keeping him talking, I ignored the threat and pressed on. "Does Martha know?"

"Of course not, idiot. She thinks I'm happy as a lark being her golden-haired boy, even though she lives in *my* apartment. Just like you live in little Brentie's. The Porters are a couple of leeches, living off young men." Realizing that he'd given his identity away, he snorted. "So you put two and two together, you tricky old bugger. I knew you'd caught me after I kissed your ex goodbye the other night." Martha's farewell. Loud laughter ricocheted off the hall walls, bursting into the bedroom. "Remember."

He changed his voice again. A smooth southern accent this time. "But it's your turn to remember, big boy."

I immediately recognized the voice. I wanted to run. To get the Hell out of there.

"Are you ready, ex-Chief Inspector Kevin J. Porter? Are you ready for *remembrances*? Turn around."

My breathing stopped. I remembered. I lifted my head slowly and turned to face the darkened hallway. The flickering candlelight picked up a young redheaded man, wearing mirrored sunglasses. As he slowly walked towards the bedroom, I saw his naked chest, buffed and bronzed. When he finally stepped fully into the bedroom, wearing only a tight pair of crotch-cleaving leather pants, I stopped breathing. I caught a glint of my own mortality reflected in his sunglasses.

Handsome and assured, he gave me a full, open-mouthed smile. He sauntered into the room, close to the bed.

My blood ran cold. Remembering. Remembering. Remembering. How could I ever forget him? Now twelve years older, but still remarkably youthful.

"Do you need a hint? Don't tell me the great Detective Porter needs a hint?"

I could only stare in disbelief. I had lost the power to speak.

Mae West's unique tones filled the room. "Well, hello, Officer. Is that a gun in your pocket, or are you just happy to see me?"

"Rusty. Rusty Towers!" Standing there was the same man who got me fired from the Force twelve years ago. "But I thought you were..."

"Yes?" he questioned in the familiar deep sexy voice. "Who did you think I was?"

"I thought you were Hank!"

"Click click. The old brain's slowing down, Porter. Rusty Towers died a natural death after I finished with him. He had one glorious cameo role. But didn't I play him well? So well that I thought it would be a lark to have you meet him one more time face to face. Still like to take me into the bushes, Officer?" Roaring with a hideous laugh, he took off his glasses and threw them in the suitcase. Then he snatched off his reddish-brown wig. "Bye-bye, Rusty. Hello, Thomas Henry King."

My heart froze. I could barely breathe. "What? You're Hank. Martha's husband. Hank."

He laughed fiendishly. "Hank was my longest-running part."

I shuddered in disbelief and then yelled, "Who the hell is Thomas Henry King?"

"That's for me to know and you to find out! I didn't need a dumb stage to act on. All the world's my stage, and you lot are merely players for me to have fun with."

I had to regain my senses and interrupt this fiend, "You're right. My old brain is slowing down. I had forgotten about Rusty." *A lie. Rusty has haunted me to this day.*

"Why don't you tell your little flit what you tried to do to poor innocent Rusty twelve years ago? I'm sure he'd like to know what kind of a pervert he's been living with for the past eight years."

I did not know what to say, lying there naked, remembering the shame that I still carried.

"You wanted to suck my cock," he screamed, "or fuck me or do whatever you old fag queens do to good-looking young men. My Mommie warned me about degenerates like you. And after I got to know Martha, she let it drop that you were homosexual. So, I decided to teach you a lesson. Instead of killing you in the bushes, and you bet your sweet ass I could have killed you in a second with your pants around your ankles, I got you fired. And I stole your wife away from you." He held a self-satisfied pause, allowing me to let this bit of truth sink in. "And now I'm going to kill your lover."

Brent was beside himself. He struggled to push me off him. Raising his head, he yelled, "When I met Kev, he was a naïve, closeted gay man. I have been *proud* to live with this dear man, loving him, supporting him, teaching him. And now I'm proud to die with him."

The fiend began to tremble. "Shut up," he screamed. It was obvious that he couldn't bear witnessing this expression of unconditional male love.

Brent continued, "He told me about that incident with Rusty. You are a bigoted, murdering homophobe. And you know what they say about homophobes?"

"Shut up, ass-wipe," he screamed.

"They're latent homosexuals."

"It's not true," he bellowed over the din of the music.

I tried one more taunt to gain supremacy. My trump card in this hellish nightmare that had become reality. "Didn't you know Shakespeare was a queer?"

The maniac's eyes became an iridescent green as if his brain had suddenly caught on fire. "Liar!" he hissed. "You son-of-a-bitch *liar*."

"Why do you think he left his wife and kids?" I was undaunted. "Who do you think was the dark lady of his sonnets?"

"A young woman, you idiot!" he croaked.

"A young man," I laughed. "Everyone knows that. Didn't you know that, Brent?"

Brent was on my wave-length. "Sure. Everyone knows that."

"I thought you were an authority on Shakespeare."

"Only his plays," he whispered. I watched him shrivel into himself, realizing that he couldn't stand it if his lifelong hero had been homosexual. He slapped his open palms over his ears, trying to block out my taunts, and screamed. "No! No! No!"

I was gaining power. "You didn't know Shakespeare was one of us? Just like me. Just like all those good gay men you killed. Just like your daddy. Just like you, Thomas Henry King!"

He opened his mouth and howled in agony. "No-o-o-o!"

"Your mother was right all the time."

"No-o-o-o!"

"Happy Hallowmas," I shouted.

"The play's over." He lifted his gun.

A shot exploded. A split second later, another blast filled the room.

Chapter
Forty

MY LIFE FLASHED before me. Two deafening gun blasts and the sound of shattering glass filled the room. The smell of gunpowder invaded my nostrils.

I could feel Brent's trembling body under me. I looked down; his eyes were bulging out of their sockets. We were alive.

I looked to my right.

In the doorway, still in attack position with both hands clutching his Smith and Wesson nine millimeter, Bear stood motionless.

"Well, you sure as hell took your time," I said with a sting.

He said nothing. I yelled, "Bear! Bear! Get hold of yourself." He blinked. I continued staring at him.

Finally, he replied, "Did you see that?"

"What?"

"Look," he pointed.

I raised my head and turned to my left. The full-length mirror had a huge hole in it with shards of glass radiating from it. The rest of the mirror was spattered with blood, bits of hair, bone, and brain tissue. I raised myself a little higher and saw Hank sprawled on the floor at the foot of the bed, the muzzle of his gun stuck in his mouth. "*He* blew the back off his own head?" I asked incredulously. Bear nodded. Blood pumped out of Hank's head. I edged my way up further and saw a gaping hole near his shoulder. The blood stain on the white carpet grew larger as I watched. "Holy shit! Who shot first?" I asked.

"I did," answered the stunned RCMP Sergeant. "He was ready to pop you. I had to shoot to save yer lives. Both of ya. After I shot, he stared at me for a split second, and grinned. His face and eyes turned green, and I swear to God smoke came out of his mouth when he opened it. Instead of takin' me out, he put the muzzle of his gun in his mouth and squeezed the trigger. I've never seen anything like it. He grinned, Kev. He wuz possessed. That maniac grinned at me and then he blew his brains out. His eyes glowed. I swear they did." And then Bear said deliberately, "I looked into the eyes of Satan tonight."

"Maybe you're right. If you want to tell Joan you shot the Devil tonight just as he was leaving Hank's body, so be it."

"Jeez. There'll be an inquiry, won't there, Kev?"

"You're right. In those seconds after you shot Hank, he took his own life. He wanted to be in control of his final curtain call. That poor demented son of a bitch committed suicide so he could deprive you of the satisfaction of bringing him in."

We were quiet for a minute, as we tried to make sense of what had just happened. "Even in death, he taunts us."

"It happened exactly as I told ya," snapped Spivic. Averting his eyes from two naked men, he walked around the foot of the bed and up to the bedside table. He picked up a decorator box and turned off the camcorder that had filmed the entire events of the night. "This'll prove my innocence. This'll show I didn't shoot a dead man. Right? That wuz a good idea of yers, Chief. Did we git enough?"

"More than enough. Christ Almighty, you really cut it short. I expected you to storm in long ago. What the hell kept you?"

"You were in charge, Chief. You destroyed him. And you helped too, young man," he said to Brent who peaked up from under me. "I jist finished him off."

Gun still in his hand, he knelt beside the remains of Hank. "He's dead, all right." *An understatement if ever there was one.* "He's not gonna suddenly jump up 'n' scare the shit out o' us like in one of them slasher movies."

Bear started to walk to the other side of the room.

"Turn off his camcorder, too."

Bear walked over to the armoire and snapped the Off button.

"Now get the hell out of here so we can shower and dress."

Bear became more relaxed. "Sorry about the mess. Yer gonna need a new carpet. And mirror. And by the looks of the guck over everything, yer gonna be cleanin' fer a week of Thursdays."

"Yeah, yeah," I answered, starting to get off Brent, who by this time was totally traumatized.

"Please," ordered Bear, "don't git off o' him. One shock is all I can take t'night." He walked around the bed to go downstairs, stopping briefly in the doorway. "Nice ass ya got there, Chief."

WHEN BEAR DISAPPEARED, I took a deep breath and let it out slowly. As I did so, I began to feel stronger. I looked at my terrified lover and gave him a gentle smile before I got up.

I tried to ignore the devastation in the room. Instead, I released Brent from his harness and led him, quivering, to the shower. He kept his eyes closed, not wanting to see Hank's body or the bloody mess on the carpet, walls, lounge, and bed. We showered quickly. I hosed him off as he stood silently, allowing me to take care of him. Brent was still in a state of shock and perhaps still high. He'd recover, and when he did, I knew that he was going to give me the third degree for weeks to come. And I deserved it. Putting my lover through Hell to catch a serial killer. *Maybe I can convince him that he just had a bad trip.* Not!

After I dried Brent down, I did the same for myself and threw on a pair of jeans and a T-shirt while he stood shivering. Then I dressed Brent in his. I aimed him towards the hall, but he resisted going back into the bedroom. His head buried in my shoulder, I carried him to the landing. "Wait here." He completely freaked out when I went back into the bedroom and bent over Thomas Henry King's body. His face was now serene, even peaceful. Perhaps for the first time. What kind of a childhood had this poor creature been forced to endure? I went through his pockets but found nothing. Brent moaned. I walked over to the suitcase and found what I wanted, his set of our keys. I joined Brent on the landing and kissed him gently. "It's okay, hon. Let's go downstairs." I put my arm around his unsteady body and we descended, one quivering step at a time.

Turning the corner towards the living room, we saw, sitting there in our lazyboys, as smug as they pleased, Bear and Abby. Brent's eyes scowled. I steered him over to the sofa and we both sat down, Brent glued next to me. I could tell that he had no intention of being out of my sight for the rest of the night.

"Quite an operation," Abby beamed. "Plan B worked like a charm."

Unexpectedly, Brent erupted. "Are you three saying that this entire night was a set-up? Plan B, for God's sake! What the hell was Plan A? Scoop up *my* battered brains?" I tried to console him, but there was no stopping him now. He stood and pointed an accusing finger at us all. "You used my place as the scene for your sting operation. And *me* as your scapegoat."

"My, he is astute." Abby smiled. "He's not only a pretty face, he has a pretty..."

"Cut the crap and tell me how you set this whole thing up." He stood in the middle of the living room, still frightened yet now enraged.

"Where'd ya want us to begin?" asked Bear.

"Duh! The beginning." Brent's hysteria was on the rise, poor darling.

"First off, "Abby started, "we have known for at least the last week, that you were going to be his next victim."

"His victim? When did you find out Hank or Thomas or Rusty or whatever the fuck he called himself was the killer and I was next on his list?"

"Kev put it all together," Bear chirped in.

"You *knew*?" Brent spat, striding over to me.

"Not totally," I admitted. "I never saw Rusty in Hank. Never.

The only time I saw Rusty was twelve years ago and then he was in his car, wearing those mirrored sunglasses. And the first time I saw Hank was seven years ago."

"Seven years ago on Halloween. Outside Celebrities," interrupted Brent. "I was there. Remember? He was a sheep. And Martha was Little Bo Peep." Nonplussed, Bear and Abby looked at each other.

"And this Thanksgiving was the second time I met Hank," I added. "I accepted him for who he was. Martha's young husband."

"Whatever." Bear shrugged. "When Kev phoned me this afternoon, he told me he knew that Hank wuz the murderer, and fer me to check out his car and then make the arrest. That was our Plan A and," he mumbled, "it kind o' fizzled."

"*I can't hear you!*" Brent screamed. He was still demanding answers and was striding around the living room.

"I wuz looking for a brown Toyota but Hank repainted his. When I went back later, I couldn't even find the car. Or him. I jist had to wait for Kev's call. Then we put Plan B into action, which was the sting. So I hopped it over here to join Abby out on the downstairs balcony."

"While I went to see if Martha was okay," I added lamely.

Anyways," Bear beamed, "it all worked out good."

Brent confronted me. "Why did you leave me when we were at Mars? In the clutches of a *known* murderer!"

"I knew he wouldn't do anything drastic at Mars."

"Drastic? I was kidnapped, for Christ's sake, and where were you? Running off to Martha's." I looked up, feeling guilty. "I could have been killed at any minute with that maniac on the loose. You should have taken him out at Mars. Or why didn't you tell *me* about your *Plan B?*" We all sat quietly, knowing that we deserved this dressing-down. Brent continued ranting. "I could have died of heart failure before I died of a bullet. If you knew he was bringing me here, why did you go to Martha's instead of to me?"

"Two reasons. I still wasn't convinced that Catwoman was Martha. I could never get a full word out of her. I even thought she might be a he. Hank could have had an accomplice. And I honestly thought Sammy had overdosed and Martha needed me." I leapt at my last lame excuse. "And I talked to Martha on the phone. Not exactly *on* the phone. But I heard her crying. From a distance. It was only when I was standing outside their place and found out no one was home that I realized Hank had impersonated Martha. He had been the one crying, begging me to come over."

Brent was listening, but not accepting my explanation. "And what's the goddammed second reason you didn't come here to save me from that maniac?"

"I'm sorry, love, but we had to hear him confess before we could put him away for good." I looked at Bear. "Bear and Abby were already here on the downstairs deck by the time you got here. I was confident that you were in no real immediate danger. I was positive that Hank would delay his little surprise until I came. He was after me as much as you. In fact, more so."

"So you deliberately allowed Hank to take me hostage?"

"I'm afraid so."

"Kev hid an envelope with keys 'n' codes fer us near the front gate."

"Part of Plan B." Another sarcastic throw-away from Brent.

"Correct. Abby came in right after the two of ya left fer the party to set up the sting," explained Bear. "I slipped back in before you and Hank arrived. You weren't in no danger whatsoever."

Abby continued, "We were watching the proceedings on a small monitor out on the downstairs deck." She looked at Brent. "We saw you and Hank come into the bedroom. It's all on film. And when Kev arrived, we saw him look out on the deck before he went upstairs."

"I gave him an all-clear sign before he went up to save ya," smiled Bear. "And then I followed him up the steps as back-up."

"And when Kev got into the bedroom, he played to Hank's vanity and got the confession we needed," said Abby.

"Over and over again. He confessed to fourteen murders, for God's sake. Were you waiting for two more? Ours?" Brent was still hyper.

"Brent. You held up really well. Congratulations," Abby said.

"Ha!" Brent wasn't going to be won over that easily.

Bear interceded. "I wuz ready to come in at a split-second notice. I wuz standing right outside yer bedroom door, listenin' to everything. Brent, we had to get his full confession on video."

"Don't forget," Abby insisted, "I could see and hear everything that was taking place in the bedroom too, and I was always in direct communication with Sergeant Spivic."

"That's right. Abby wuz my eyes. When she whispered 'GO,' I wuz in there like a dirty shirt with my gun blastin'." Bear smiled proudly. "But the bastard turned his gun on hisself after I popped him in the shoulder."

"Satisfied?" I asked Brent.

Brent walked over to me. We all watched him, not really knowing whether or not he was going to attack, but he sat down next to me. He looked up and said in a plaintive voice, "But why me? Why did he use me?"

"That seems obvious," I said softly. "It's clear that he was out to get me. As Rusty Towers, he took my job from me. As Hank, he took my wife from me. And as the Thomas Henry King, he was ready to take you away from me whenever he chose. Think of the thrill it would have given him to see you arrested and found guilty of all his murders. Nothing would have given him more pleasure than seeing me lose the man I love to a life of imprisonment."

"A sick wacko," said Brent. "But, Kev, he was going to shoot both of us. We were a second away from dying in each other's arms."

"I think I have that one figured out, too," I said. "I think he'd have set up our deaths like a murder/suicide. He'd leave a confession, written ostensibly by you, admitting all your crimes. You should search that suitcase, Bear, for a suicide note. After he shot us both, he'd walk out with his snuff film."

"And, case closed," Bear put in.

"Wait a minute." Brent looked at me. "How did you know that the killer was Hank?"

"Last weekend. Remember how chummy Hank was?" I looked at Brent.

"Yeah, I suppose so. What does that prove?"

"Before you and Hank went out for a drink, he kissed Martha passionately and *she* asked, 'Is that to remember me by?' Then Hank looked at me sort of funny and winked. But I didn't clue into anything until you kissed me this afternoon before you went out. You said 'That's for remembrance.'" *Was it only this afternoon? It seemed a lifetime ago.* "So, really, *you* discovered the most important piece of this jigsaw puzzle."

"Really?" Brent looked confused yet sounded confident at the same time. Always eager to be on the winning side, his tone had a touch of self-congratulatory victory.

"And when I went to the library to check a Shakespearean concordance, sure enough, all of the messages on the backs of the Polaroids, with either the word 'remember' or 'remembrance' in them, were quotations from different Shakespeare plays. 'That's for remembrance' comes from *Hamlet*, Act 4, scene 5, line 174." I would guess that Hank used that line on Martha many times."

"My lover's become a Shakespearean scholar." A small smile crossed Brent's lips.

"Ya betcha," Bear laughed.

I continued, "When I got home, I checked our itinerary calendars, and sure enough, at the same times of the last five murders when you were at your various volleyball tournaments, Martha and Hank were visiting one of our kids. Or more exactly, Martha visited; Hank stalked and murdered his next prey."

"Are you saying he deliberately planned these murders while I was in the same cities?"

"Yeah, Brent. It appears that way," answered Bear. "That creep's bin plannin' to implicate ya fer years. Seven years ago he carried some of yer pubic hairs to London so he'd have a fall guy to take the rap if ever the heat got too much fer him. He even planted one of yer hairs at each murder scene as well."

"And all the time he was using my ex as a cover," I added.

"You're forgetting Martha," Brent said. "She's still at Mars, waiting for Hank to take her home." I was on my feet. "We've got to go, now."

AS WE LEFT our apartment, the Vancouver Police were already arriving on the scene. The media had already set up camp. The street was filling with bewildered, inquisitive neighbors. They and the police would be there for hours.

Abby trotted down the street to get her cruiser, leaving Brent and me standing on the sidewalk. We watched Bear in front of a TV camera. He was being interviewed by his favorite Vancouver Police media officer. "Well, Sergeant Spivic, it's been quite a day for you. How does it feel to have finally apprehended the killer responsible for the death of Nancy Henderson?"

"Well, Annie, right off the bat I wanna let the women of this city..."

Abby pulled up and we got into the cruiser.

CAUGHT IN THE headlights of Abby's car, a blinded Catwoman peered out from the empty sidewalk in front of Mars. She had lost all her kittenish confidence and looked startled, vulnerable. We all got out and hurried to her. "Martha," I said, taking her trembling hands in mine. "I've got some bad news."

"Sammy? Has something happened to Sammy?"

"No. No."

She stared at Abby in her Mountie uniform. "Is it Hank? Is he...?" Martha collapsed in my arms.

I half-carried her to the cruiser. Abby drove us all to Martha's apartment. On the way, we filled her in with only the most relevant details concerning what had happened since she had last seen Hank at Mars. Weeping silently, she sat motionless, staring out the front window. Her feline face, once so beautifully made up, was streaked with tears, mascara, and unglued cat whiskers.

Unconsciously, she licked her lips, taking in salty black tears. I handed her my hanky.

As soon as we entered the apartment, Martha padded silently into the bathroom. She appeared fragile and tentative. The energetic, volatile adversary of Batman and Robin had disappeared. When she closed the door, we listened, concerned. "Martha? Are you going to be okay? Do you need any help?" No response. "Martha?" I said loudly.

"Kev, I want to clean up. Let me be alone for a while." We heard the shower turn on.

Abby yelled, "Do you mind if we look around?"

"Do what you have to do."

With Brent tagging along, Abby and I searched the kitchen, den, and living room. "There's nothing here. Let's check out the bedroom, Abby," I suggested. I whispered to Brent, "Why don't you sit on the couch and wait for me. I won't be long." I led him to the sofa then walked into the bedroom. Hesitantly, Abby followed me.

I knew what I was looking for but didn't quite know how or where I was going to find it. And I certainly didn't want Brent to see anything that would further freak him out.

Everything in the bedroom looked perfectly normal. I looked at the two closet doors. I opened one which contained Martha's clothes and gave it a quick examination, feeling down the walls. Nothing out of the ordinary. I opened the other door. This was Hank's closet; its heavy fragrance of potpourri filled my lungs. In the middle of the clothes rail, I saw a makeup smock over a shirt and a familiar pair of pants. I recognized the pants. They were mine. I hadn't seen them in years. *How the hell did he get hold of a pair of my pants?* I snapped on the closet lights and pushed Hank's clothes to the right and left. I inspected every inch of the walls inside his closet. I was positive I'd find a secret doorway. Nothing. I started all over again, inspecting every inch of the wall. I looked at Abby who hadn't a clue what I was up to. "Well, there goes that theory."

We both jumped when a loud ringing filled the apartment. "What the hell was that?" Abby yelled.

From the living room, Martha explained apologetically, "Sorry. It's the intercom. Hank likes the volume turned up."

As we walked back to the living room, Martha, wrapped in her bathrobe and looking more like herself, picked up the phone, "Yes?" I had the notion that she thought it might be Hank. She looked at me sadly. "It's Sergeant Spivic. He wants to come up."

"Buzz him in." After Martha did so, I added, "Better put out some food." Martha went over to the kitchen area.

Within a minute Bear was at the door. "Turn on the TV. Channel 11. There's a special police report." Brent turned on the TV and we caught the beginning of the interview.

"Sergeant Spivic, it's been quite a day for you. How does it feel to have finally apprehended the killer responsible for the death of Nancy Henderson?"

Martha collapsed on one of the dining room chairs. Abby reached out to console her. Brent glued himself to me.

"Well, Annie, right off the bat I wanna tell the women of this city that they can sleep more better in their beds t'night, knowin' that this maniac is no more. He confessed that he wuz the serial killer I've bin lookin' fer. And Annie, he didn't limit hisself to Vancouver. The lunatic admitted that he killed fourteen people around the world!"

Both Martha and Anne Wyner on the TV, exclaimed, "Fourteen?" Recovering, Anne asked Bear, "So, Sergeant Spivic, you shot and killed this man during your apprehension of him?"

We all stared at the screen and listened to Bear's long explanation. Finally the VPD media officer spoke directly into the camera as if to bring the interview to a halt. "Well, that will be the end of the so-called Clean Fiend."

"Not exactly," smirked Bear. He looked directly into the camera. "You homosexual guys out there can sleep a lot more easier t'night too."

Anne Wyner's ears perked. "What are you getting at, Sergeant Spivic?"

"The Vancouver Police don't need to worry no more about them six homosexual cases that they ain't been able t'close. By t'morra night with the evidence I gathered, I'll close them cases, too. All I need to do is..."

ON THE OTHER side of the wall directly behind where Kevin J. Porter was sitting, a single spotlight focused on two figures. Horror filling their staring eyes, encrusted blood covering their bodies, empty bleeding mouths gaping wide, Marigold and Sweetcakes hung on the wall as Thomas Henry King's final, vengeful trophies.

FORTHCOMING TITLES

published by
Quest Books

The Three
by Meghan O'Brien

Alone in rural Indiana with only the clothes on her back, twenty-five-year-old Anna is almost ready to give up on trying to live in a world that has seen the recent slaughter of her childhood tribe and the murder, only a year later, of her best friend and only surviving tribe mate. When Anna interrupts an attack on a beautiful woman lounging by a lake, she is subsequently drawn into the relationship of two other survivors of the sickness: young, idealistic Elin, who welcomes Anna into their makeshift family with open arms, and her lover, the older, more jaded Kael, whose dark and brooding nature initially keeps Anna at bay.

While Anna and Elin fall into affectionate interaction that quickly turns romantic — with Kael's permission — Anna and Kael have a more difficult time learning to live with one another. Their mutual love for Elin sees them through a rough start, and soon they develop a tentative, but genuine, friendship.

The threesome is journeying south for the winter season when an unexpected accident leaves Elin severely injured and unable to defend herself from the constant threat of attack that is a part of their everyday lives. Making the decision to nurse Elin back to health in the relative safety of a city, Kael and Anna soon find that tensions rise as their relationship is strained by their concern over Elin's condition and Kael's resulting emotional distance from Anna.

When Elin is threatened yet again, this time by a group of religious fanatics who believe that a woman's duty in the post-apocalyptic world is to bear children and work towards repopulating the earth, Kael and Anna's fragile bond will be tested once again as they find the need to work together to save the woman they both love.

Mind Games
by Nancy Griffis

Betrayed and almost killed by her police partner, PsiAgent Rebecca Curtains is understandably reluctant to take on a new one, despite the danger in working alone. When she finds out that the Violent Crimes loner, Detective Genie marshall, is scheduled to be the replacement, reluctance turns to outright apprehension.

In becoming partners with the resident telepath, Detective Genie Marshall has been given a second chance to become a 'real' cop again, and she knows it. After the death of her last partner, Genie has worked alone, not wanting to risk herself like that again. It won't make her any more popular with the other detectives, but then, being popular has never been on Genie's list. Get the job done right, and with as little bloodshed as possible, has always been her motto.

After a rocky start, the two women forge a strong partnership that allows them to solve crimes faster and more accurately than ever. The partnership grows into something deeper than friendship as they begin a journey that brings the hidden aspects of their lives to the surface. When Rebecca is attacked, telepathically and physically, it's a race to discover who's behind it; the leader of UnderTEM, a group bent on wiping out all telepaths, or a random psycho with telepathic powers of his or her own.

It is only by trusting in each other, and their new bond, that they'll find the killer. If they don't, Rebecca's very sanity will be the cost of failure.

Other QUEST Publications

Gabrielle Goldsby	Wall of Silence	1-932300-01-5	$ 20.95
Trish Kocialski	Blue Holes To Terror	1-930928-61-0	$ 16.99
Trish Kocialski	Deadly Challenge	1-930928-76-9	$ 14.95
Trish Kocialski	Forces of Evil	1-932300-10-4	$ 14.95
Trish Kocialski	The Visitors	1-932300-27-9	$ 14.95
Lori L. Lake	Gun Shy	1-930928-43-2	$ 18.95
Lori L. Lake	Have Gun We'll Travel	1-932300-33-3	$ 18.95
Lori L. Lake	Under the Gun	1-930928-44-0	$ 22.95
Helen M. Macpherson	Colder Than Ice	1-932300-29-5	$ 18.95
C. Paradee	Deep Cover	1-932300-23-6	$ 17.95
Talaran	Vendetta	1-930928-56-4	$ 15.99
C N Winters	Irrefutable Evidence	1-930928-88-2	$ 15.95

See <u>www.JohnFParker.com</u> where you will find some interesting additional material about *Come Clean* and the author.

VISIT US ONLINE AT

www.regalcrest.biz

At the Regal Crest Website You'll Find

- The latest news about forthcoming titles and new releases

- Our complete backlist of romance, mystery, thriller and adventure titles

- Information about your favorite authors

- Current bestsellers

Regal Crest titles are available from all progressive booksellers and online at StarCrossed Productions, (www.scp-inc.biz), or at www.amazon.com, www.bamm.com, www.barnesandnoble.com, and many others.

Printed in the United States
67812LVS00005B/68

9 781932 300437